THE GREAT COW RACE

THE GREAT COW RACE

BY JEFF SMITH

WITH COLOR BY STEVE HAMAKER

An Imprint of

SCHOLASTIC

All rights reserved. Published by Graphix, an imprint of Scholastic Inc., *Publishers since 1920.* SCHOLASTIC, GRAPHIX, and associated logos are trademarks and/or registered trademarks of Scholastic Inc.

Library of Congress Cataloging-in-Publication Data is available.
ISBN-13 978-0-439-70624-7 — ISBN-10 0-439-70624-6 (hardcover)
ISBN 0-439-70639-4 (paperback)

ACKNOWLEDGMENTS
Harvestar Family Crest designed by Charles Vess
Map of *The Valley* by Mark Crilley

30 29 28 27 26 25   17 18
First Scholastic edition, August 2005
Book design by David Saylor
Printed in Malaysia 108
Scholastic Inc., 557 Broadway, New York, NY 10012.

This book is for Dan Root

CONTENTS

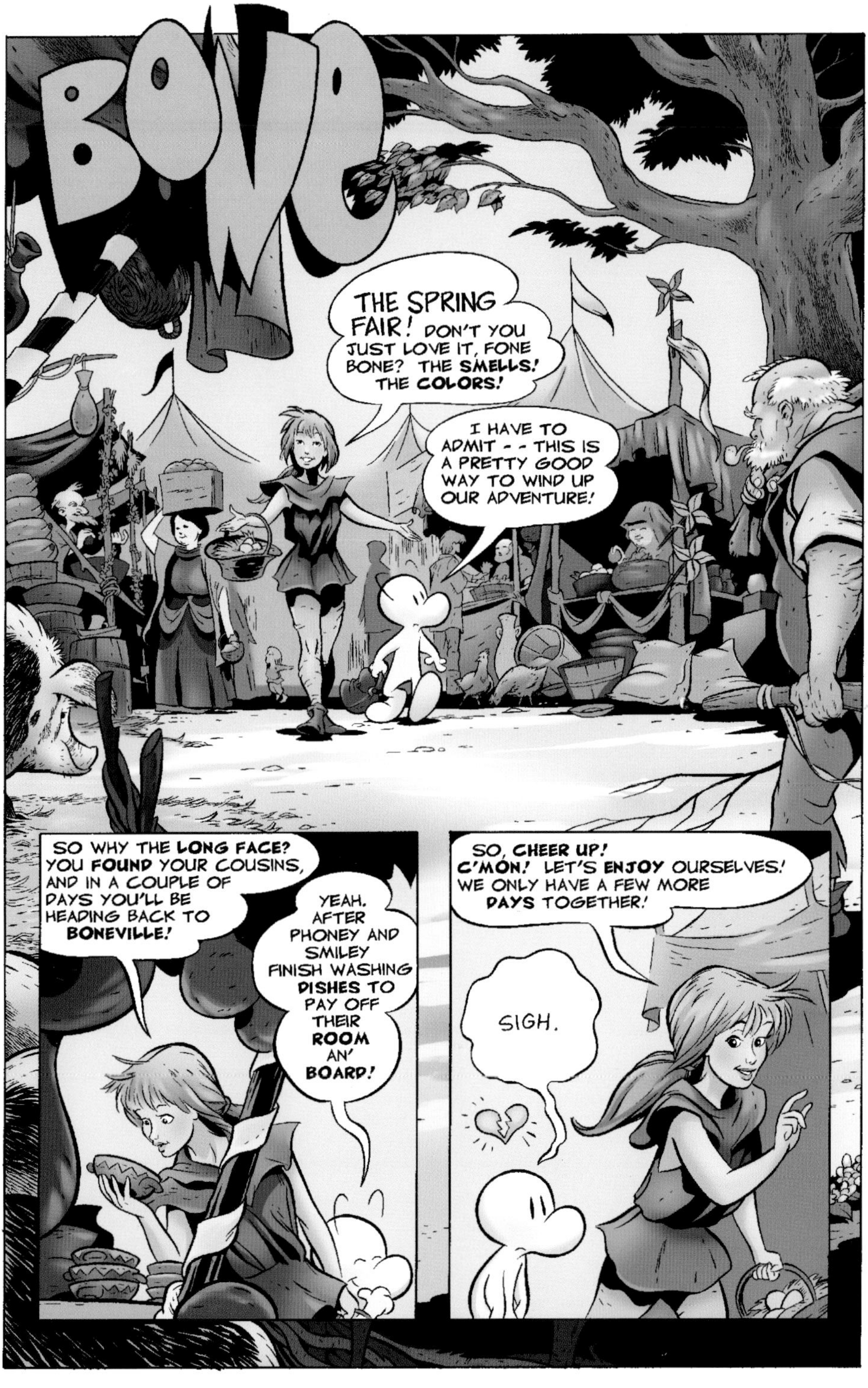
BONE
THE SPRING FAIR! DON'T YOU JUST LOVE IT, FONE BONE? THE SMELLS! THE COLORS!
I HAVE TO ADMIT - - THIS IS A PRETTY GOOD WAY TO WIND UP OUR ADVENTURE!
SO WHY THE LONG FACE? YOU FOUND YOUR COUSINS, AND IN A COUPLE OF DAYS YOU'LL BE HEADING BACK TO BONEVILLE!
YEAH. AFTER PHONEY AND SMILEY FINISH WASHING DISHES TO PAY OFF THEIR ROOM AN' BOARD!
SO, CHEER UP! C'MON! LET'S ENJOY OURSELVES! WE ONLY HAVE A FEW MORE DAYS TOGETHER!
SIGH.

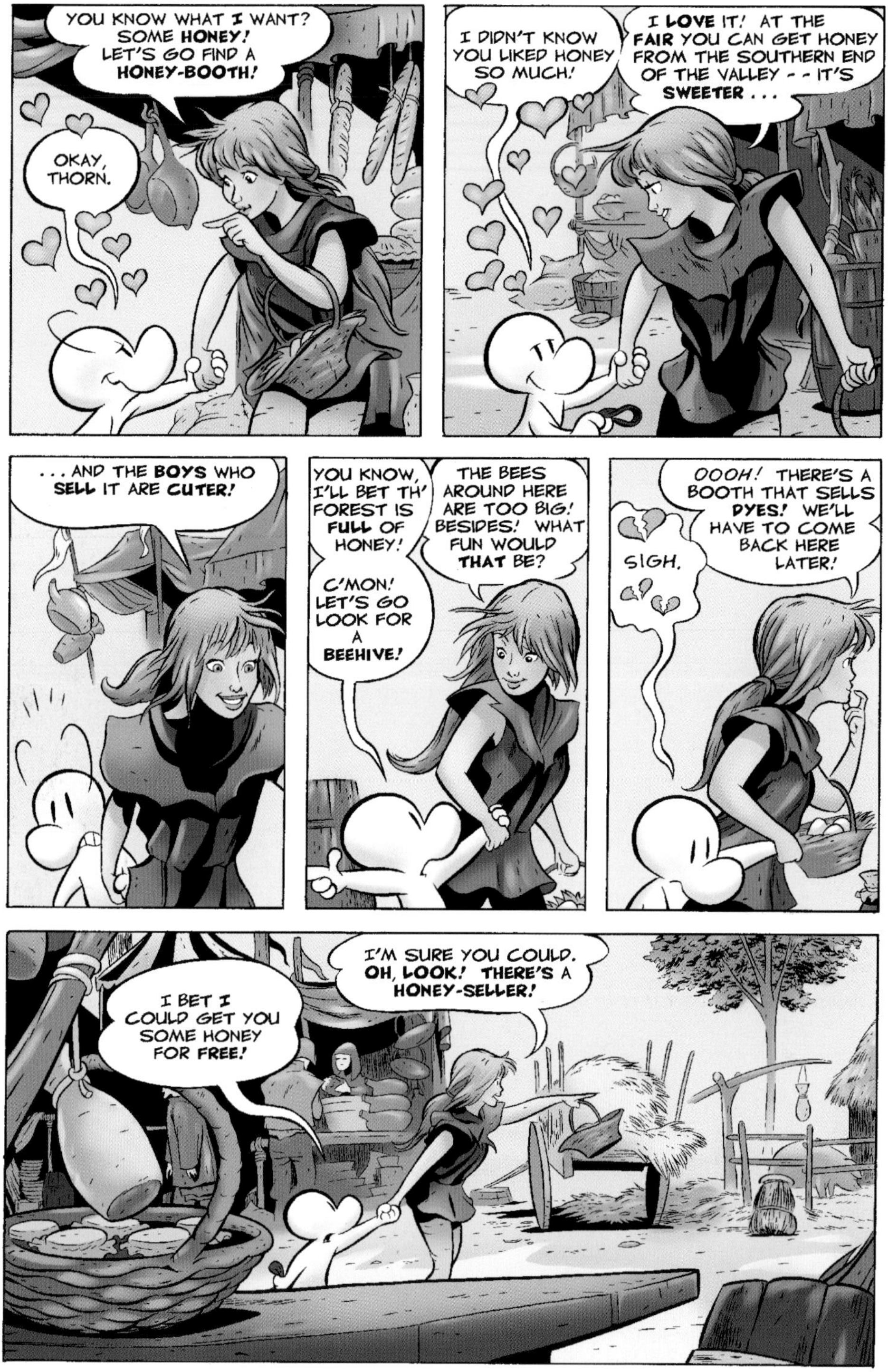
YOU KNOW WHAT I WANT? SOME HONEY! LET'S GO FIND A HONEY-BOOTH!
OKAY, THORN.
I DIDN'T KNOW YOU LIKED HONEY SO MUCH!
I LOVE IT! AT THE FAIR YOU CAN GET HONEY FROM THE SOUTHERN END OF THE VALLEY -- IT'S SWEETER ...
... AND THE BOYS WHO SELL IT ARE CUTER!
YOU KNOW, I'LL BET TH' FOREST IS FULL OF HONEY!
THE BEES AROUND HERE ARE TOO BIG! BESIDES! WHAT FUN WOULD THAT BE?
C'MON! LET'S GO LOOK FOR A BEEHIVE!
SIGH.
OOOH! THERE'S A BOOTH THAT SELLS DYES! WE'LL HAVE TO COME BACK HERE LATER!
I BET I COULD GET YOU SOME HONEY FOR FREE!
I'M SURE YOU COULD. OH, LOOK! THERE'S A HONEY-SELLER!

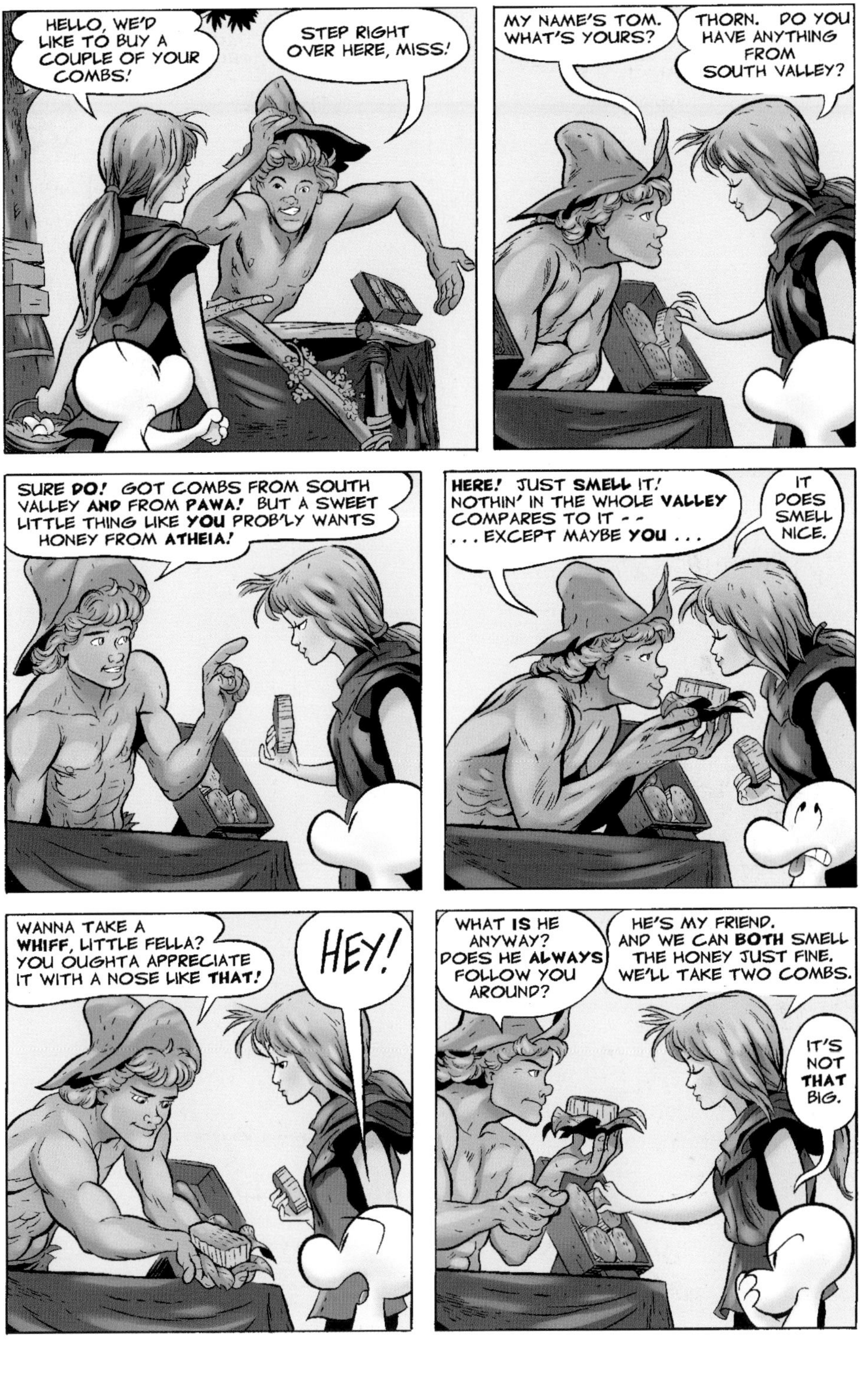
HELLO, WE'D LIKE TO BUY A COUPLE OF YOUR COMBS!
STEP RIGHT OVER HERE, MISS!
MY NAME'S TOM. WHAT'S YOURS?
THORN. DO YOU HAVE ANYTHING FROM SOUTH VALLEY?
SURE DO! GOT COMBS FROM SOUTH VALLEY AND FROM PAWA! BUT A SWEET LITTLE THING LIKE YOU PROB'LY WANTS HONEY FROM ATHEIA!
HERE! JUST SMELL IT! NOTHIN' IN THE WHOLE VALLEY COMPARES TO IT - - . . . EXCEPT MAYBE YOU . . .
IT DOES SMELL NICE.
WANNA TAKE A WHIFF, LITTLE FELLA? YOU OUGHTA APPRECIATE IT WITH A NOSE LIKE THAT!
HEY!
WHAT IS HE ANYWAY? DOES HE ALWAYS FOLLOW YOU AROUND?
HE'S MY FRIEND. AND WE CAN BOTH SMELL THE HONEY JUST FINE. WE'LL TAKE TWO COMBS.
IT'S NOT THAT BIG.

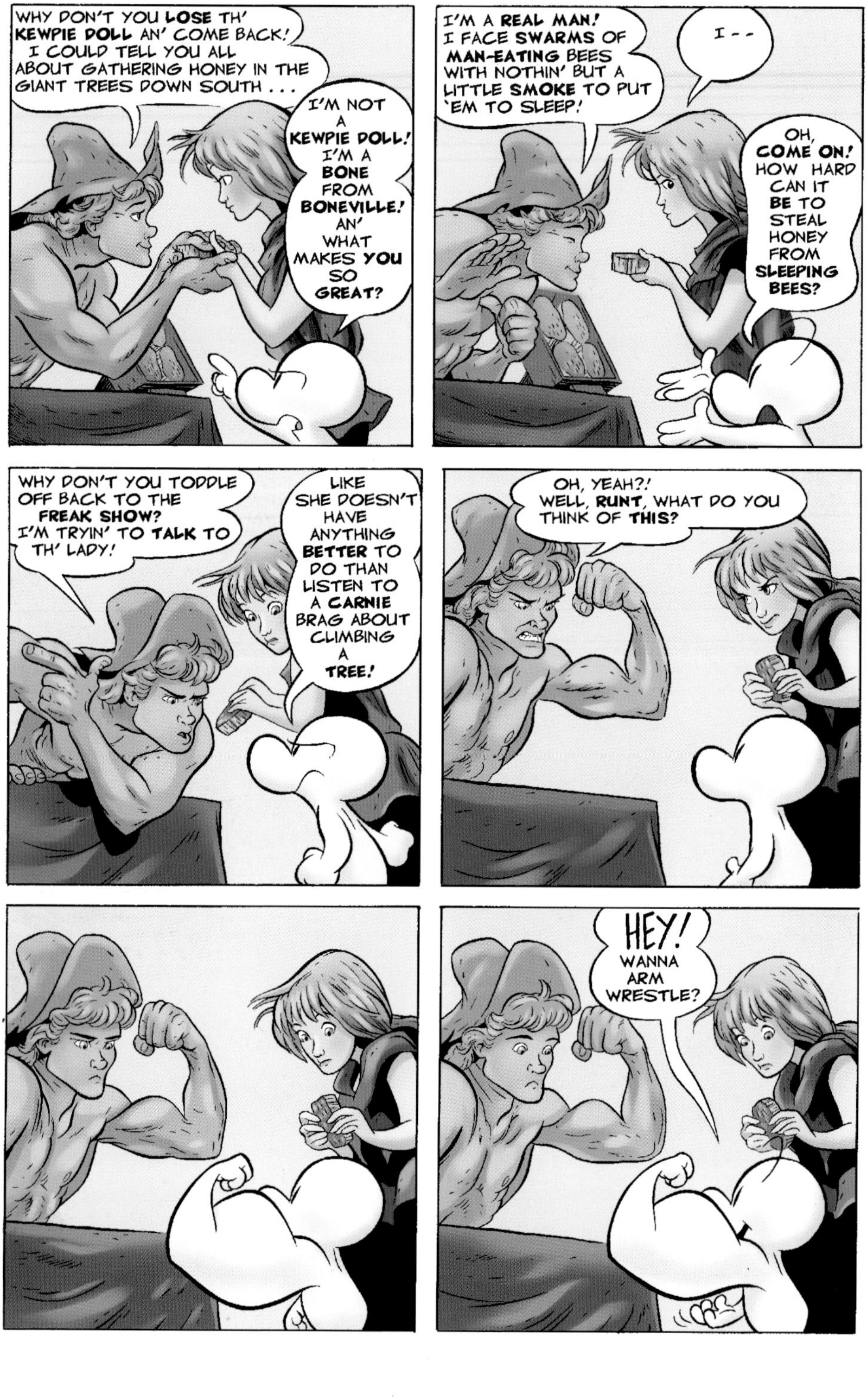
WHY DON'T YOU LOSE TH' KEWPIE DOLL AN' COME BACK! I COULD TELL YOU ALL ABOUT GATHERING HONEY IN THE GIANT TREES DOWN SOUTH . . .
I'M NOT A KEWPIE DOLL! I'M A BONE FROM BONEVILLE! AN' WHAT MAKES YOU SO GREAT?
I'M A REAL MAN! I FACE SWARMS OF MAN-EATING BEES WITH NOTHIN' BUT A LITTLE SMOKE TO PUT 'EM TO SLEEP!
I --
OH, COME ON! HOW HARD CAN IT BE TO STEAL HONEY FROM SLEEPING BEES?
WHY DON'T YOU TODDLE OFF BACK TO THE FREAK SHOW? I'M TRYIN' TO TALK TO TH' LADY!
LIKE SHE DOESN'T HAVE ANYTHING BETTER TO DO THAN LISTEN TO A CARNIE BRAG ABOUT CLIMBING A TREE!
OH, YEAH?! WELL, RUNT, WHAT DO YOU THINK OF THIS?
HEY! WANNA ARM WRESTLE?

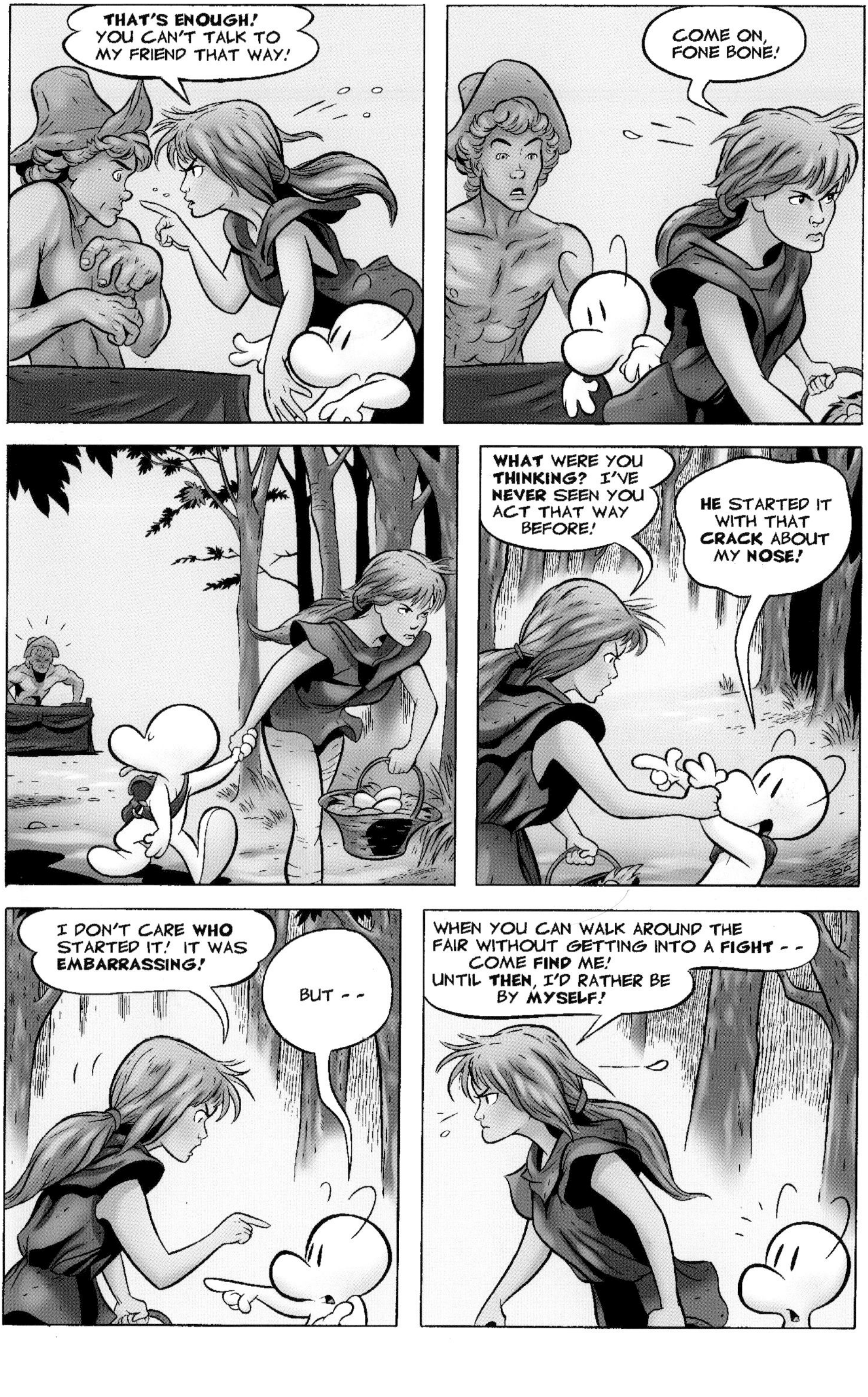
THAT'S ENOUGH! YOU CAN'T TALK TO MY FRIEND THAT WAY!
COME ON, FONE BONE!
WHAT WERE YOU THINKING? I'VE NEVER SEEN YOU ACT THAT WAY BEFORE!
HE STARTED IT WITH THAT CRACK ABOUT MY NOSE!
I DON'T CARE WHO STARTED IT! IT WAS EMBARRASSING!
BUT - -
WHEN YOU CAN WALK AROUND THE FAIR WITHOUT GETTING INTO A FIGHT - - COME FIND ME! UNTIL THEN, I'D RATHER BE BY MYSELF!

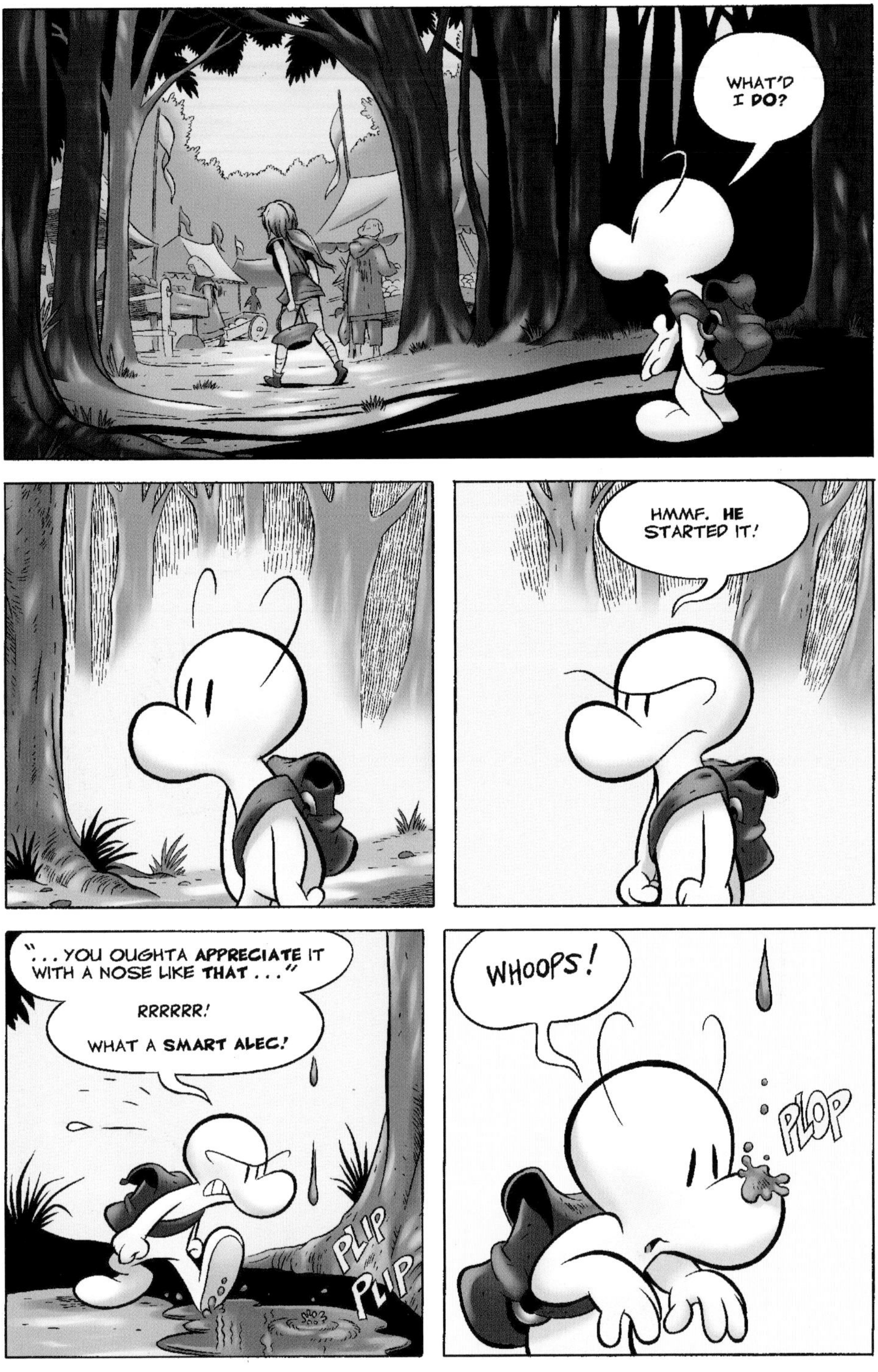
WHAT'D I DO?
HMMF. HE STARTED IT!
"...YOU OUGHTA APPRECIATE IT WITH A NOSE LIKE THAT..."
RRRRRR!
WHAT A SMART ALEC!
PLIP
PLIP
WHOOPS!
PLOP

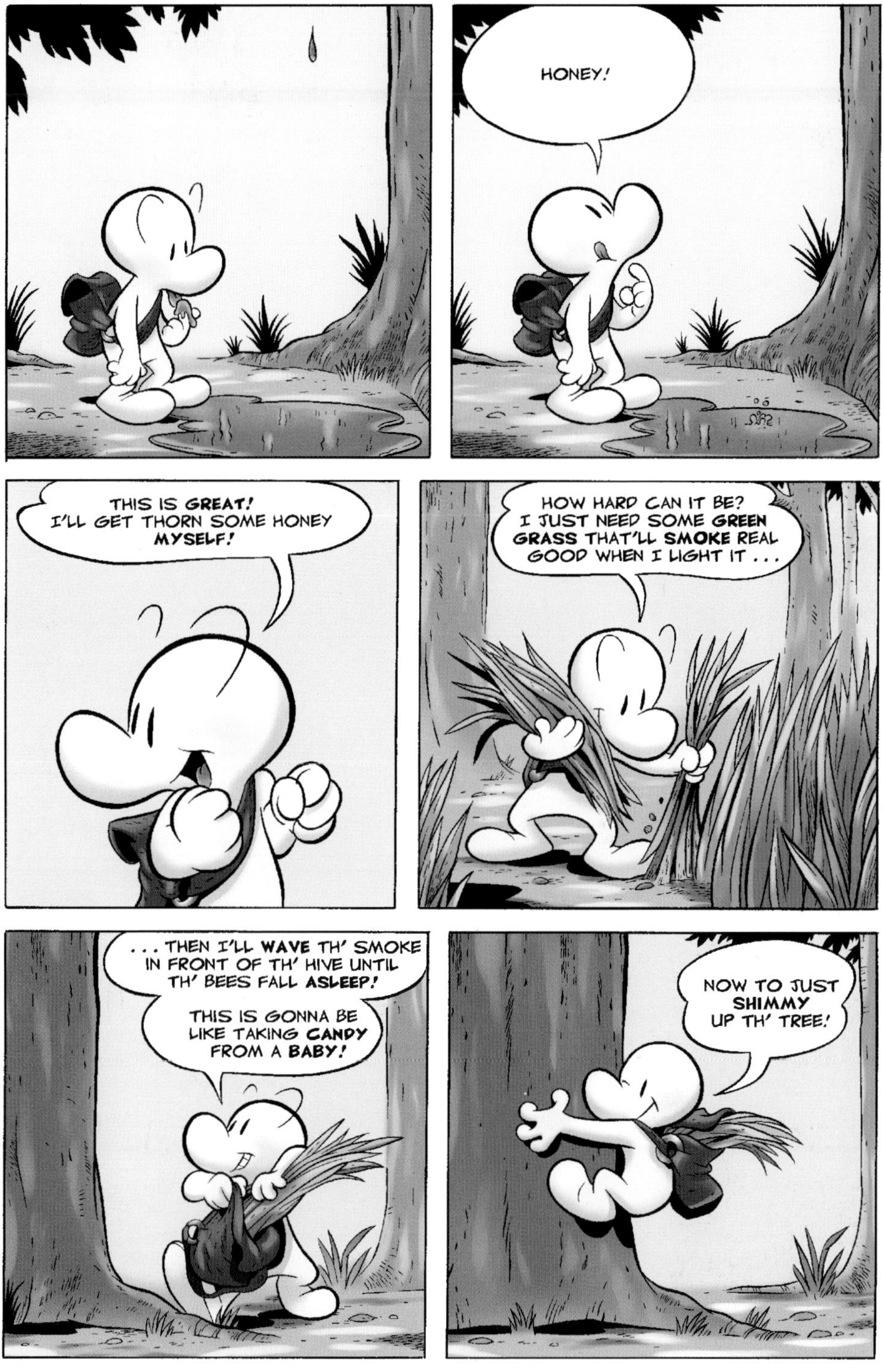
HONEY!
THIS IS GREAT! I'LL GET THORN SOME HONEY MYSELF!
HOW HARD CAN IT BE? I JUST NEED SOME GREEN GRASS THAT'LL SMOKE REAL GOOD WHEN I LIGHT IT . . .
. . . THEN I'LL WAVE TH' SMOKE IN FRONT OF TH' HIVE UNTIL TH' BEES FALL ASLEEP!
THIS IS GONNA BE LIKE TAKING CANDY FROM A BABY!
NOW TO JUST SHIMMY UP TH' TREE!

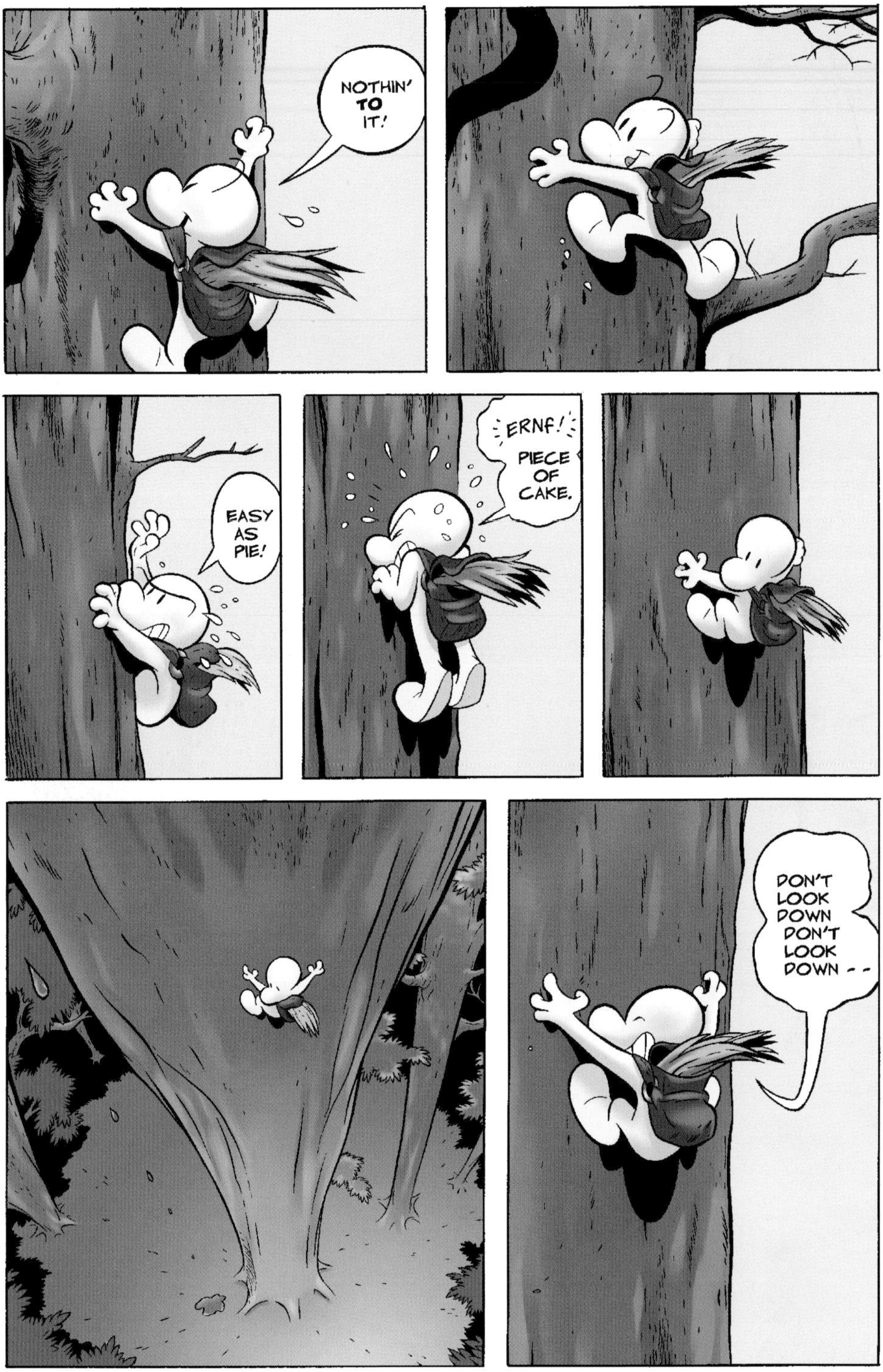
NOTHIN' TO IT!
EASY AS PIE!
ERNF!
PIECE OF CAKE.
DON'T LOOK DOWN DON'T LOOK DOWN - -

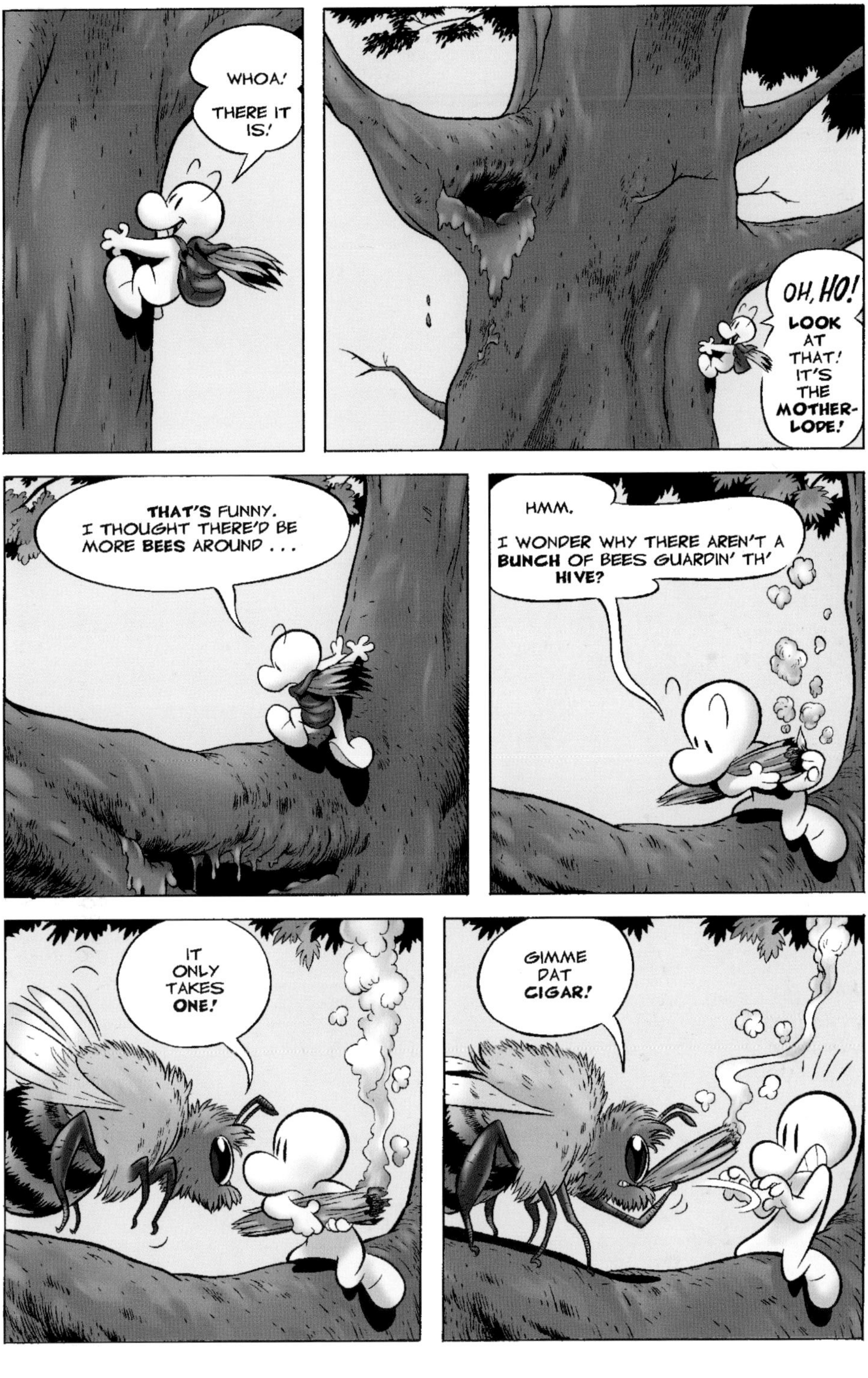
WHOA!
THERE IT IS!
OH, HO! LOOK AT THAT! IT'S THE MOTHER-LODE!
THAT'S FUNNY. I THOUGHT THERE'D BE MORE BEES AROUND . . .
HMM.
I WONDER WHY THERE AREN'T A BUNCH OF BEES GUARDIN' TH' HIVE?
IT ONLY TAKES ONE!
GIMME DAT CIGAR!

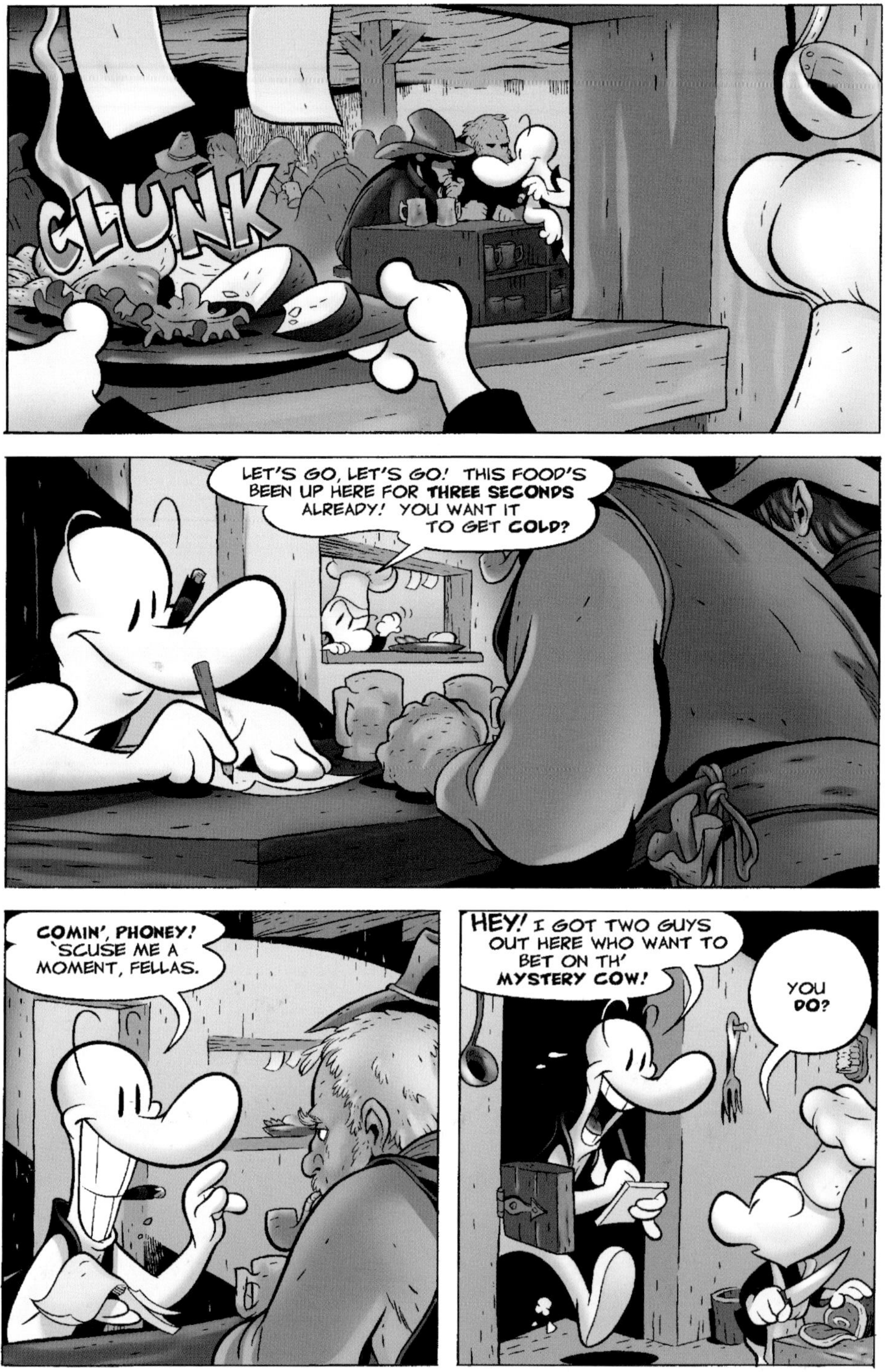
CLUNK
LET'S GO, LET'S GO! THIS FOOD'S BEEN UP HERE FOR THREE SECONDS ALREADY! YOU WANT IT TO GET COLD?
COMIN', PHONEY! 'SCUSE ME A MOMENT, FELLAS.
HEY! I GOT TWO GUYS OUT HERE WHO WANT TO BET ON TH' MYSTERY COW!
YOU DO?

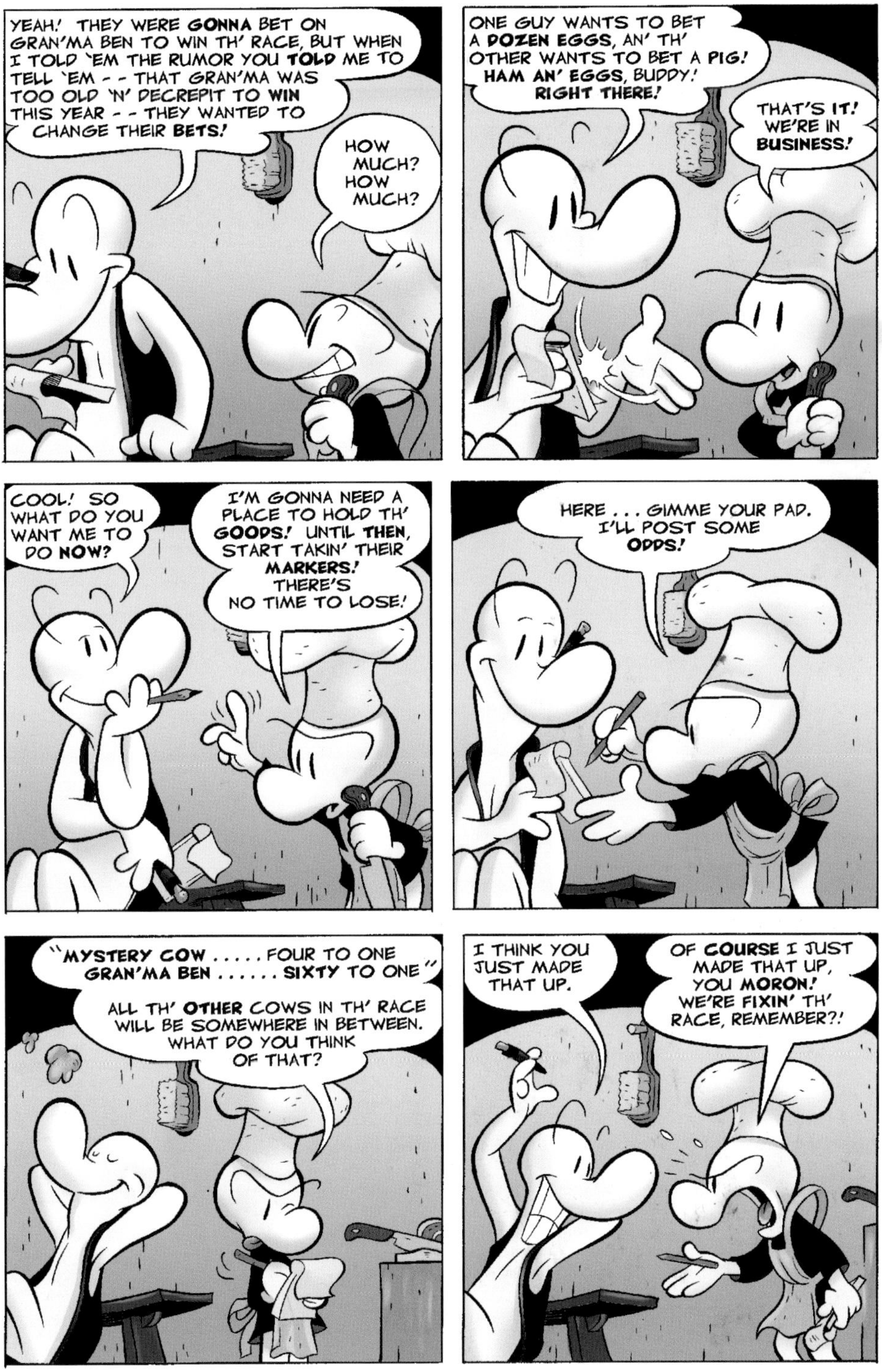
YEAH! THEY WERE GONNA BET ON GRAN'MA BEN TO WIN TH' RACE, BUT WHEN I TOLD 'EM THE RUMOR YOU TOLD ME TO TELL 'EM - - THAT GRAN'MA WAS TOO OLD 'N' DECREPIT TO WIN THIS YEAR - - THEY WANTED TO CHANGE THEIR BETS!
HOW MUCH? HOW MUCH?
ONE GUY WANTS TO BET A DOZEN EGGS, AN' TH' OTHER WANTS TO BET A PIG! HAM AN' EGGS, BUDDY! RIGHT THERE!
THAT'S IT! WE'RE IN BUSINESS!
COOL! SO WHAT DO YOU WANT ME TO DO NOW?
I'M GONNA NEED A PLACE TO HOLD TH' GOODS! UNTIL THEN, START TAKIN' THEIR MARKERS! THERE'S NO TIME TO LOSE!
HERE . . . GIMME YOUR PAD. I'LL POST SOME ODDS!
"MYSTERY COW . . . . . FOUR TO ONE GRAN'MA BEN . . . . . . SIXTY TO ONE"
ALL TH' OTHER COWS IN TH' RACE WILL BE SOMEWHERE IN BETWEEN. WHAT DO YOU THINK OF THAT?
I THINK YOU JUST MADE THAT UP.
OF COURSE I JUST MADE THAT UP, YOU MORON! WE'RE FIXIN' TH' RACE, REMEMBER?!

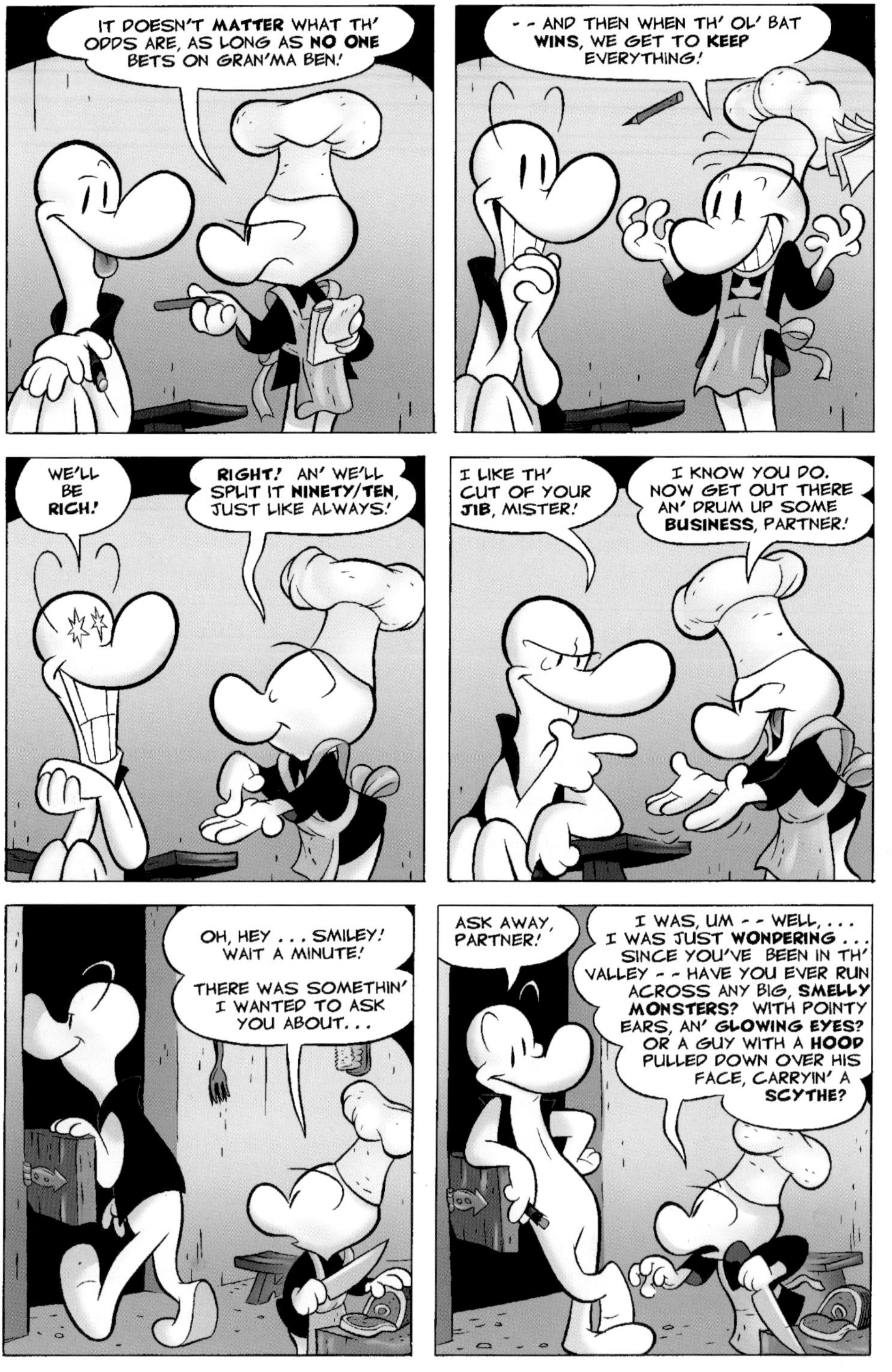
IT DOESN'T MATTER WHAT TH' ODDS ARE, AS LONG AS NO ONE BETS ON GRAN'MA BEN!
- - AND THEN WHEN TH' OL' BAT WINS, WE GET TO KEEP EVERYTHING!
WE'LL BE RICH!
RIGHT! AN' WE'LL SPLIT IT NINETY/TEN, JUST LIKE ALWAYS!
I LIKE TH' CUT OF YOUR JIB, MISTER!
I KNOW YOU DO. NOW GET OUT THERE AN' DRUM UP SOME BUSINESS, PARTNER!
OH, HEY . . . SMILEY! WAIT A MINUTE!
THERE WAS SOMETHIN' I WANTED TO ASK YOU ABOUT. . .
ASK AWAY, PARTNER!
I WAS, UM - - WELL, . . . I WAS JUST WONDERING . . . SINCE YOU'VE BEEN IN TH' VALLEY - - HAVE YOU EVER RUN ACROSS ANY BIG, SMELLY MONSTERS? WITH POINTY EARS, AN' GLOWING EYES? OR A GUY WITH A HOOD PULLED DOWN OVER HIS FACE, CARRYIN' A SCYTHE?

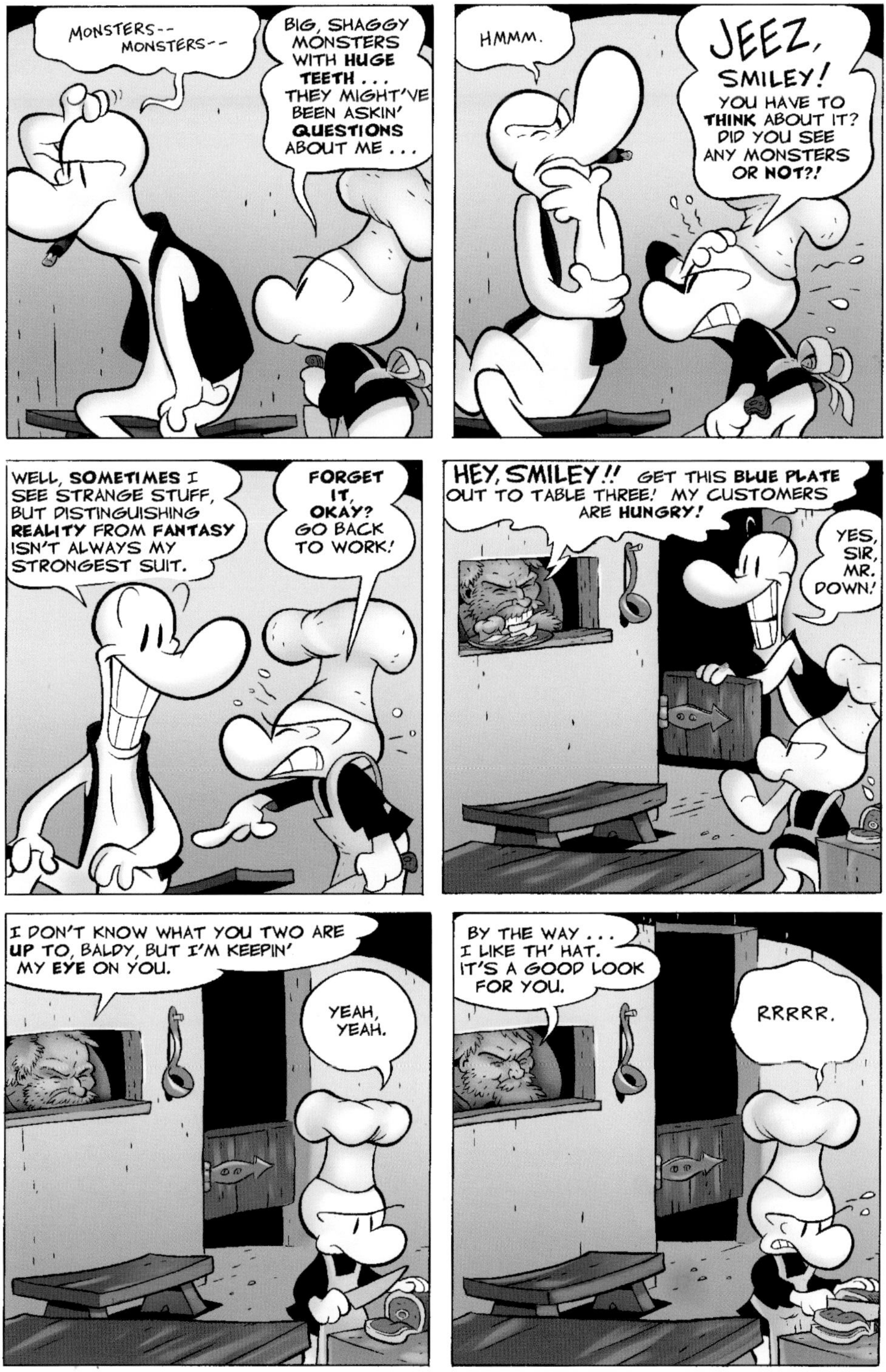
MONSTERS-- MONSTERS--
BIG, SHAGGY MONSTERS WITH HUGE TEETH . . . THEY MIGHT'VE BEEN ASKIN' QUESTIONS ABOUT ME . . .
HMMM.
JEEZ, SMILEY! YOU HAVE TO THINK ABOUT IT? DID YOU SEE ANY MONSTERS OR NOT?!
WELL, SOMETIMES I SEE STRANGE STUFF, BUT DISTINGUISHING REALITY FROM FANTASY ISN'T ALWAYS MY STRONGEST SUIT.
FORGET IT, OKAY? GO BACK TO WORK!
HEY, SMILEY!! GET THIS BLUE PLATE OUT TO TABLE THREE! MY CUSTOMERS ARE HUNGRY!
YES, SIR, MR. DOWN!
I DON'T KNOW WHAT YOU TWO ARE UP TO, BALDY, BUT I'M KEEPIN' MY EYE ON YOU.
YEAH, YEAH.
BY THE WAY . . . I LIKE TH' HAT. IT'S A GOOD LOOK FOR YOU.
RRRRR.

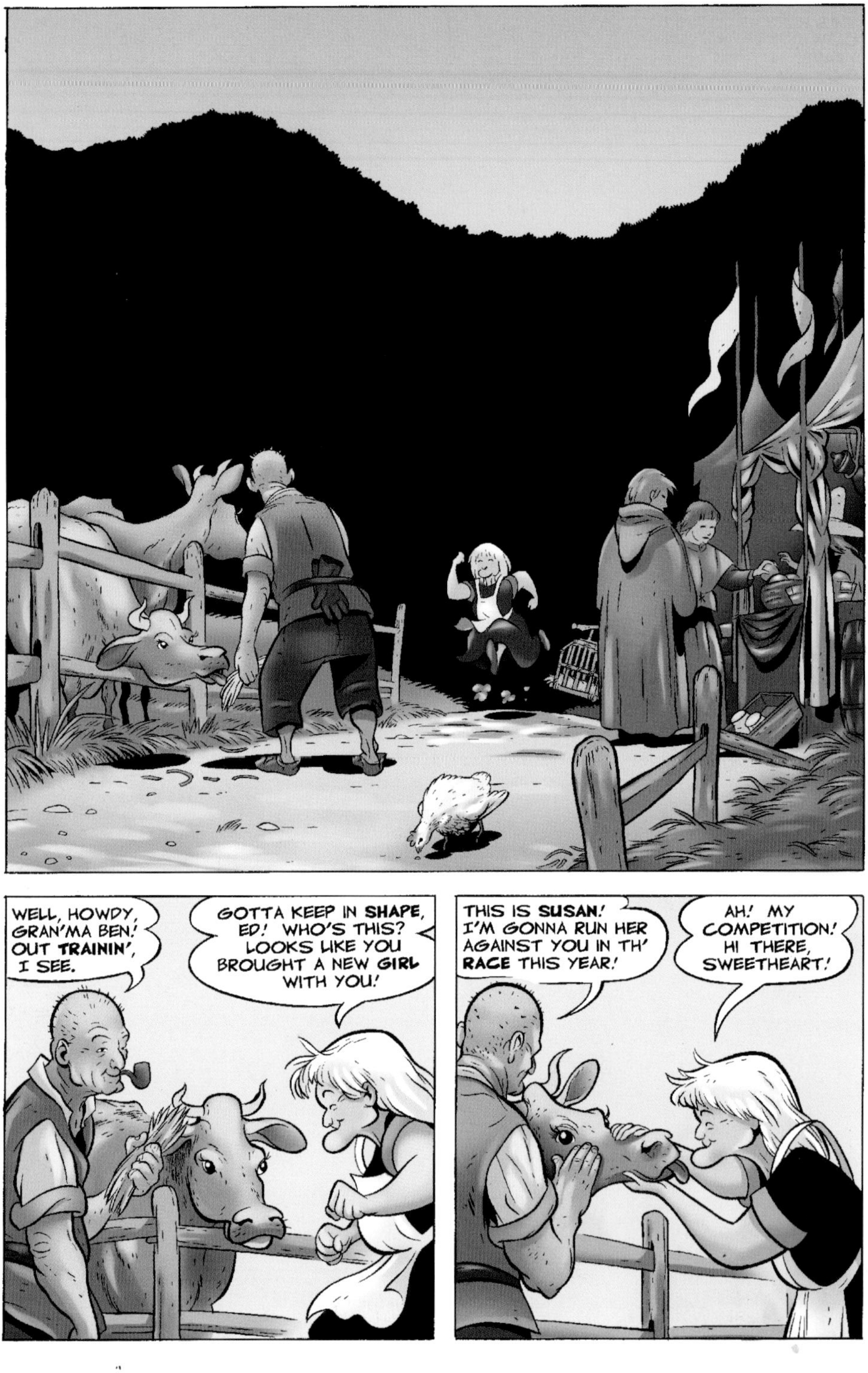
WELL, HOWDY, GRAN'MA BEN! OUT TRAININ', I SEE.
GOTTA KEEP IN SHAPE, ED! WHO'S THIS? LOOKS LIKE YOU BROUGHT A NEW GIRL WITH YOU!
THIS IS SUSAN! I'M GONNA RUN HER AGAINST YOU IN TH' RACE THIS YEAR!
AH! MY COMPETITION! HI THERE, SWEETHEART!

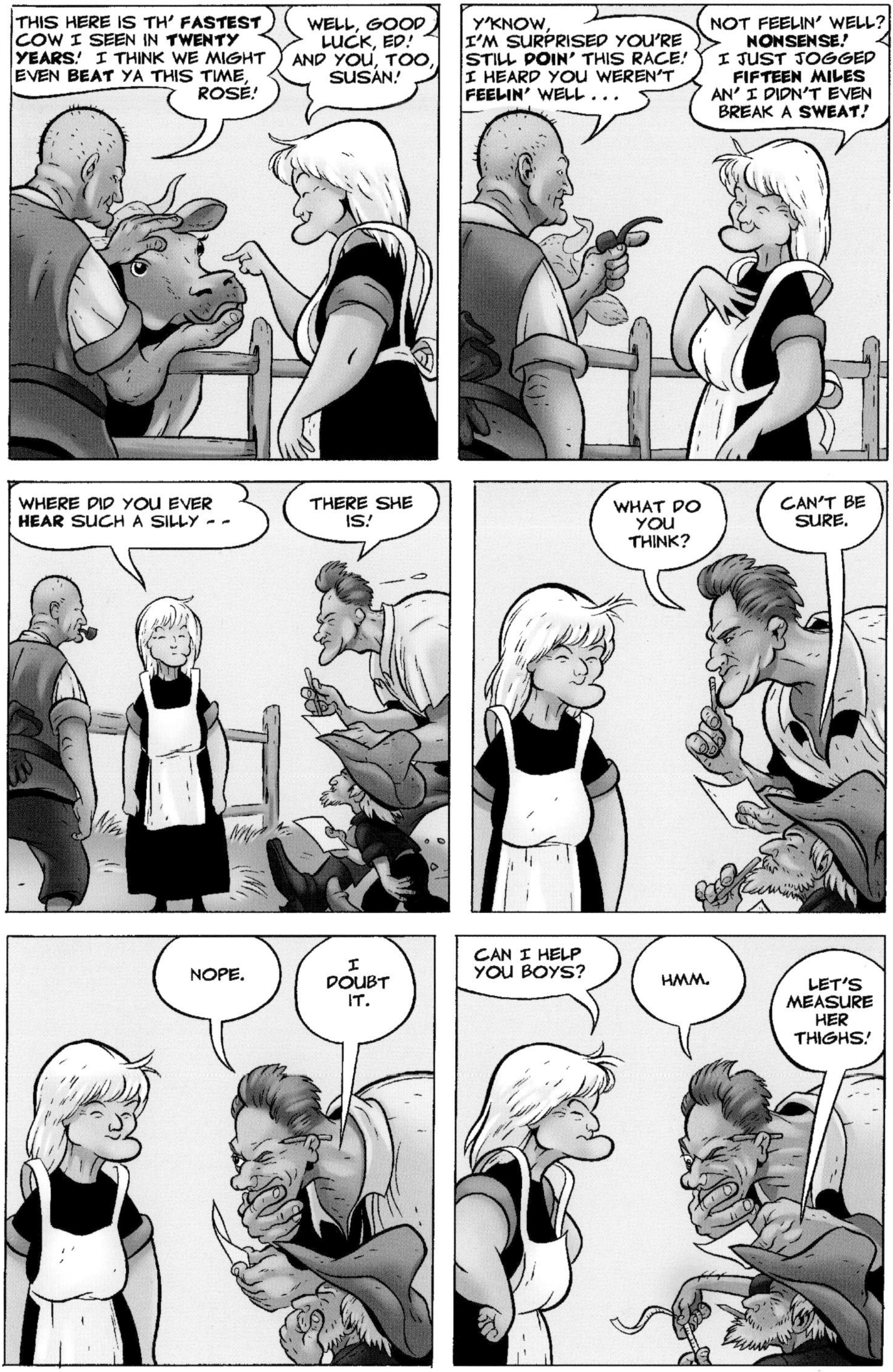
THIS HERE IS TH' FASTEST COW I SEEN IN TWENTY YEARS! I THINK WE MIGHT EVEN BEAT YA THIS TIME, ROSE!
WELL, GOOD LUCK, ED! AND YOU, TOO, SUSAN!
Y'KNOW, I'M SURPRISED YOU'RE STILL DOIN' THIS RACE! I HEARD YOU WEREN'T FEELIN' WELL . . .
NOT FEELIN' WELL? NONSENSE! I JUST JOGGED FIFTEEN MILES AN' I DIDN'T EVEN BREAK A SWEAT!
WHERE DID YOU EVER HEAR SUCH A SILLY - -
THERE SHE IS!
WHAT DO YOU THINK?
CAN'T BE SURE.
NOPE.
I DOUBT IT.
CAN I HELP YOU BOYS?
HMM.
LET'S MEASURE HER THIGHS!

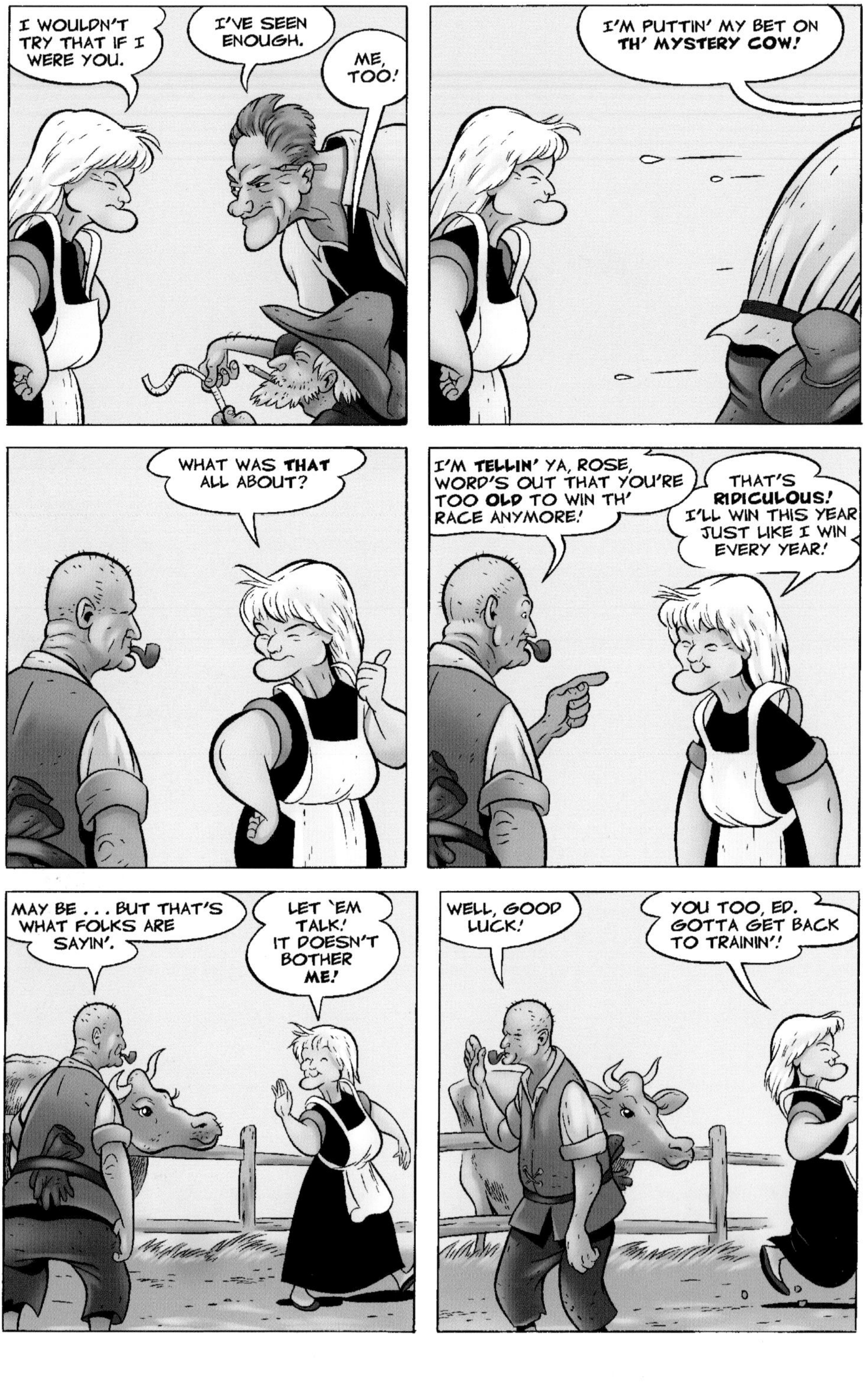
I WOULDN'T TRY THAT IF I WERE YOU.
I'VE SEEN ENOUGH.
ME, TOO!
I'M PUTTIN' MY BET ON TH' MYSTERY COW!
WHAT WAS THAT ALL ABOUT?
I'M TELLIN' YA, ROSE, WORD'S OUT THAT YOU'RE TOO OLD TO WIN TH' RACE ANYMORE!
THAT'S RIDICULOUS! I'LL WIN THIS YEAR JUST LIKE I WIN EVERY YEAR!
MAY BE . . . BUT THAT'S WHAT FOLKS ARE SAYIN'.
LET 'EM TALK! IT DOESN'T BOTHER ME!
WELL, GOOD LUCK!
YOU TOO, ED. GOTTA GET BACK TO TRAININ'!

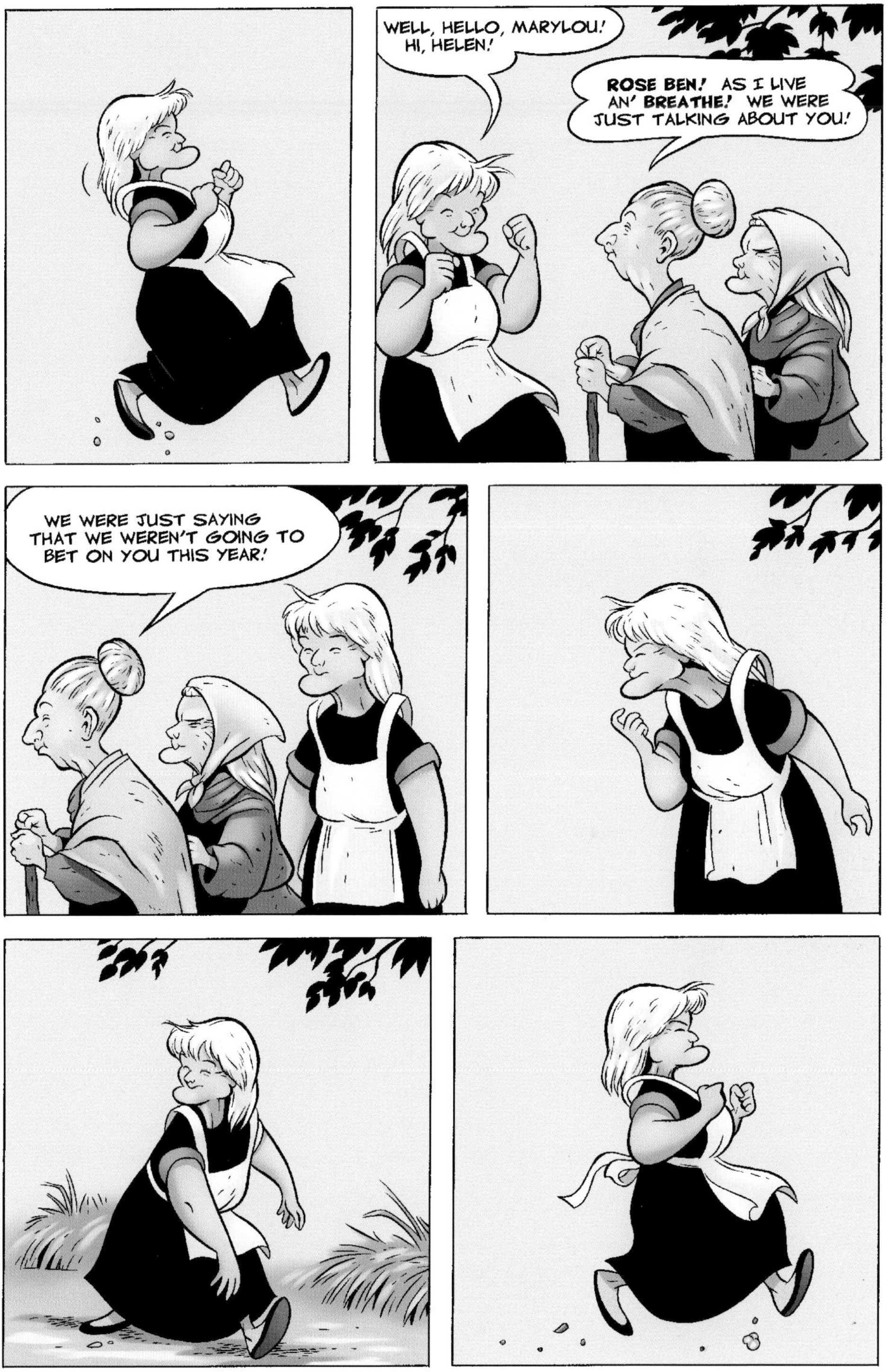
WELL, HELLO, MARYLOU! HI, HELEN!
ROSE BEN! AS I LIVE AN' BREATHE! WE WERE JUST TALKING ABOUT YOU!
WE WERE JUST SAYING THAT WE WEREN'T GOING TO BET ON YOU THIS YEAR!

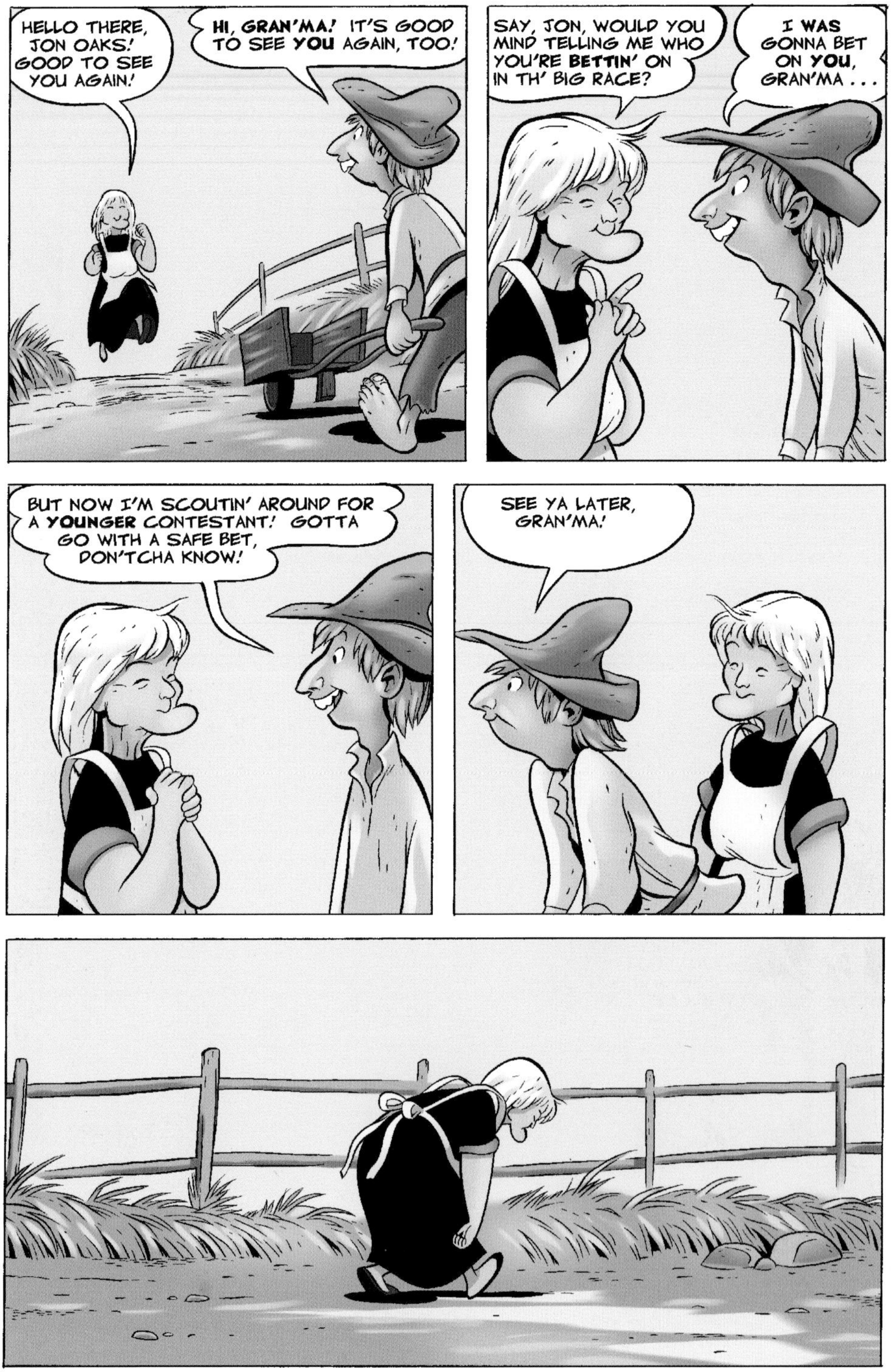
HELLO THERE, JON OAKS! GOOD TO SEE YOU AGAIN!
HI, GRAN'MA! IT'S GOOD TO SEE YOU AGAIN, TOO!
SAY, JON, WOULD YOU MIND TELLING ME WHO YOU'RE BETTIN' ON IN TH' BIG RACE?
I WAS GONNA BET ON YOU, GRAN'MA . . .
BUT NOW I'M SCOUTIN' AROUND FOR A YOUNGER CONTESTANT! GOTTA GO WITH A SAFE BET, DON'TCHA KNOW!
SEE YA LATER, GRAN'MA!

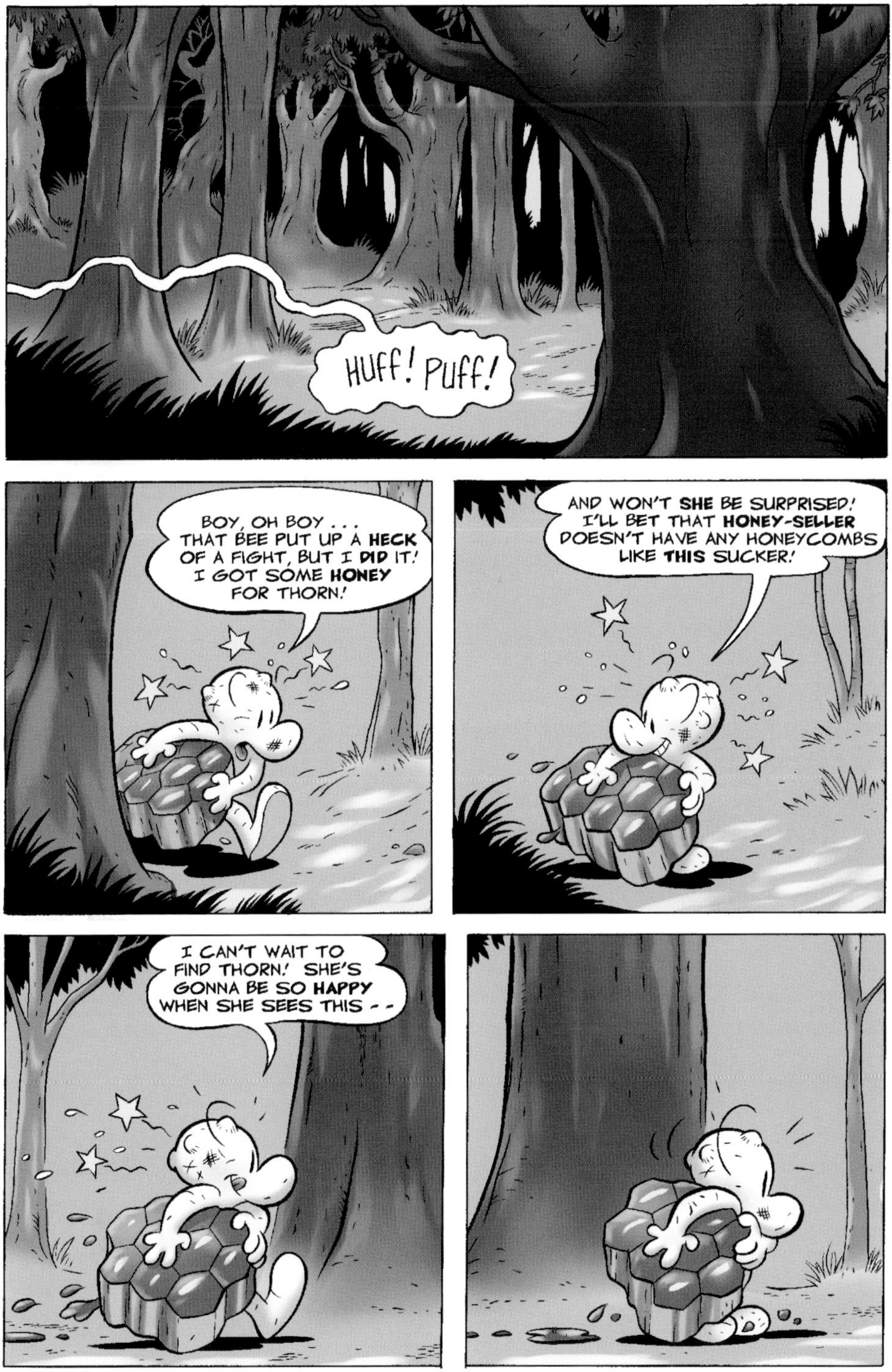
HUFF! PUFF!
BOY, OH BOY . . . THAT BEE PUT UP A HECK OF A FIGHT, BUT I DID IT! I GOT SOME HONEY FOR THORN!
AND WON'T SHE BE SURPRISED! I'LL BET THAT HONEY-SELLER DOESN'T HAVE ANY HONEYCOMBS LIKE THIS SUCKER!
I CAN'T WAIT TO FIND THORN! SHE'S GONNA BE SO HAPPY WHEN SHE SEES THIS - -

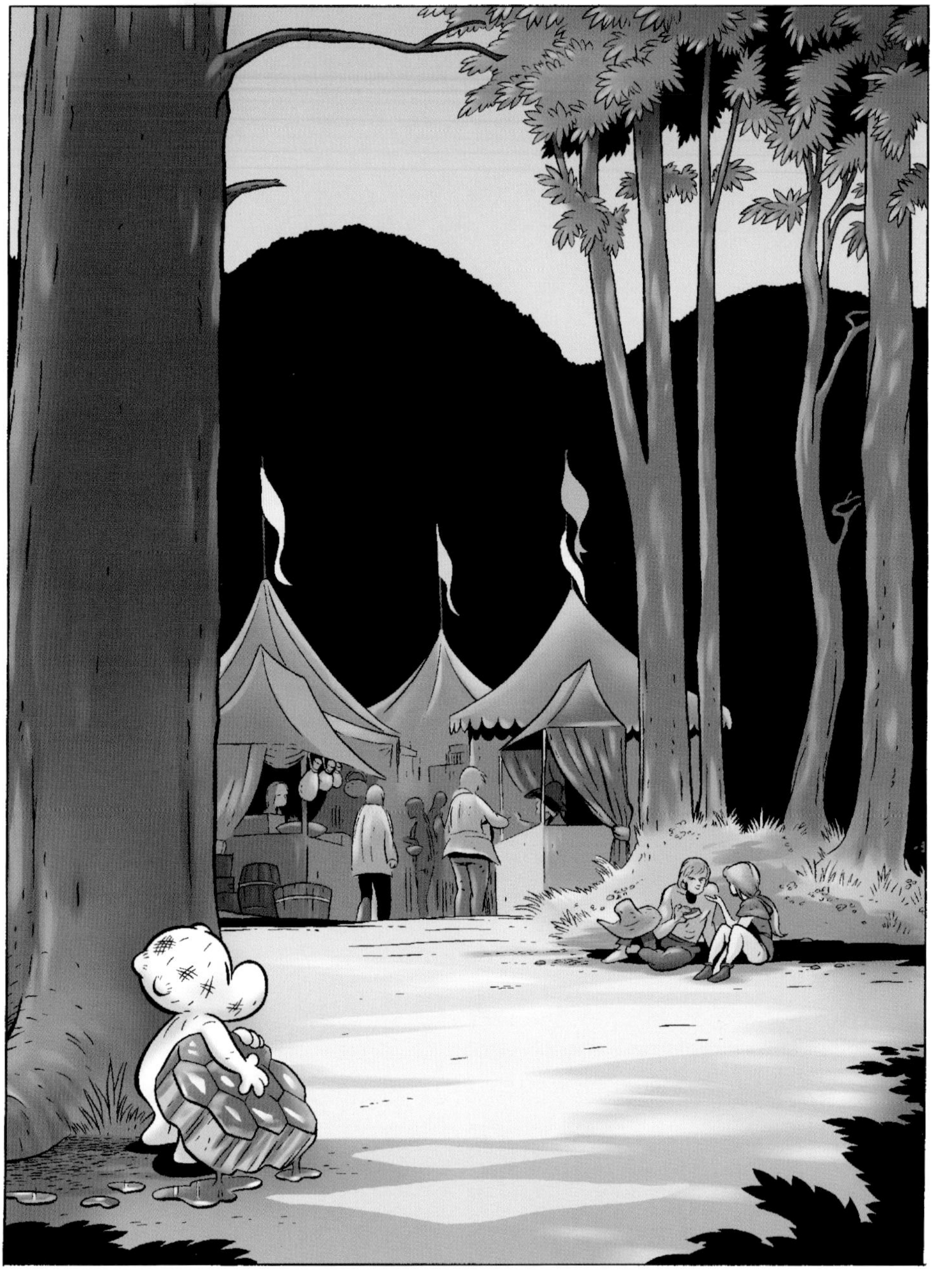

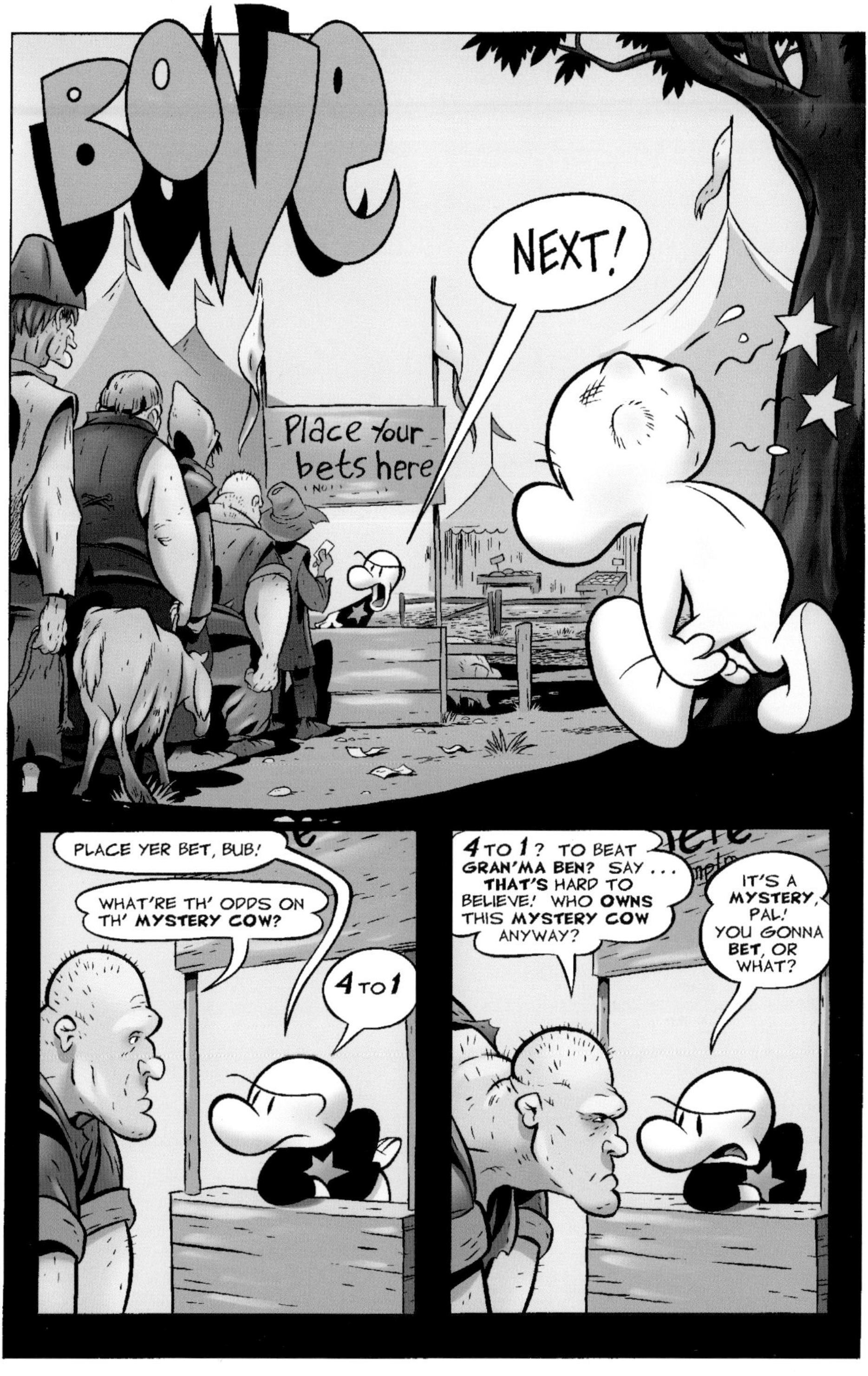
BONE
NEXT!
Place your bets here
PLACE YER BET, BUB!
WHAT'RE TH' ODDS ON TH' MYSTERY COW?
4 TO 1
4 TO 1? TO BEAT GRAN'MA BEN? SAY... THAT'S HARD TO BELIEVE! WHO OWNS THIS MYSTERY COW ANYWAY?
IT'S A MYSTERY, PAL! YOU GONNA BET, OR WHAT?

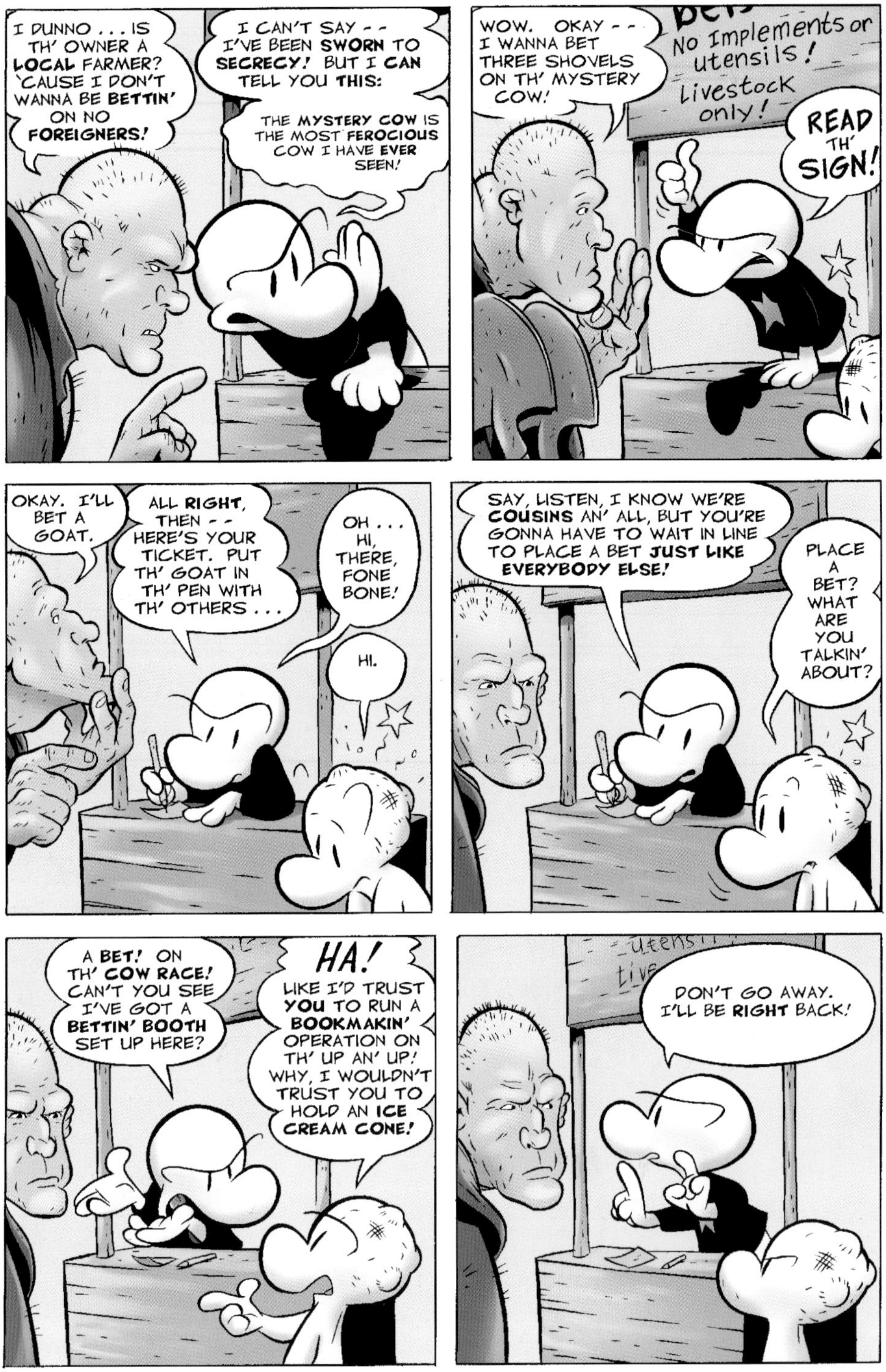
I DUNNO . . . IS TH' OWNER A LOCAL FARMER? 'CAUSE I DON'T WANNA BE BETTIN' ON NO FOREIGNERS!
I CAN'T SAY - - I'VE BEEN SWORN TO SECRECY! BUT I CAN TELL YOU THIS:
THE MYSTERY COW IS THE MOST FEROCIOUS COW I HAVE EVER SEEN!
WOW. OKAY - - I WANNA BET THREE SHOVELS ON TH' MYSTERY COW!
No Implements or utensils! Livestock only!
READ TH' SIGN!
OKAY. I'LL BET A GOAT.
ALL RIGHT, THEN - - HERE'S YOUR TICKET. PUT TH' GOAT IN TH' PEN WITH TH' OTHERS . . .
OH . . . HI, THERE, FONE BONE!
HI.
SAY, LISTEN, I KNOW WE'RE COUSINS AN' ALL, BUT YOU'RE GONNA HAVE TO WAIT IN LINE TO PLACE A BET JUST LIKE EVERYBODY ELSE!
PLACE A BET? WHAT ARE YOU TALKIN' ABOUT?
A BET! ON TH' COW RACE! CAN'T YOU SEE I'VE GOT A BETTIN' BOOTH SET UP HERE?
HA!
LIKE I'D TRUST YOU TO RUN A BOOKMAKIN' OPERATION ON TH' UP AN' UP! WHY, I WOULDN'T TRUST YOU TO HOLD AN ICE CREAM CONE!
DON'T GO AWAY. I'LL BE RIGHT BACK!

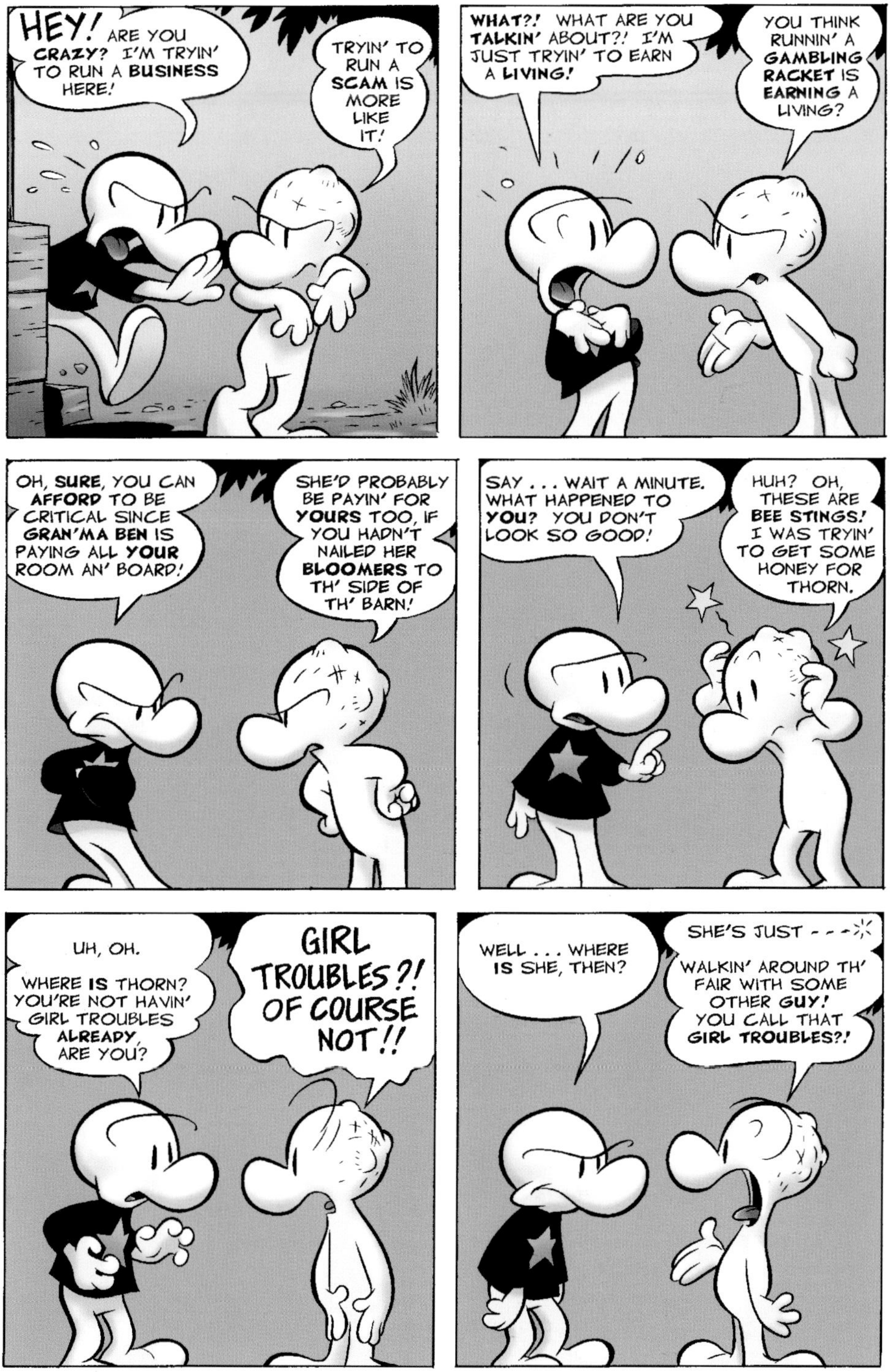
HEY! ARE YOU CRAZY? I'M TRYIN' TO RUN A BUSINESS HERE!
TRYIN' TO RUN A SCAM IS MORE LIKE IT!
WHAT?! WHAT ARE YOU TALKIN' ABOUT?! I'M JUST TRYIN' TO EARN A LIVING!
YOU THINK RUNNIN' A GAMBLING RACKET IS EARNING A LIVING?
OH, SURE, YOU CAN AFFORD TO BE CRITICAL SINCE GRAN'MA BEN IS PAYING ALL YOUR ROOM AN' BOARD!
SHE'D PROBABLY BE PAYIN' FOR YOURS TOO, IF YOU HADN'T NAILED HER BLOOMERS TO TH' SIDE OF TH' BARN!
SAY . . . WAIT A MINUTE. WHAT HAPPENED TO YOU? YOU DON'T LOOK SO GOOD!
HUH? OH, THESE ARE BEE STINGS! I WAS TRYIN' TO GET SOME HONEY FOR THORN.
UH, OH.
WHERE IS THORN? YOU'RE NOT HAVIN' GIRL TROUBLES ALREADY, ARE YOU?
GIRL TROUBLES?! OF COURSE NOT!!
WELL . . . WHERE IS SHE, THEN?
SHE'S JUST - - -
WALKIN' AROUND TH' FAIR WITH SOME OTHER GUY! YOU CALL THAT GIRL TROUBLES?!

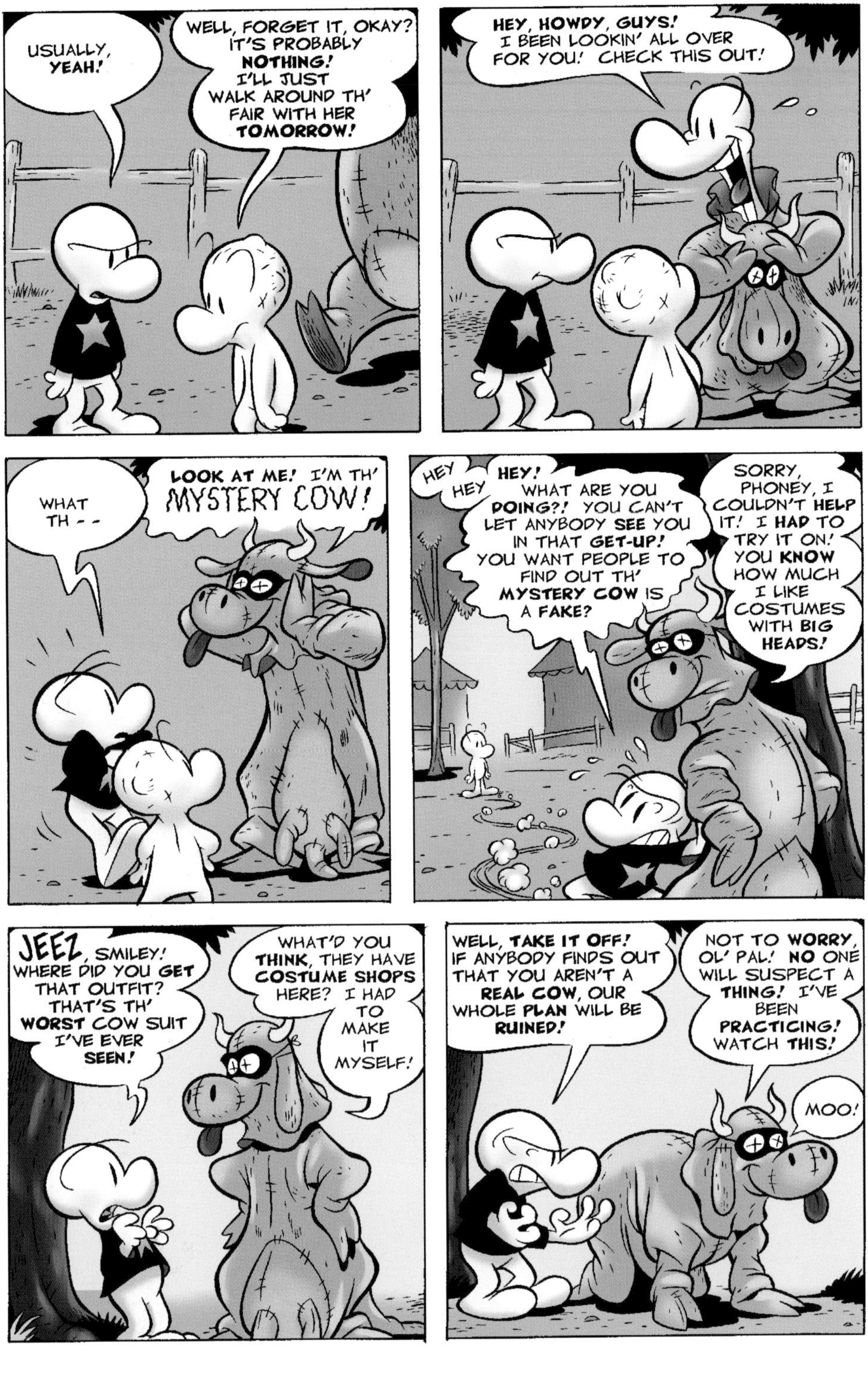
USUALLY, YEAH!
WELL, FORGET IT, OKAY? IT'S PROBABLY NOTHING! I'LL JUST WALK AROUND TH' FAIR WITH HER TOMORROW!
HEY, HOWDY, GUYS! I BEEN LOOKIN' ALL OVER FOR YOU! CHECK THIS OUT!
WHAT TH --
LOOK AT ME! I'M TH' MYSTERY COW!
HEY HEY HEY! WHAT ARE YOU DOING?! YOU CAN'T LET ANYBODY SEE YOU IN THAT GET-UP! YOU WANT PEOPLE TO FIND OUT TH' MYSTERY COW IS A FAKE?
SORRY, PHONEY, I COULDN'T HELP IT! I HAD TO TRY IT ON! YOU KNOW HOW MUCH I LIKE COSTUMES WITH BIG HEADS!
JEEZ, SMILEY! WHERE DID YOU GET THAT OUTFIT? THAT'S TH' WORST COW SUIT I'VE EVER SEEN!
WHAT'D YOU THINK, THEY HAVE COSTUME SHOPS HERE? I HAD TO MAKE IT MYSELF!
WELL, TAKE IT OFF! IF ANYBODY FINDS OUT THAT YOU AREN'T A REAL COW, OUR WHOLE PLAN WILL BE RUINED!
NOT TO WORRY, OL' PAL! NO ONE WILL SUSPECT A THING! I'VE BEEN PRACTICING! WATCH THIS!
MOO!

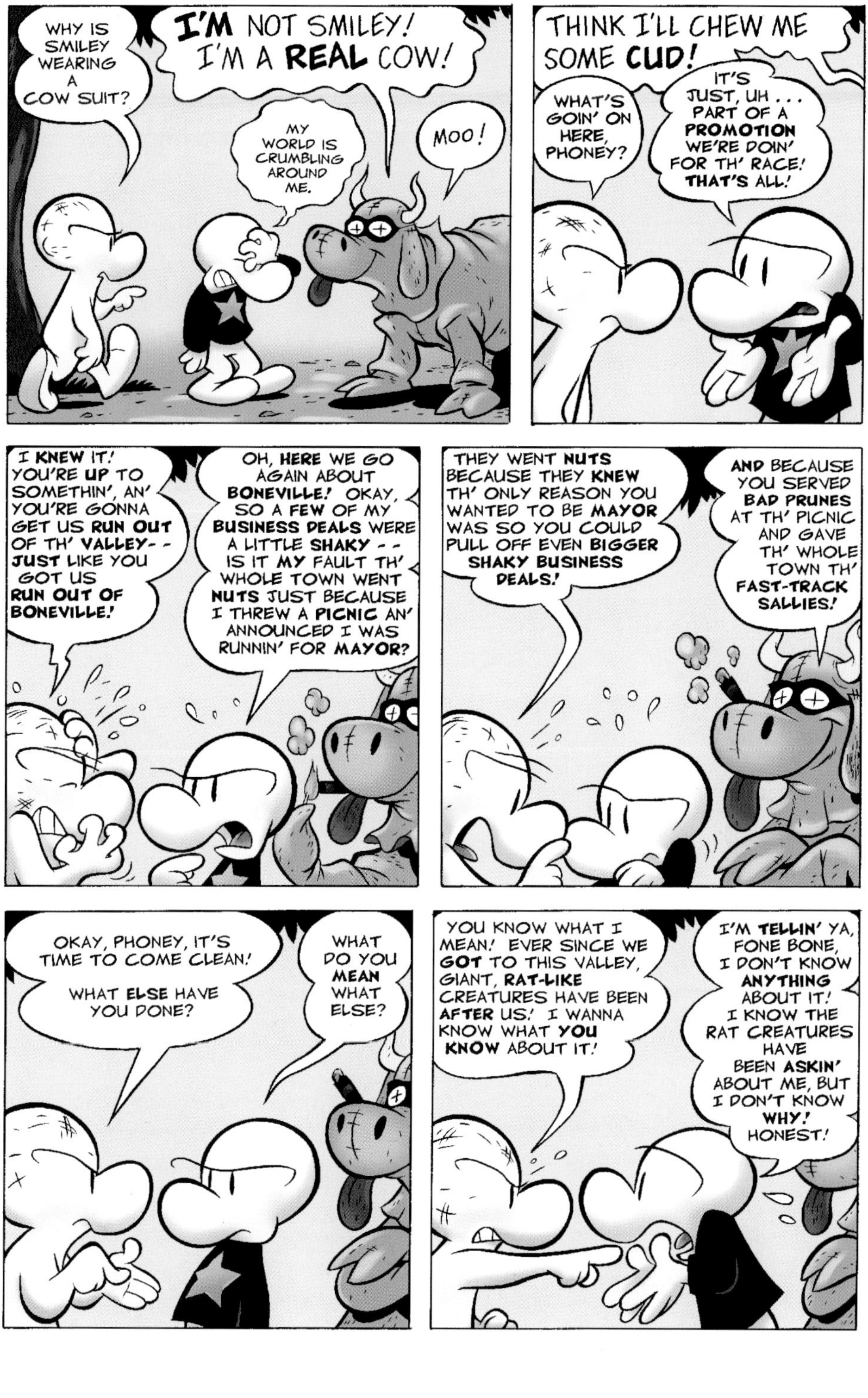
WHY IS SMILEY WEARING A COW SUIT?
I'M NOT SMILEY! I'M A REAL COW!
MY WORLD IS CRUMBLING AROUND ME.
MOO!
THINK I'LL CHEW ME SOME CUD!
WHAT'S GOIN' ON HERE, PHONEY?
IT'S JUST, UH . . . PART OF A PROMOTION WE'RE DOIN' FOR TH' RACE! THAT'S ALL!
I KNEW IT! YOU'RE UP TO SOMETHIN', AN' YOU'RE GONNA GET US RUN OUT OF TH' VALLEY-- JUST LIKE YOU GOT US RUN OUT OF BONEVILLE!
OH, HERE WE GO AGAIN ABOUT BONEVILLE! OKAY, SO A FEW OF MY BUSINESS DEALS WERE A LITTLE SHAKY -- IS IT MY FAULT TH' WHOLE TOWN WENT NUTS JUST BECAUSE I THREW A PICNIC AN' ANNOUNCED I WAS RUNNIN' FOR MAYOR?
THEY WENT NUTS BECAUSE THEY KNEW TH' ONLY REASON YOU WANTED TO BE MAYOR WAS SO YOU COULD PULL OFF EVEN BIGGER SHAKY BUSINESS DEALS!
AND BECAUSE YOU SERVED BAD PRUNES AT TH' PICNIC AND GAVE TH' WHOLE TOWN TH' FAST-TRACK SALLIES!
OKAY, PHONEY, IT'S TIME TO COME CLEAN!
WHAT ELSE HAVE YOU DONE?
WHAT DO YOU MEAN WHAT ELSE?
YOU KNOW WHAT I MEAN! EVER SINCE WE GOT TO THIS VALLEY, GIANT, RAT-LIKE CREATURES HAVE BEEN AFTER US! I WANNA KNOW WHAT YOU KNOW ABOUT IT!
I'M TELLIN' YA, FONE BONE, I DON'T KNOW ANYTHING ABOUT IT! I KNOW THE RAT CREATURES HAVE BEEN ASKIN' ABOUT ME, BUT I DON'T KNOW WHY! HONEST!

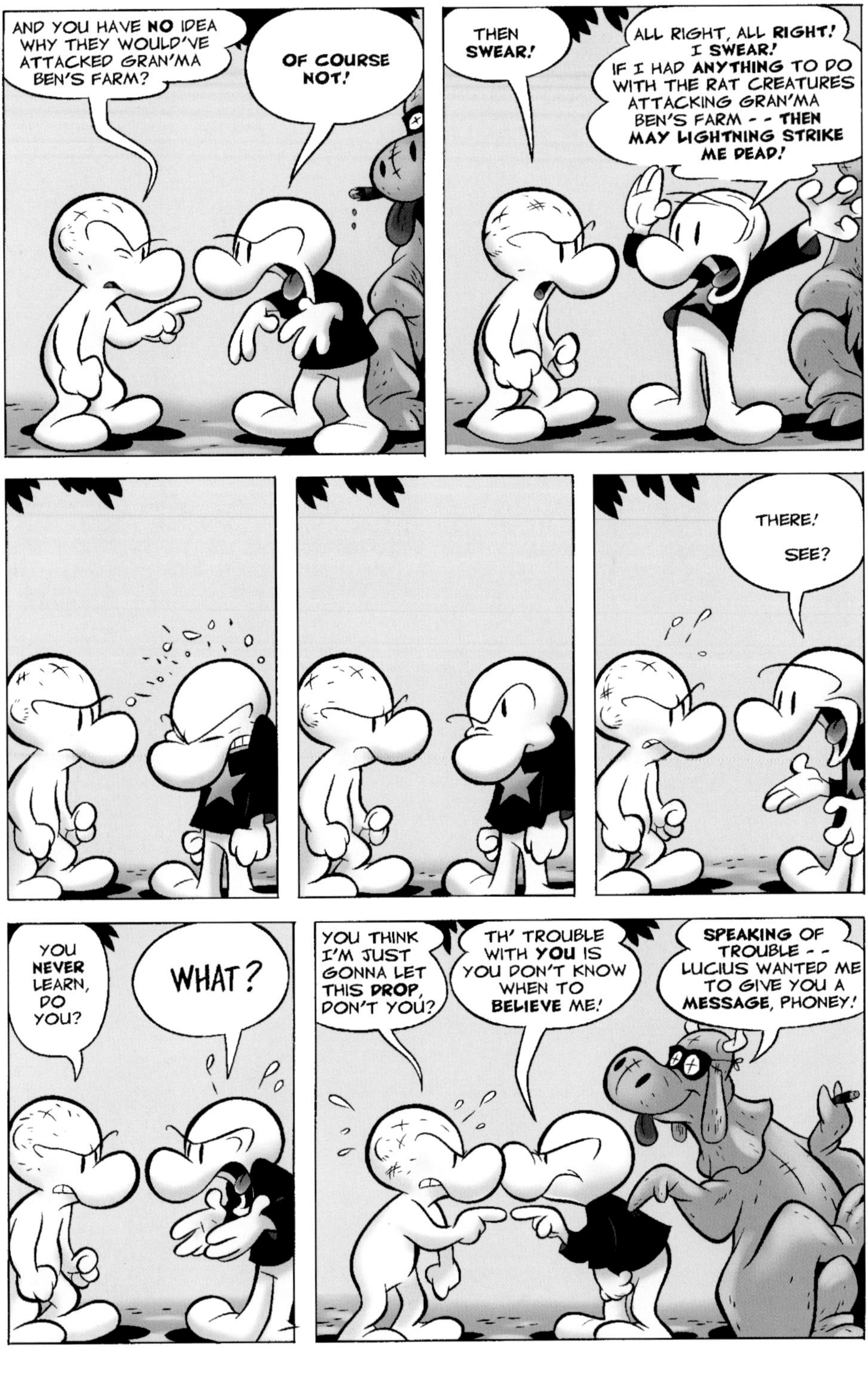
AND YOU HAVE NO IDEA WHY THEY WOULD'VE ATTACKED GRAN'MA BEN'S FARM?
OF COURSE NOT!
THEN SWEAR!
ALL RIGHT, ALL RIGHT! I SWEAR! IF I HAD ANYTHING TO DO WITH THE RAT CREATURES ATTACKING GRAN'MA BEN'S FARM - - THEN MAY LIGHTNING STRIKE ME DEAD!
THERE! SEE?
YOU NEVER LEARN, DO YOU?
WHAT?
YOU THINK I'M JUST GONNA LET THIS DROP, DON'T YOU?
TH' TROUBLE WITH YOU IS YOU DON'T KNOW WHEN TO BELIEVE ME!
SPEAKING OF TROUBLE - - LUCIUS WANTED ME TO GIVE YOU A MESSAGE, PHONEY!

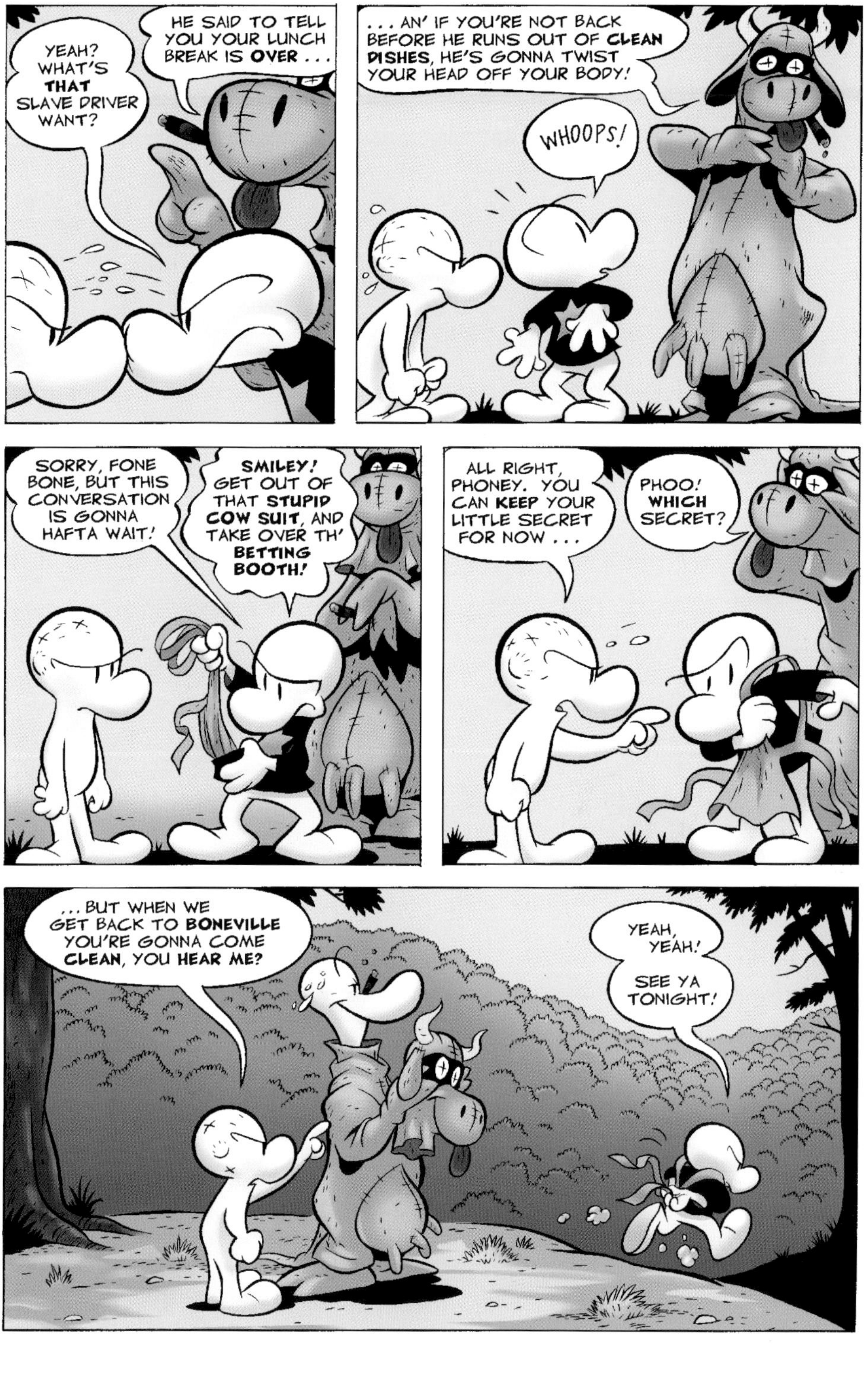
YEAH? WHAT'S THAT SLAVE DRIVER WANT?
HE SAID TO TELL YOU YOUR LUNCH BREAK IS OVER . . .
. . . AN' IF YOU'RE NOT BACK BEFORE HE RUNS OUT OF CLEAN DISHES, HE'S GONNA TWIST YOUR HEAD OFF YOUR BODY!
WHOOPS!
SORRY, FONE BONE, BUT THIS CONVERSATION IS GONNA HAFTA WAIT!
SMILEY! GET OUT OF THAT STUPID COW SUIT, AND TAKE OVER TH' BETTING BOOTH!
ALL RIGHT, PHONEY. YOU CAN KEEP YOUR LITTLE SECRET FOR NOW . . .
PHOO! WHICH SECRET?
. . . BUT WHEN WE GET BACK TO BONEVILLE YOU'RE GONNA COME CLEAN, YOU HEAR ME?
YEAH, YEAH!
SEE YA TONIGHT!

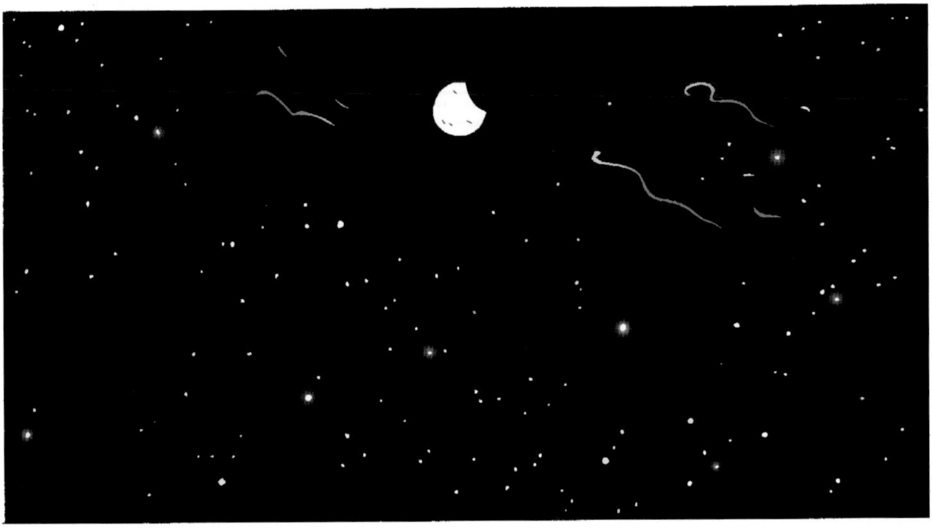

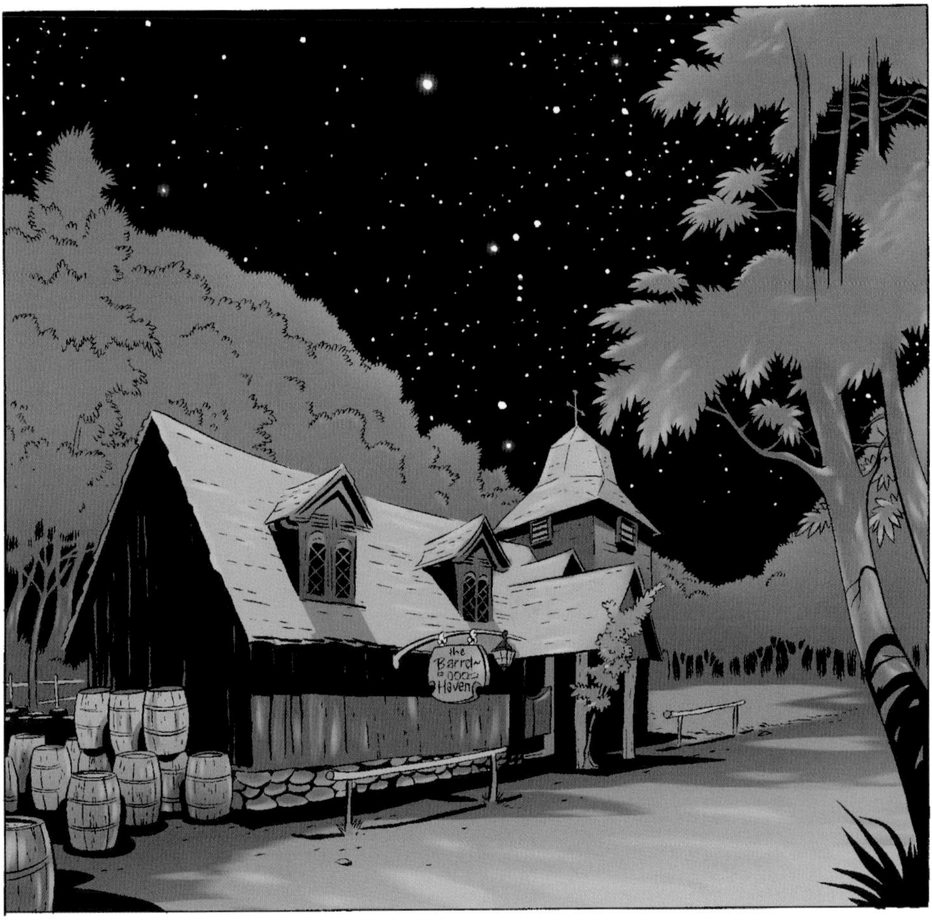
the
Barrel
Haven

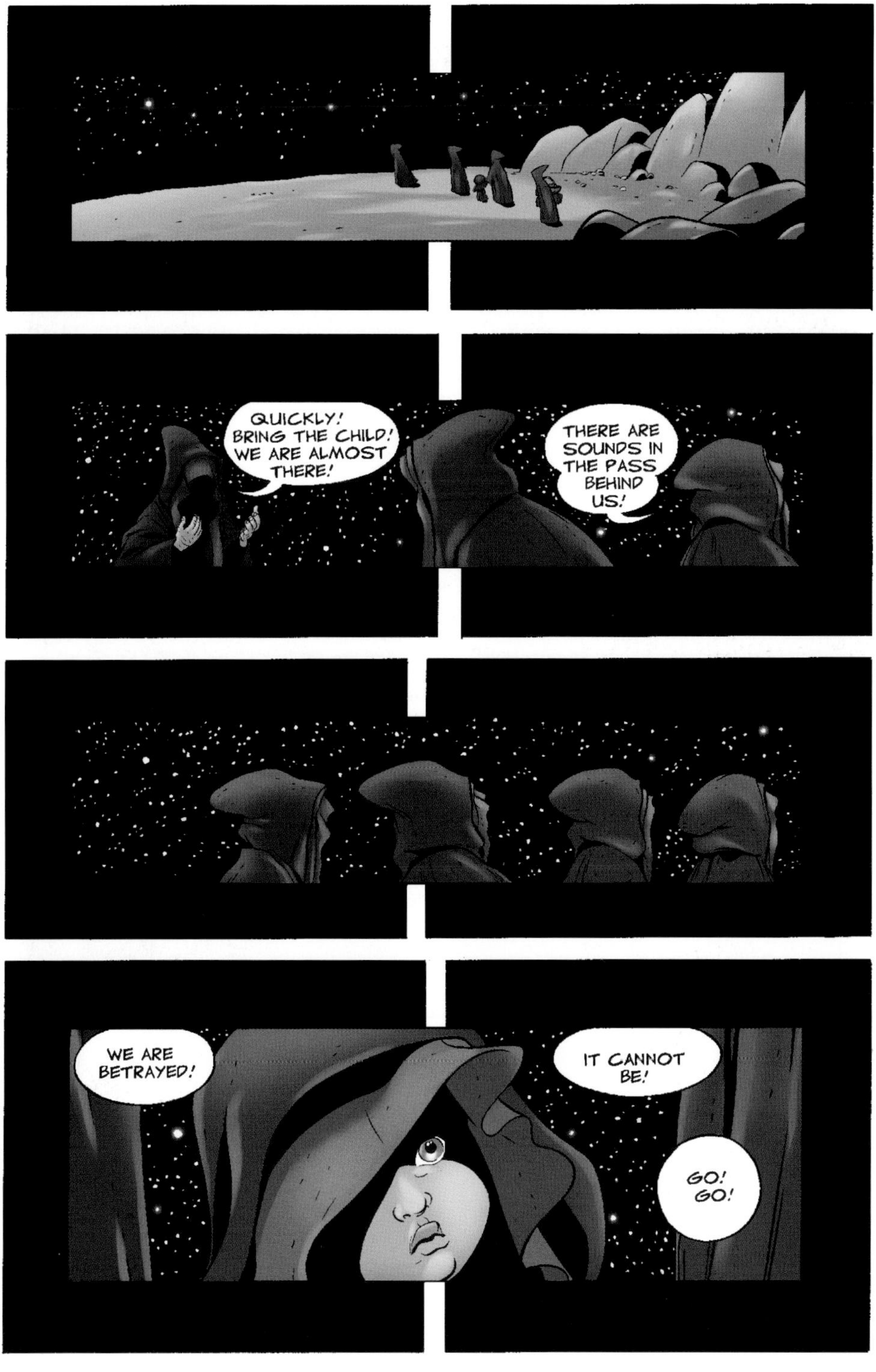
QUICKLY! BRING THE CHILD! WE ARE ALMOST THERE!
THERE ARE SOUNDS IN THE PASS BEHIND US!
WE ARE BETRAYED!
IT CANNOT BE!
GO! GO!

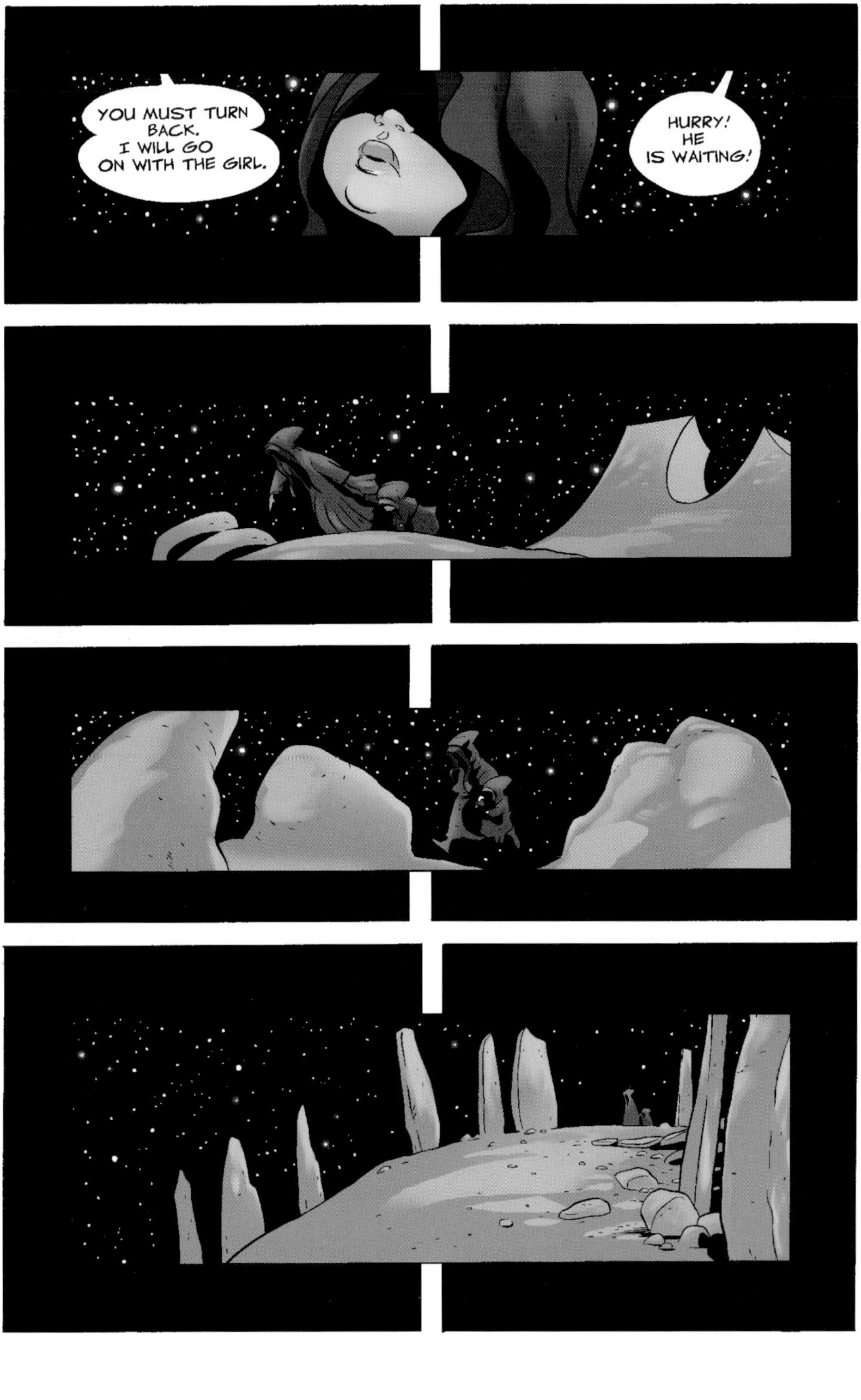
YOU MUST TURN BACK. I WILL GO ON WITH THE GIRL.
HURRY! HE IS WAITING!

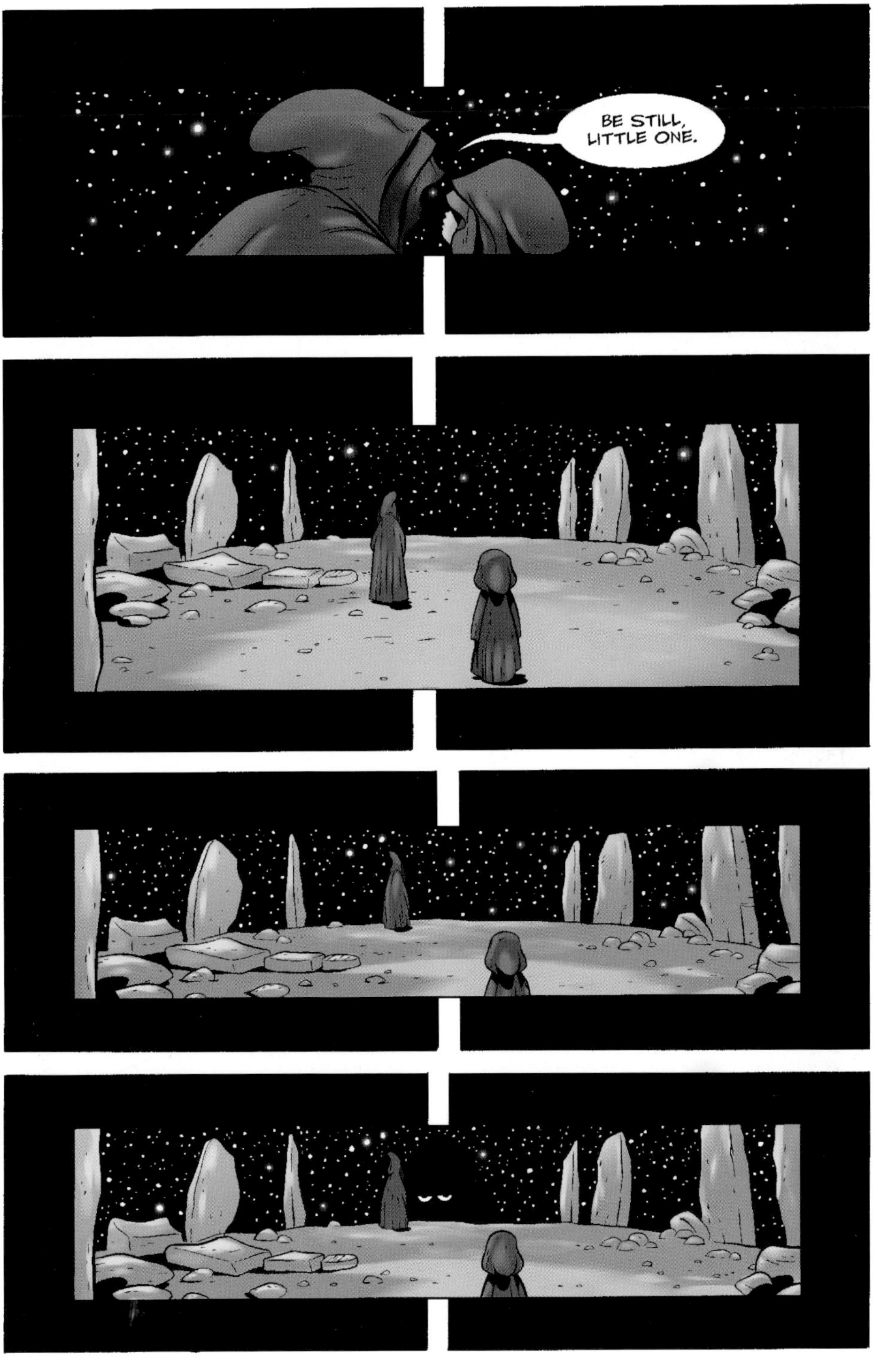
BE STILL, LITTLE ONE.

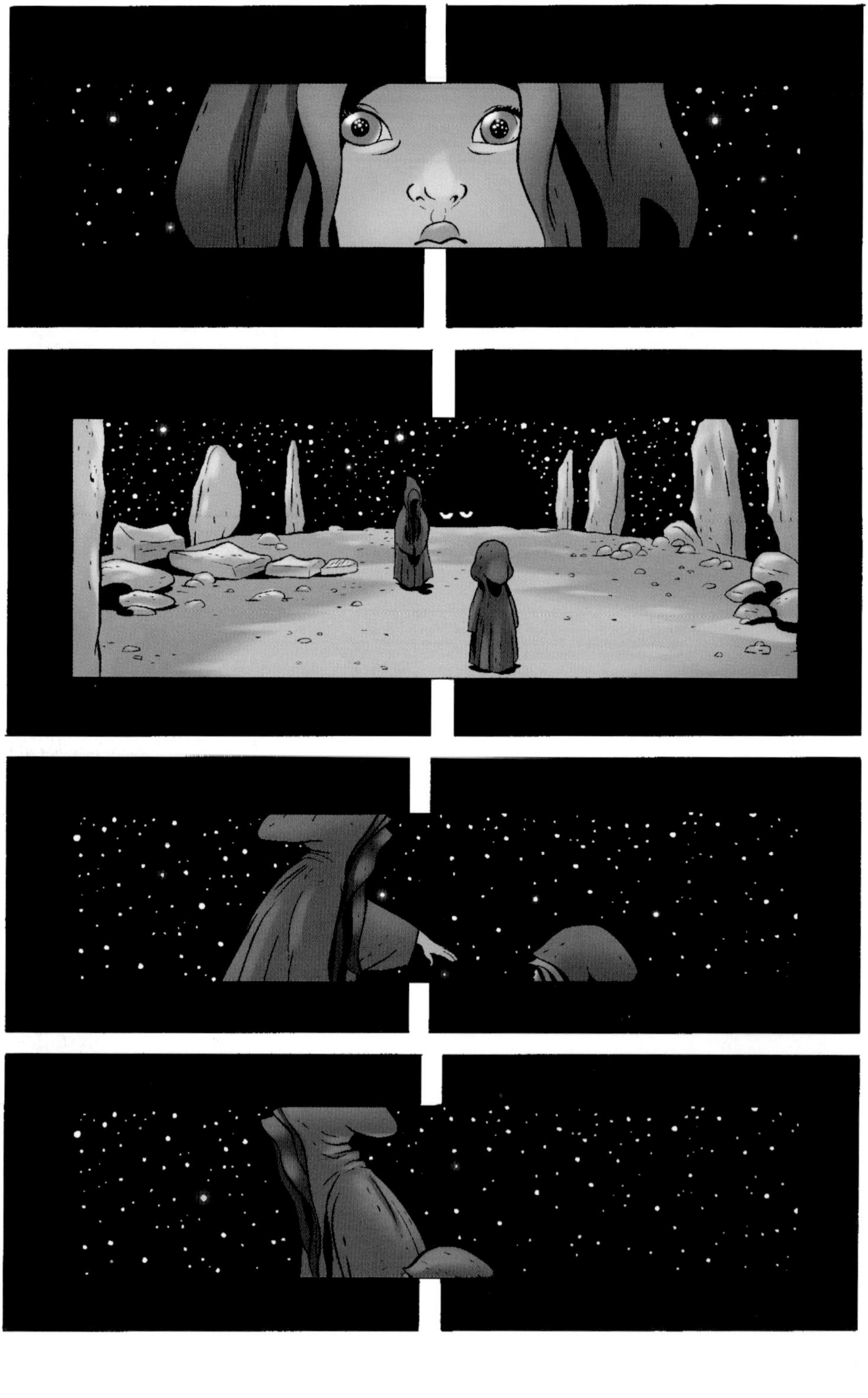

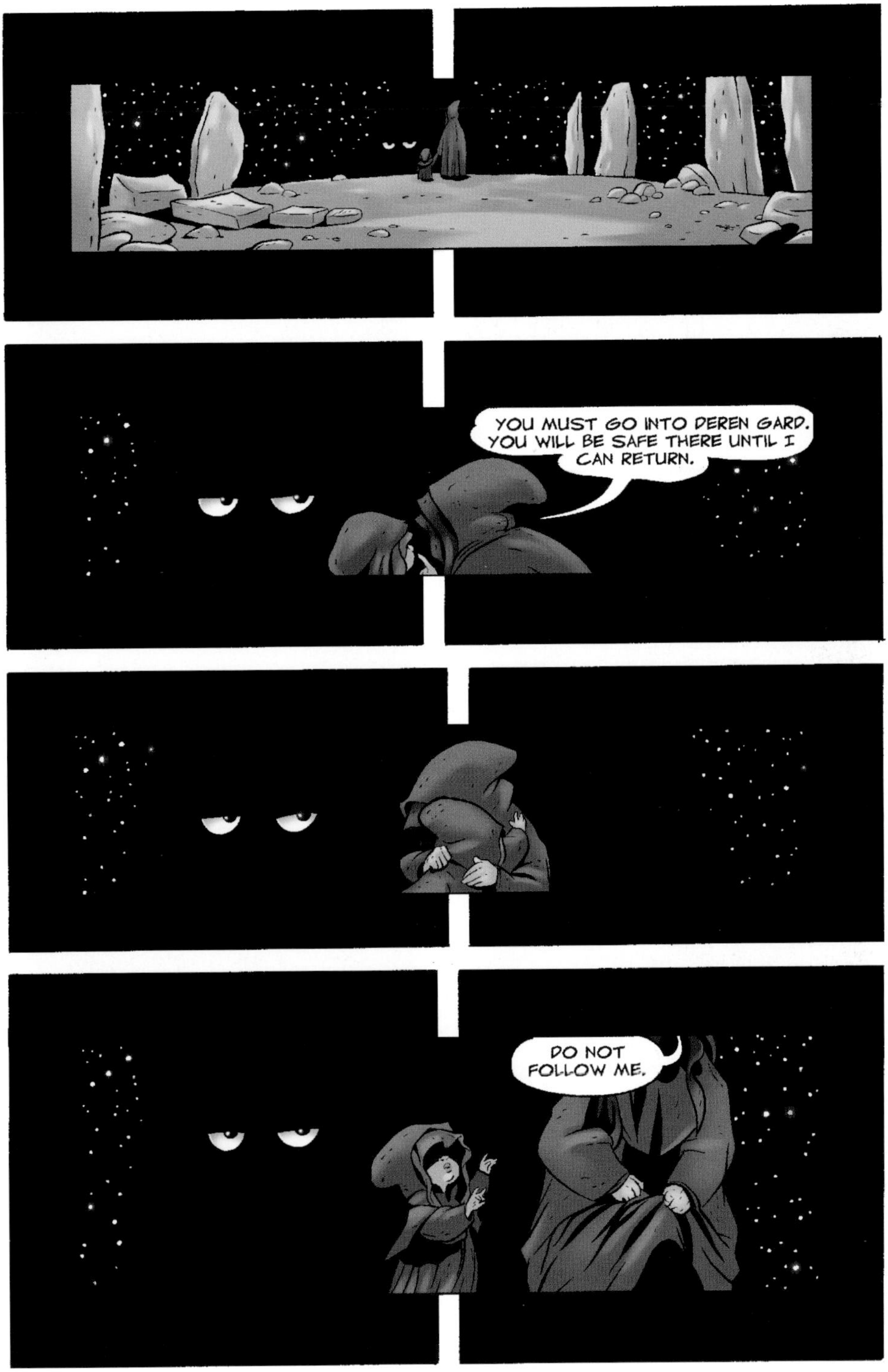
YOU MUST GO INTO DEREN GARD. YOU WILL BE SAFE THERE UNTIL I CAN RETURN.
DO NOT FOLLOW ME.

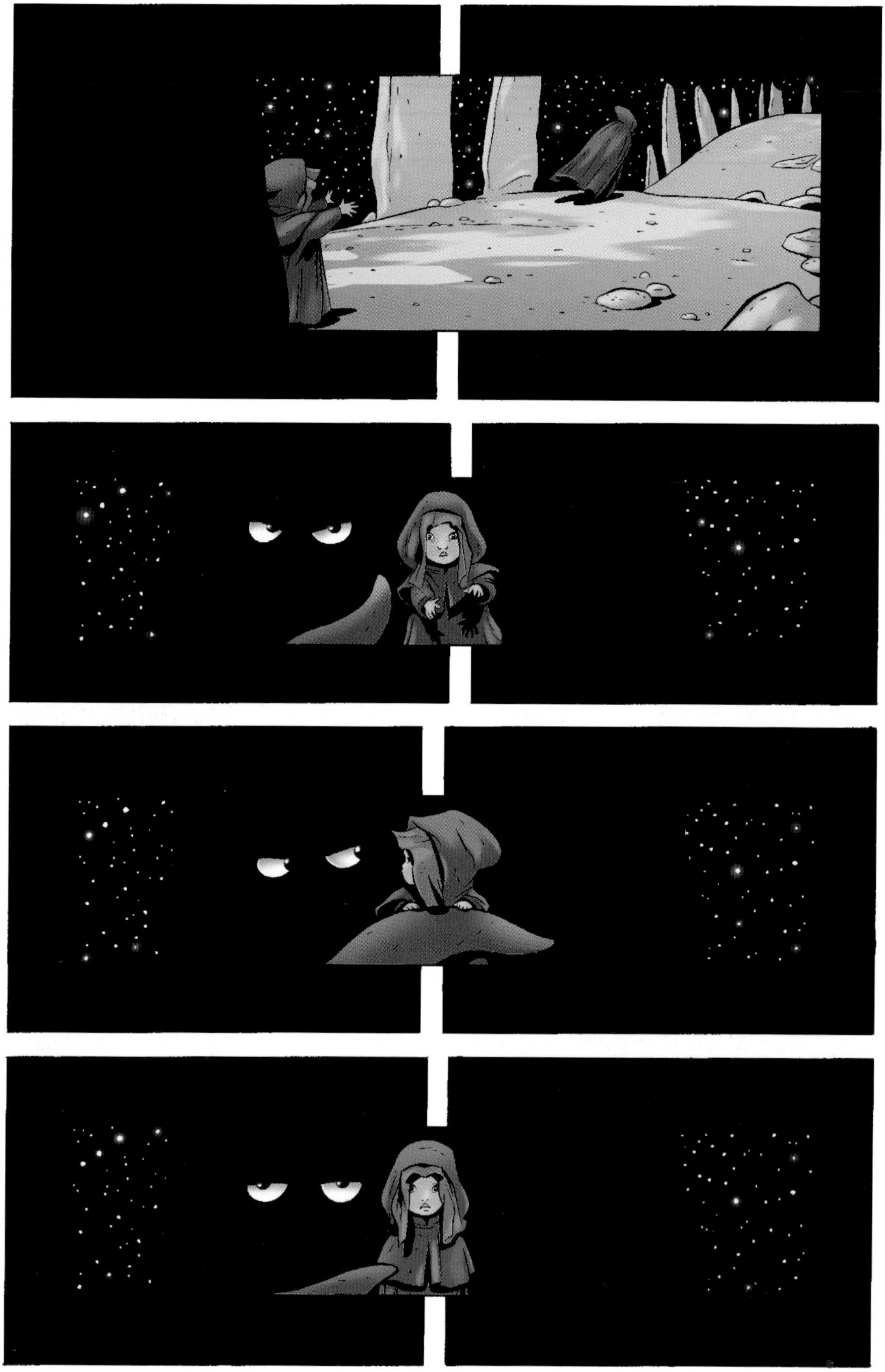

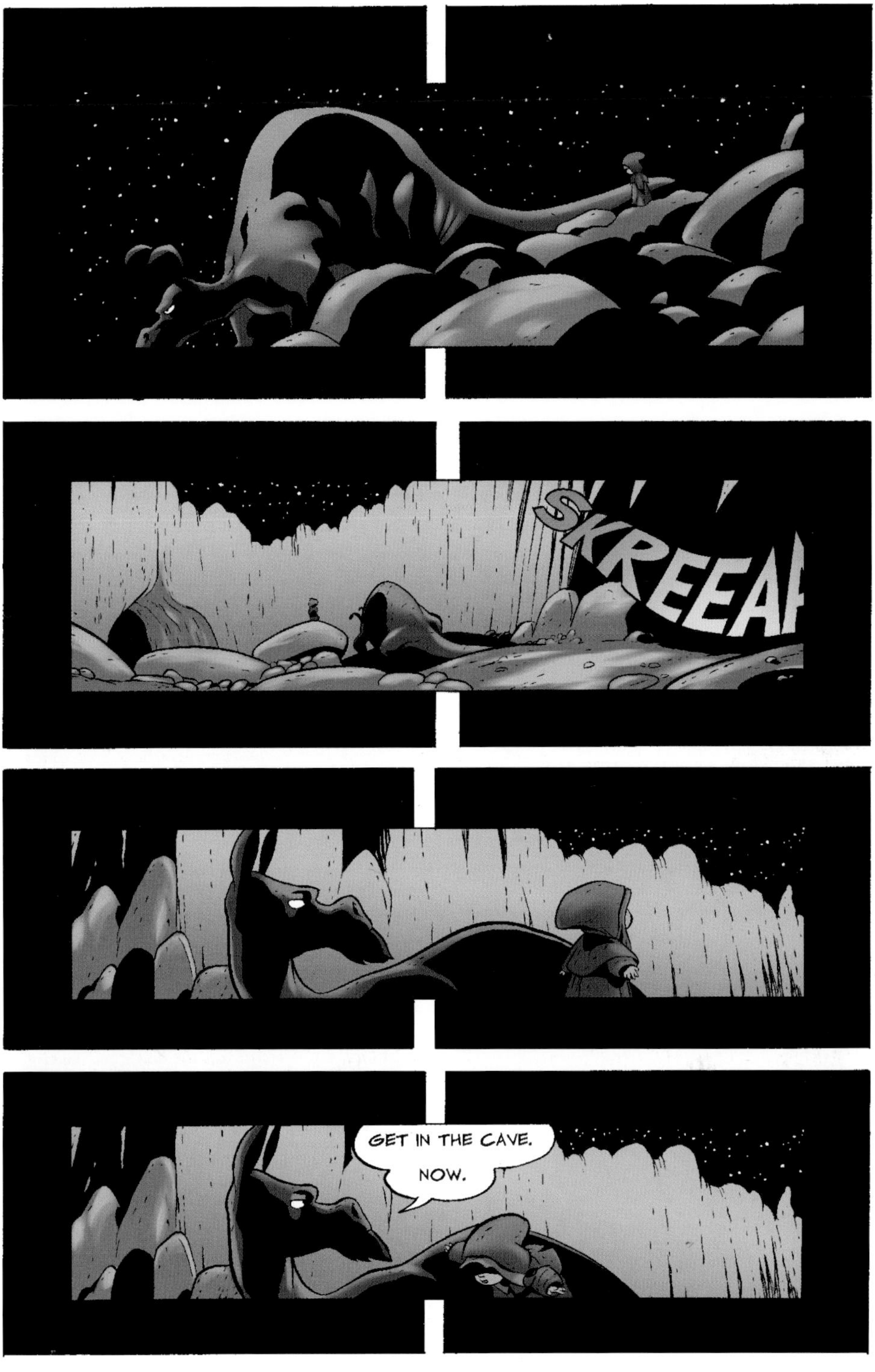
SKREEAP
GET IN THE CAVE. NOW.

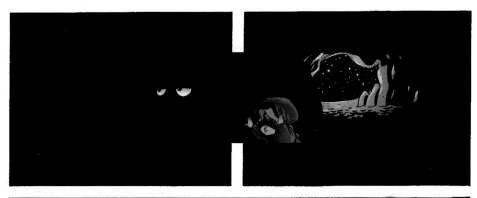

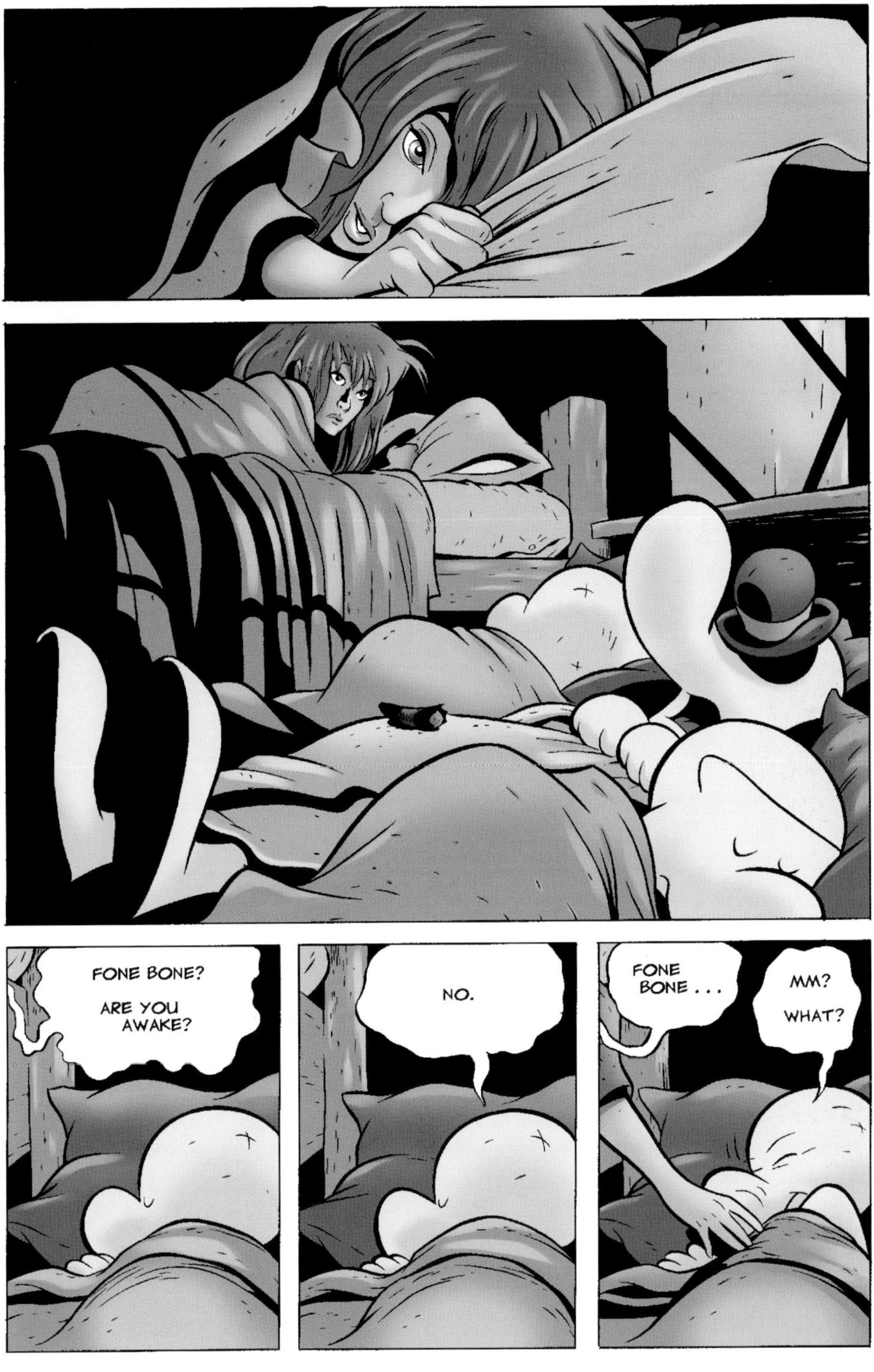
FONE BONE?
ARE YOU AWAKE?
NO.
FONE BONE . . .
MM?
WHAT?

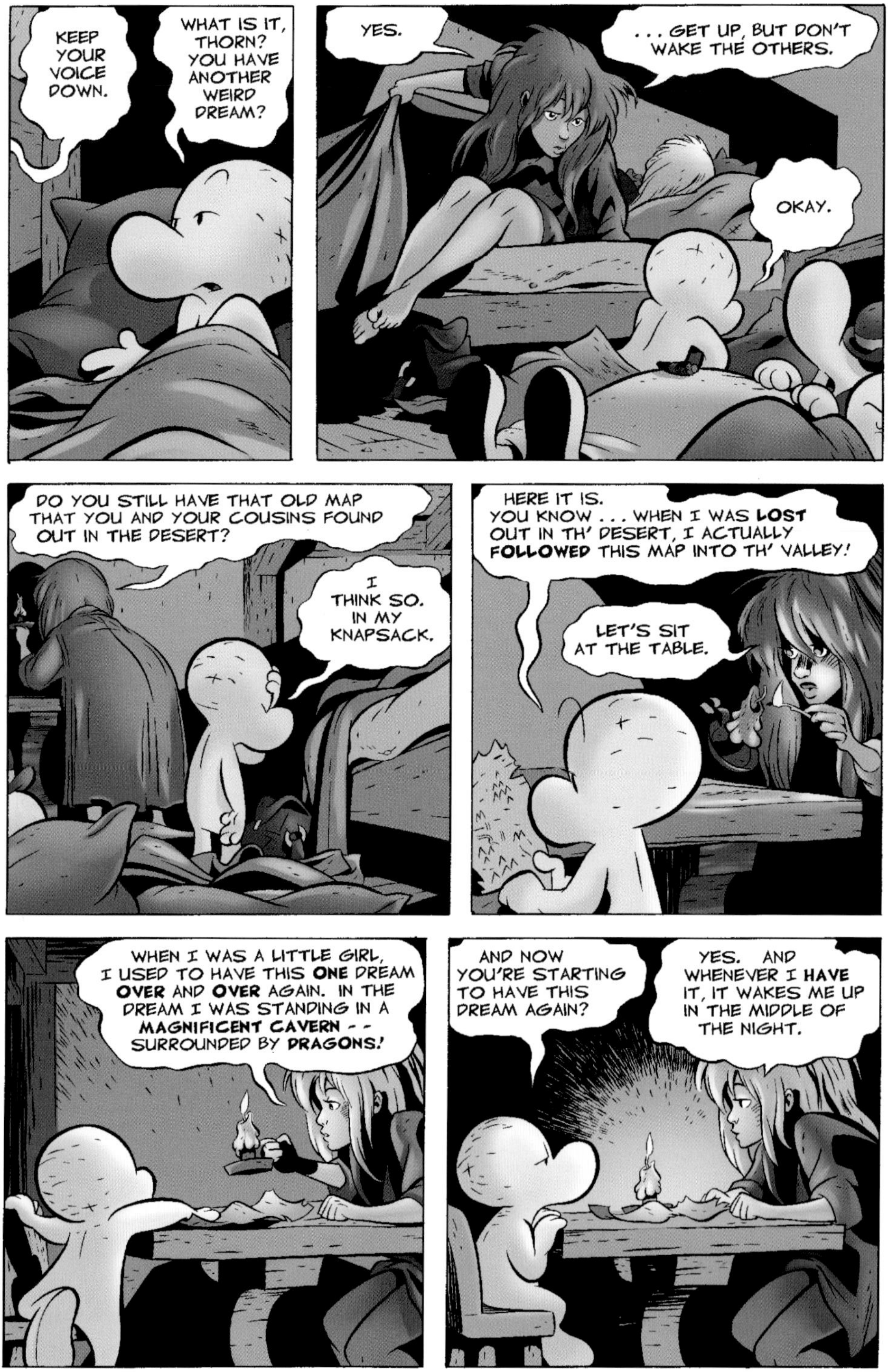
KEEP YOUR VOICE DOWN.
WHAT IS IT, THORN? YOU HAVE ANOTHER WEIRD DREAM?
YES.
. . . GET UP, BUT DON'T WAKE THE OTHERS.
OKAY.
DO YOU STILL HAVE THAT OLD MAP THAT YOU AND YOUR COUSINS FOUND OUT IN THE DESERT?
I THINK SO. IN MY KNAPSACK.
HERE IT IS. YOU KNOW . . . WHEN I WAS **LOST** OUT IN TH' DESERT, I ACTUALLY **FOLLOWED** THIS MAP INTO TH' VALLEY!
LET'S SIT AT THE TABLE.
WHEN I WAS A LITTLE GIRL, I USED TO HAVE THIS **ONE** DREAM **OVER** AND **OVER** AGAIN. IN THE DREAM I WAS STANDING IN A **MAGNIFICENT CAVERN** - - SURROUNDED BY **DRAGONS**!
AND NOW YOU'RE STARTING TO HAVE THIS DREAM AGAIN?
YES. AND WHENEVER I **HAVE** IT, IT WAKES ME UP IN THE MIDDLE OF THE NIGHT.

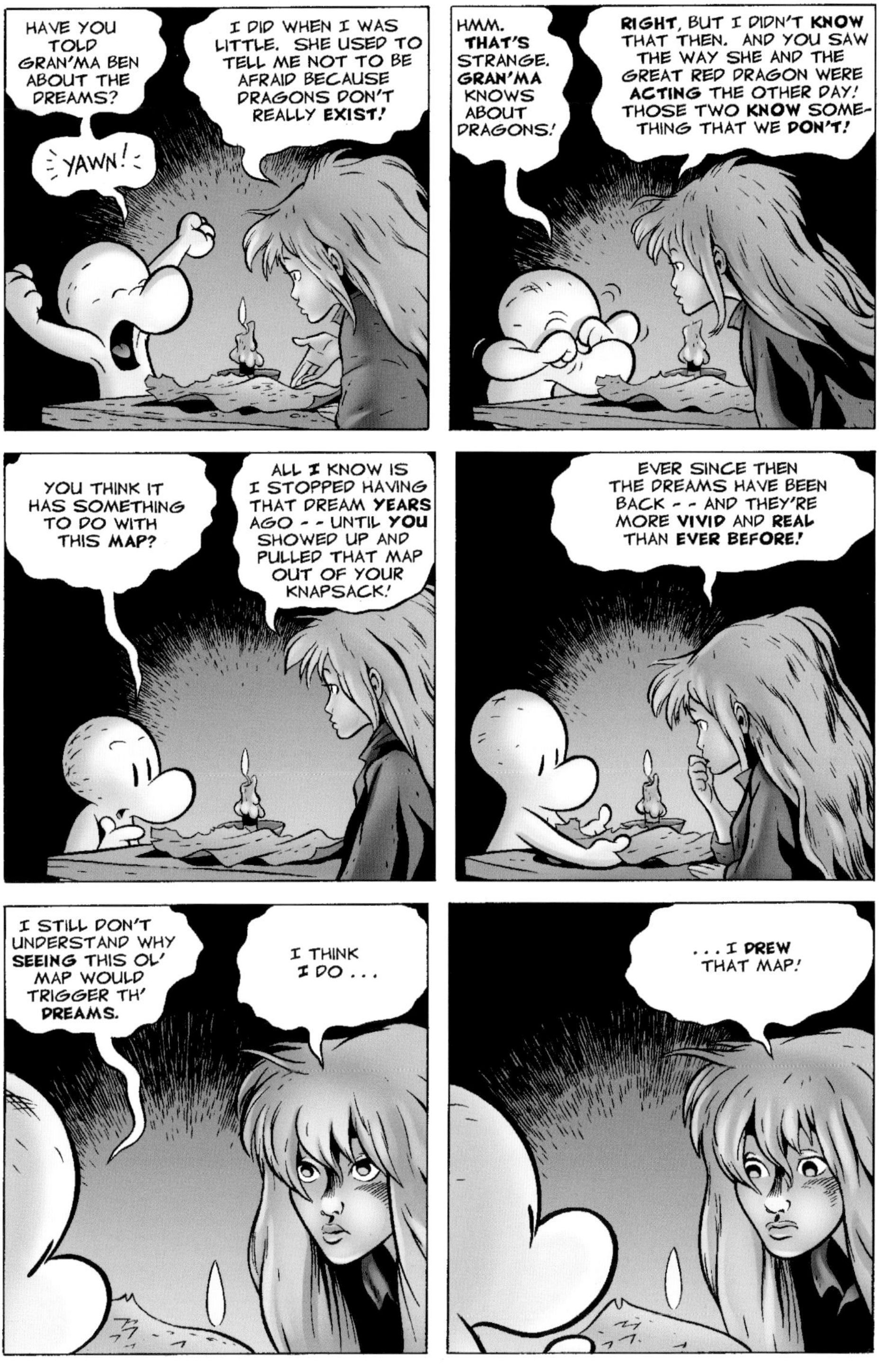
HAVE YOU TOLD GRAN'MA BEN ABOUT THE DREAMS?
YAWN!
I DID WHEN I WAS LITTLE. SHE USED TO TELL ME NOT TO BE AFRAID BECAUSE DRAGONS DON'T REALLY EXIST!
HMM. THAT'S STRANGE. GRAN'MA KNOWS ABOUT DRAGONS!
RIGHT, BUT I DIDN'T KNOW THAT THEN. AND YOU SAW THE WAY SHE AND THE GREAT RED DRAGON WERE ACTING THE OTHER DAY! THOSE TWO KNOW SOMETHING THAT WE DON'T!
YOU THINK IT HAS SOMETHING TO DO WITH THIS MAP?
ALL I KNOW IS I STOPPED HAVING THAT DREAM YEARS AGO - - UNTIL YOU SHOWED UP AND PULLED THAT MAP OUT OF YOUR KNAPSACK!
EVER SINCE THEN THE DREAMS HAVE BEEN BACK - - AND THEY'RE MORE VIVID AND REAL THAN EVER BEFORE!
I STILL DON'T UNDERSTAND WHY SEEING THIS OL' MAP WOULD TRIGGER TH' DREAMS.
I THINK I DO . . .
. . . I DREW THAT MAP!

YOU'RE KIDDING!

NO. I'M PRETTY SURE. I'M STARTING TO REMEMBER IT.

I DREW THAT MAP WHEN I WAS IN THE CAVE WITH THE DRAGONS.

WHOA.

WAIT A MINUTE. WHAT ARE YOU SAYING? YOU REALLY **WERE** IN A CAVERN WITH A BUNCH OF DRAGONS? I THOUGHT IT WAS A **DREAM!**

OH, I DON'T KNOW, FONE BONE!

IT'S SO CONFUSING!

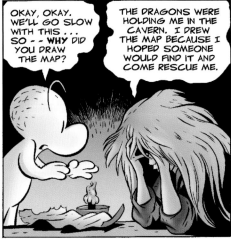

OKAY, OKAY. WE'LL GO SLOW WITH THIS . . . SO - - **WHY** DID YOU DRAW THE MAP?

THE DRAGONS WERE HOLDING ME IN THE CAVERN. I DREW THE MAP BECAUSE I HOPED SOMEONE WOULD FIND IT AND COME RESCUE ME.

WHAT DO YOU **MEAN** HOLDING? WERE YOU A **PRISONER?**

I DON'T REMEMBER ANYMORE . . . BUT AT THE TIME I WANTED TO ESCAPE.

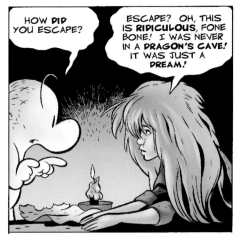

HOW **DID** YOU ESCAPE?

ESCAPE? OH, THIS IS **RIDICULOUS**, FONE BONE! I WAS NEVER IN A **DRAGON'S CAVE!** IT WAS JUST A **DREAM!**

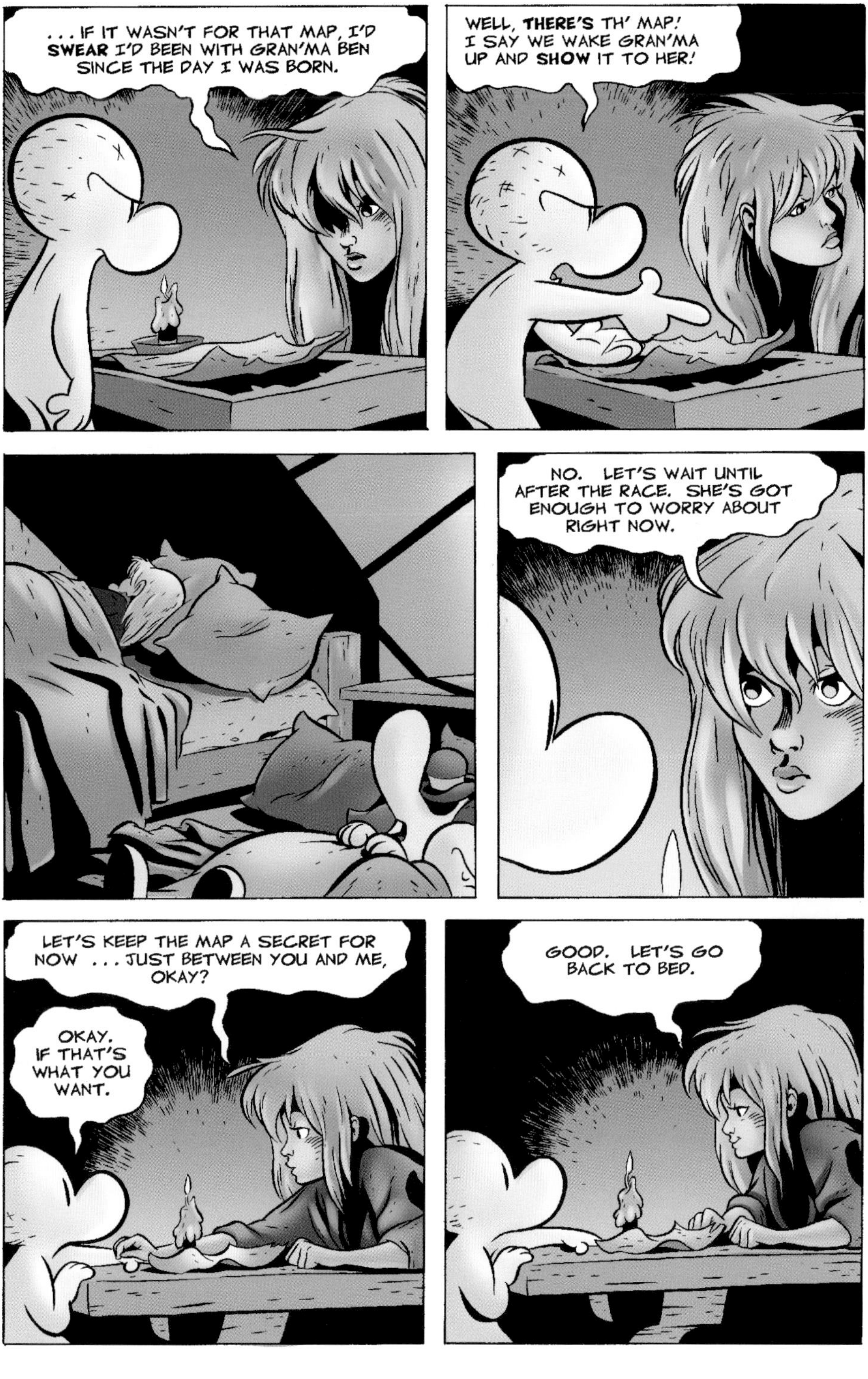
. . . IF IT WASN'T FOR THAT MAP, I'D SWEAR I'D BEEN WITH GRAN'MA BEN SINCE THE DAY I WAS BORN.
WELL, THERE'S TH' MAP! I SAY WE WAKE GRAN'MA UP AND SHOW IT TO HER!
NO. LET'S WAIT UNTIL AFTER THE RACE. SHE'S GOT ENOUGH TO WORRY ABOUT RIGHT NOW.
LET'S KEEP THE MAP A SECRET FOR NOW . . . JUST BETWEEN YOU AND ME, OKAY?
OKAY. IF THAT'S WHAT YOU WANT.
GOOD. LET'S GO BACK TO BED.

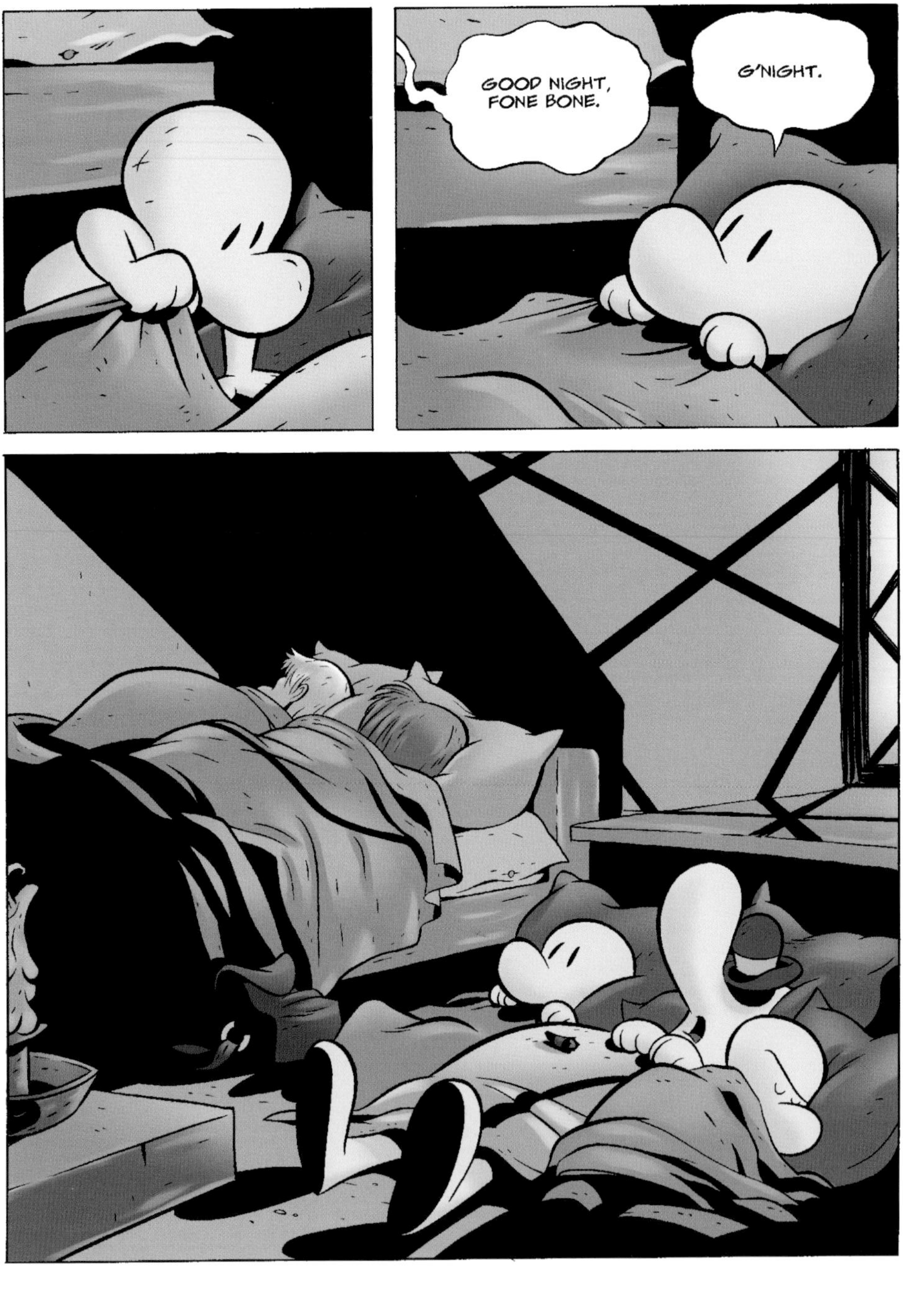
GOOD NIGHT, FONE BONE.
G'NIGHT.

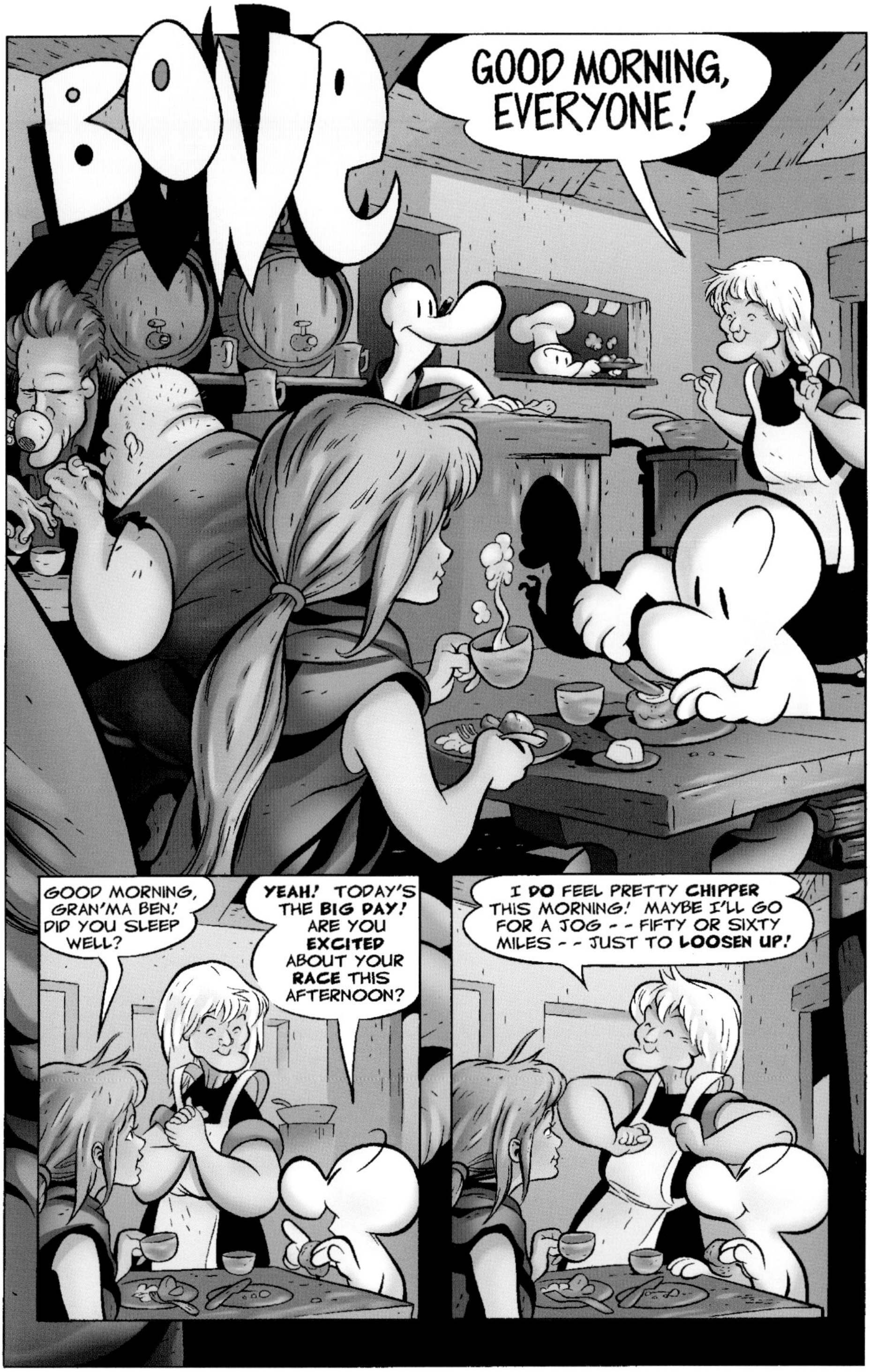
BONE
GOOD MORNING, EVERYONE!
GOOD MORNING, GRAN'MA BEN! DID YOU SLEEP WELL?
YEAH! TODAY'S THE BIG DAY! ARE YOU EXCITED ABOUT YOUR RACE THIS AFTERNOON?
I DO FEEL PRETTY CHIPPER THIS MORNING! MAYBE I'LL GO FOR A JOG - - FIFTY OR SIXTY MILES - - JUST TO LOOSEN UP!

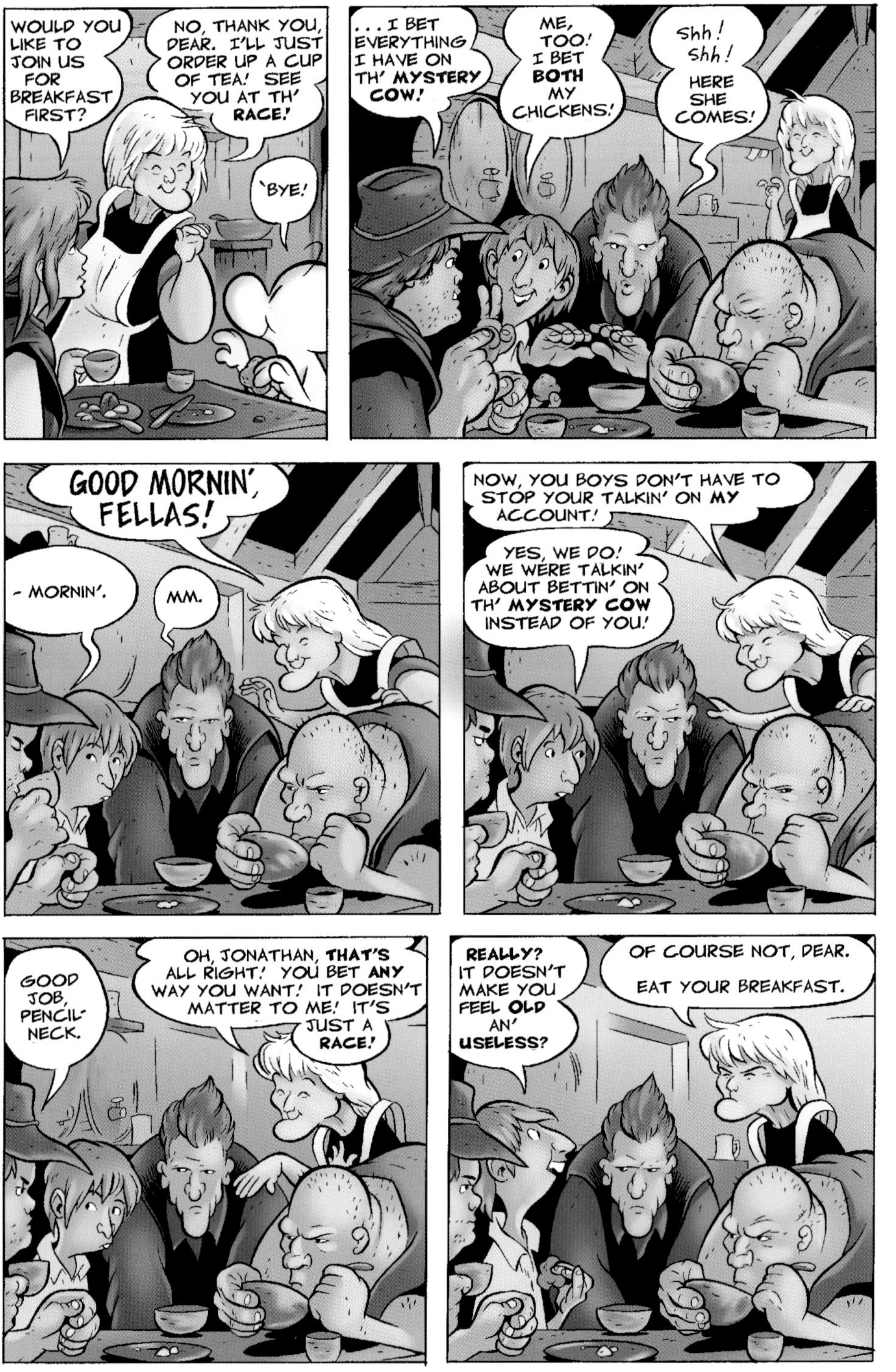
WOULD YOU LIKE TO JOIN US FOR BREAKFAST FIRST?
NO, THANK YOU, DEAR. I'LL JUST ORDER UP A CUP OF TEA! SEE YOU AT TH' RACE!
'BYE!
. . . I BET EVERYTHING I HAVE ON TH' MYSTERY COW!
ME, TOO! I BET BOTH MY CHICKENS!
Shh! Shh! HERE SHE COMES!
GOOD MORNIN', FELLAS!
- MORNIN'.
MM.
NOW, YOU BOYS DON'T HAVE TO STOP YOUR TALKIN' ON MY ACCOUNT!
YES, WE DO! WE WERE TALKIN' ABOUT BETTIN' ON TH' MYSTERY COW INSTEAD OF YOU!
GOOD JOB, PENCIL-NECK.
OH, JONATHAN, THAT'S ALL RIGHT! YOU BET ANY WAY YOU WANT! IT DOESN'T MATTER TO ME! IT'S JUST A RACE!
REALLY? IT DOESN'T MAKE YOU FEEL OLD AN' USELESS?
OF COURSE NOT, DEAR.
EAT YOUR BREAKFAST.

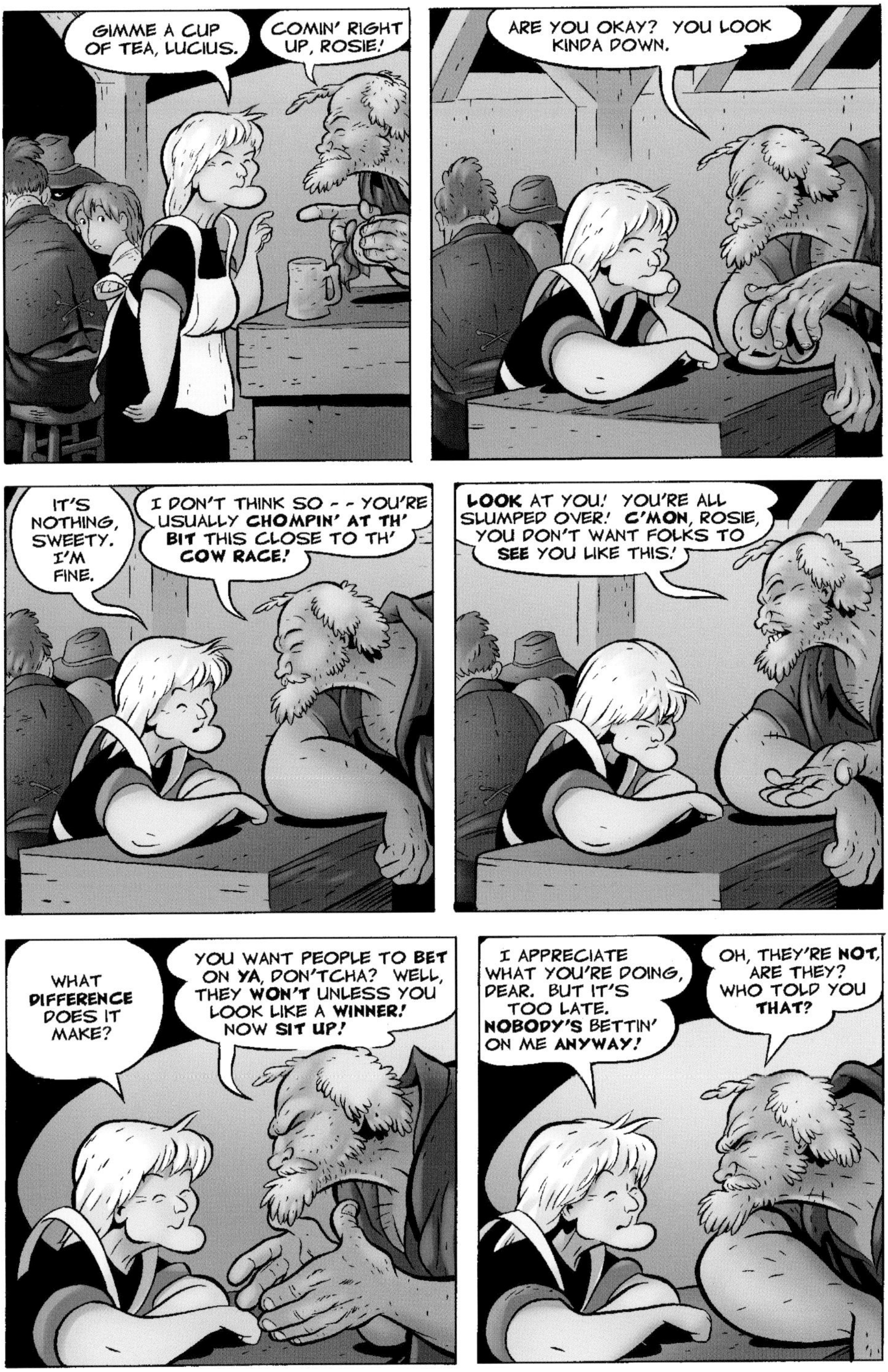
GIMME A CUP OF TEA, LUCIUS.
COMIN' RIGHT UP, ROSIE!
ARE YOU OKAY? YOU LOOK KINDA DOWN.
IT'S NOTHING, SWEETY. I'M FINE.
I DON'T THINK SO - - YOU'RE USUALLY CHOMPIN' AT TH' BIT THIS CLOSE TO TH' COW RACE!
LOOK AT YOU! YOU'RE ALL SLUMPED OVER! C'MON, ROSIE, YOU DON'T WANT FOLKS TO SEE YOU LIKE THIS!
WHAT DIFFERENCE DOES IT MAKE?
YOU WANT PEOPLE TO BET ON YA, DON'TCHA? WELL, THEY WON'T UNLESS YOU LOOK LIKE A WINNER! NOW SIT UP!
I APPRECIATE WHAT YOU'RE DOING, DEAR. BUT IT'S TOO LATE. NOBODY'S BETTIN' ON ME ANYWAY!
OH, THEY'RE NOT, ARE THEY? WHO TOLD YOU THAT?

EVERYBODY! YOU **MUST'VE** HEARD TALK IN TH' BAR.

YEAH, WELL, I DON'T LISTEN . . .

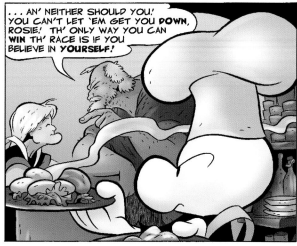

. . . AN' NEITHER SHOULD YOU! YOU CAN'T LET 'EM GET YOU **DOWN**, ROSIE! TH' ONLY WAY YOU CAN **WIN** TH' RACE IS IF YOU BELIEVE IN **YOURSELF!**

HE'S **RIGHT**, GRAN'MA! DON'T LISTEN TO TH' **RABBLE!** THINK **POSITIVE!**

SINCE WHEN ARE **YOU** ONE OF MY **BOOSTERS**, PHONEY BONE?

I'M A **FRIEND**, GRAN'MA! AN' I **CARE!**

PAY NO ATTENTION TO WHAT THESE FARMERS ARE SAYING! YOU CAN **WIN!** I HAVE FAITH IN YOU!

WHAT ARE YOU UP TO, YOU LITTLE RUNT?

NOTHING! CAN'T A **FRIEND** WISH A FRIEND **LUCK?**

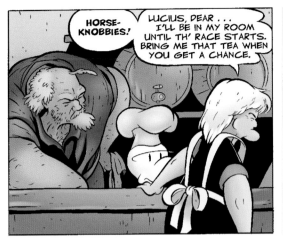

HORSE-KNOBBIES!

LUCIUS, DEAR . . . I'LL BE IN MY ROOM UNTIL TH' RACE STARTS. BRING ME THAT TEA WHEN YOU GET A CHANCE.

POOR OL' SAP! SHE'S GONNA GET **CREAMED** THIS AFTERNOON! IF YA WANT **MY** ADVICE, YOU'RE BETTER OFF BETTIN' ON TH' **MYSTERY COW!**

SPEAKING OF WHICH . . . A **WELL-TO-DO** MAN LIKE YOURSELF **MUST** BE THINKING OF MAKING A **WAGER** ON TH' RACE -- A REALLY, REALLY **BIG WAGER!** LIKE . . . OH, SAY . . . **YOUR ENTIRE BAR!**

. . . BUT THERE'S NO **RUSH!** WHEN YOU'RE READY TO BET -- YOU KNOW WHERE TO FIND ME! I'LL BE TAKING BETS RIGHT UP TO THE STARTING BELL! THINK ABOUT IT!

HMM.

BOY! THAT WAS **DELICIOUS!** LUCIUS'S MENU CERTAINLY HAS **IMPROVED** SINCE HE HIRED YOUR COUSINS TO WORK IN THE **KITCHEN!**

YEAH, PHONEY ALWAYS WAS A **GOOD** COOK ...

SAY, UM ... THORN? YOU WANNA WALK AROUND TH' **FAIR** TOGETHER TODAY?

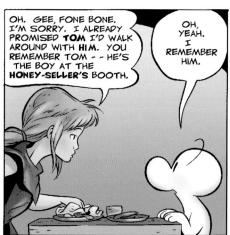

OH. GEE, FONE BONE. I'M SORRY. I ALREADY PROMISED **TOM** I'D WALK AROUND WITH **HIM.** YOU REMEMBER TOM -- HE'S THE BOY AT THE **HONEY-SELLER'S** BOOTH.

OH, YEAH. I REMEMBER HIM.

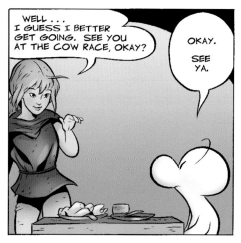

WELL ... I GUESS I BETTER GET GOING. SEE YOU AT THE COW RACE, OKAY?

OKAY. SEE YA.

HEY! WHAT'S THIS I HEAR ABOUT NOBODY BETTIN' ON ROSE? WHAT'S TH' **MATTER** WITH YOU GUYS? YOU TRYIN' TO HURT HER **FEELINGS?!**

NAW! WE AIN'T TRYIN' TO HURT HER FEELIN'S. BUT **YOU** HEARD TH' RUMORS. GRAN'MA BEN IS **WASHED UP!**

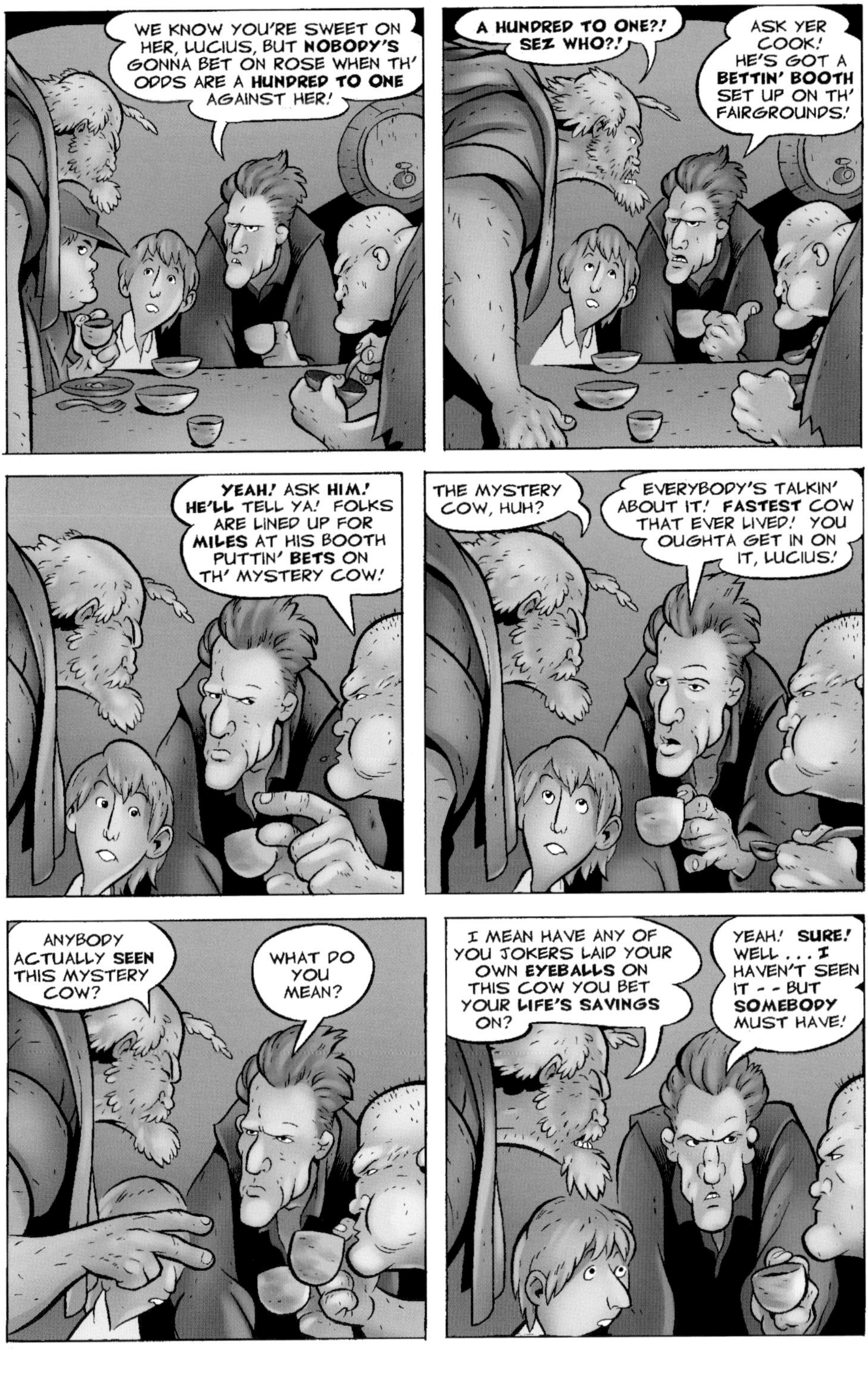
WE KNOW YOU'RE SWEET ON HER, LUCIUS, BUT NOBODY'S GONNA BET ON ROSE WHEN TH' ODDS ARE A HUNDRED TO ONE AGAINST HER!
A HUNDRED TO ONE?! SEZ WHO?!
ASK YER COOK! HE'S GOT A BETTIN' BOOTH SET UP ON TH' FAIRGROUNDS!
YEAH! ASK HIM! HE'LL TELL YA! FOLKS ARE LINED UP FOR MILES AT HIS BOOTH PUTTIN' BETS ON TH' MYSTERY COW!
THE MYSTERY COW, HUH?
EVERYBODY'S TALKIN' ABOUT IT! FASTEST COW THAT EVER LIVED! YOU OUGHTA GET IN ON IT, LUCIUS!
ANYBODY ACTUALLY SEEN THIS MYSTERY COW?
WHAT DO YOU MEAN?
I MEAN HAVE ANY OF YOU JOKERS LAID YOUR OWN EYEBALLS ON THIS COW YOU BET YOUR LIFE'S SAVINGS ON?
YEAH! SURE! WELL . . . I HAVEN'T SEEN IT - - BUT SOMEBODY MUST HAVE!

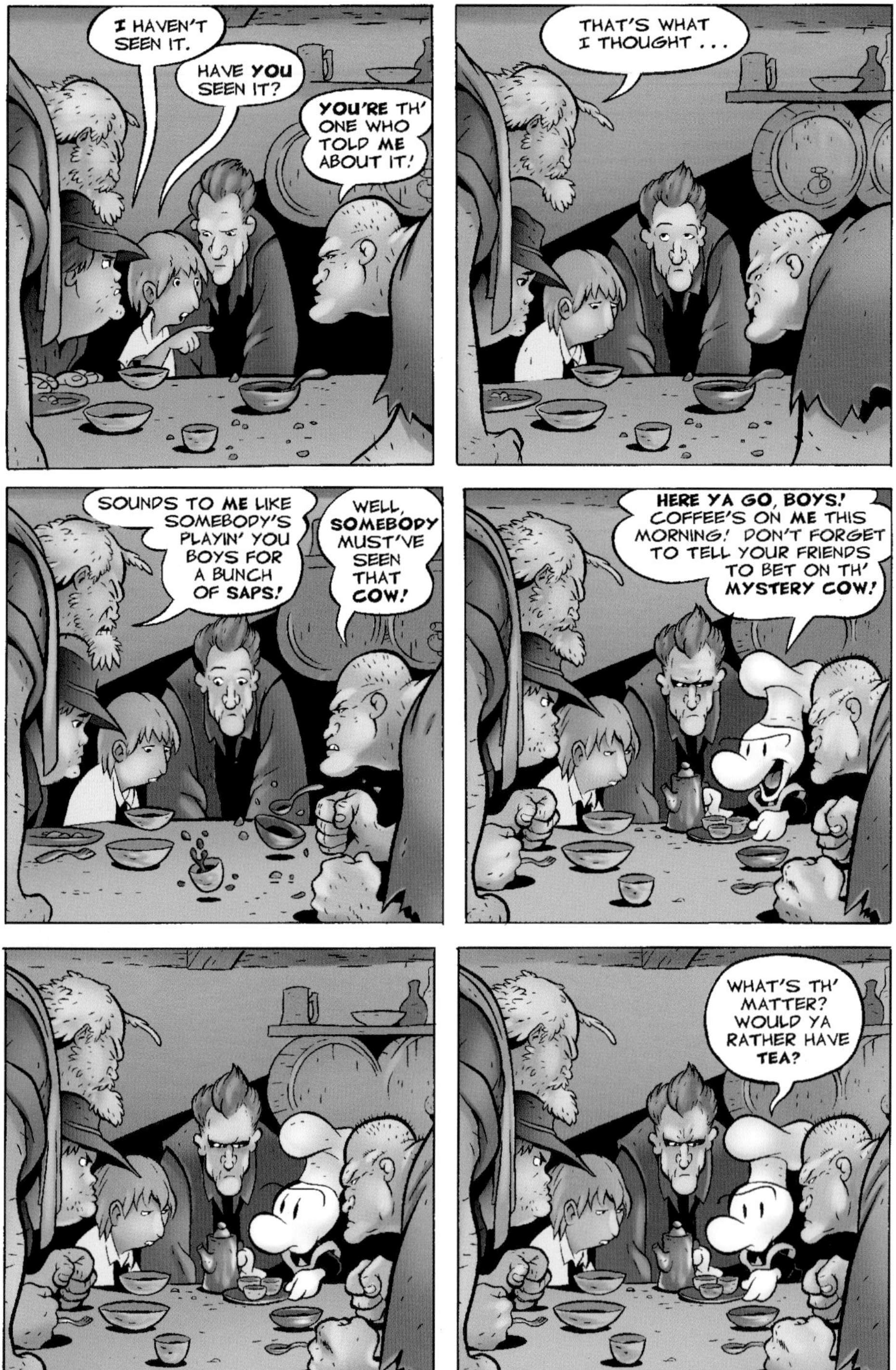
I HAVEN'T SEEN IT.
HAVE YOU SEEN IT?
YOU'RE TH' ONE WHO TOLD ME ABOUT IT!
THAT'S WHAT I THOUGHT . . .
SOUNDS TO ME LIKE SOMEBODY'S PLAYIN' YOU BOYS FOR A BUNCH OF SAPS!
WELL, SOMEBODY MUST'VE SEEN THAT COW!
HERE YA GO, BOYS! COFFEE'S ON ME THIS MORNING! DON'T FORGET TO TELL YOUR FRIENDS TO BET ON TH' MYSTERY COW!
WHAT'S TH' MATTER? WOULD YA RATHER HAVE TEA?

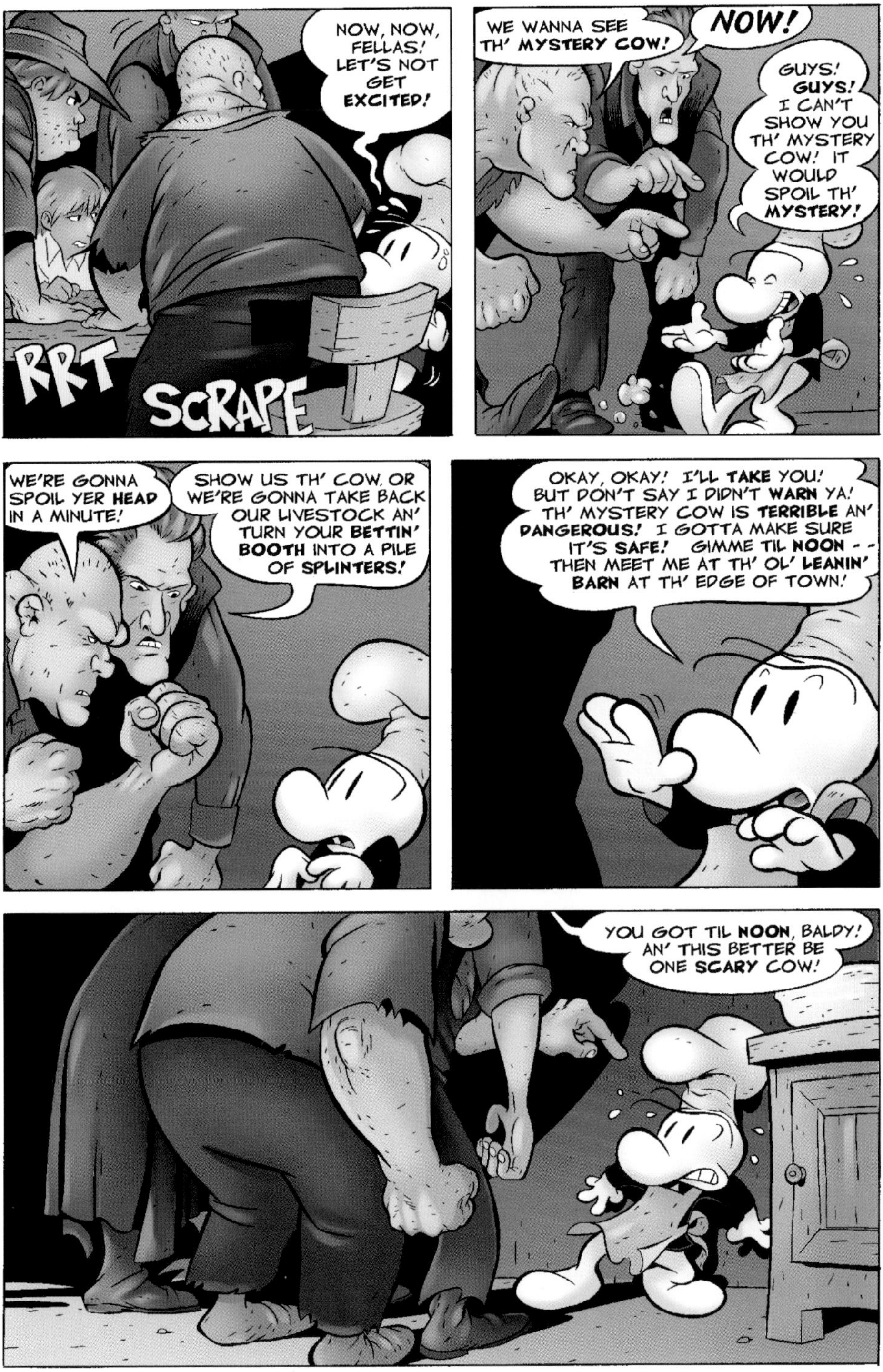
NOW, NOW, FELLAS! LET'S NOT GET EXCITED!
RRT
SCRAPE
WE WANNA SEE TH' MYSTERY COW!
NOW!
GUYS! GUYS! I CAN'T SHOW YOU TH' MYSTERY COW! IT WOULD SPOIL TH' MYSTERY!
WE'RE GONNA SPOIL YER HEAD IN A MINUTE!
SHOW US TH' COW, OR WE'RE GONNA TAKE BACK OUR LIVESTOCK AN' TURN YOUR BETTIN' BOOTH INTO A PILE OF SPLINTERS!
OKAY, OKAY! I'LL TAKE YOU! BUT DON'T SAY I DIDN'T WARN YA! TH' MYSTERY COW IS TERRIBLE AN' DANGEROUS! I GOTTA MAKE SURE IT'S SAFE! GIMME TIL NOON - - THEN MEET ME AT TH' OL' LEANIN' BARN AT TH' EDGE OF TOWN!
YOU GOT TIL NOON, BALDY! AN' THIS BETTER BE ONE SCARY COW!

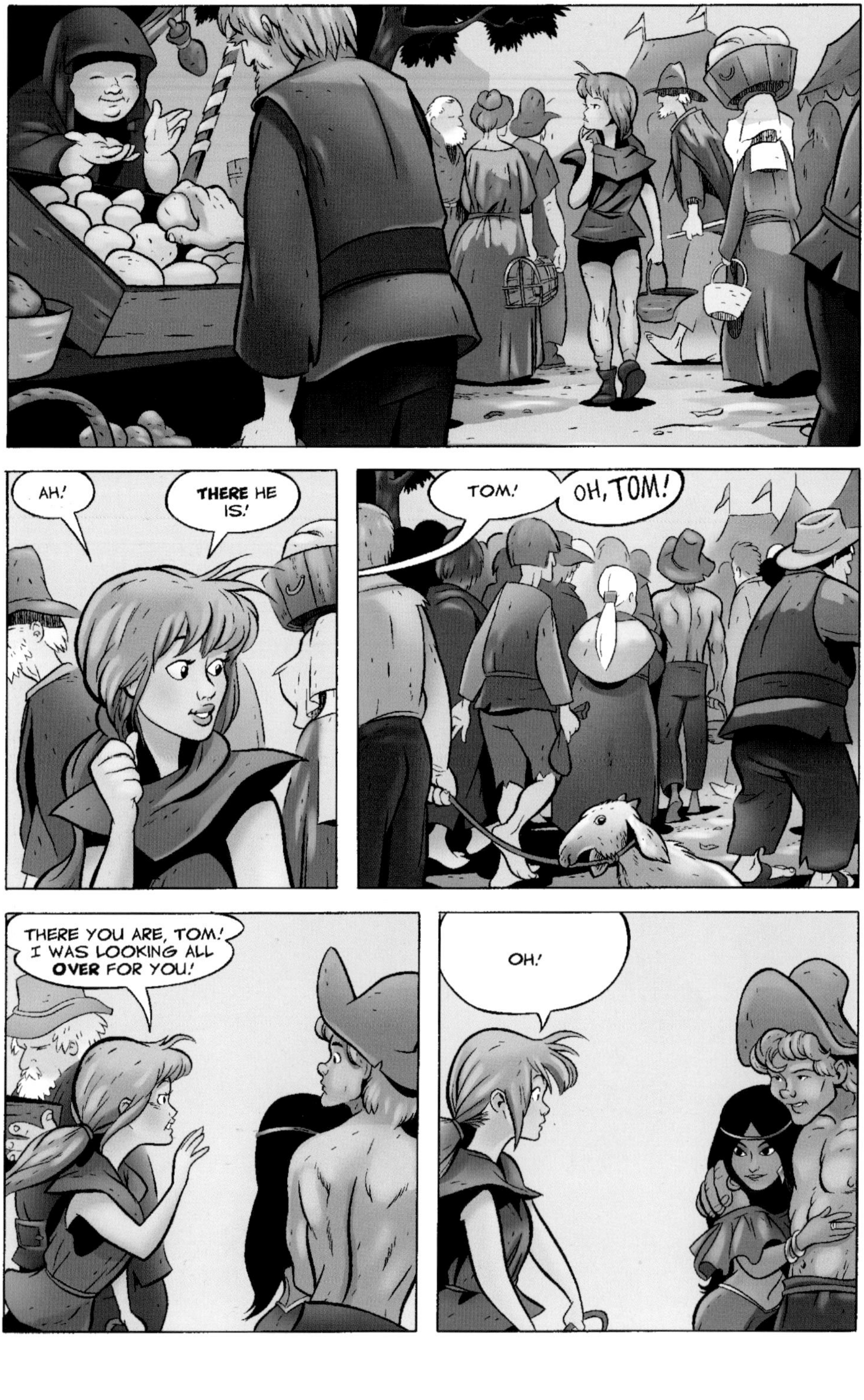
AH!
THERE HE IS!
TOM!
OH, TOM!
THERE YOU ARE, TOM! I WAS LOOKING ALL OVER FOR YOU!
OH!

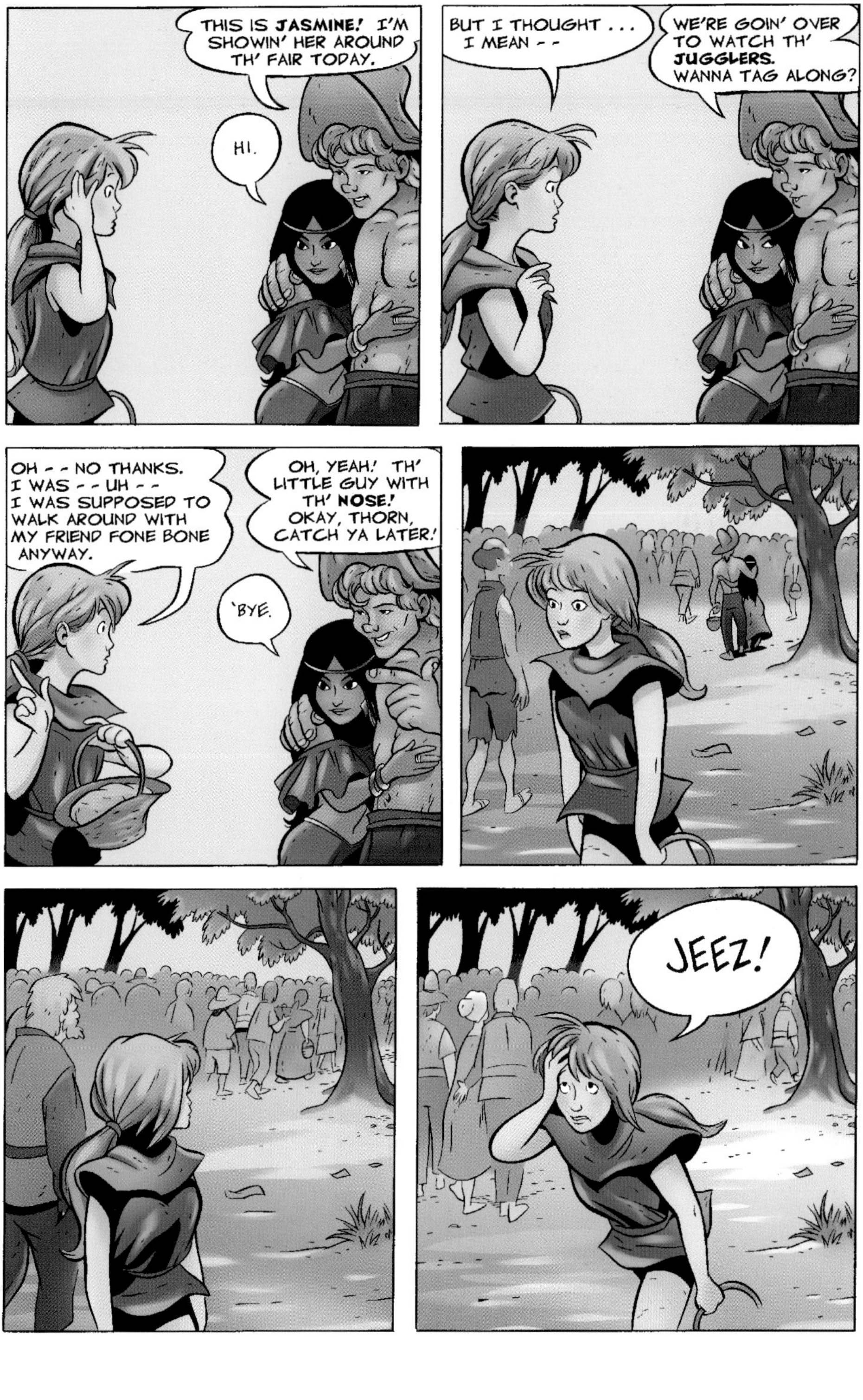
THIS IS JASMINE! I'M SHOWIN' HER AROUND TH' FAIR TODAY.
HI.
BUT I THOUGHT . . . I MEAN - -
WE'RE GOIN' OVER TO WATCH TH' JUGGLERS. WANNA TAG ALONG?
OH - - NO THANKS. I WAS - - UH - - I WAS SUPPOSED TO WALK AROUND WITH MY FRIEND FONE BONE ANYWAY.
OH, YEAH! TH' LITTLE GUY WITH TH' NOSE! OKAY, THORN, CATCH YA LATER!
'BYE.
JEEZ!

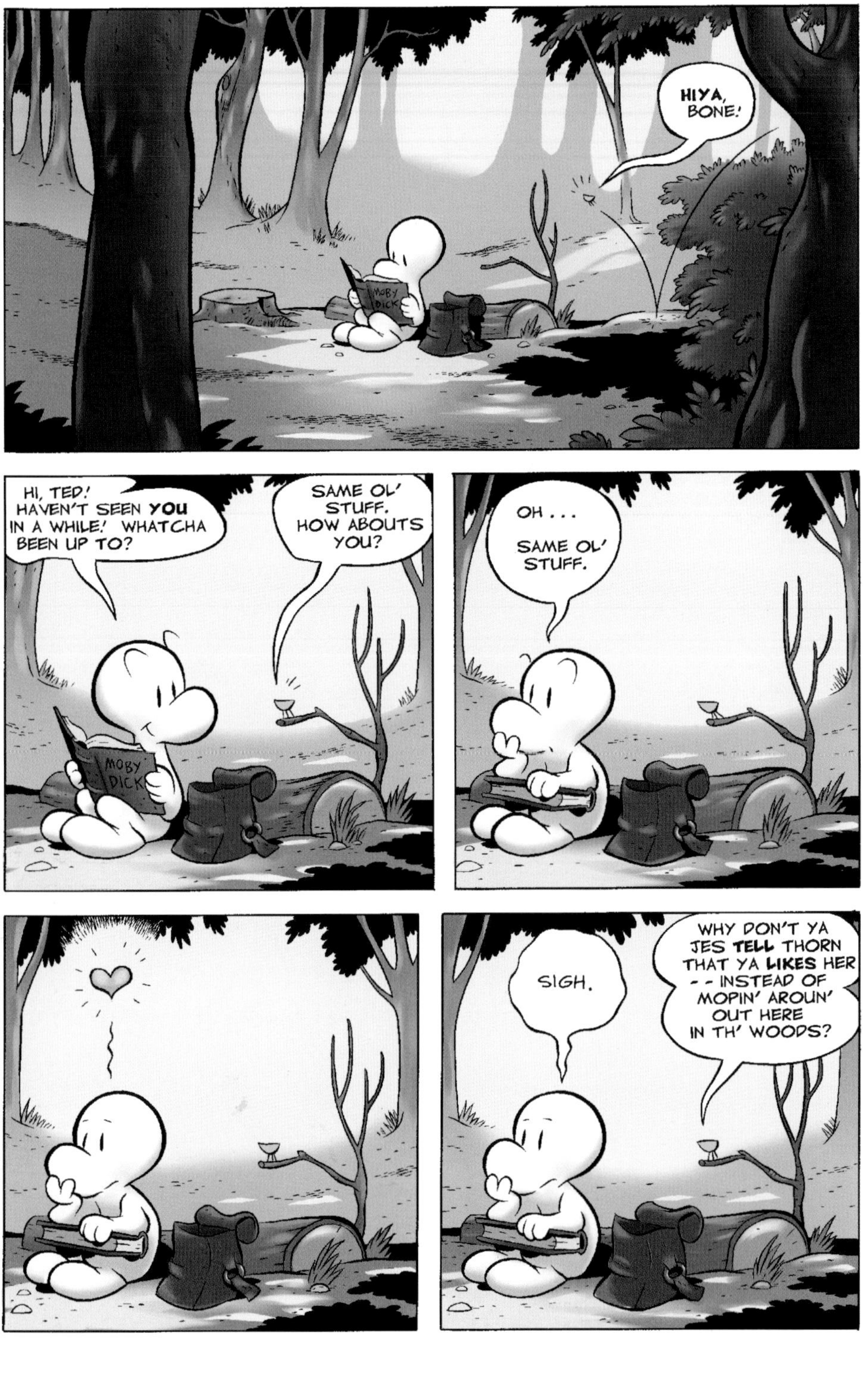
HIYA, BONE!
MOBY DICK
HI, TED! HAVEN'T SEEN YOU IN A WHILE! WHATCHA BEEN UP TO?
SAME OL' STUFF. HOW ABOUTS YOU?
MOBY DICK
OH . . .
SAME OL' STUFF.
SIGH.
WHY DON'T YA JES TELL THORN THAT YA LIKES HER - - INSTEAD OF MOPIN' AROUN' OUT HERE IN TH' WOODS?

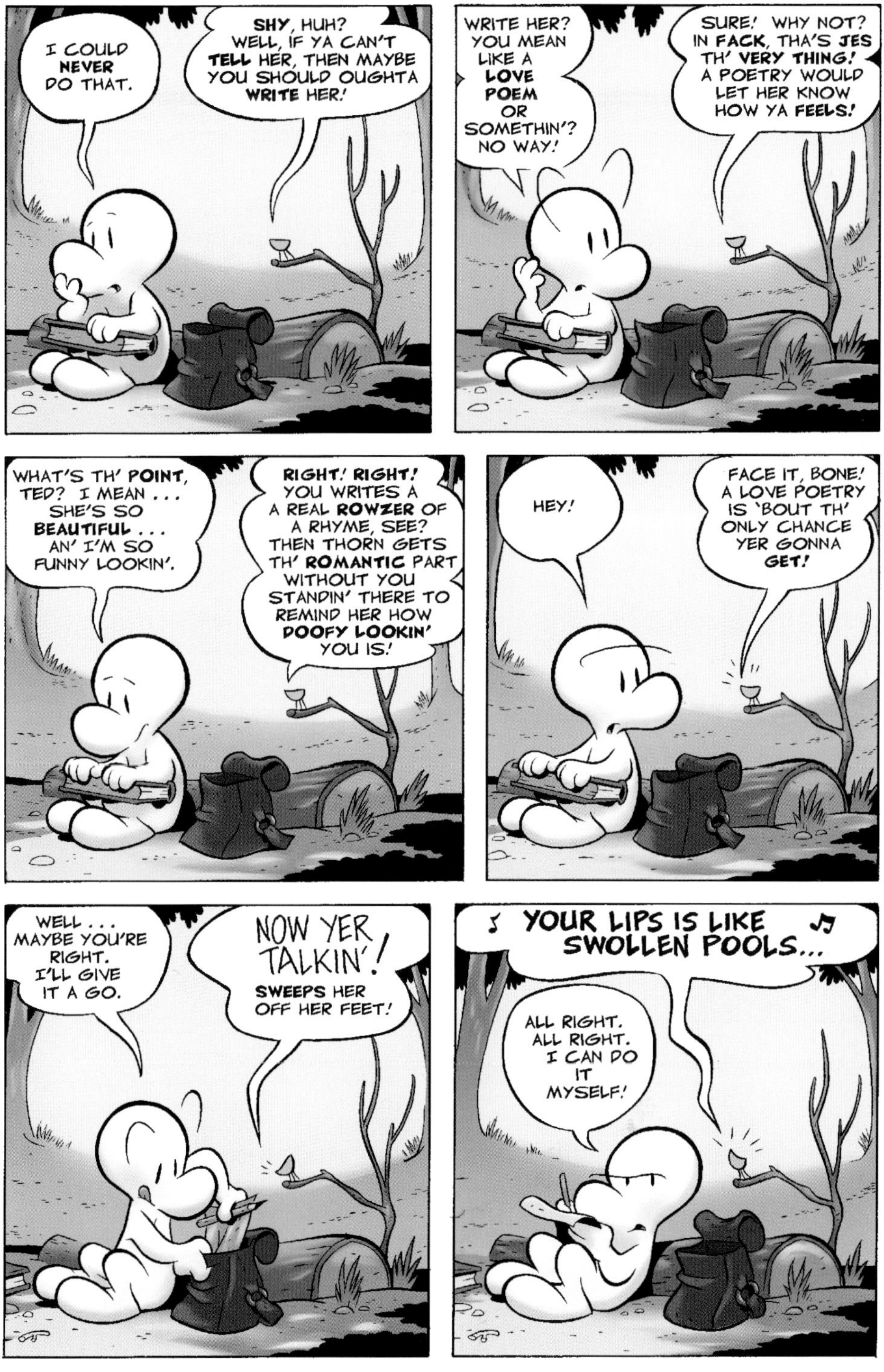
I COULD NEVER DO THAT.
SHY, HUH? WELL, IF YA CAN'T TELL HER, THEN MAYBE YOU SHOULD OUGHTA WRITE HER!
WRITE HER? YOU MEAN LIKE A LOVE POEM OR SOMETHIN'? NO WAY!
SURE! WHY NOT? IN FACK, THA'S JES TH' VERY THING! A POETRY WOULD LET HER KNOW HOW YA FEELS!
WHAT'S TH' POINT, TED? I MEAN . . . SHE'S SO BEAUTIFUL . . . AN' I'M SO FUNNY LOOKIN'.
RIGHT! RIGHT! YOU WRITES A A REAL ROWZER OF A RHYME, SEE? THEN THORN GETS TH' ROMANTIC PART WITHOUT YOU STANDIN' THERE TO REMIND HER HOW DOOFY LOOKIN' YOU IS!
HEY!
FACE IT, BONE! A LOVE POETRY IS 'BOUT TH' ONLY CHANCE YER GONNA GET!
WELL . . . MAYBE YOU'RE RIGHT. I'LL GIVE IT A GO.
NOW YER TALKIN'! SWEEPS HER OFF HER FEET!
YOUR LIPS IS LIKE SWOLLEN POOLS...
ALL RIGHT. ALL RIGHT. I CAN DO IT MYSELF!

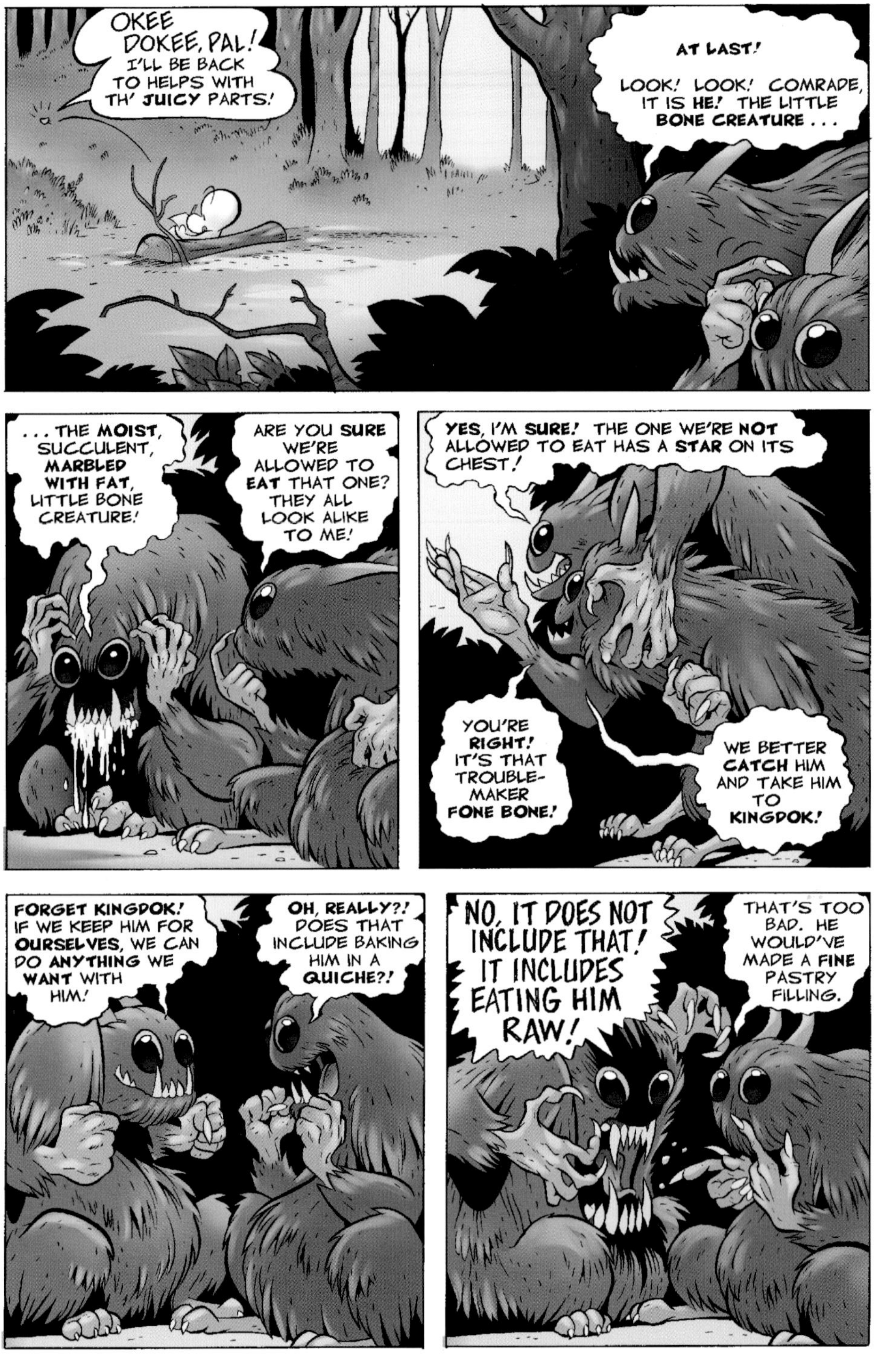
OKEE DOKEE, PAL! I'LL BE BACK TO HELPS WITH TH' JUICY PARTS!
AT LAST!
LOOK! LOOK! COMRADE, IT IS HE! THE LITTLE BONE CREATURE . . .
. . . THE MOIST, SUCCULENT, MARBLED WITH FAT, LITTLE BONE CREATURE!
ARE YOU SURE WE'RE ALLOWED TO EAT THAT ONE? THEY ALL LOOK ALIKE TO ME!
YES, I'M SURE! THE ONE WE'RE NOT ALLOWED TO EAT HAS A STAR ON ITS CHEST!
YOU'RE RIGHT! IT'S THAT TROUBLE-MAKER FONE BONE!
WE BETTER CATCH HIM AND TAKE HIM TO KINGDOK!
FORGET KINGDOK! IF WE KEEP HIM FOR OURSELVES, WE CAN DO ANYTHING WE WANT WITH HIM!
OH, REALLY?! DOES THAT INCLUDE BAKING HIM IN A QUICHE?!
NO, IT DOES NOT INCLUDE THAT! IT INCLUDES EATING HIM RAW!
THAT'S TOO BAD. HE WOULD'VE MADE A FINE PASTRY FILLING.

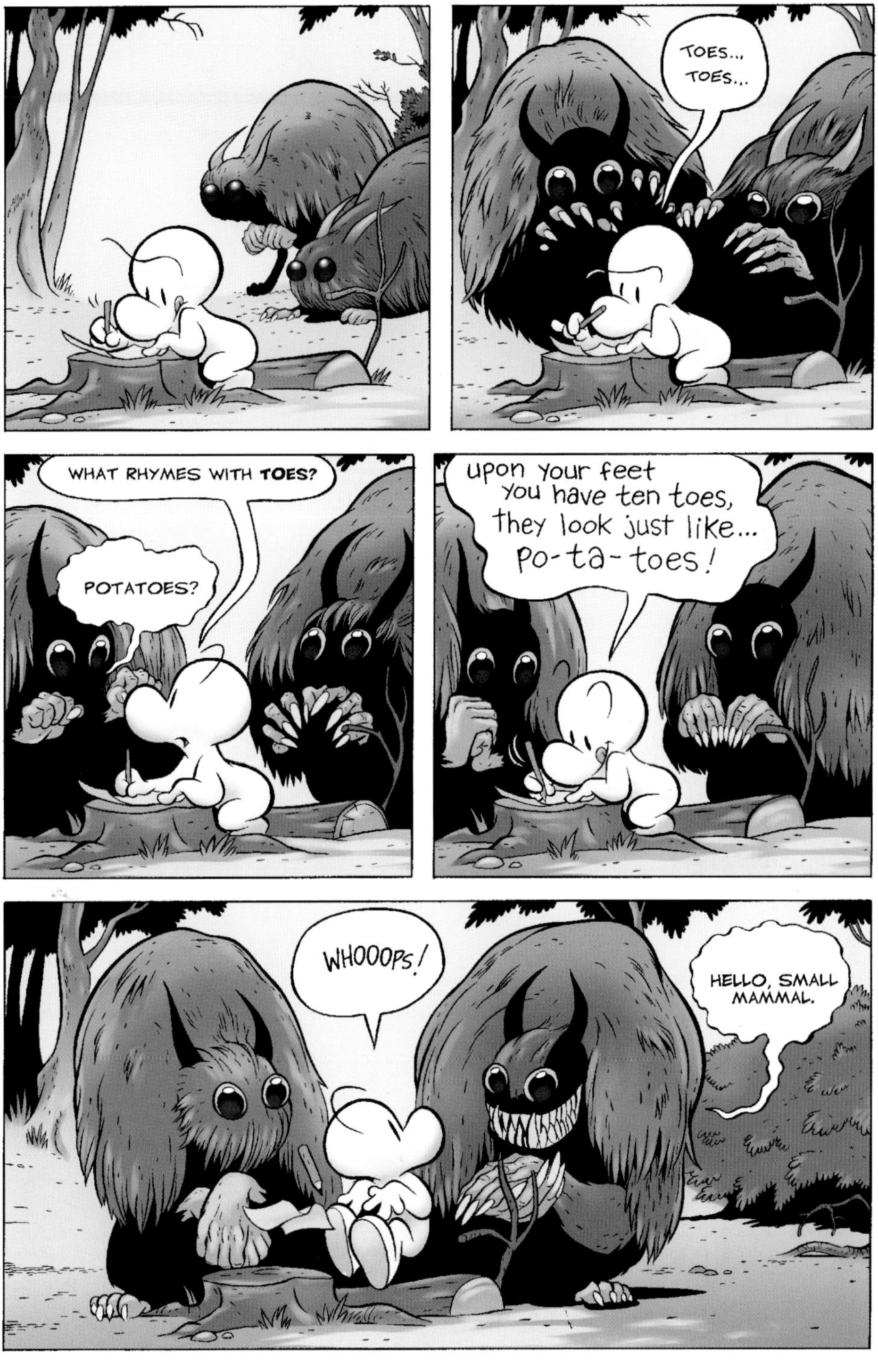
TOES...
TOES...
WHAT RHYMES WITH **TOES?**
POTATOES?
upon your feet
you have ten toes,
they look just like...
po-ta-toes!
WHOOOPS!
HELLO, SMALL
MAMMAL.

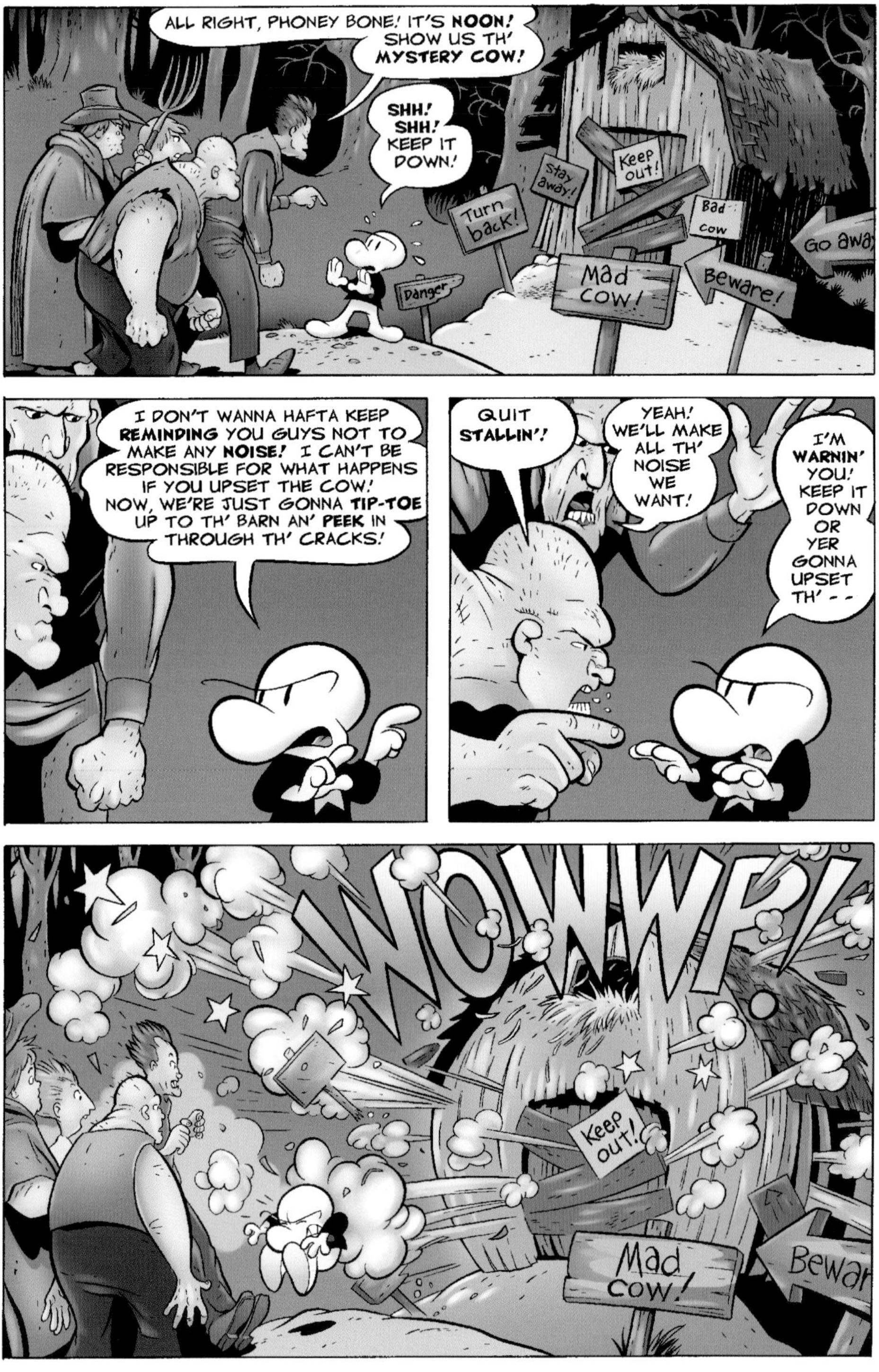
ALL RIGHT, PHONEY BONE! IT'S NOON! SHOW US TH' MYSTERY COW!
SHH! SHH! KEEP IT DOWN!
Turn back!
Stay away!
Keep out!
Bad cow
Go away
Danger
Mad cow!
Beware!
I DON'T WANNA HAFTA KEEP REMINDING YOU GUYS NOT TO MAKE ANY NOISE! I CAN'T BE RESPONSIBLE FOR WHAT HAPPENS IF YOU UPSET THE COW! NOW, WE'RE JUST GONNA TIP-TOE UP TO TH' BARN AN' PEEK IN THROUGH TH' CRACKS!
QUIT STALLIN'!
YEAH! WE'LL MAKE ALL TH' NOISE WE WANT!
I'M WARNIN' YOU! KEEP IT DOWN OR YER GONNA UPSET TH' - -
WOWWP!
Keep out!
Mad cow!
Bewar

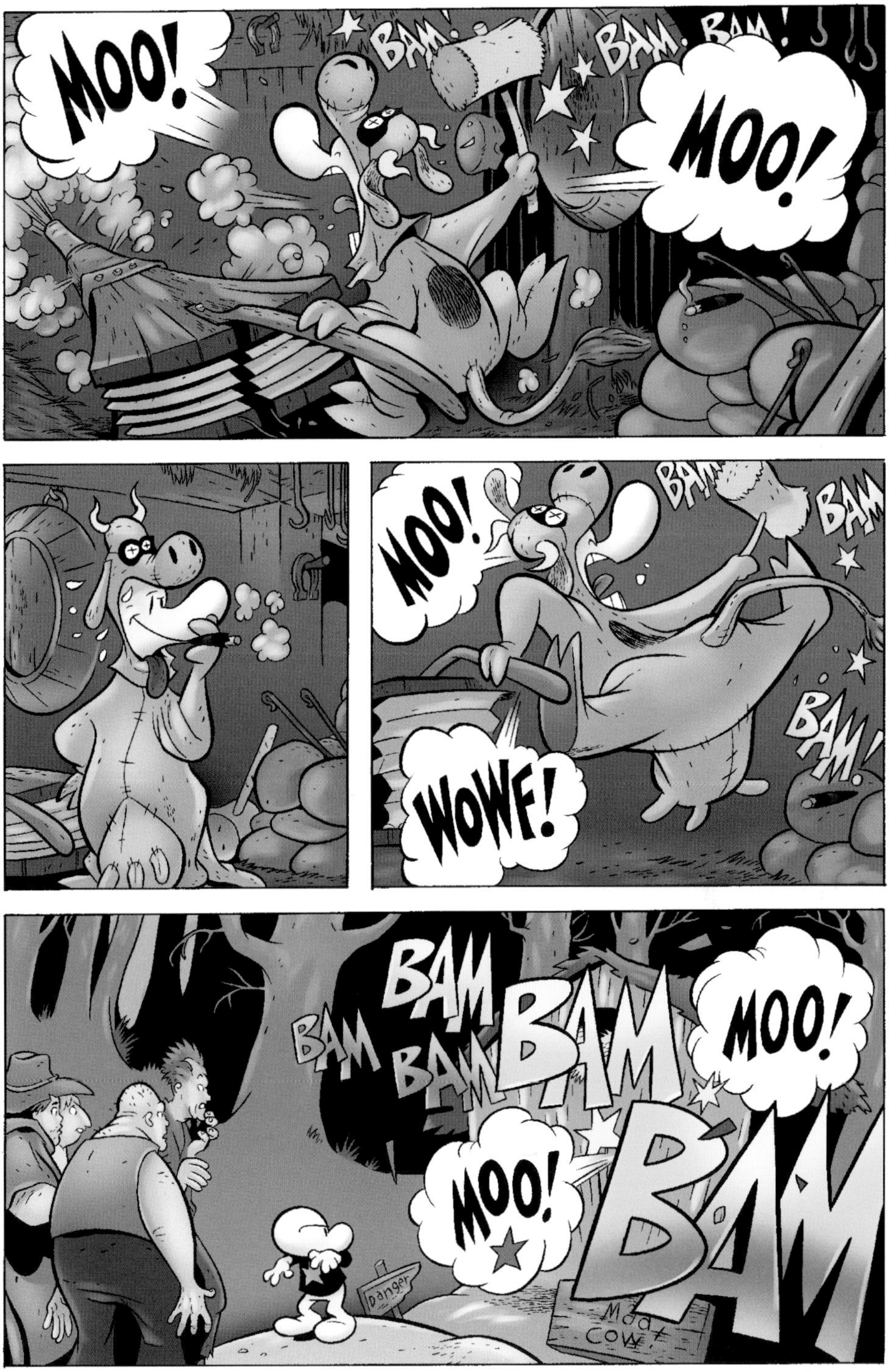
MOO!
BAM!
BAM! BAM!
MOO!
MOO!
BAM
BAM
WOWF!
BAM!
BAM
BAM
BAM
BAM
MOO!
MOO!
BAM
danger
Mad Cow!

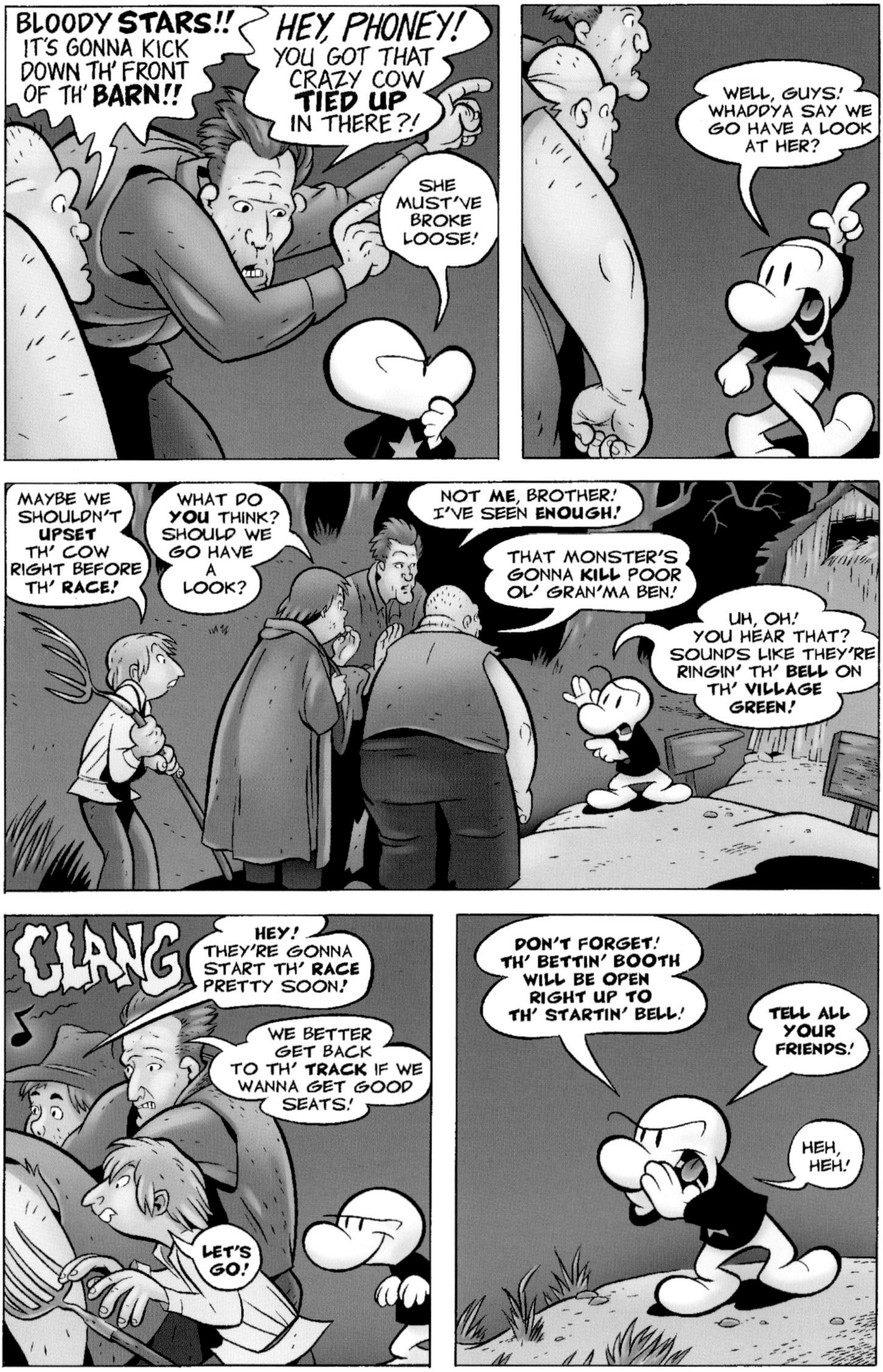
BLOODY STARS!! IT'S GONNA KICK DOWN TH' FRONT OF TH' BARN!!
HEY, PHONEY! YOU GOT THAT CRAZY COW TIED UP IN THERE?!
SHE MUST'VE BROKE LOOSE!
WELL, GUYS! WHADDYA SAY WE GO HAVE A LOOK AT HER?
MAYBE WE SHOULDN'T UPSET TH' COW RIGHT BEFORE TH' RACE!
WHAT DO YOU THINK? SHOULD WE GO HAVE A LOOK?
NOT ME, BROTHER! I'VE SEEN ENOUGH!
THAT MONSTER'S GONNA KILL POOR OL' GRAN'MA BEN!
UH, OH! YOU HEAR THAT? SOUNDS LIKE THEY'RE RINGIN' TH' BELL ON TH' VILLAGE GREEN!
CLANG
HEY! THEY'RE GONNA START TH' RACE PRETTY SOON!
WE BETTER GET BACK TO TH' TRACK IF WE WANNA GET GOOD SEATS!
LET'S GO!
DON'T FORGET! TH' BETTIN' BOOTH WILL BE OPEN RIGHT UP TO TH' STARTIN' BELL!
TELL ALL YOUR FRIENDS!
HEH, HEH!

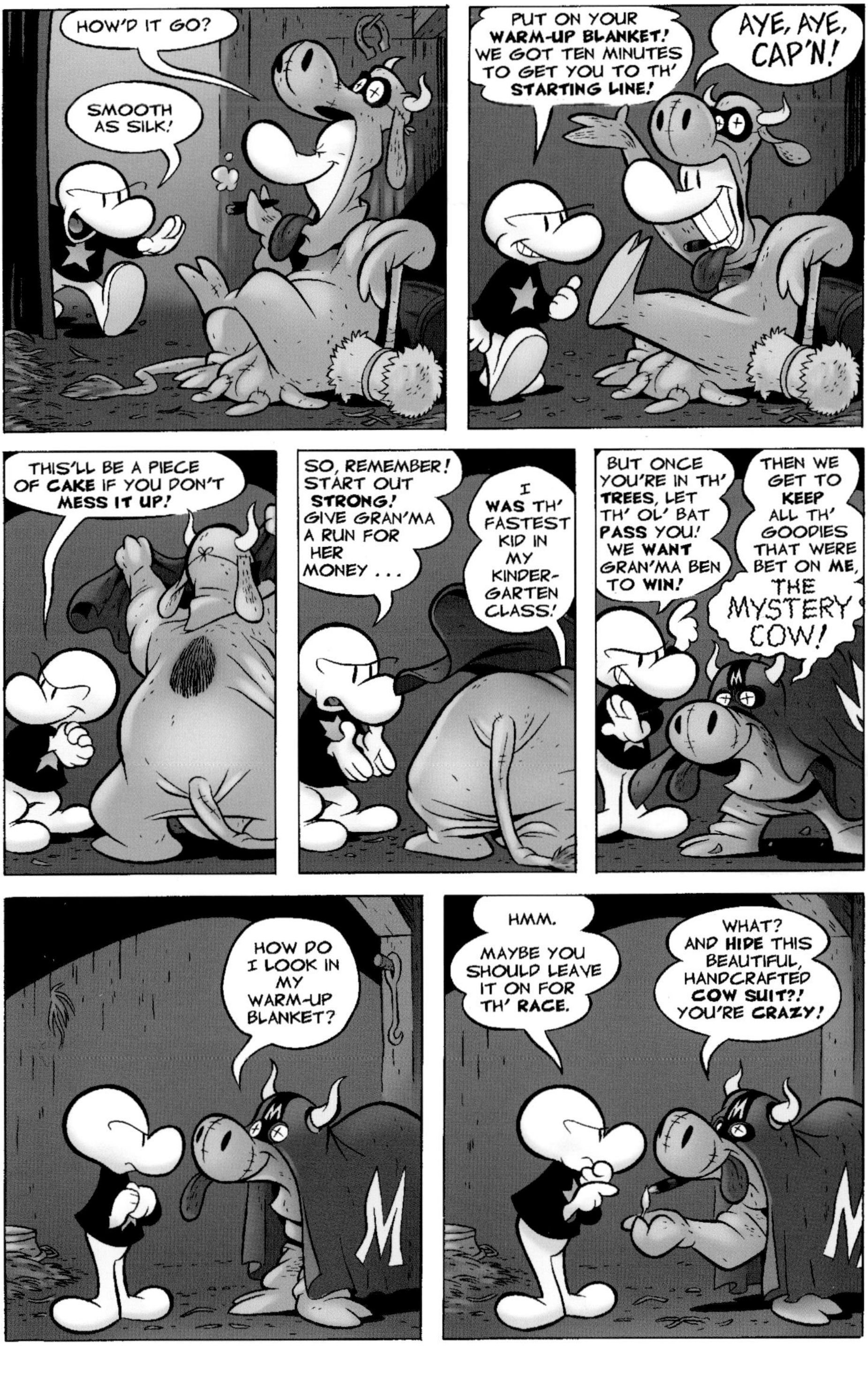
HOW'D IT GO?
SMOOTH AS SILK!
PUT ON YOUR WARM-UP BLANKET! WE GOT TEN MINUTES TO GET YOU TO TH' STARTING LINE!
AYE, AYE, CAP'N!
THIS'LL BE A PIECE OF CAKE IF YOU DON'T MESS IT UP!
SO, REMEMBER! START OUT STRONG! GIVE GRAN'MA A RUN FOR HER MONEY . . .
I WAS TH' FASTEST KID IN MY KINDER-GARTEN CLASS!
BUT ONCE YOU'RE IN TH' TREES, LET TH' OL' BAT PASS YOU! WE WANT GRAN'MA BEN TO WIN!
THEN WE GET TO KEEP ALL TH' GOODIES THAT WERE BET ON ME, THE MYSTERY COW!
HOW DO I LOOK IN MY WARM-UP BLANKET?
HMM.
MAYBE YOU SHOULD LEAVE IT ON FOR TH' RACE.
WHAT? AND HIDE THIS BEAUTIFUL, HANDCRAFTED COW SUIT?! YOU'RE CRAZY!

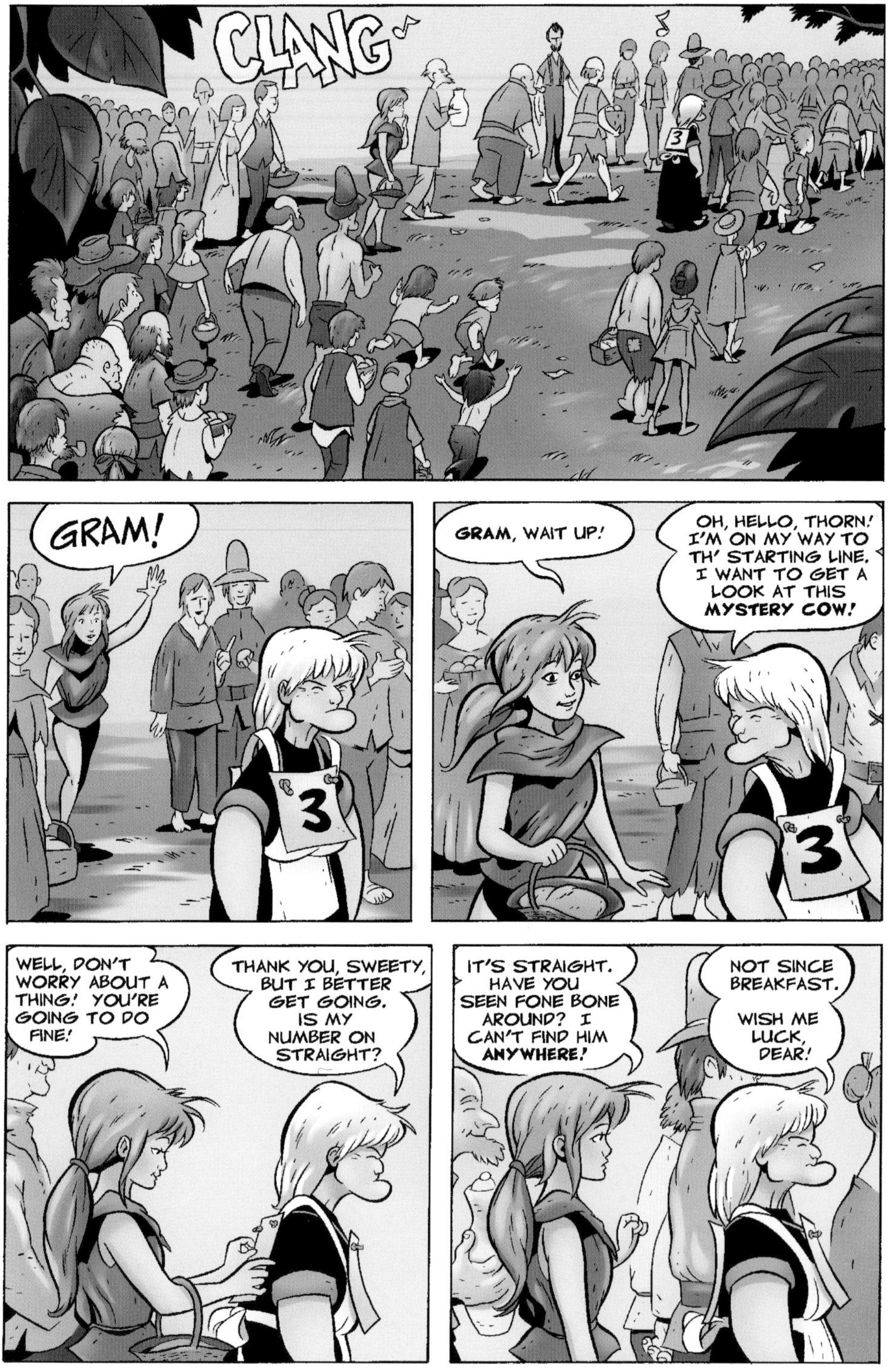
CLANG
GRAM!
GRAM, WAIT UP!
OH, HELLO, THORN! I'M ON MY WAY TO TH' STARTING LINE. I WANT TO GET A LOOK AT THIS MYSTERY COW!
3
3
WELL, DON'T WORRY ABOUT A THING! YOU'RE GOING TO DO FINE!
THANK YOU, SWEETY, BUT I BETTER GET GOING. IS MY NUMBER ON STRAIGHT?
IT'S STRAIGHT. HAVE YOU SEEN FONE BONE AROUND? I CAN'T FIND HIM ANYWHERE!
NOT SINCE BREAKFAST.
WISH ME LUCK, DEAR!

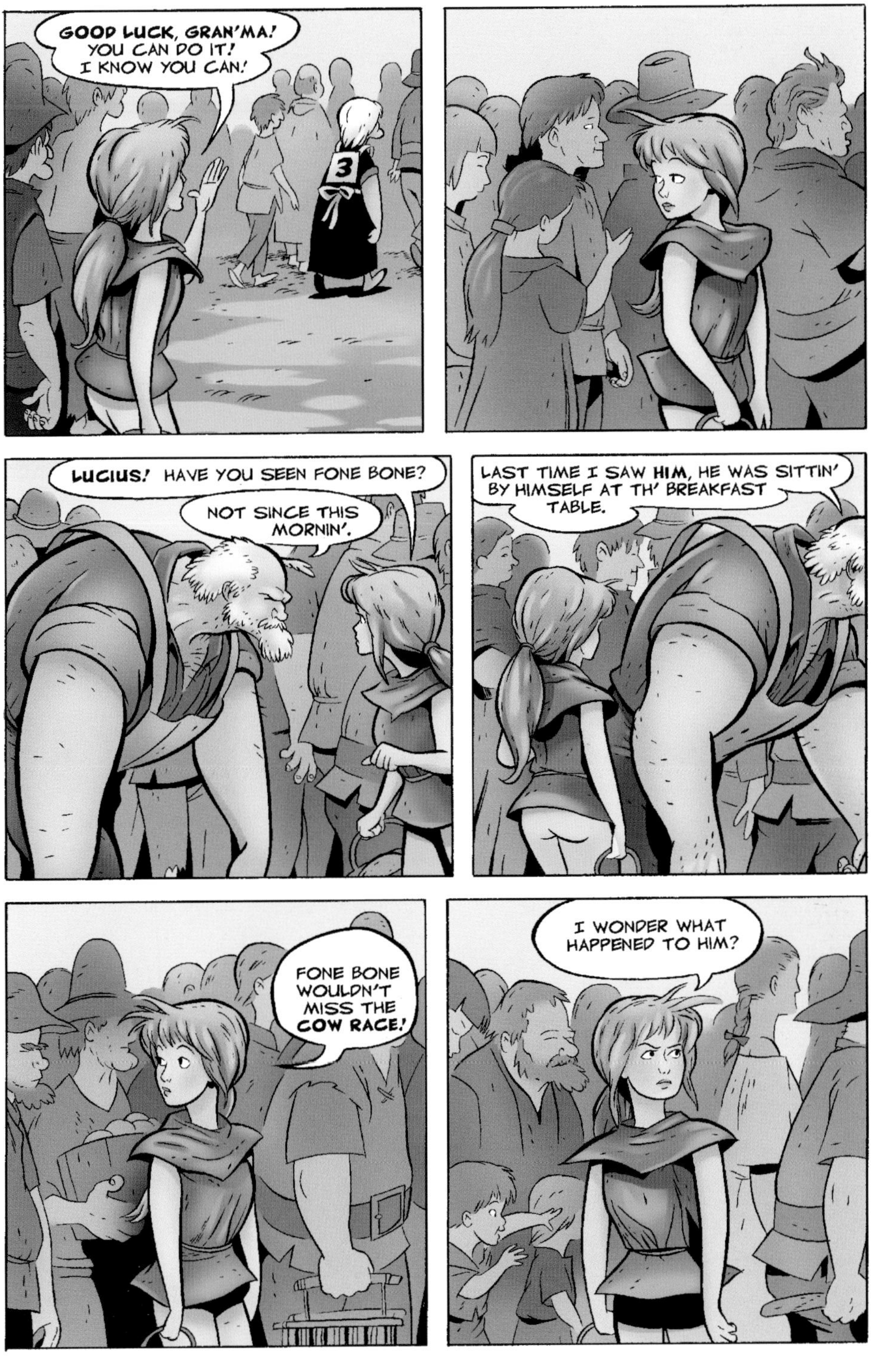
GOOD LUCK, GRAN'MA! YOU CAN DO IT! I KNOW YOU CAN!
LUCIUS! HAVE YOU SEEN FONE BONE?
NOT SINCE THIS MORNIN'.
LAST TIME I SAW HIM, HE WAS SITTIN' BY HIMSELF AT TH' BREAKFAST TABLE.
FONE BONE WOULDN'T MISS THE COW RACE!
I WONDER WHAT HAPPENED TO HIM?

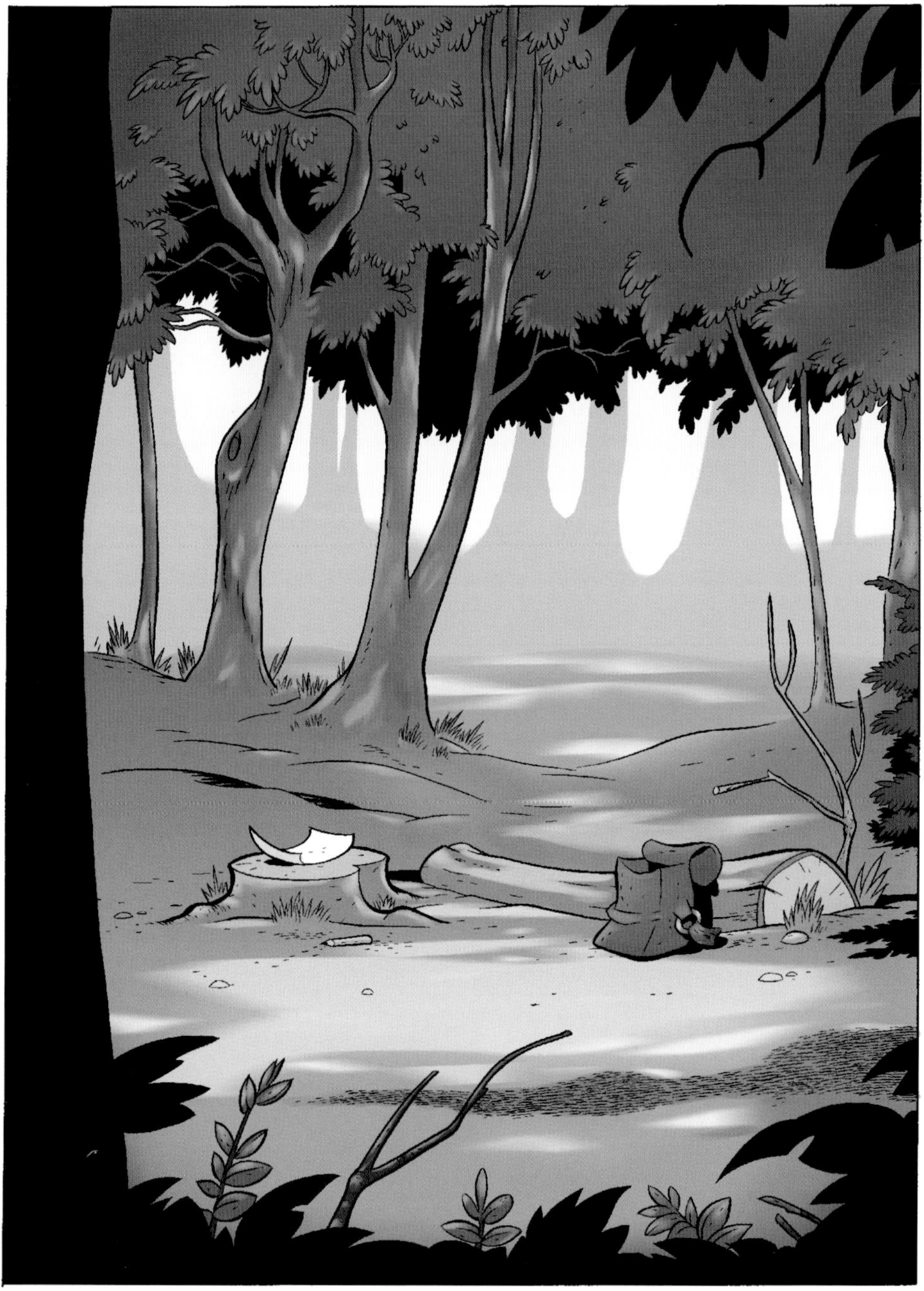

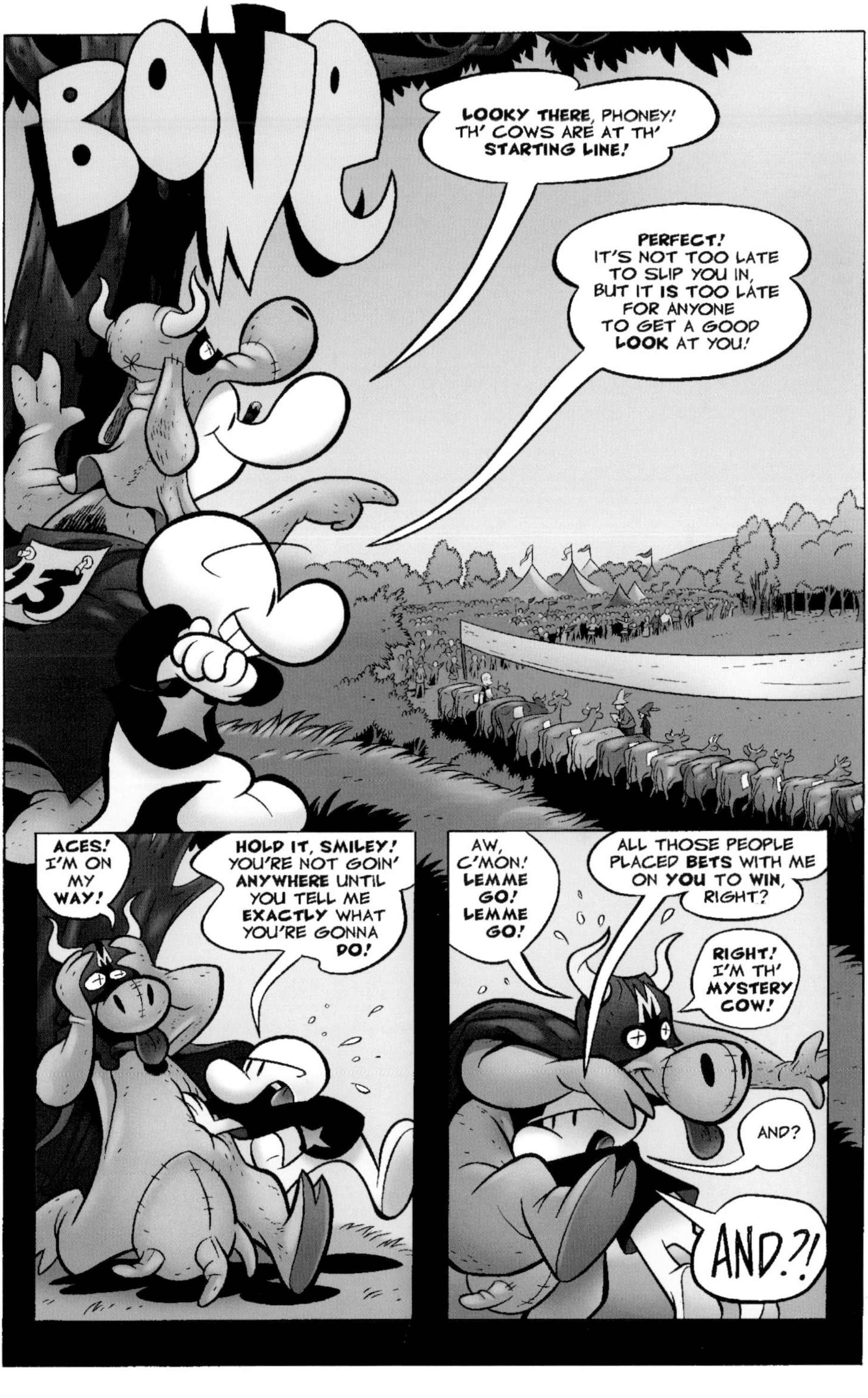
BONE
LOOKY THERE, PHONEY! TH' COWS ARE AT TH' STARTING LINE!
PERFECT! IT'S NOT TOO LATE TO SLIP YOU IN, BUT IT IS TOO LATE FOR ANYONE TO GET A GOOD LOOK AT YOU!
13
ACES! I'M ON MY WAY!
HOLD IT, SMILEY! YOU'RE NOT GOIN' ANYWHERE UNTIL YOU TELL ME EXACTLY WHAT YOU'RE GONNA DO!
AW, C'MON! LEMME GO! LEMME GO!
ALL THOSE PEOPLE PLACED BETS WITH ME ON YOU TO WIN, RIGHT?
RIGHT! I'M TH' MYSTERY COW!
AND?
AND?!

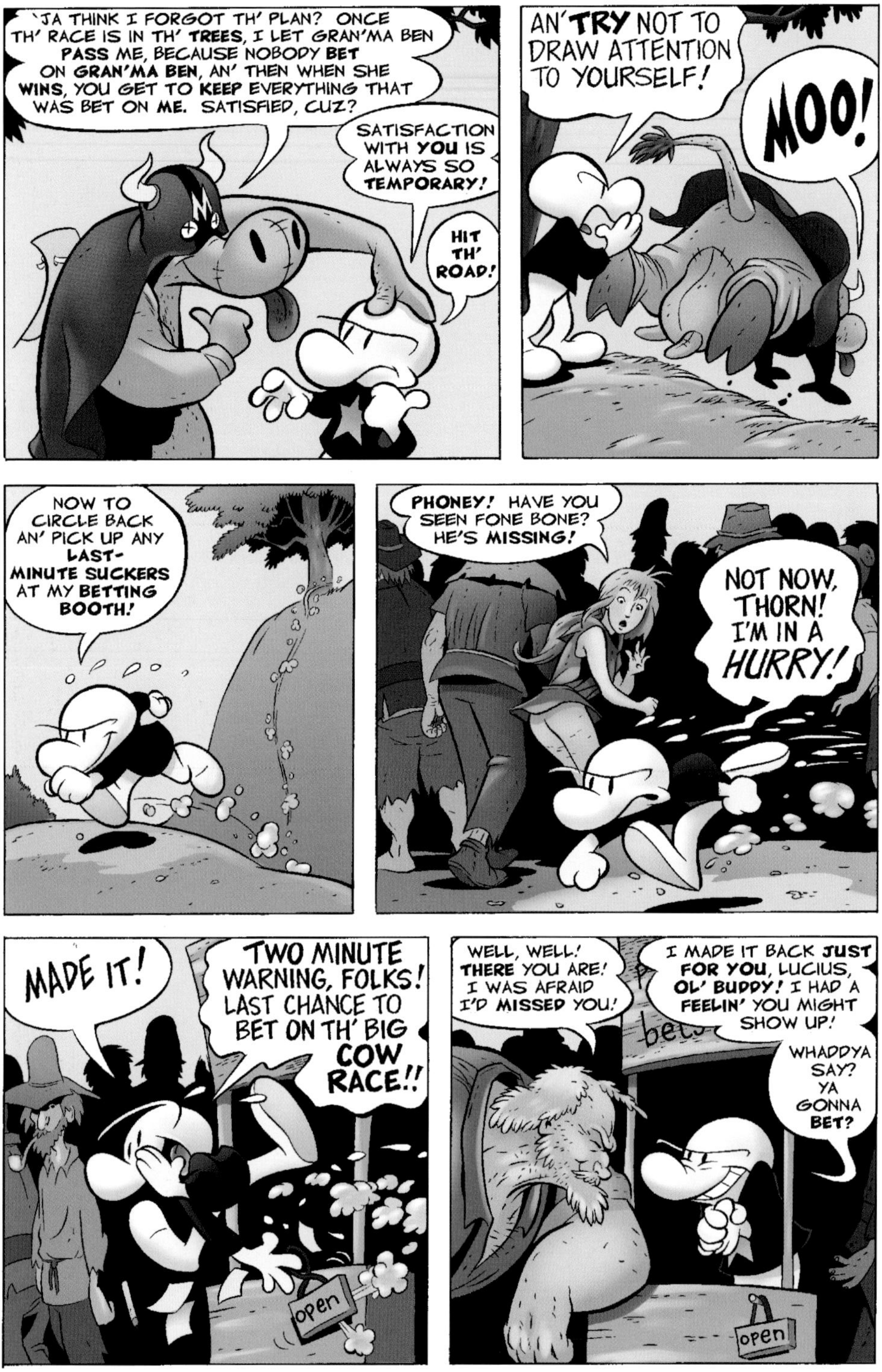
`JA THINK I FORGOT TH' PLAN? ONCE TH' RACE IS IN TH' TREES, I LET GRAN'MA BEN PASS ME, BECAUSE NOBODY BET ON GRAN'MA BEN, AN' THEN WHEN SHE WINS, YOU GET TO KEEP EVERYTHING THAT WAS BET ON ME. SATISFIED, CUZ?
SATISFACTION WITH YOU IS ALWAYS SO TEMPORARY!
HIT TH' ROAD!
AN' TRY NOT TO DRAW ATTENTION TO YOURSELF!
MOO!
NOW TO CIRCLE BACK AN' PICK UP ANY LAST-MINUTE SUCKERS AT MY BETTING BOOTH!
PHONEY! HAVE YOU SEEN FONE BONE? HE'S MISSING!
NOT NOW, THORN! I'M IN A HURRY!
MADE IT!
TWO MINUTE WARNING, FOLKS! LAST CHANCE TO BET ON TH' BIG COW RACE!!
open
WELL, WELL! THERE YOU ARE! I WAS AFRAID I'D MISSED YOU!
I MADE IT BACK JUST FOR YOU, LUCIUS, OL' BUDDY! I HAD A FEELIN' YOU MIGHT SHOW UP!
WHADDYA SAY? YA GONNA BET?
open

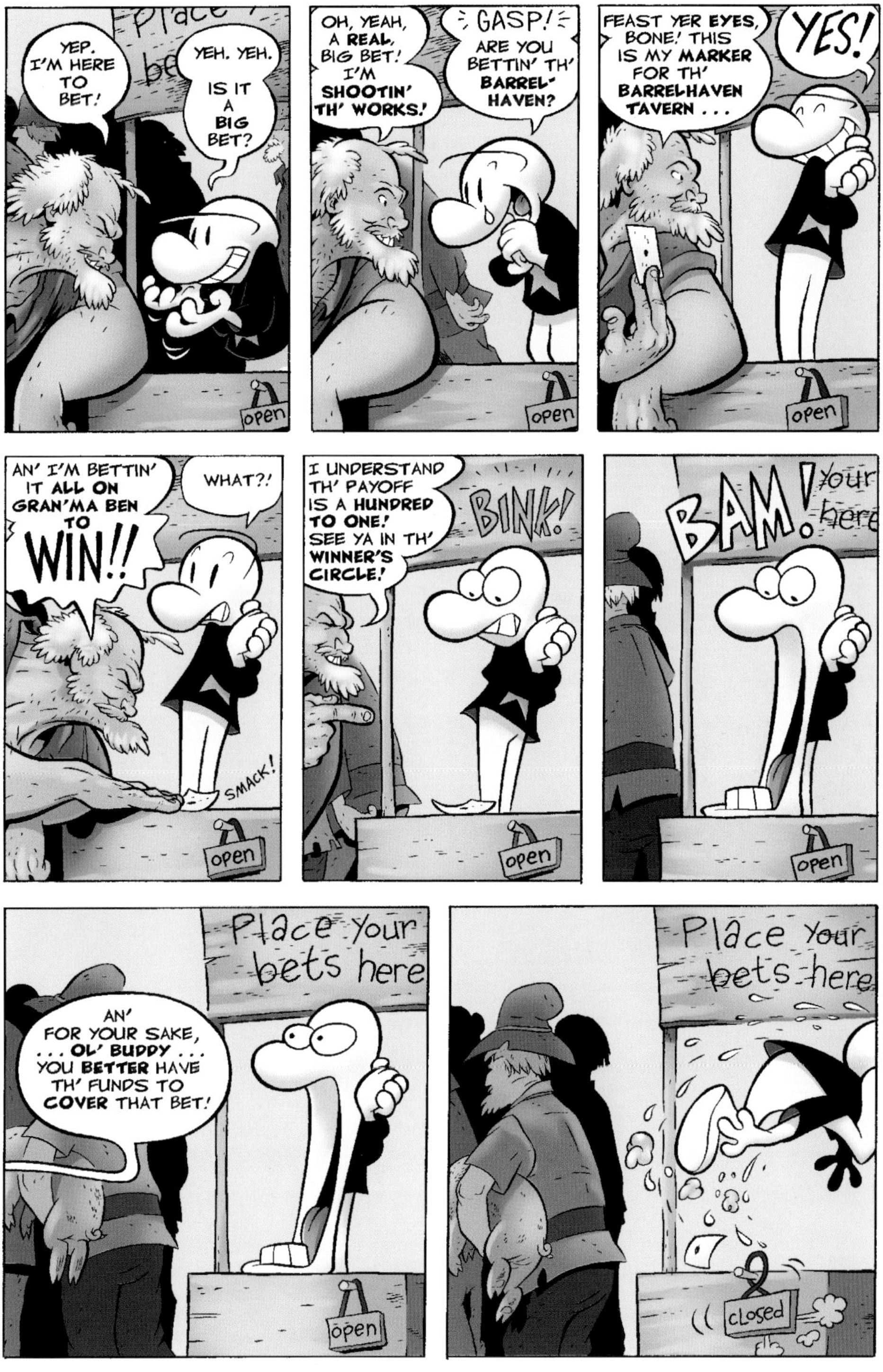
YEP. I'M HERE TO BET!
YEH. YEH. IS IT A BIG BET?
OH, YEAH, A REAL, BIG BET! I'M SHOOTIN' TH' WORKS!
GASP! ARE YOU BETTIN' TH' BARREL-HAVEN?
FEAST YER EYES, BONE! THIS IS MY MARKER FOR TH' BARRELHAVEN TAVERN . . .
YES!
open
AN' I'M BETTIN' IT ALL ON GRAN'MA BEN TO WIN!!
WHAT?!
SMACK!
I UNDERSTAND TH' PAYOFF IS A HUNDRED TO ONE! SEE YA IN TH' WINNER'S CIRCLE!
BINK!
BAM!
AN' FOR YOUR SAKE, . . . OL' BUDDY . . . YOU BETTER HAVE TH' FUNDS TO COVER THAT BET!
Place your bets here
closed

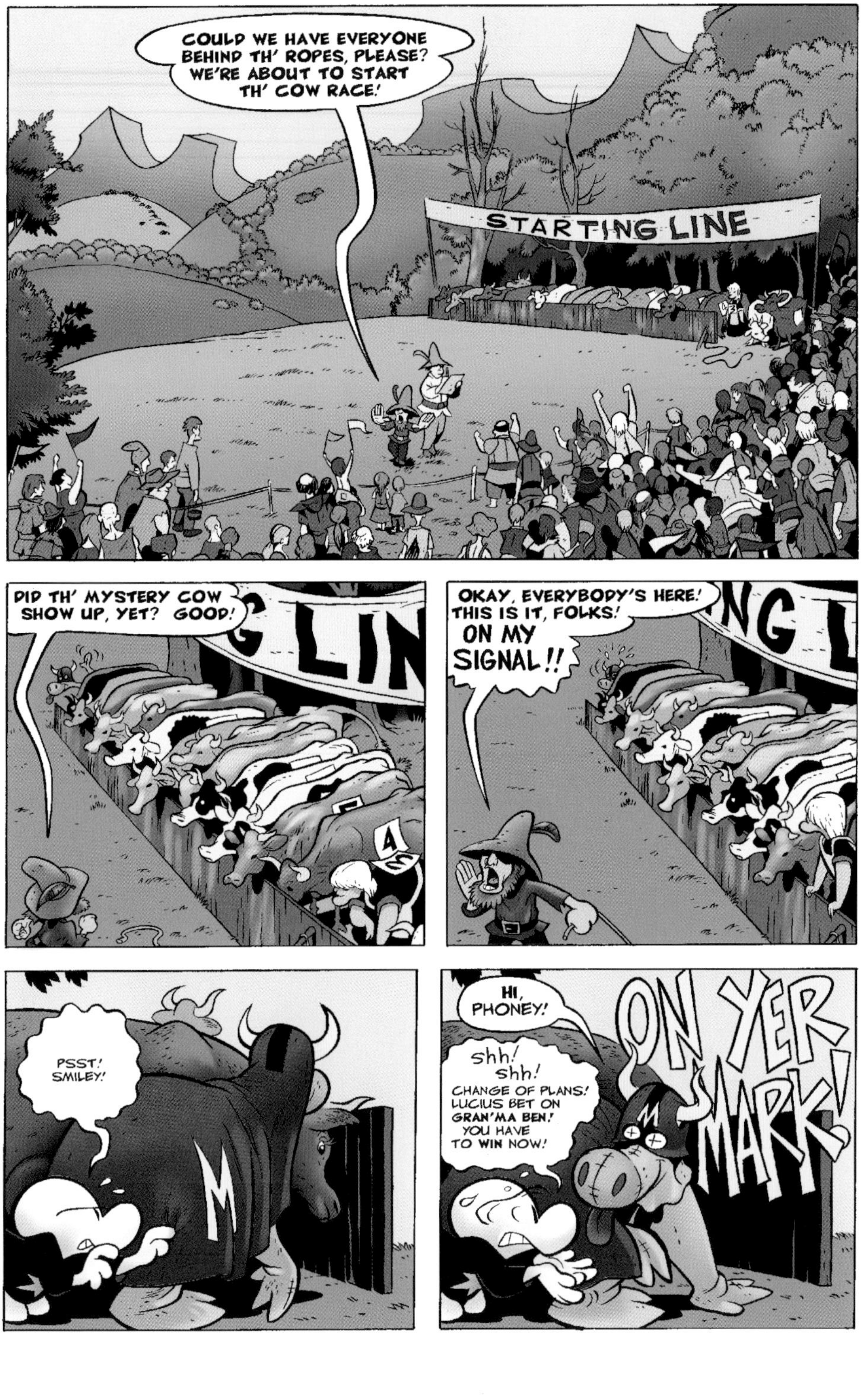
COULD WE HAVE EVERYONE BEHIND TH' ROPES, PLEASE? WE'RE ABOUT TO START TH' COW RACE!
STARTING LINE
DID TH' MYSTERY COW SHOW UP, YET? GOOD!
OKAY, EVERYBODY'S HERE! THIS IS IT, FOLKS! ON MY SIGNAL!!
PSST! SMILEY!
HI, PHONEY!
shh! shh! CHANGE OF PLANS! LUCIUS BET ON GRAN'MA BEN! YOU HAVE TO WIN NOW!
ON YER MARK!

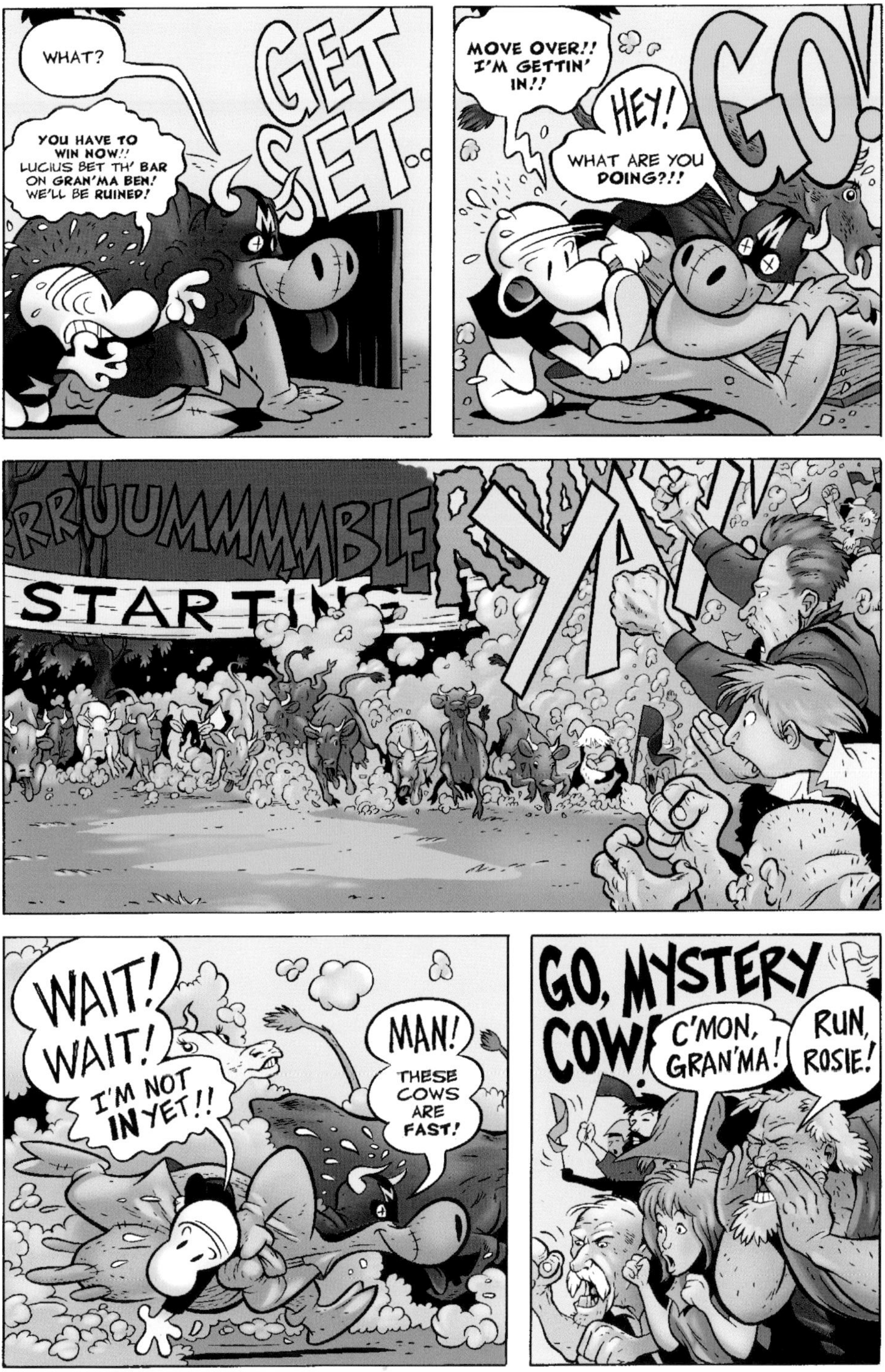
WHAT?
YOU HAVE TO WIN NOW!! LUCIUS BET TH' BAR ON GRAN'MA BEN! WE'LL BE RUINED!
GET SET
MOVE OVER!! I'M GETTIN' IN!!
HEY!
WHAT ARE YOU DOING?!!
GO!
RRUUMMMMMBLE
STARTING
WAIT! WAIT! I'M NOT IN YET!!
MAN! THESE COWS ARE FAST!
GO, MYSTERY COW!
C'MON, GRAN'MA!
RUN, ROSIE!

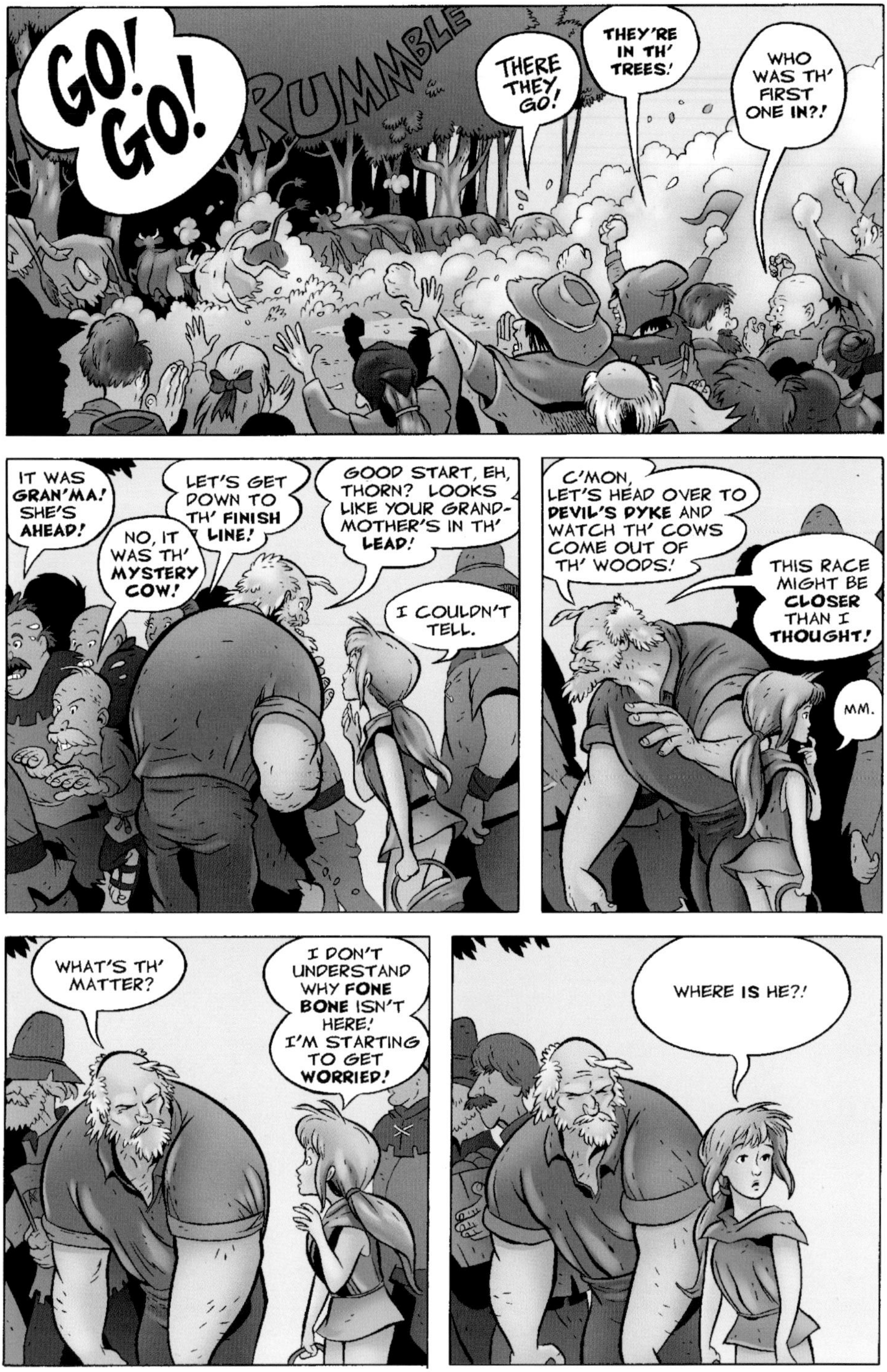
GO! GO!
RUMMBLE
THERE THEY GO!
THEY'RE IN TH' TREES!
WHO WAS TH' FIRST ONE IN?!
IT WAS GRAN'MA! SHE'S AHEAD!
NO, IT WAS TH' MYSTERY COW!
LET'S GET DOWN TO TH' FINISH LINE!
GOOD START, EH, THORN? LOOKS LIKE YOUR GRAND-MOTHER'S IN TH' LEAD!
I COULDN'T TELL.
C'MON, LET'S HEAD OVER TO DEVIL'S DYKE AND WATCH TH' COWS COME OUT OF TH' WOODS!
THIS RACE MIGHT BE CLOSER THAN I THOUGHT!
MM.
WHAT'S TH' MATTER?
I DON'T UNDERSTAND WHY FONE BONE ISN'T HERE! I'M STARTING TO GET WORRIED!
WHERE IS HE?!

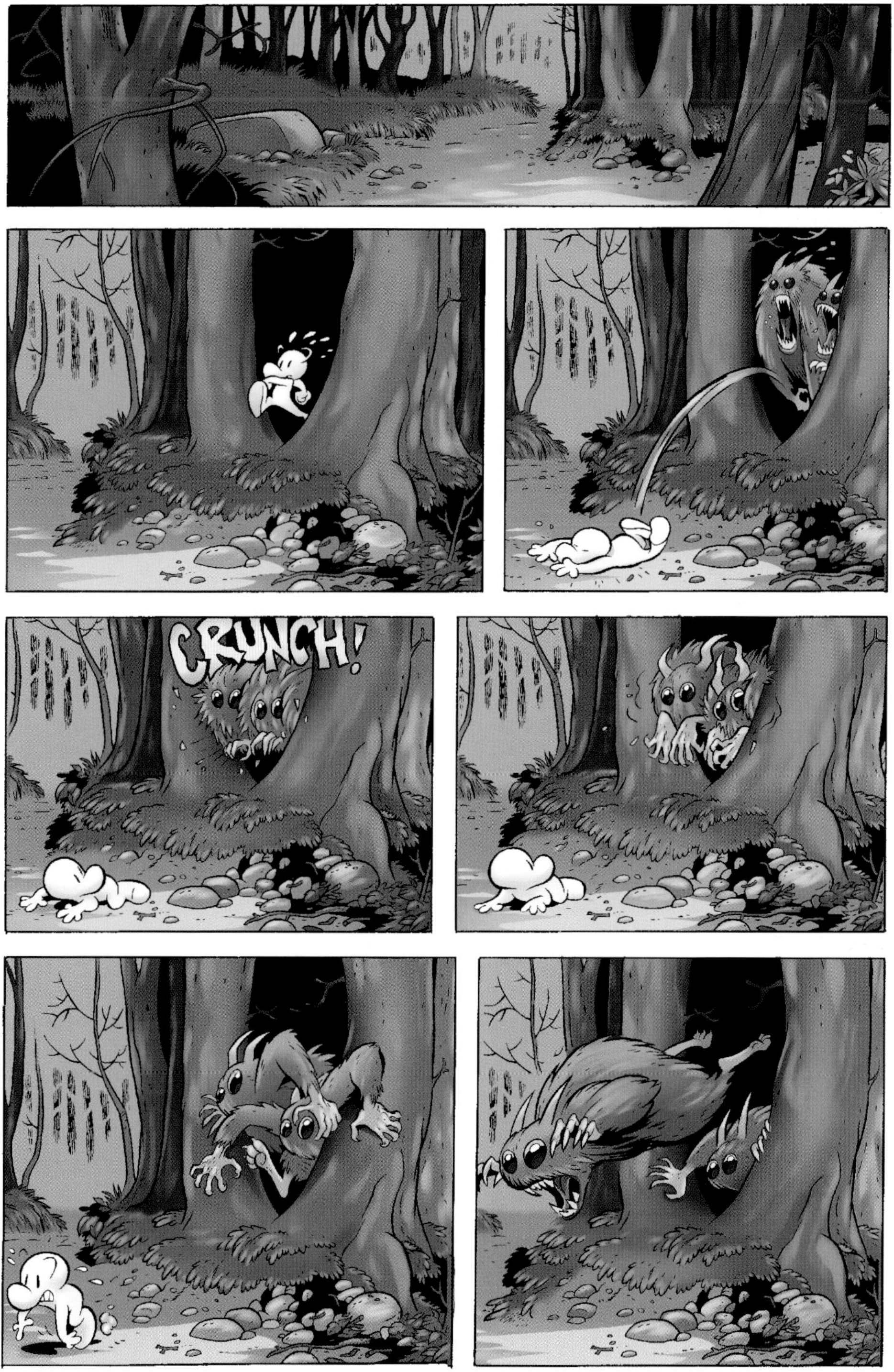
CRUNCH!

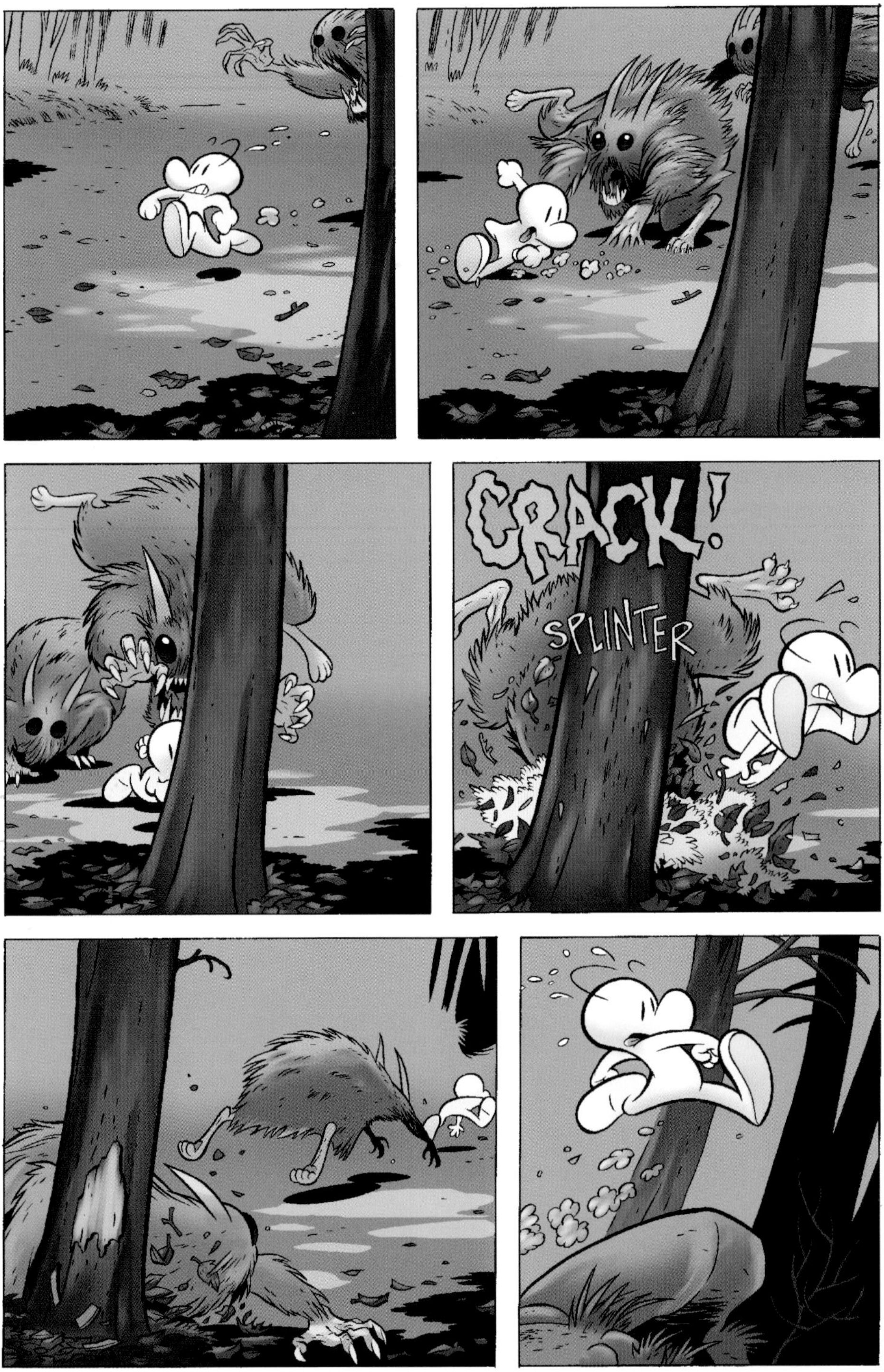
CRACK!
SPLINTER

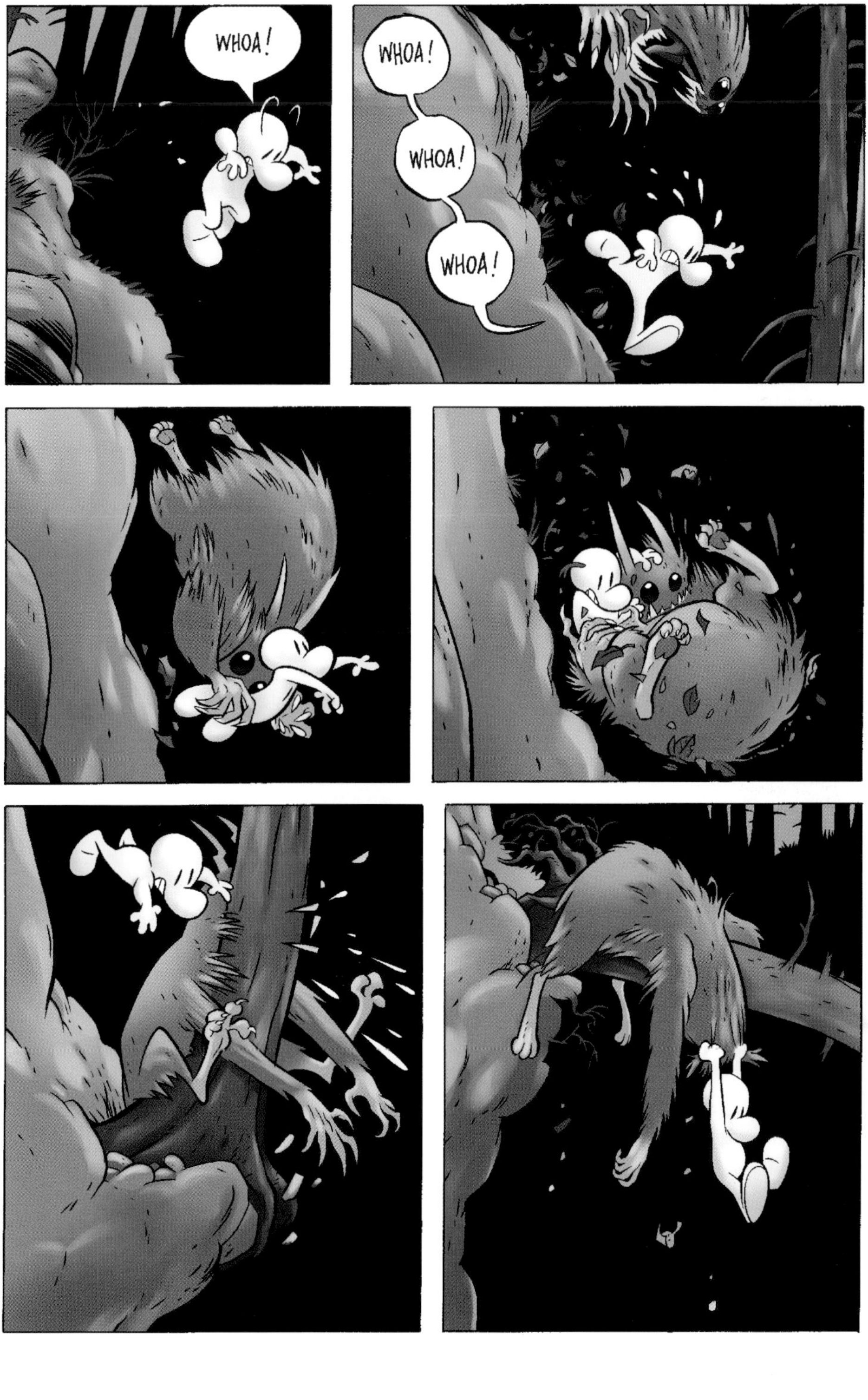
WHOA!
WHOA!
WHOA!
WHOA!

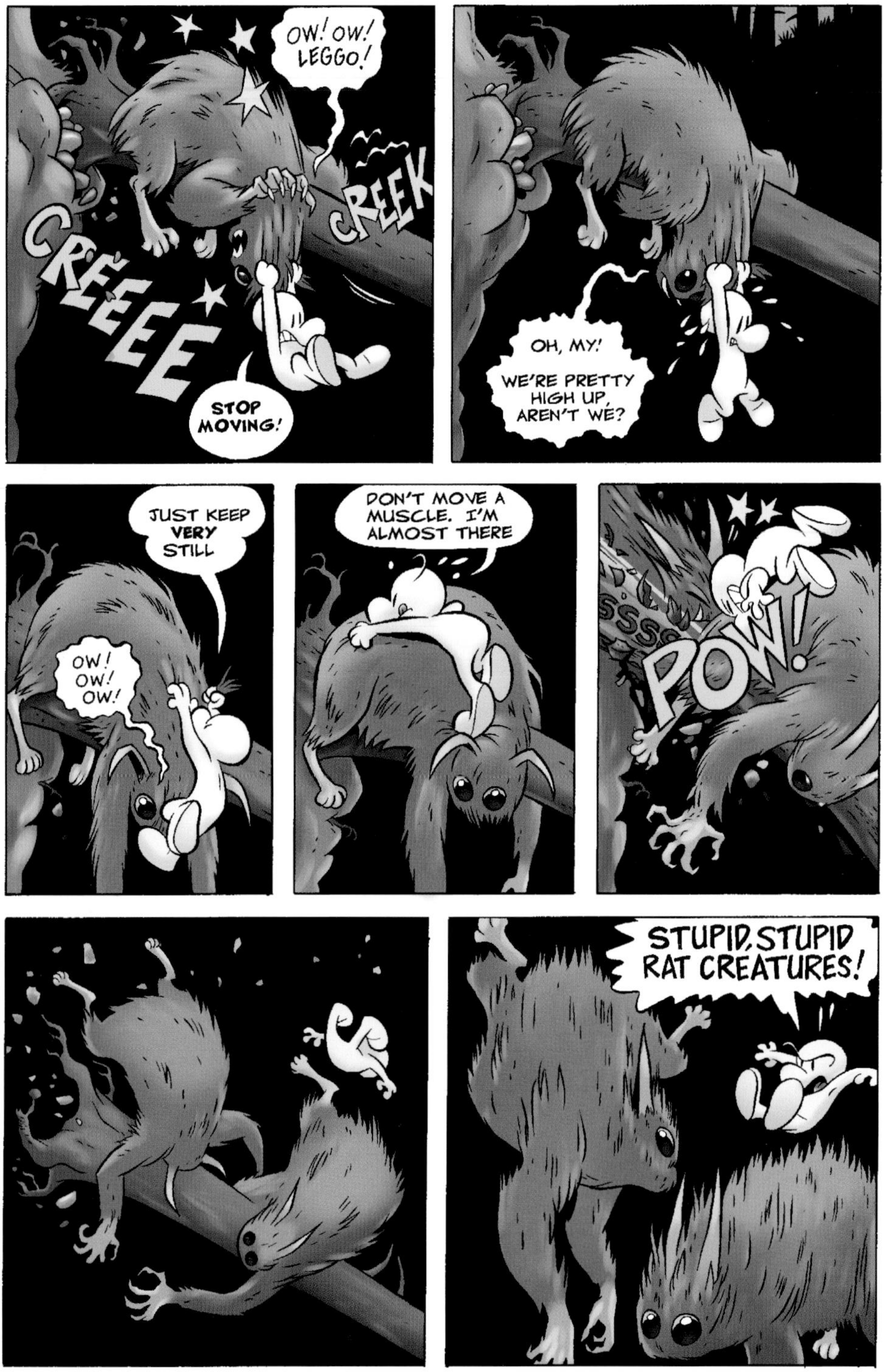
OW! OW! LEGGO!
CREEEEE
CREEK
STOP MOVING!
OH, MY!
WE'RE PRETTY HIGH UP, AREN'T WE?
JUST KEEP VERY STILL
OW! OW! OW!
DON'T MOVE A MUSCLE. I'M ALMOST THERE
POW!
STUPID, STUPID RAT CREATURES!

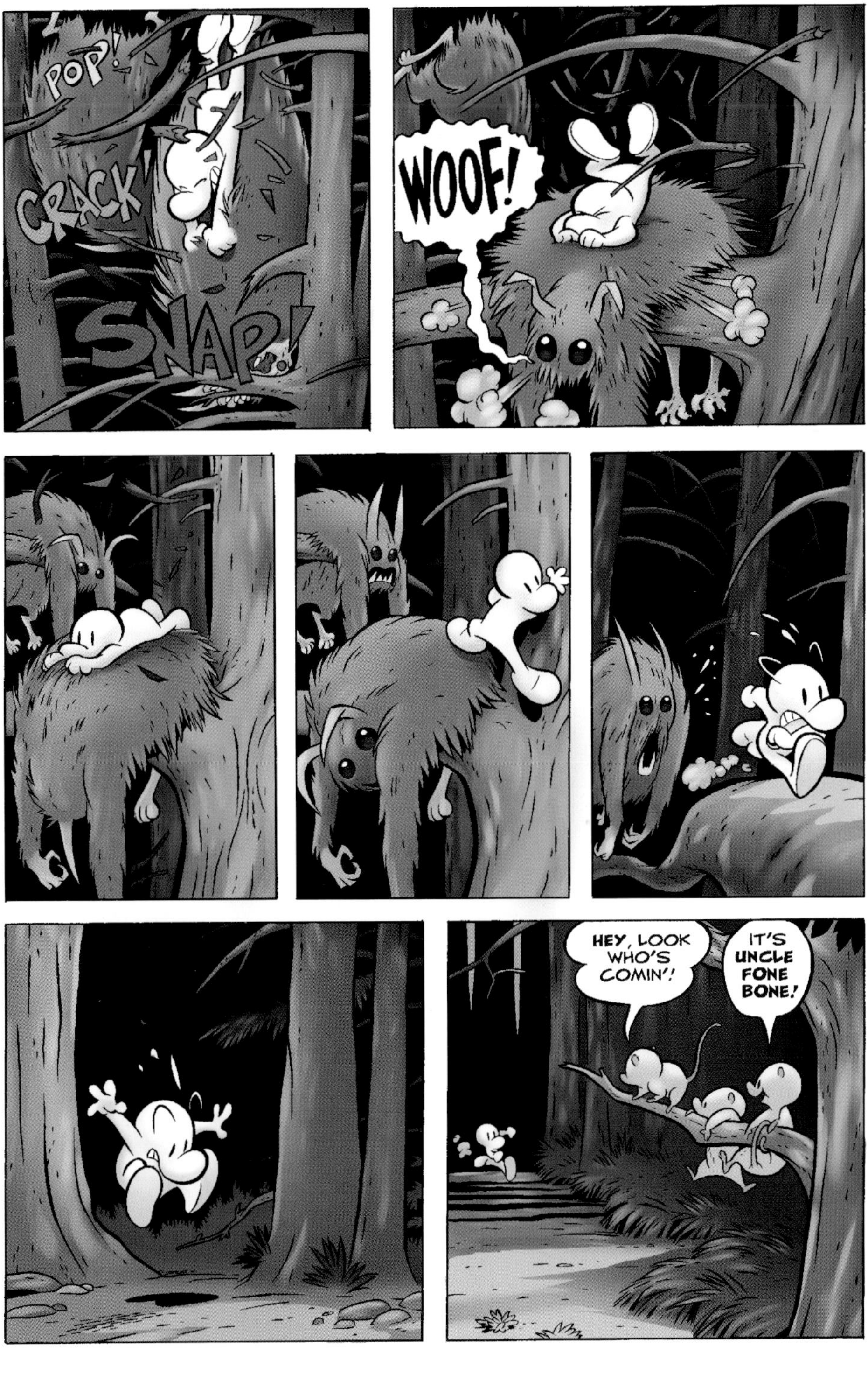
POP!
CRACK!
SNAP!
WOOF!
HEY, LOOK WHO'S COMIN'!
IT'S UNCLE FONE BONE!

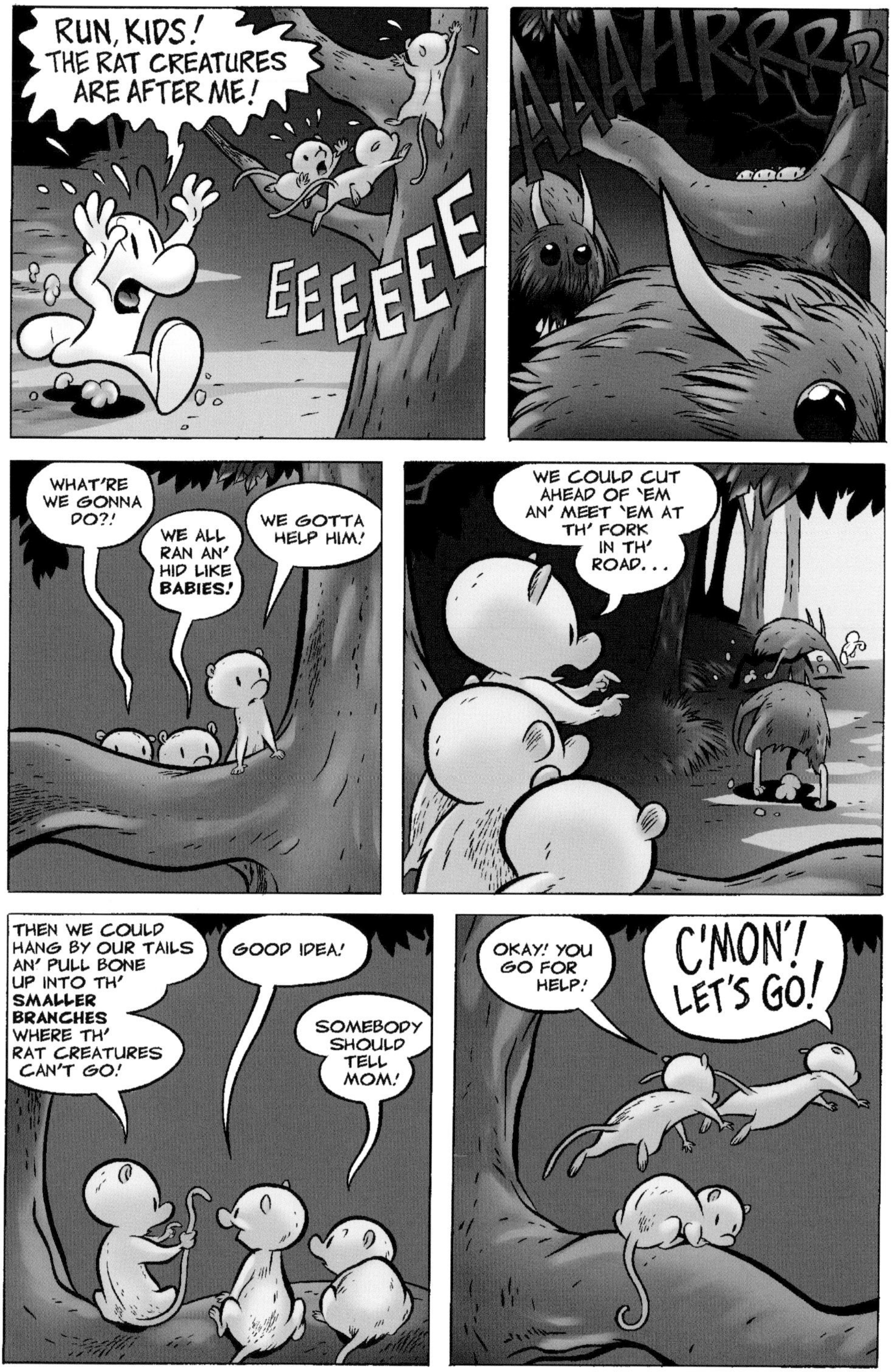
RUN, KIDS! THE RAT CREATURES ARE AFTER ME!
EEEEEE
AAAHRRRR
WHAT'RE WE GONNA DO?!
WE ALL RAN AN' HID LIKE **BABIES!**
WE GOTTA HELP HIM!
WE COULD CUT AHEAD OF 'EM AN' MEET 'EM AT TH' FORK IN TH' ROAD...
THEN WE COULD HANG BY OUR TAILS AN' PULL BONE UP INTO TH' **SMALLER BRANCHES** WHERE TH' RAT CREATURES CAN'T GO!
GOOD IDEA!
SOMEBODY SHOULD TELL MOM!
OKAY! YOU GO FOR HELP!
C'MON'! LET'S GO!

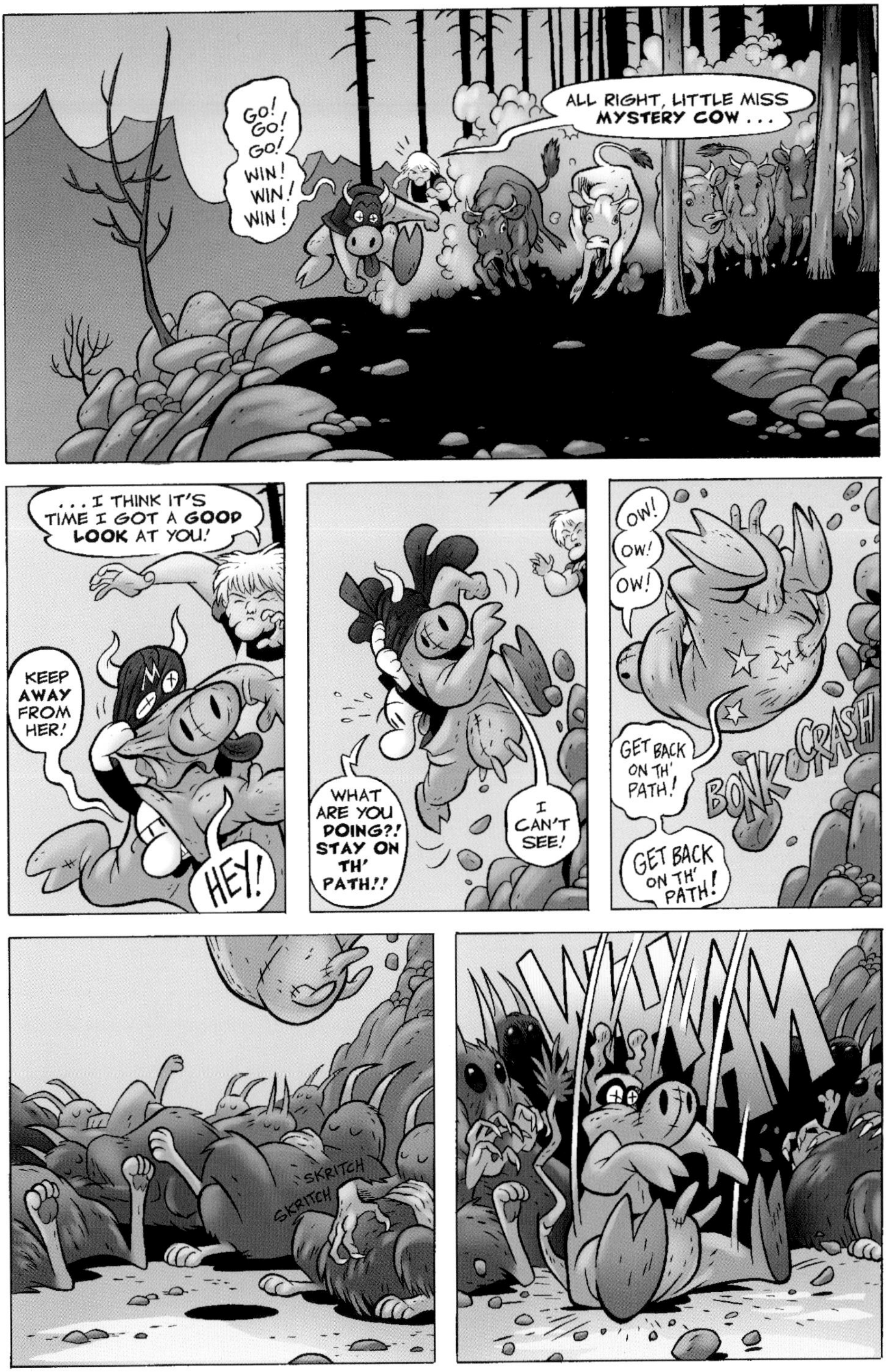
GO! GO! GO! WIN! WIN! WIN!
ALL RIGHT, LITTLE MISS MYSTERY COW . . .
. . . I THINK IT'S TIME I GOT A GOOD LOOK AT YOU!
KEEP AWAY FROM HER!
HEY!
WHAT ARE YOU DOING?! STAY ON TH' PATH!!
I CAN'T SEE!
OW! OW! OW!
GET BACK ON TH' PATH!
BONK
CRASH
GET BACK ON TH' PATH!
SKRITCH
SKRITCH

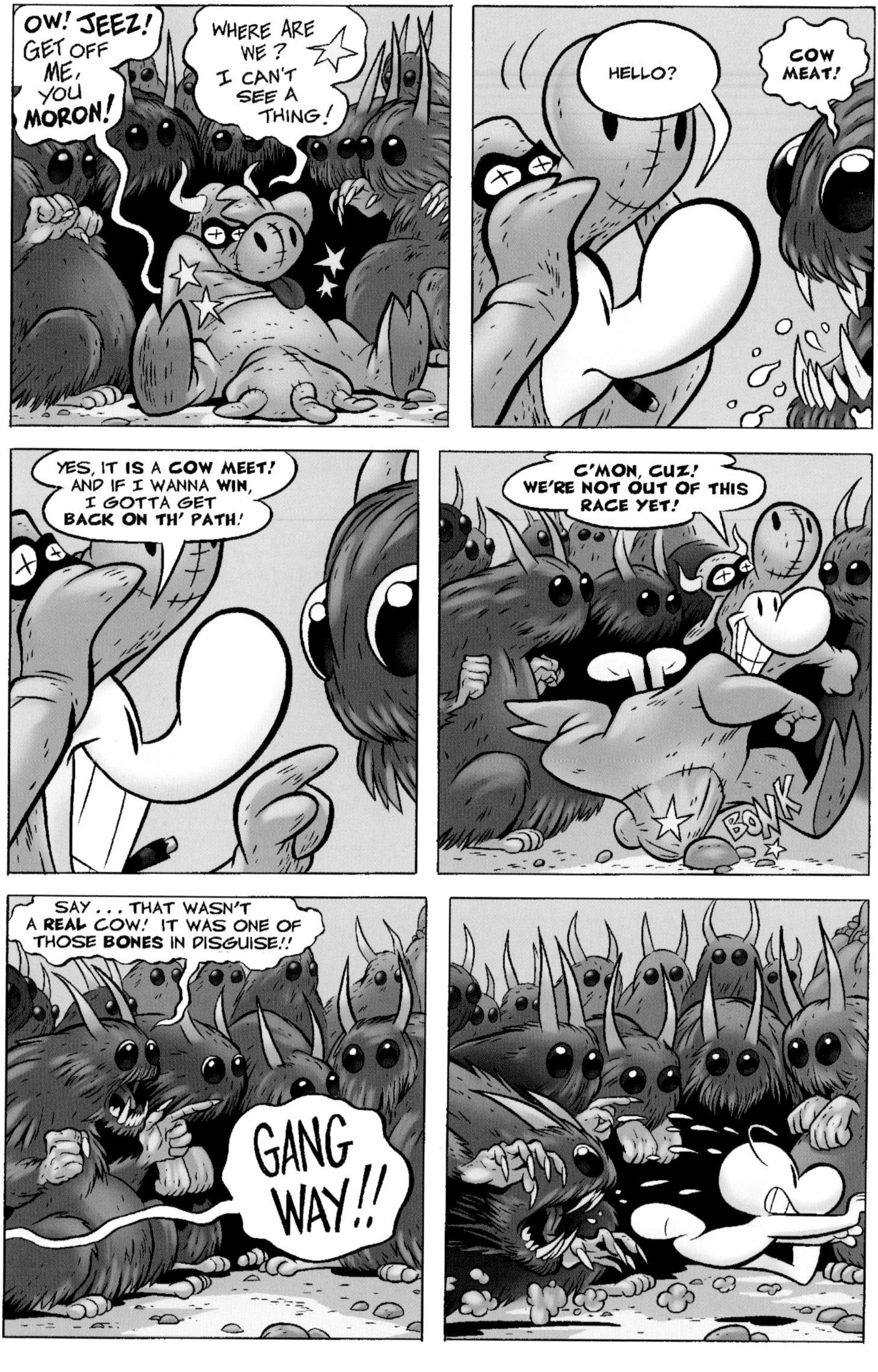
OW! JEEZ! GET OFF ME, YOU MORON!
WHERE ARE WE? I CAN'T SEE A THING!
HELLO?
COW MEAT!
YES, IT IS A COW MEET! AND IF I WANNA WIN, I GOTTA GET BACK ON TH' PATH!
C'MON, CUZ! WE'RE NOT OUT OF THIS RACE YET!
BONK
SAY . . . THAT WASN'T A REAL COW! IT WAS ONE OF THOSE BONES IN DISGUISE!!
GANG WAY!!

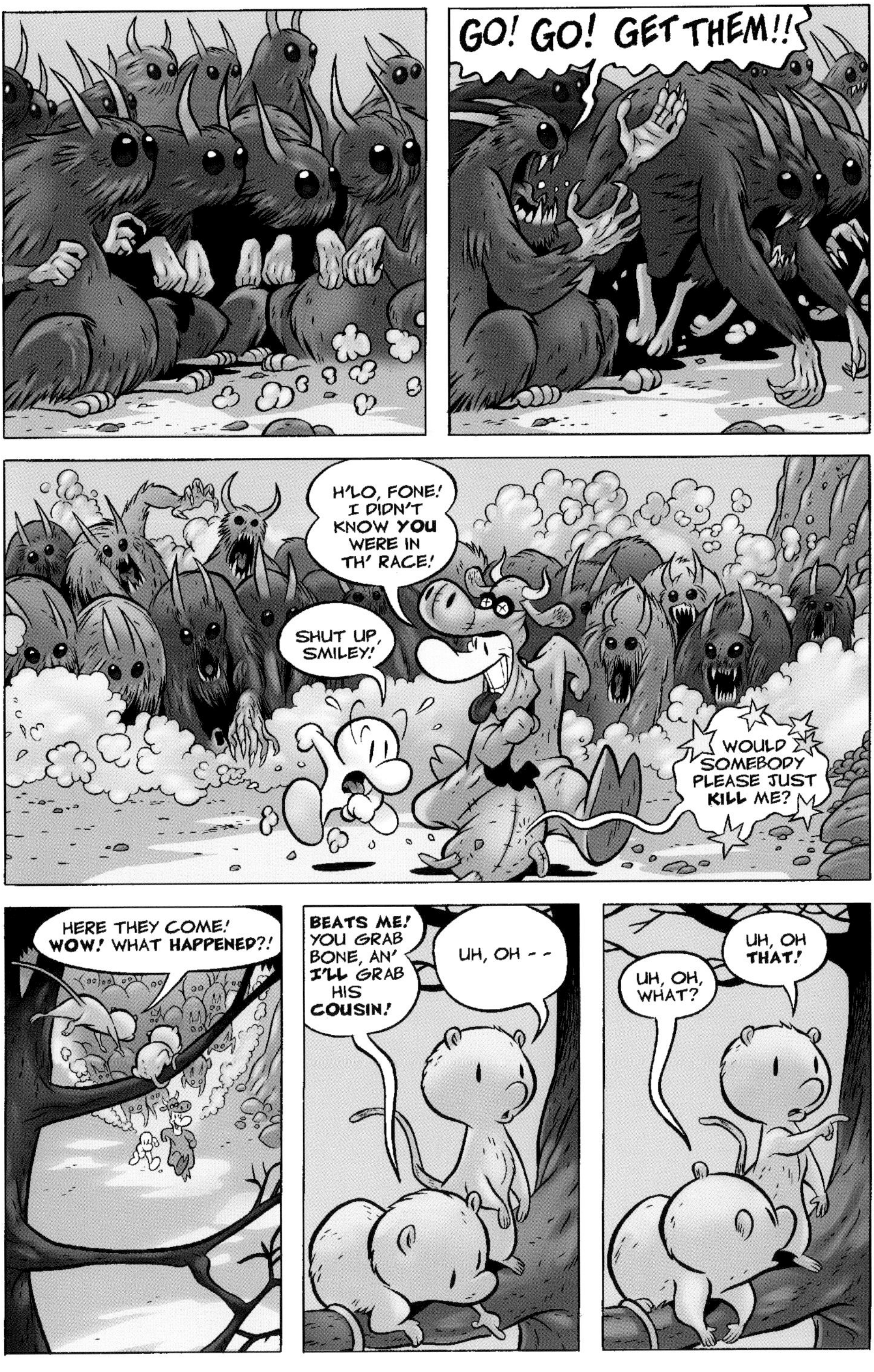
GO! GO! GET THEM!!
H'LO, FONE! I DIDN'T KNOW YOU WERE IN TH' RACE!
SHUT UP, SMILEY!
WOULD SOMEBODY PLEASE JUST KILL ME?
HERE THEY COME! WOW! WHAT HAPPENED?!
BEATS ME! YOU GRAB BONE, AN' I'LL GRAB HIS COUSIN!
UH, OH - -
UH, OH, WHAT?
UH, OH THAT!

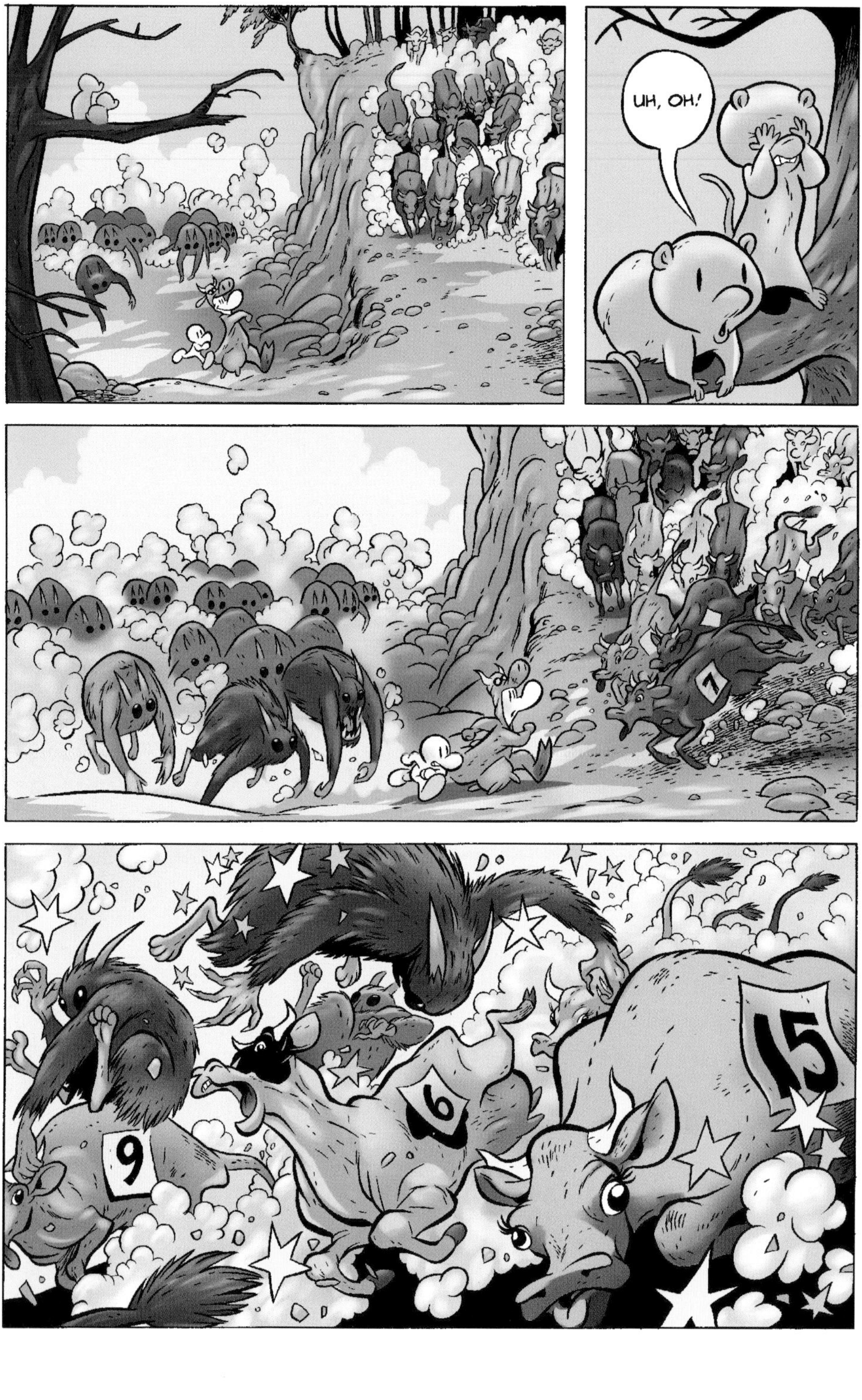
UH, OH!
9
6
15
7

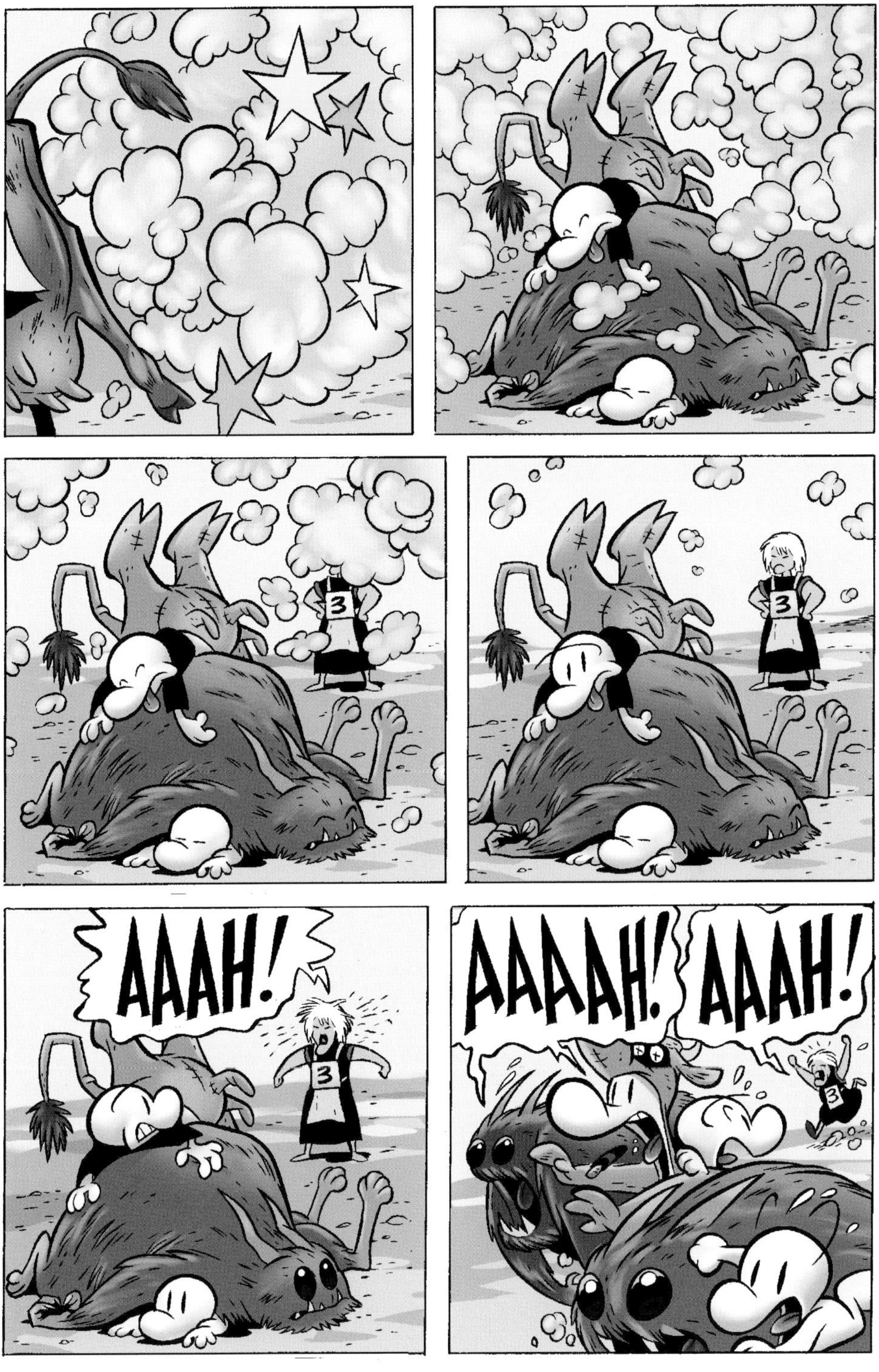
3
3
AAAH!
3
AAAAH!
AAAH!
3

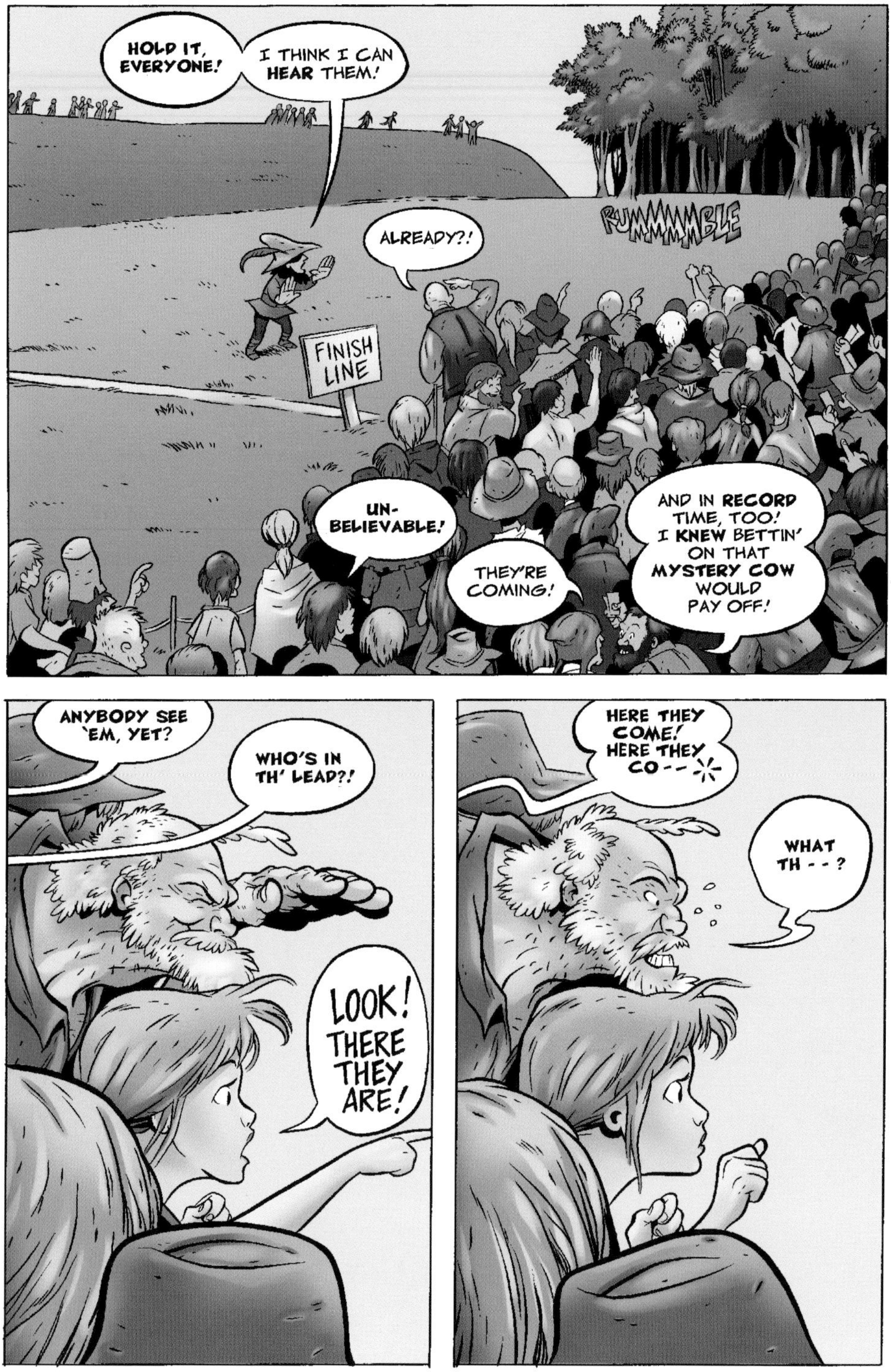
HOLD IT, EVERYONE!
I THINK I CAN HEAR THEM!
RUMMMMBLE
ALREADY?!
UN-BELIEVABLE!
THEY'RE COMING!
AND IN RECORD TIME, TOO! I KNEW BETTIN' ON THAT MYSTERY COW WOULD PAY OFF!
FINISH LINE
ANYBODY SEE 'EM, YET?
WHO'S IN TH' LEAD?!
LOOK! THERE THEY ARE!
HERE THEY COME! HERE THEY CO--
WHAT TH--?

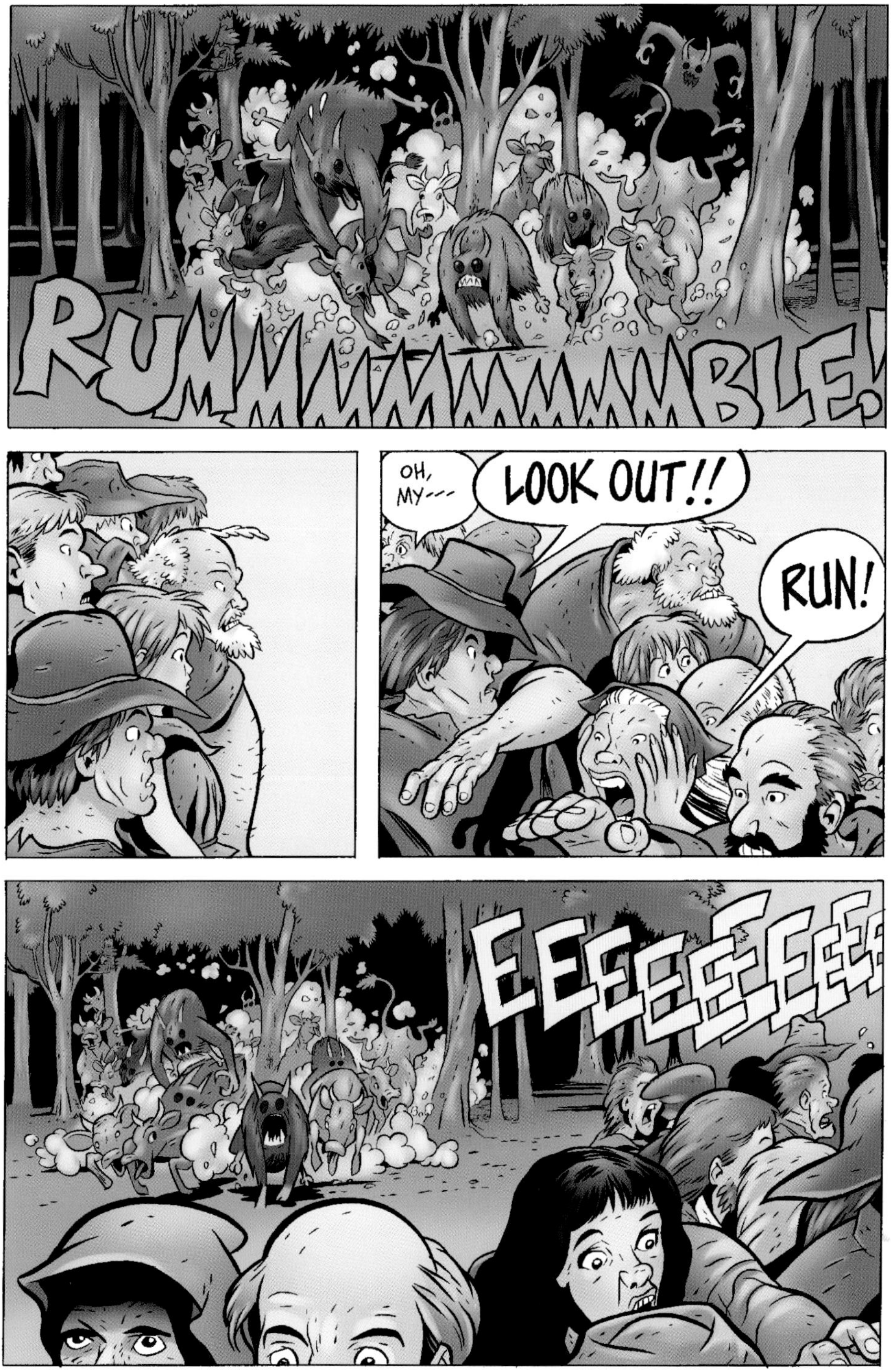
RUMMMMMMMMMBLE!
OH, MY---
LOOK OUT!!
RUN!
EEEEEEEEE

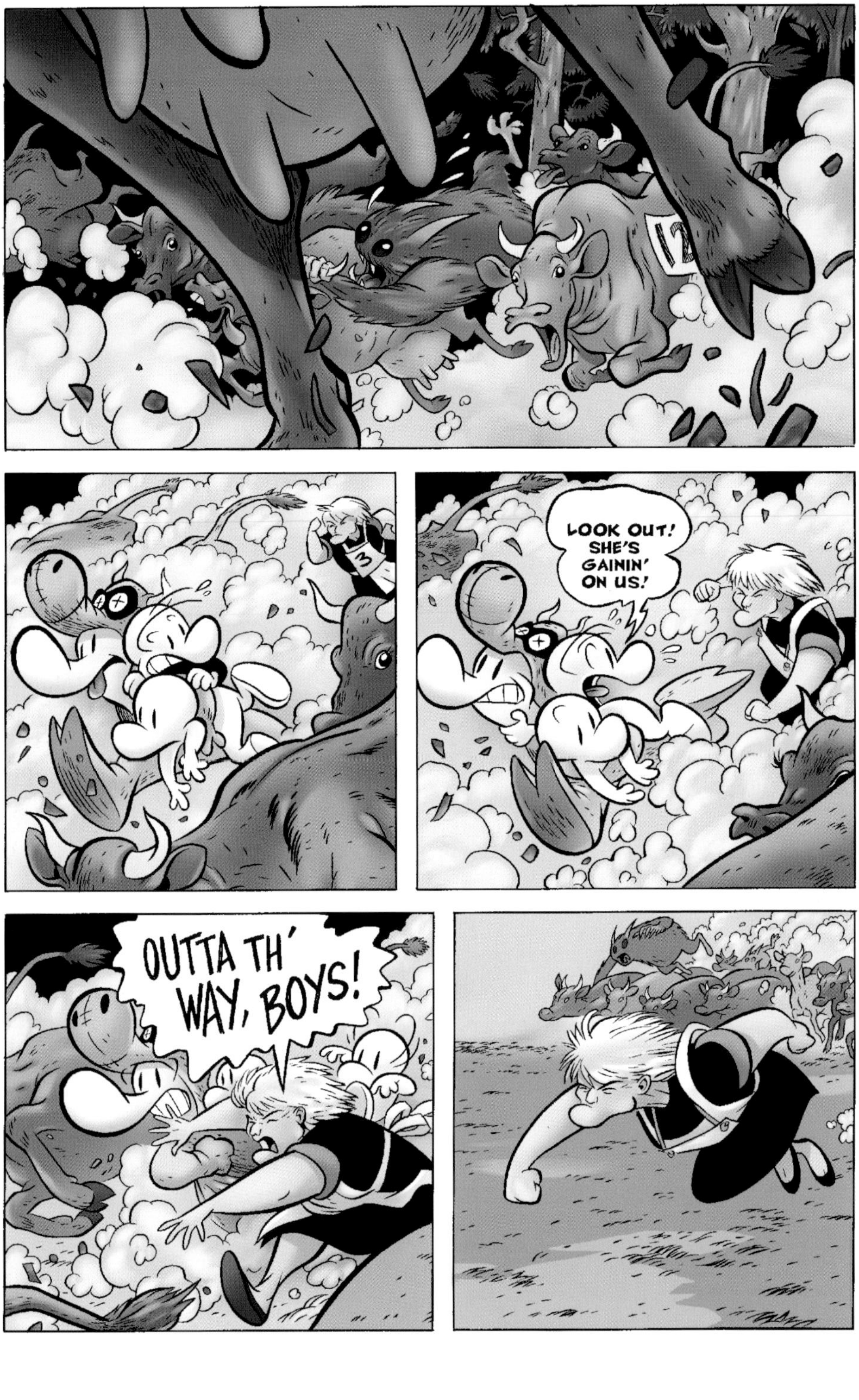
LOOK OUT! SHE'S GAININ' ON US!
OUTTA TH' WAY, BOYS!

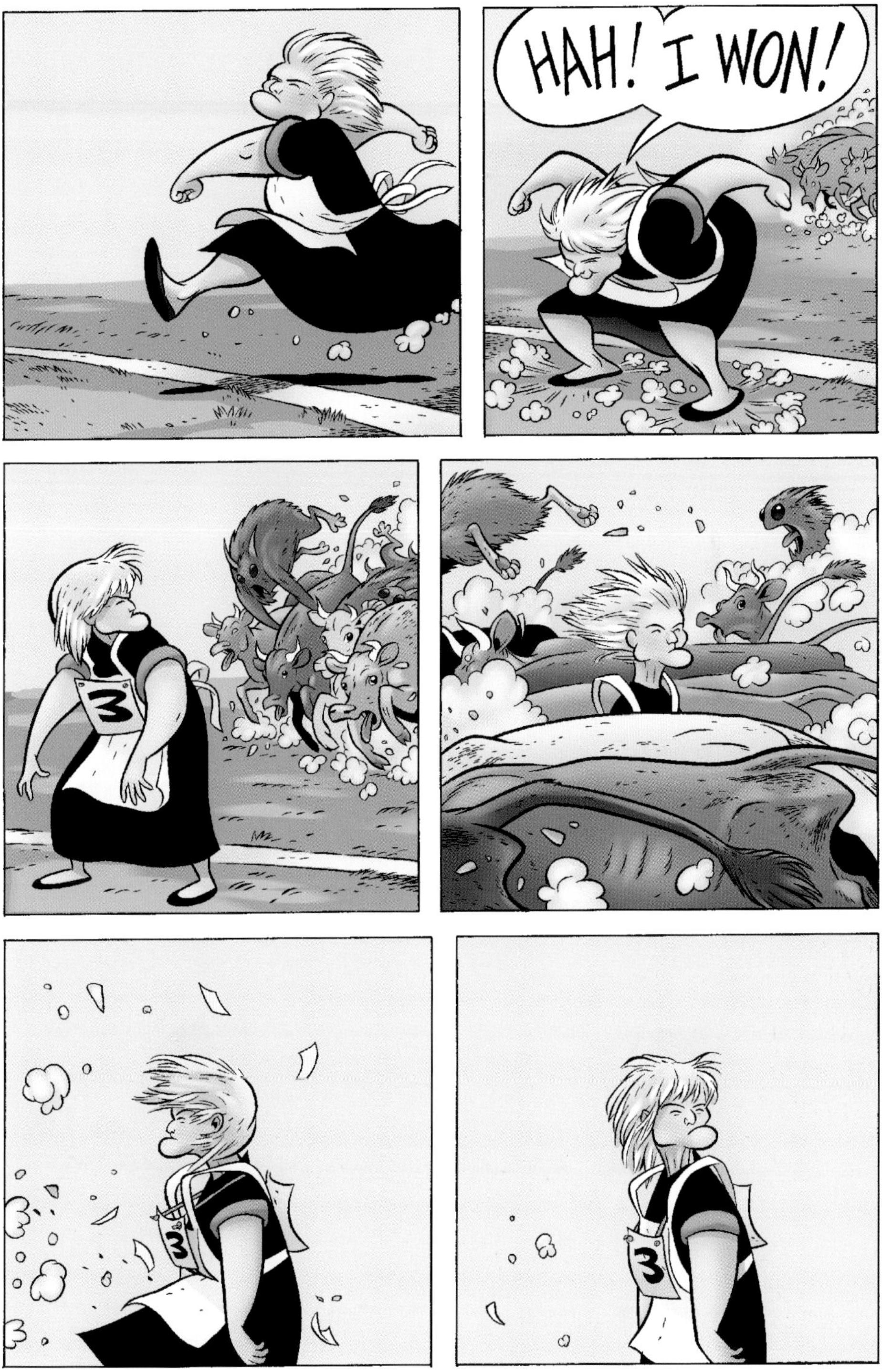
HAH! I WON!

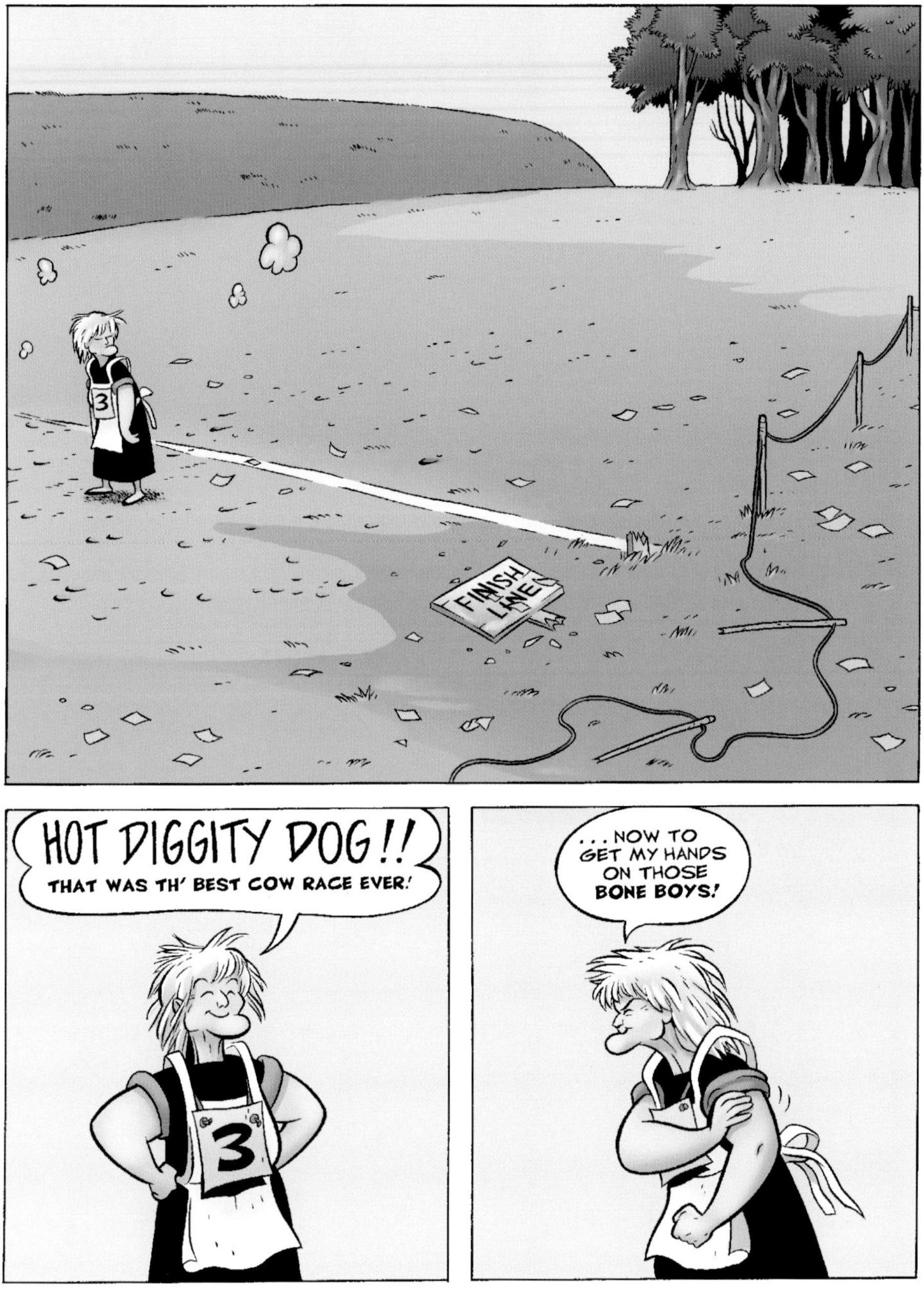
FINISH LINE
HOT DIGGITY DOG!!
THAT WAS TH' BEST COW RACE EVER!
...NOW TO GET MY HANDS ON THOSE BONE BOYS!

CHAPTER FIVE LONESOME ROAD

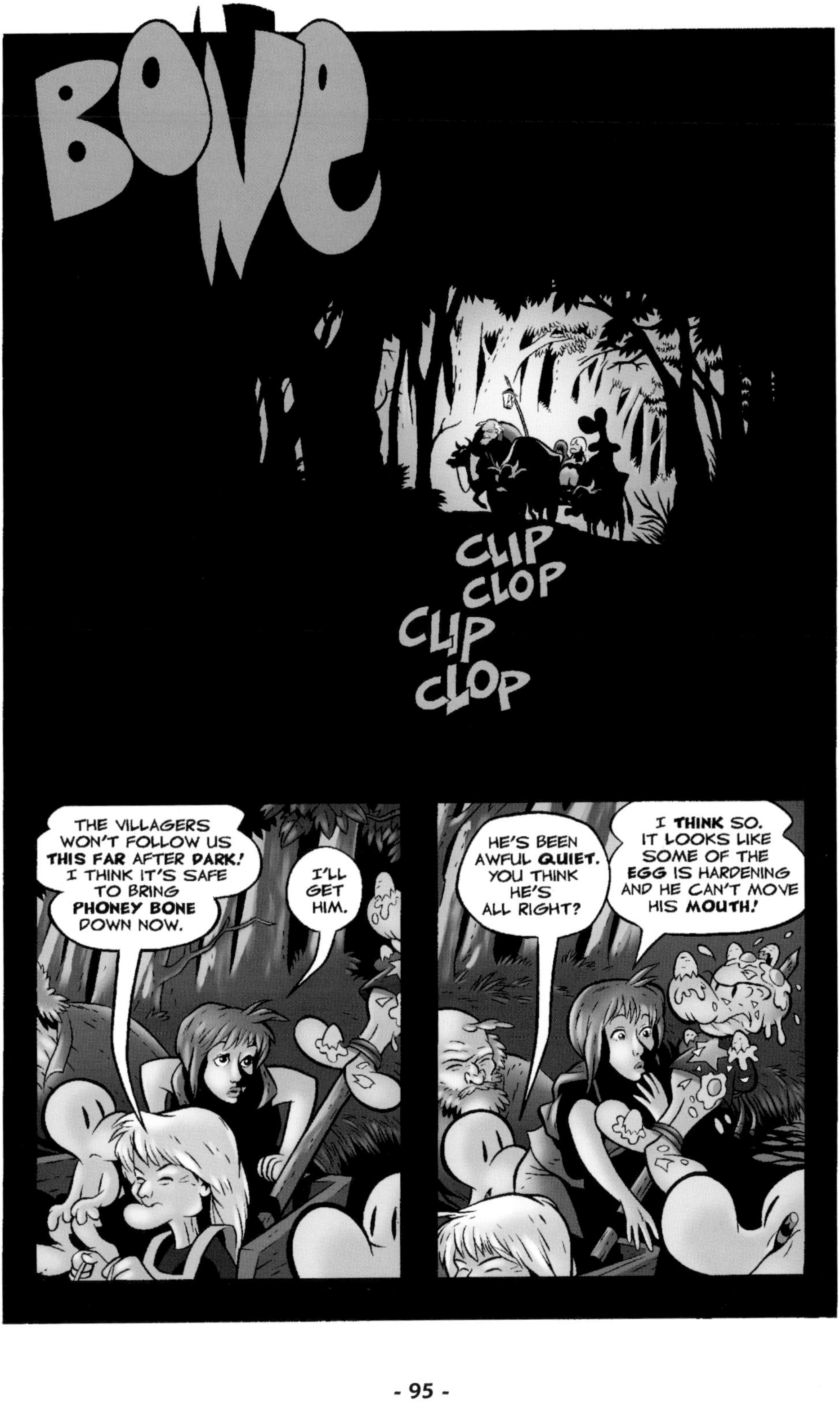

BONE
CLIP
CLOP
CLIP
CLOP
THE VILLAGERS WON'T FOLLOW US THIS FAR AFTER DARK! I THINK IT'S SAFE TO BRING PHONEY BONE DOWN NOW.
I'LL GET HIM.
HE'S BEEN AWFUL QUIET. YOU THINK HE'S ALL RIGHT?
I THINK SO. IT LOOKS LIKE SOME OF THE EGG IS HARDENING AND HE CAN'T MOVE HIS MOUTH!

I SAY WE LEAVE HIM THAT WAY.

GET HIM DOWN, THORN!

JUST A MOMENT... THERE!

IT'S ABOUT TIME!! GET ME DOWN FROM HERE!! THIS IS AN OUTRAGE! MY HANDS ARE GOIN' TO SLEEP!

I TOLD YOU TO LEAVE HIM!

PHONCIBLE P. BONE! YOU SHOULD BE GRATEFUL WE GOT YOU AWAY FROM THAT ANGRY MOB AT ALL! WHY, IF GRAN'MA HADN'T PROMISED TO COVER YOUR DEBTS FROM THE COW RACE, THINGS MIGHT'VE BEEN A LOT WORSE THAN BEING TIED TO A STAKE AND HIT WITH EGGS!

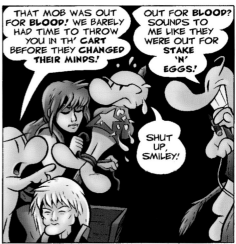

THAT MOB WAS OUT FOR BLOOD! WE BARELY HAD TIME TO THROW YOU IN TH' CART BEFORE THEY CHANGED THEIR MINDS!

OUT FOR BLOOD? SOUNDS TO ME LIKE THEY WERE OUT FOR STAKE 'N' EGGS!

SHUT UP, SMILEY!

HOW COME THEY DIDN'T TIE SMILEY TO A STAKE? HE WAS TH' ONE IN TH' COW SUIT!

AN' A STRIKING FIGURE OF A COW I MADE AT THAT!

YER BOTH IN TROUBLE!

AN' TO WORK OFF YER DEBTS, YOU AN' SMILEY ARE GONNA SPLIT YER TIME BETWEEN FARM CHORES AT GRAN'MA'S, AND WASHIN' DISHES FOR ME AT TH' TAVERN!

FOR HOW LONG?!

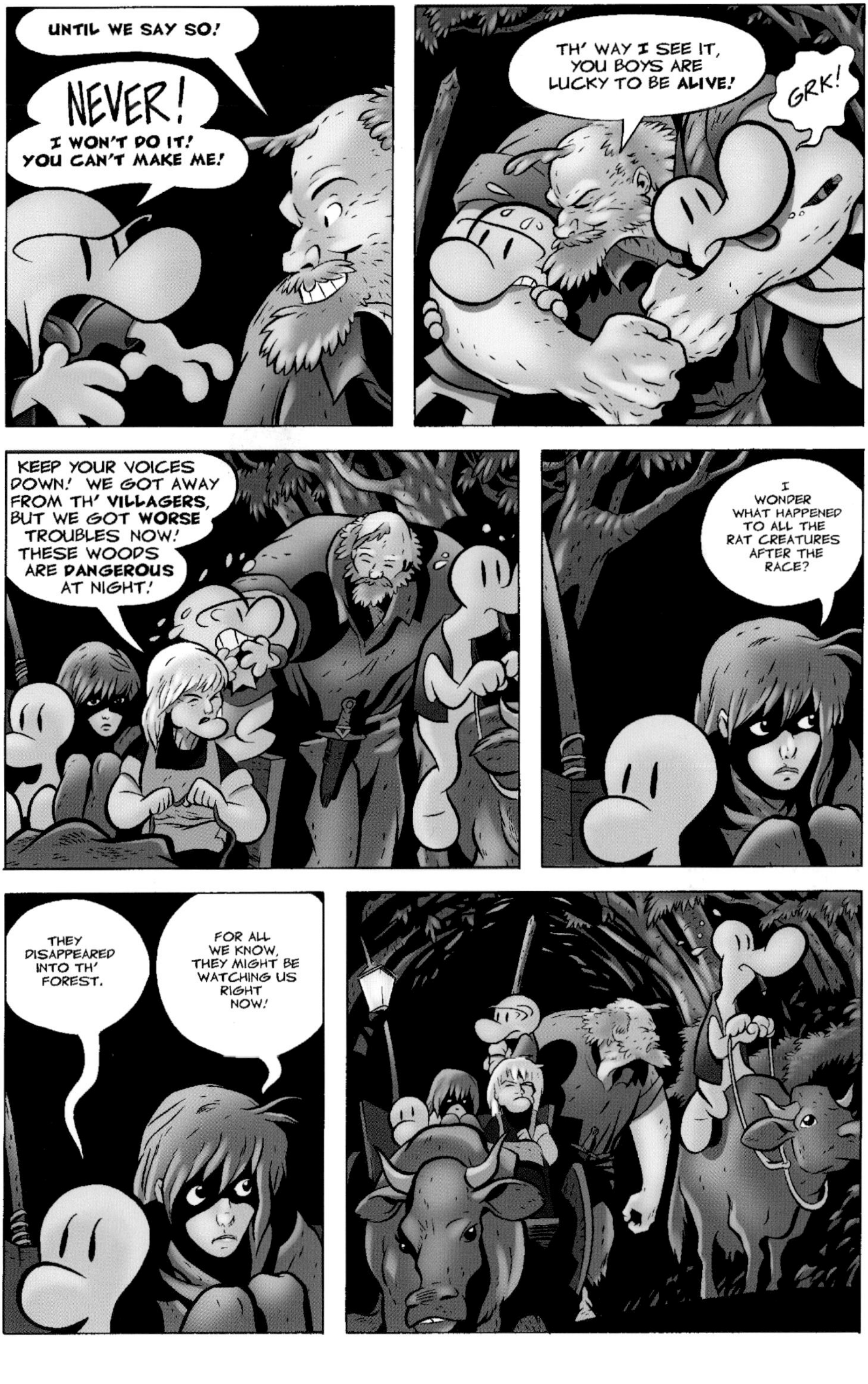
UNTIL WE SAY SO!
NEVER! I WON'T DO IT! YOU CAN'T MAKE ME!
TH' WAY I SEE IT, YOU BOYS ARE LUCKY TO BE ALIVE!
GRK!
KEEP YOUR VOICES DOWN! WE GOT AWAY FROM TH' VILLAGERS, BUT WE GOT WORSE TROUBLES NOW! THESE WOODS ARE DANGEROUS AT NIGHT!
I WONDER WHAT HAPPENED TO ALL THE RAT CREATURES AFTER THE RACE?
THEY DISAPPEARED INTO TH' FOREST.
FOR ALL WE KNOW, THEY MIGHT BE WATCHING US RIGHT NOW!

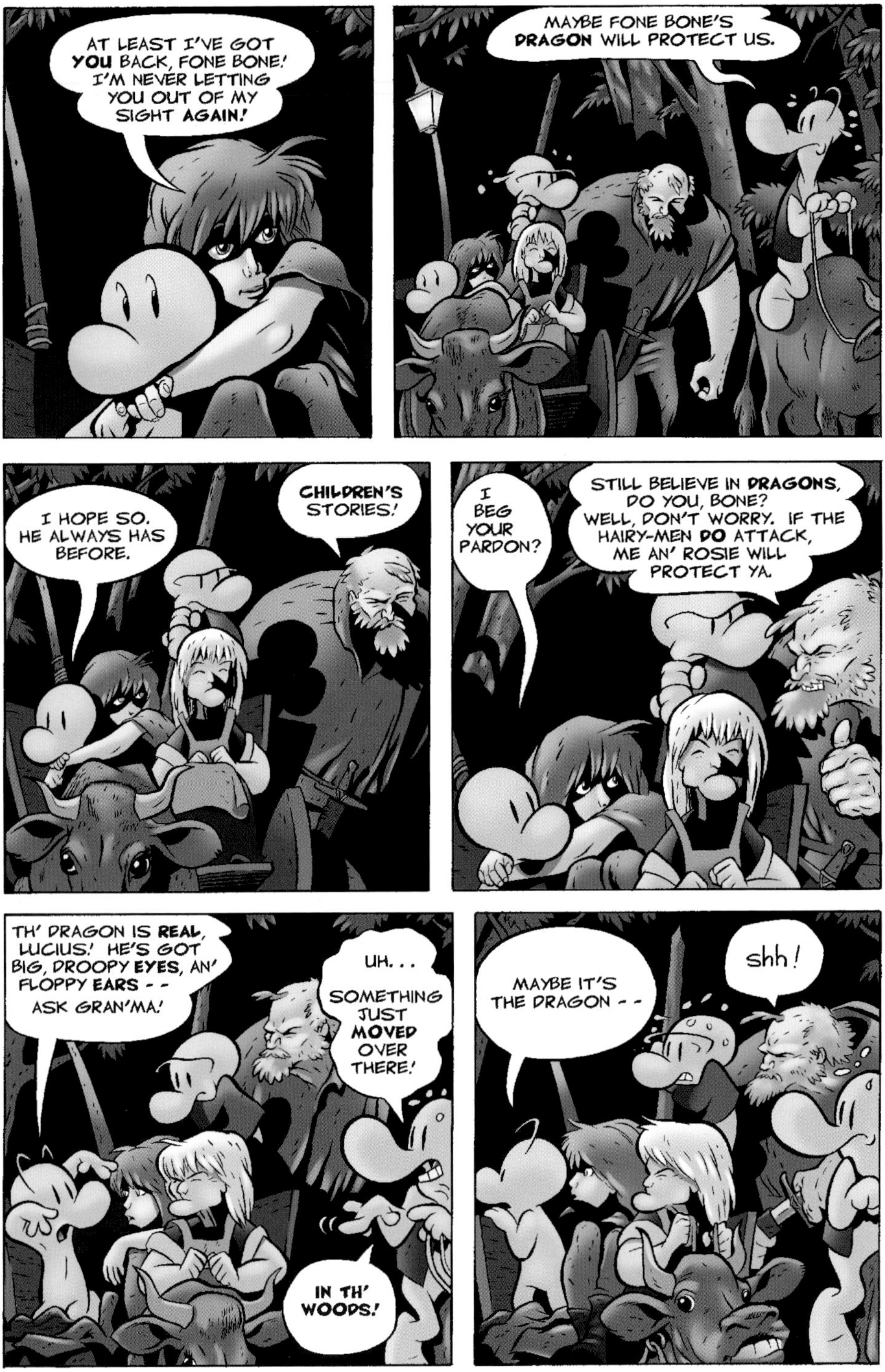
AT LEAST I'VE GOT YOU BACK, FONE BONE! I'M NEVER LETTING YOU OUT OF MY SIGHT AGAIN!
MAYBE FONE BONE'S DRAGON WILL PROTECT US.
I HOPE SO. HE ALWAYS HAS BEFORE.
CHILDREN'S STORIES!
I BEG YOUR PARDON?
STILL BELIEVE IN DRAGONS, DO YOU, BONE? WELL, DON'T WORRY. IF THE HAIRY-MEN DO ATTACK, ME AN' ROSIE WILL PROTECT YA.
TH' DRAGON IS REAL, LUCIUS! HE'S GOT BIG, DROOPY EYES, AN' FLOPPY EARS - - ASK GRAN'MA!
UH. . . SOMETHING JUST MOVED OVER THERE!
IN TH' WOODS!
MAYBE IT'S THE DRAGON - -
shh!

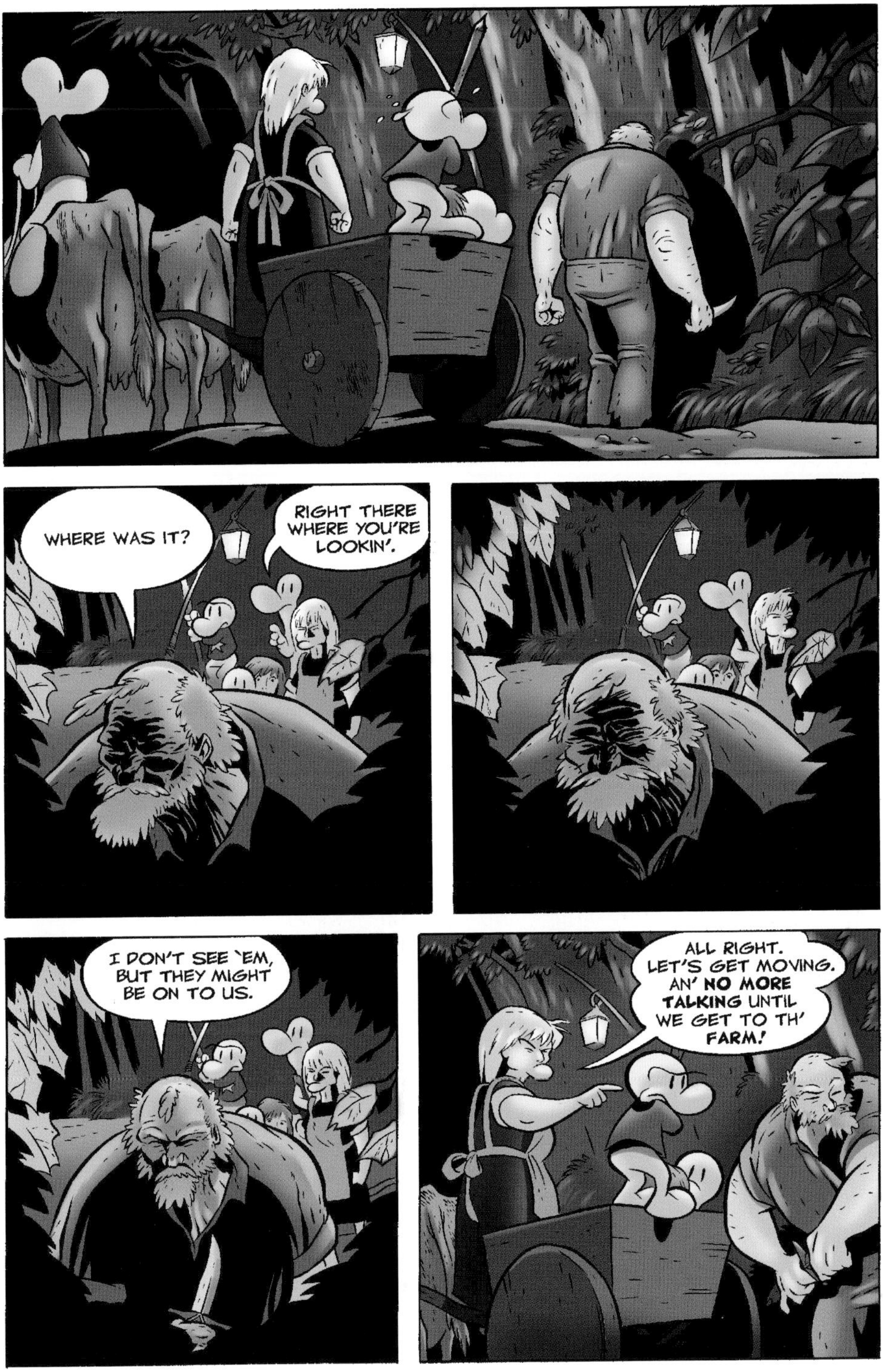
WHERE WAS IT?
RIGHT THERE WHERE YOU'RE LOOKIN'.
I DON'T SEE 'EM, BUT THEY MIGHT BE ON TO US.
ALL RIGHT. LET'S GET MOVING. AN' **NO MORE TALKING** UNTIL WE GET TO TH' **FARM!**

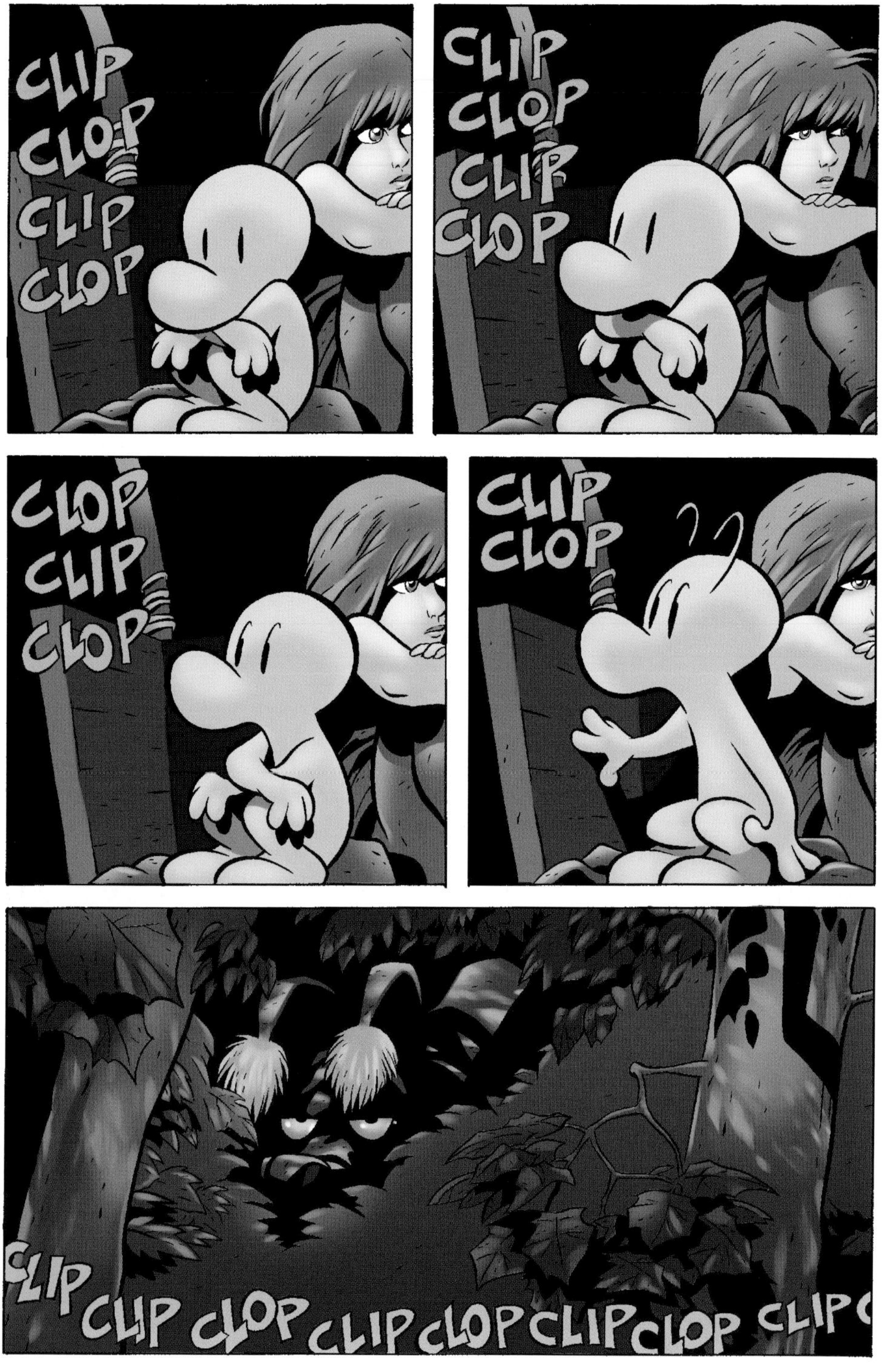
CLIP
CLOP
CLIP
CLOP
CLIP
CLOP
CLIP
CLOP
CLOP
CLIP
CLOP
CLIP
CLOP
CLIP CLIP CLOP CLIP CLOP CLIP CLOP CLIP

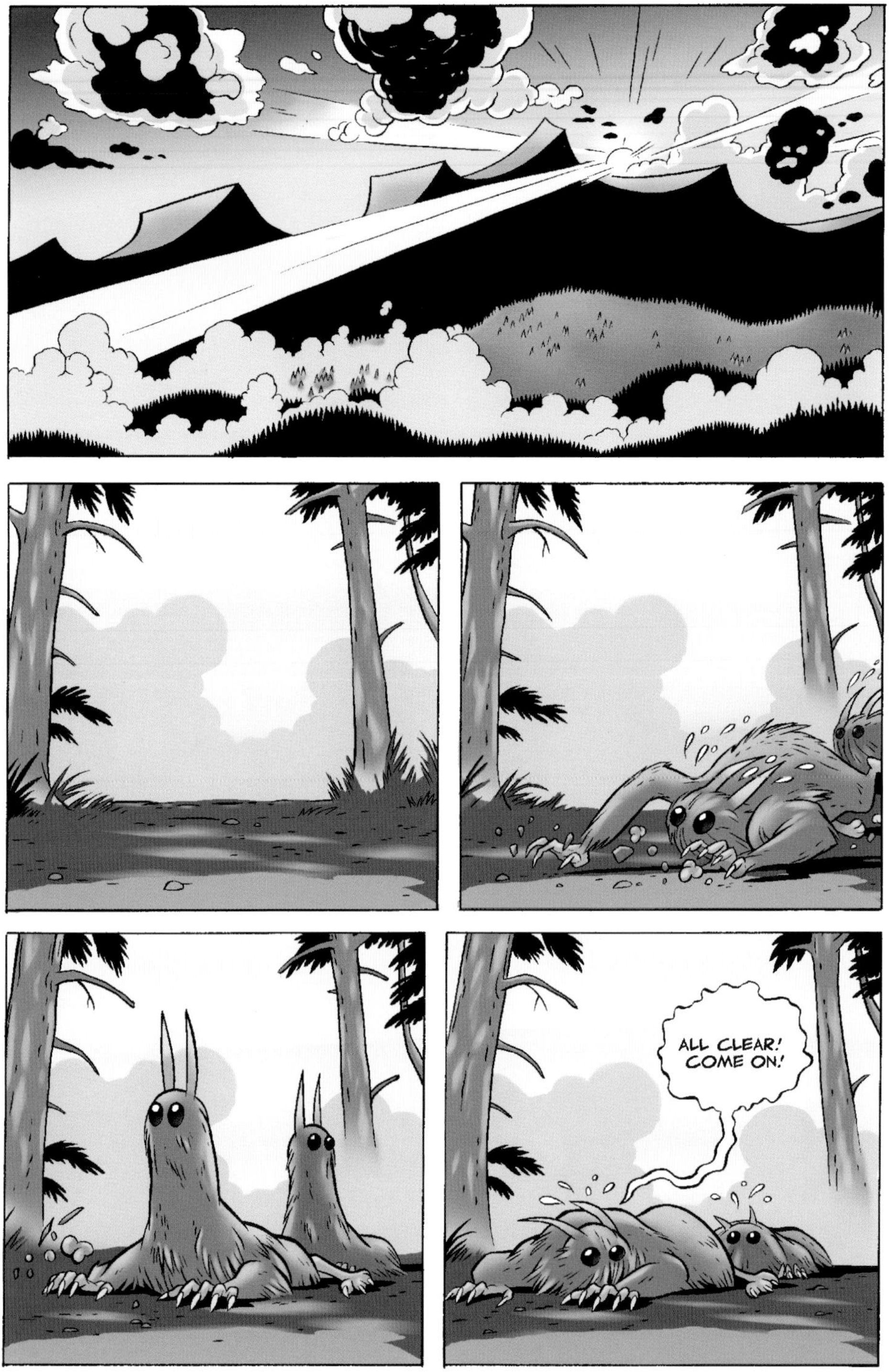
ALL CLEAR! COME ON!

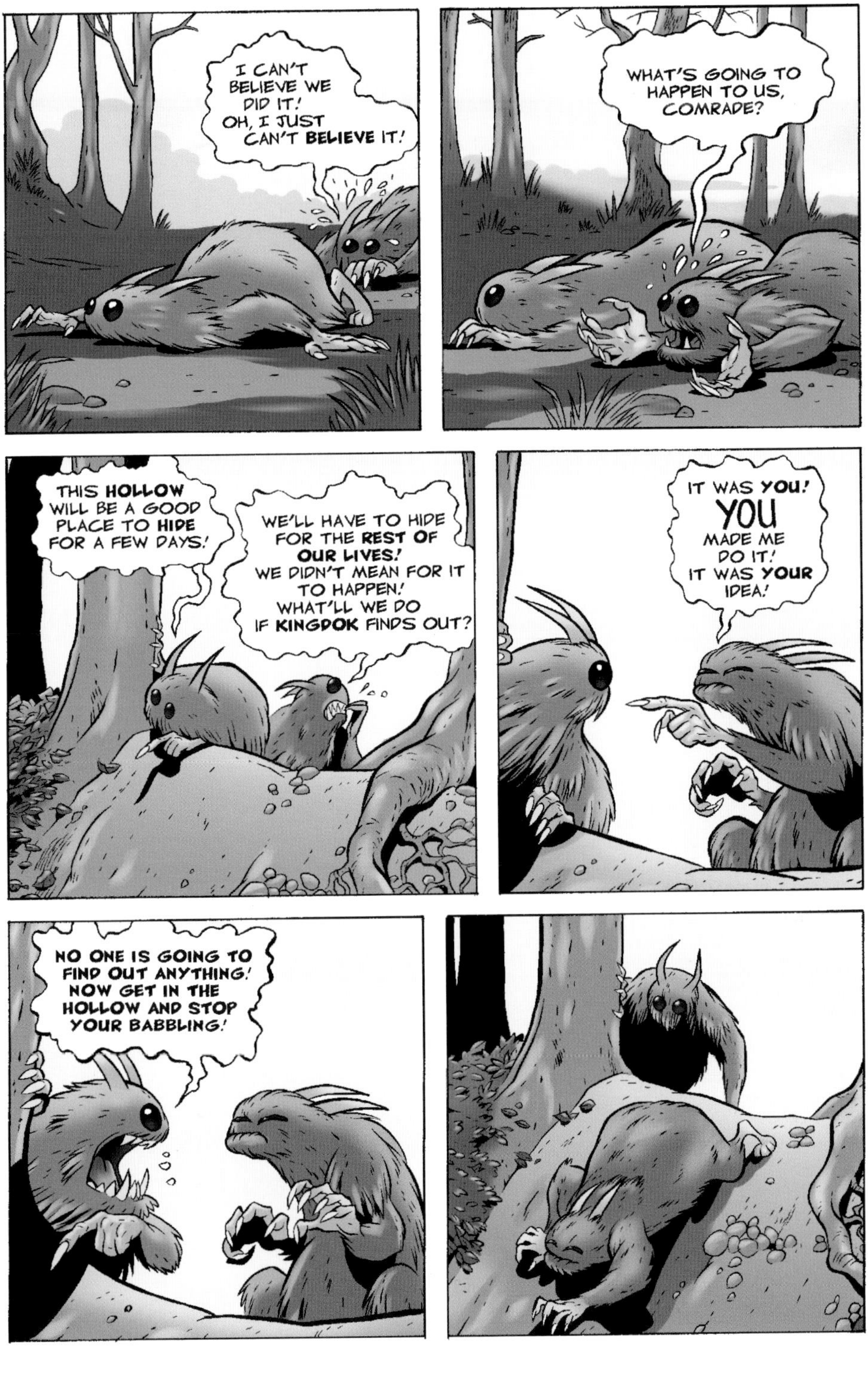
I CAN'T BELIEVE WE DID IT! OH, I JUST CAN'T BELIEVE IT!
WHAT'S GOING TO HAPPEN TO US, COMRADE?
THIS HOLLOW WILL BE A GOOD PLACE TO HIDE FOR A FEW DAYS!
WE'LL HAVE TO HIDE FOR THE REST OF OUR LIVES! WE DIDN'T MEAN FOR IT TO HAPPEN! WHAT'LL WE DO IF KINGDOK FINDS OUT?
IT WAS YOU! YOU MADE ME DO IT! IT WAS YOUR IDEA!
NO ONE IS GOING TO FIND OUT ANYTHING! NOW GET IN THE HOLLOW AND STOP YOUR BABBLING!

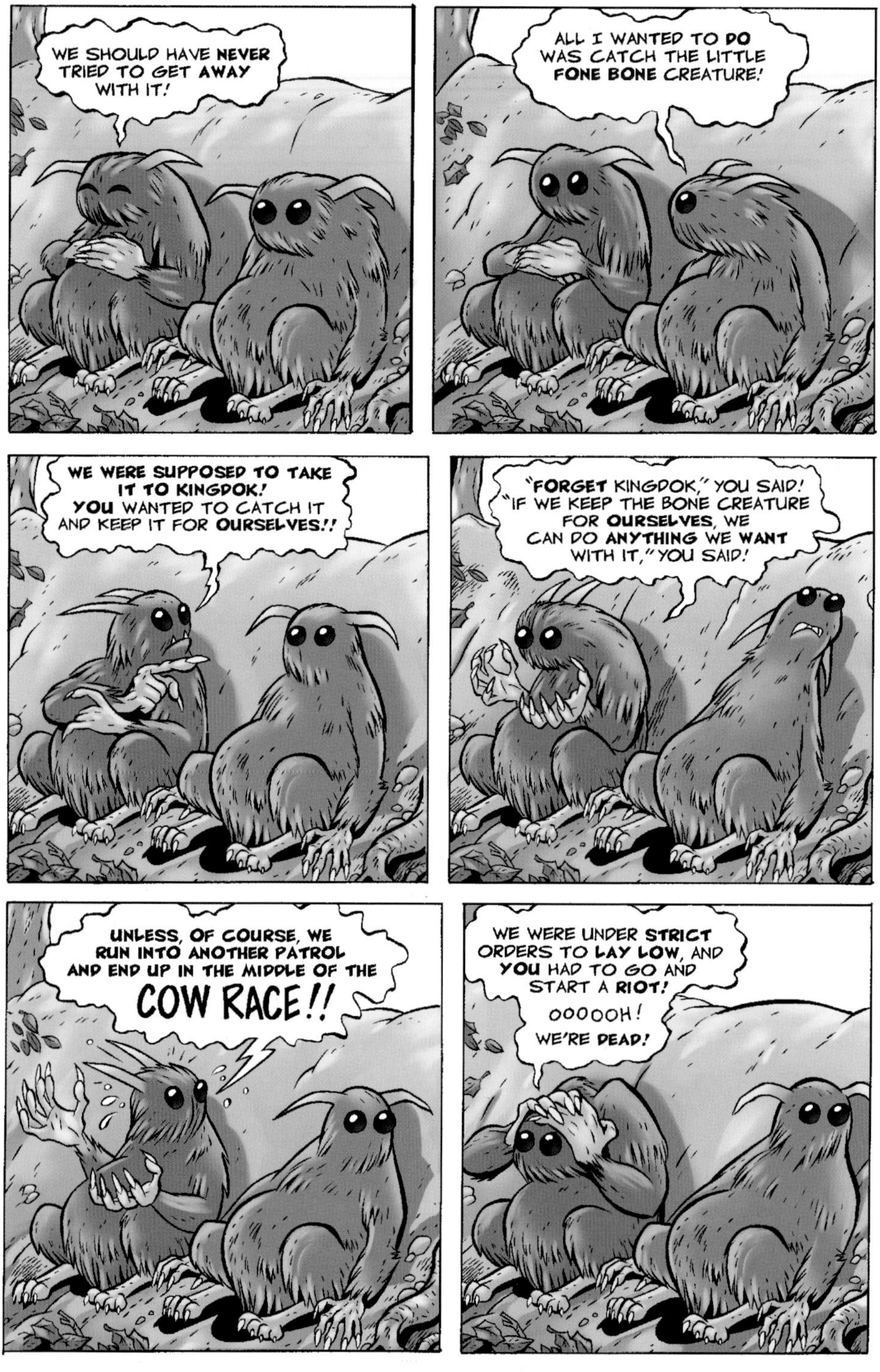
WE SHOULD HAVE NEVER TRIED TO GET AWAY WITH IT!
ALL I WANTED TO DO WAS CATCH THE LITTLE FONE BONE CREATURE!
WE WERE SUPPOSED TO TAKE IT TO KINGDOK! YOU WANTED TO CATCH IT AND KEEP IT FOR OURSELVES!!
"FORGET KINGDOK," YOU SAID! "IF WE KEEP THE BONE CREATURE FOR OURSELVES, WE CAN DO ANYTHING WE WANT WITH IT," YOU SAID!
UNLESS, OF COURSE, WE RUN INTO ANOTHER PATROL AND END UP IN THE MIDDLE OF THE COW RACE!!
WE WERE UNDER STRICT ORDERS TO LAY LOW, AND YOU HAD TO GO AND START A RIOT!
OOOOOH!
WE'RE DEAD!

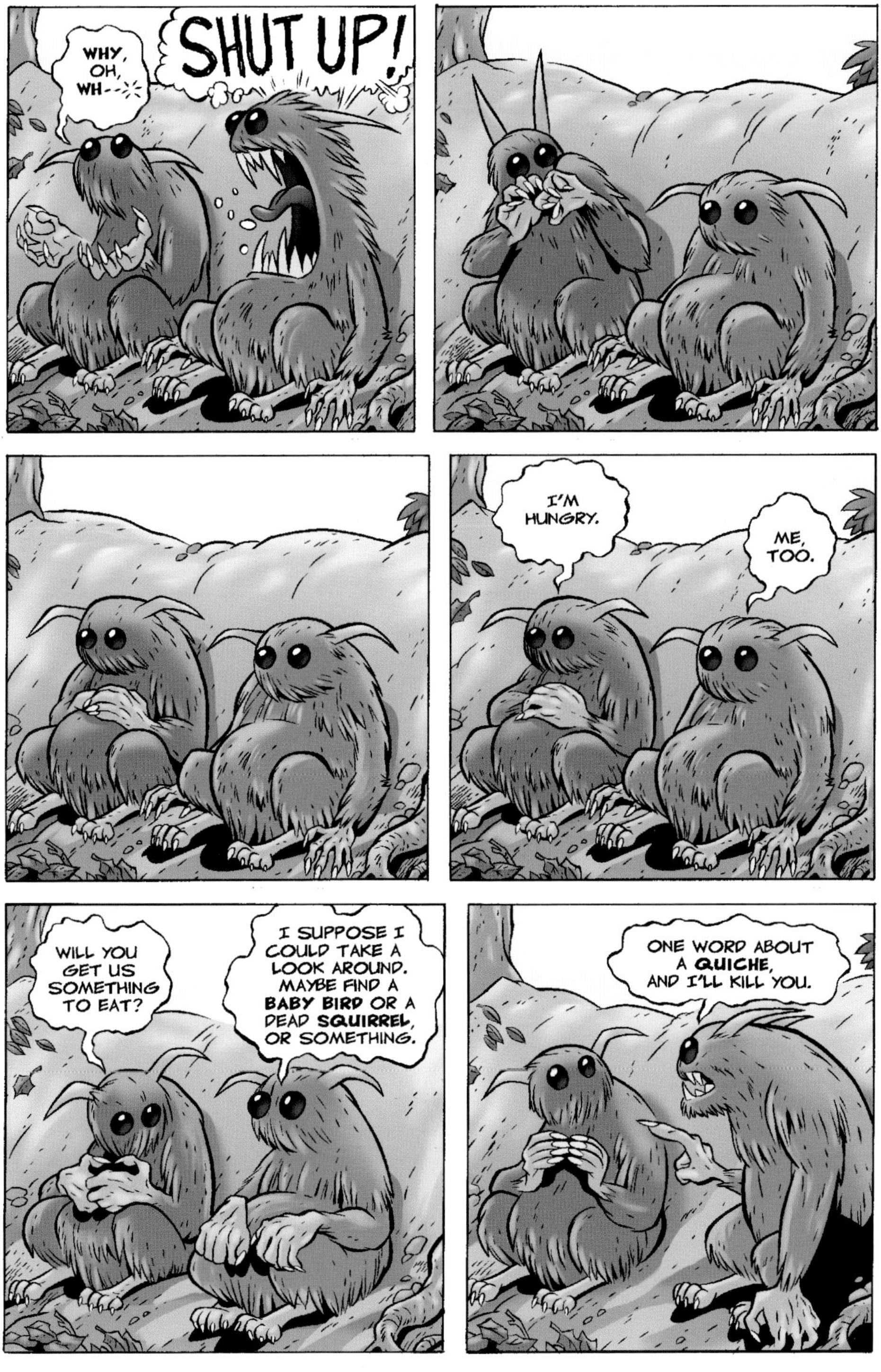
WHY, OH, WH--
SHUT UP!
I'M HUNGRY.
ME, TOO.
WILL YOU GET US SOMETHING TO EAT?
I SUPPOSE I COULD TAKE A LOOK AROUND. MAYBE FIND A **BABY BIRD** OR A DEAD **SQUIRREL**, OR SOMETHING.
ONE WORD ABOUT A **QUICHE**, AND I'LL KILL YOU.

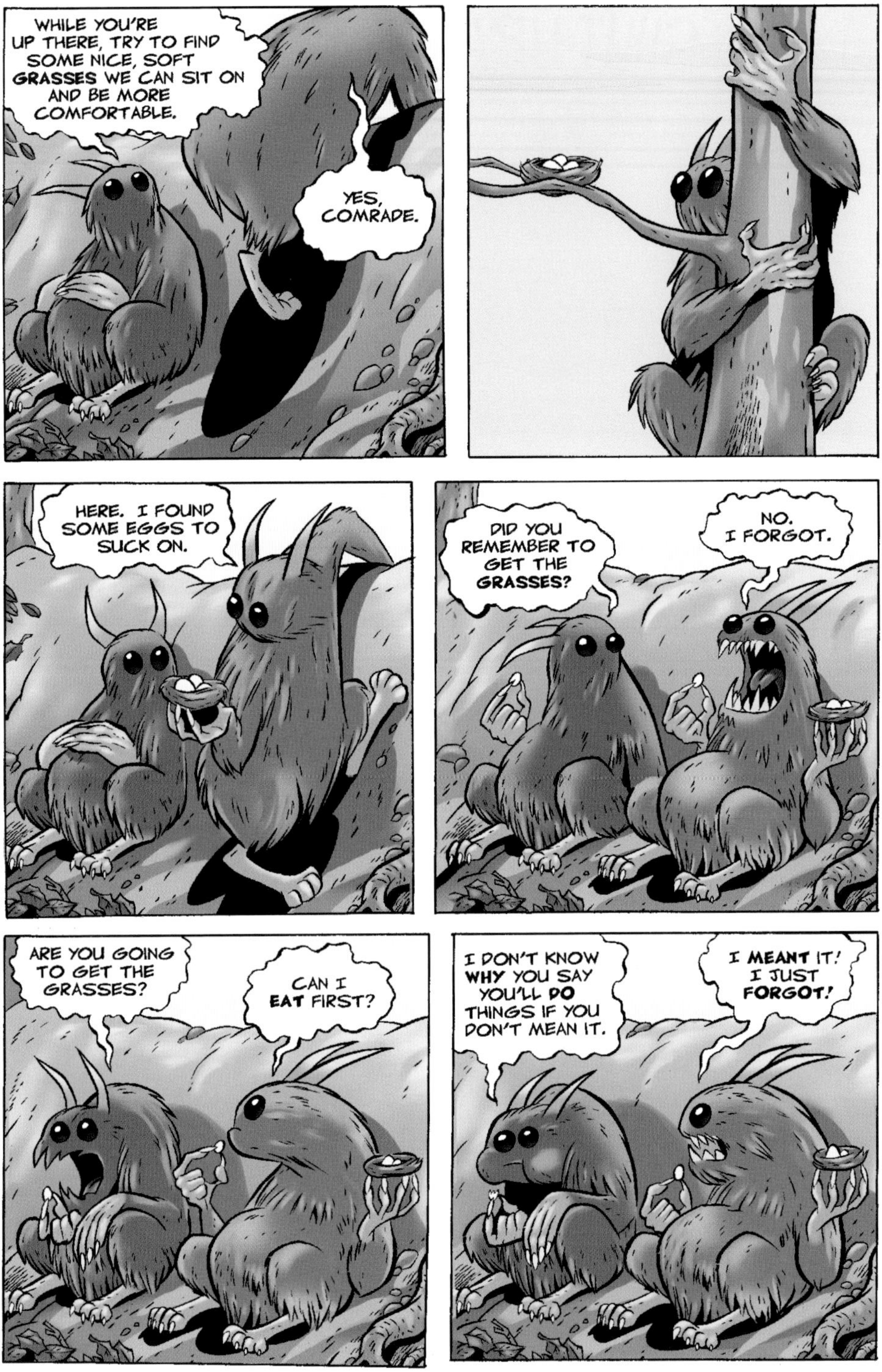
WHILE YOU'RE UP THERE, TRY TO FIND SOME NICE, SOFT **GRASSES** WE CAN SIT ON AND BE MORE COMFORTABLE.
YES, COMRADE.
HERE. I FOUND SOME EGGS TO SUCK ON.
DID YOU REMEMBER TO GET THE **GRASSES?**
NO. I FORGOT.
ARE YOU GOING TO GET THE GRASSES?
CAN I **EAT** FIRST?
I DON'T KNOW **WHY** YOU SAY YOU'LL **DO** THINGS IF YOU DON'T MEAN IT.
I **MEANT** IT! I JUST **FORGOT!**

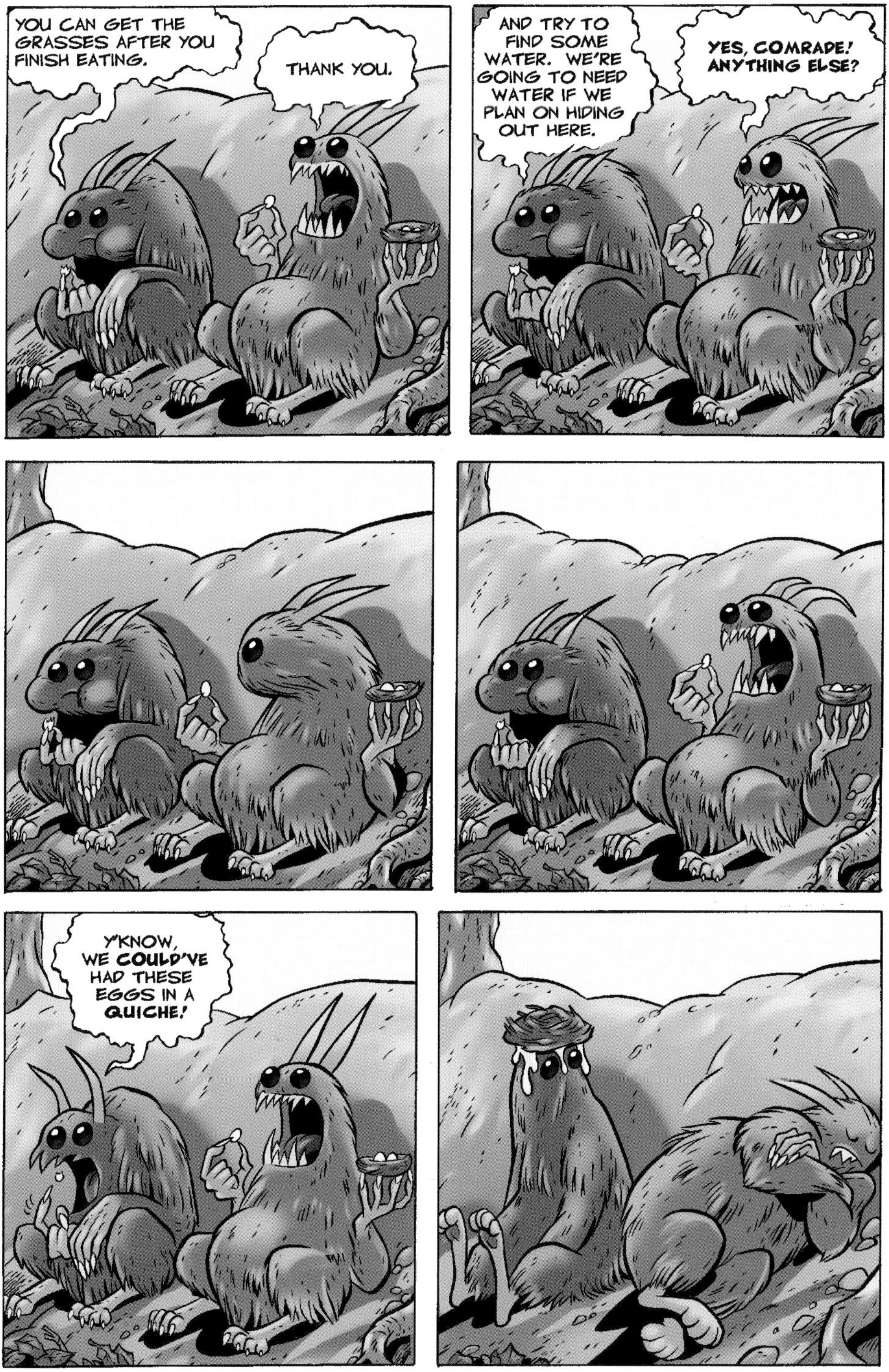
YOU CAN GET THE GRASSES AFTER YOU FINISH EATING.
THANK YOU.
AND TRY TO FIND SOME WATER. WE'RE GOING TO NEED WATER IF WE PLAN ON HIDING OUT HERE.
YES, COMRADE! ANYTHING ELSE?
Y'KNOW, WE COULD'VE HAD THESE EGGS IN A QUICHE!

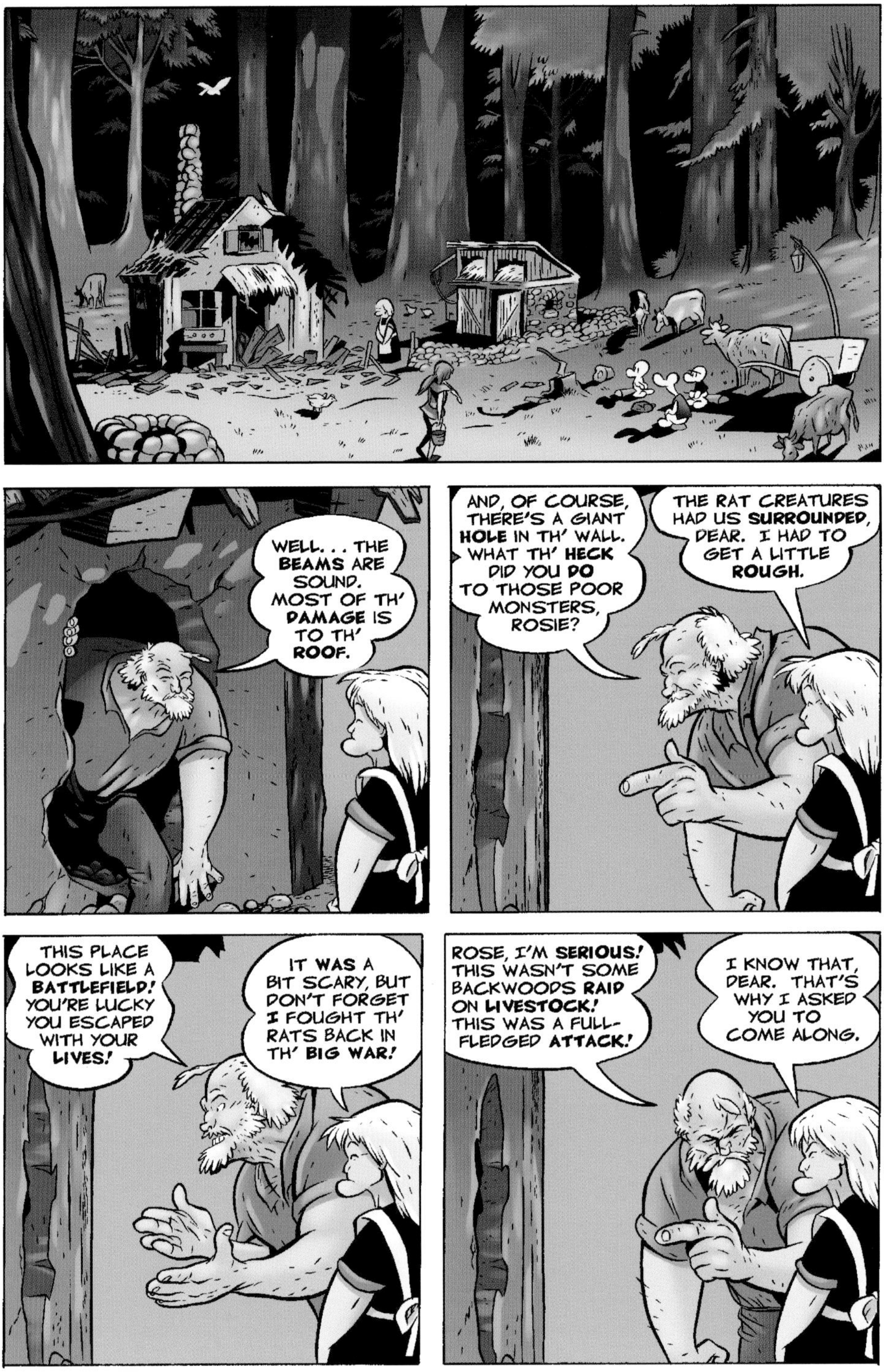
WELL. . . THE BEAMS ARE SOUND. MOST OF TH' DAMAGE IS TO TH' ROOF.
AND, OF COURSE, THERE'S A GIANT HOLE IN TH' WALL. WHAT TH' HECK DID YOU DO TO THOSE POOR MONSTERS, ROSIE?
THE RAT CREATURES HAD US SURROUNDED, DEAR. I HAD TO GET A LITTLE ROUGH.
THIS PLACE LOOKS LIKE A BATTLEFIELD! YOU'RE LUCKY YOU ESCAPED WITH YOUR LIVES!
IT WAS A BIT SCARY, BUT DON'T FORGET I FOUGHT TH' RATS BACK IN TH' BIG WAR!
ROSE, I'M SERIOUS! THIS WASN'T SOME BACKWOODS RAID ON LIVESTOCK! THIS WAS A FULL-FLEDGED ATTACK!
I KNOW THAT, DEAR. THAT'S WHY I ASKED YOU TO COME ALONG.

THAT'S **ALSO** WHY I ASKED YOU TO HELP ME RESCUE THE **BONE COUSINS** FROM TH' FOLKS THEY **SWINDLED!**

IT WAS AGAINST **MY** BETTER JUDGMENT! WHY **DID** WE SAVE THEM?

RIGHT NOW, THEY'RE THE **ONLY** CLUE I'VE **GOT**. TH' RAT CREATURES ATTACKED TH' **FARMHOUSE** BECAUSE THEY WERE **LOOKING** FOR THE **BONES!**

I KNEW IT! I **KNEW** THAT SNEAKY LITTLE RUNT **PHONEY BONE** WAS A **TROUBLEMAKER!!**

HE'S A TROUBLEMAKER, ALL RIGHT, BUT I DON'T THINK HE'S GOT ANY MORE IDEA ABOUT WHAT'S GOIN' ON THAN **WE DO!**

YOU **DON'T?**

I GRILLED HIS COUSIN **FONE BONE** TH' MORNIN' AFTER THE ATTACK. CLAIMS THEY NEVER EVEN **HEARD** OF RAT CREATURES BEFORE THEY CAME TO OUR VALLEY.

YOU **BELIEVE** HIM?

I DO. FONE BONE'S A **GOOD** ONE. AND I THINK HE HAS A **CRUSH** ON THORN!

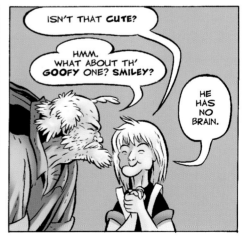

ISN'T THAT **CUTE?**

HMM. WHAT ABOUT TH' **GOOFY** ONE? SMILEY?

HE HAS NO BRAIN.

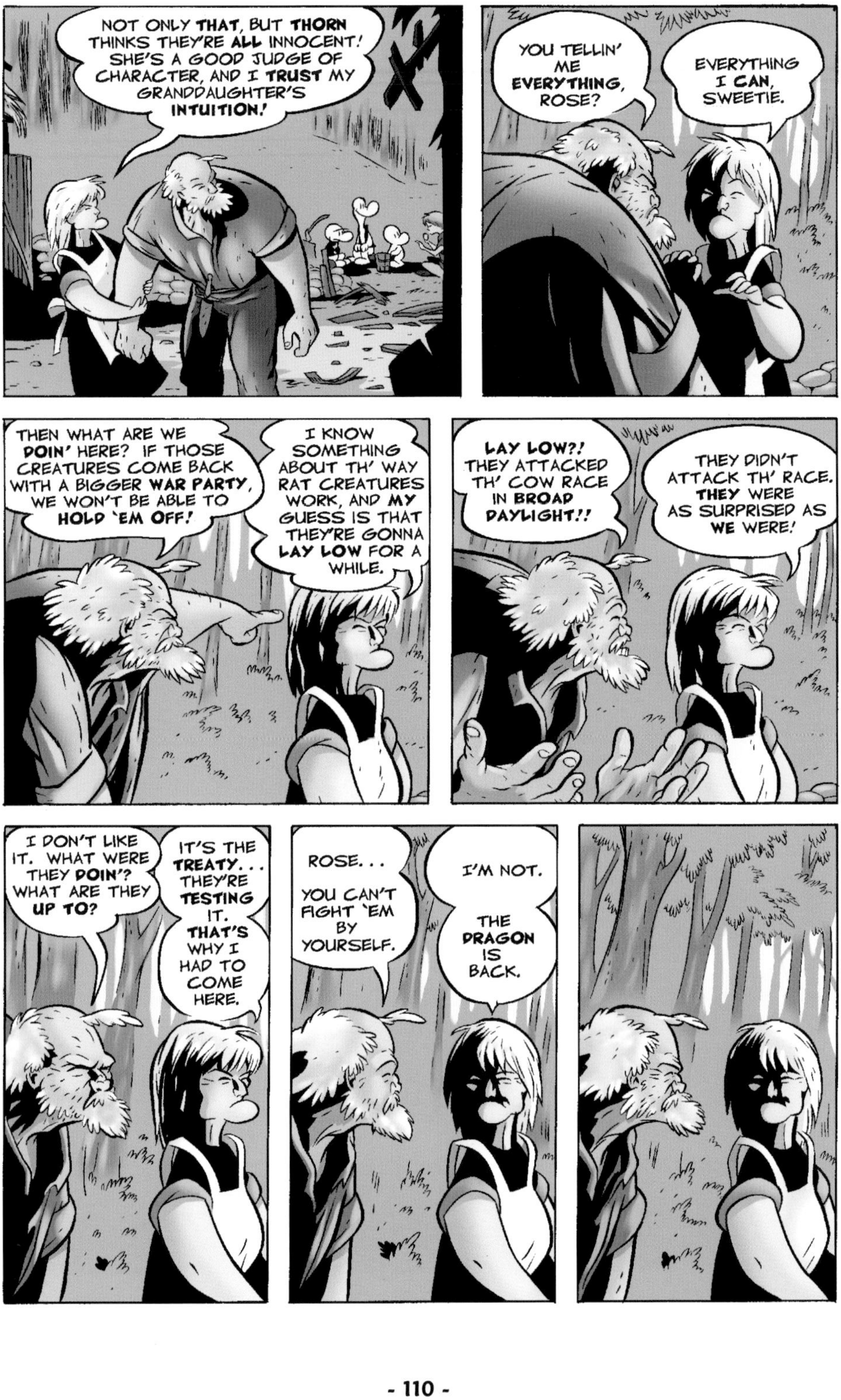
NOT ONLY THAT, BUT THORN THINKS THEY'RE ALL INNOCENT! SHE'S A GOOD JUDGE OF CHARACTER, AND I TRUST MY GRANDDAUGHTER'S INTUITION!
YOU TELLIN' ME EVERYTHING, ROSE?
EVERYTHING I CAN, SWEETIE.
THEN WHAT ARE WE DOIN' HERE? IF THOSE CREATURES COME BACK WITH A BIGGER WAR PARTY, WE WON'T BE ABLE TO HOLD 'EM OFF!
I KNOW SOMETHING ABOUT TH' WAY RAT CREATURES WORK, AND MY GUESS IS THAT THEY'RE GONNA LAY LOW FOR A WHILE.
LAY LOW?! THEY ATTACKED TH' COW RACE IN BROAD DAYLIGHT!!
THEY DIDN'T ATTACK TH' RACE. THEY WERE AS SURPRISED AS WE WERE!
I DON'T LIKE IT. WHAT WERE THEY DOIN'? WHAT ARE THEY UP TO?
IT'S THE TREATY... THEY'RE TESTING IT. THAT'S WHY I HAD TO COME HERE.
ROSE...
YOU CAN'T FIGHT 'EM BY YOURSELF.
I'M NOT.
THE DRAGON IS BACK.

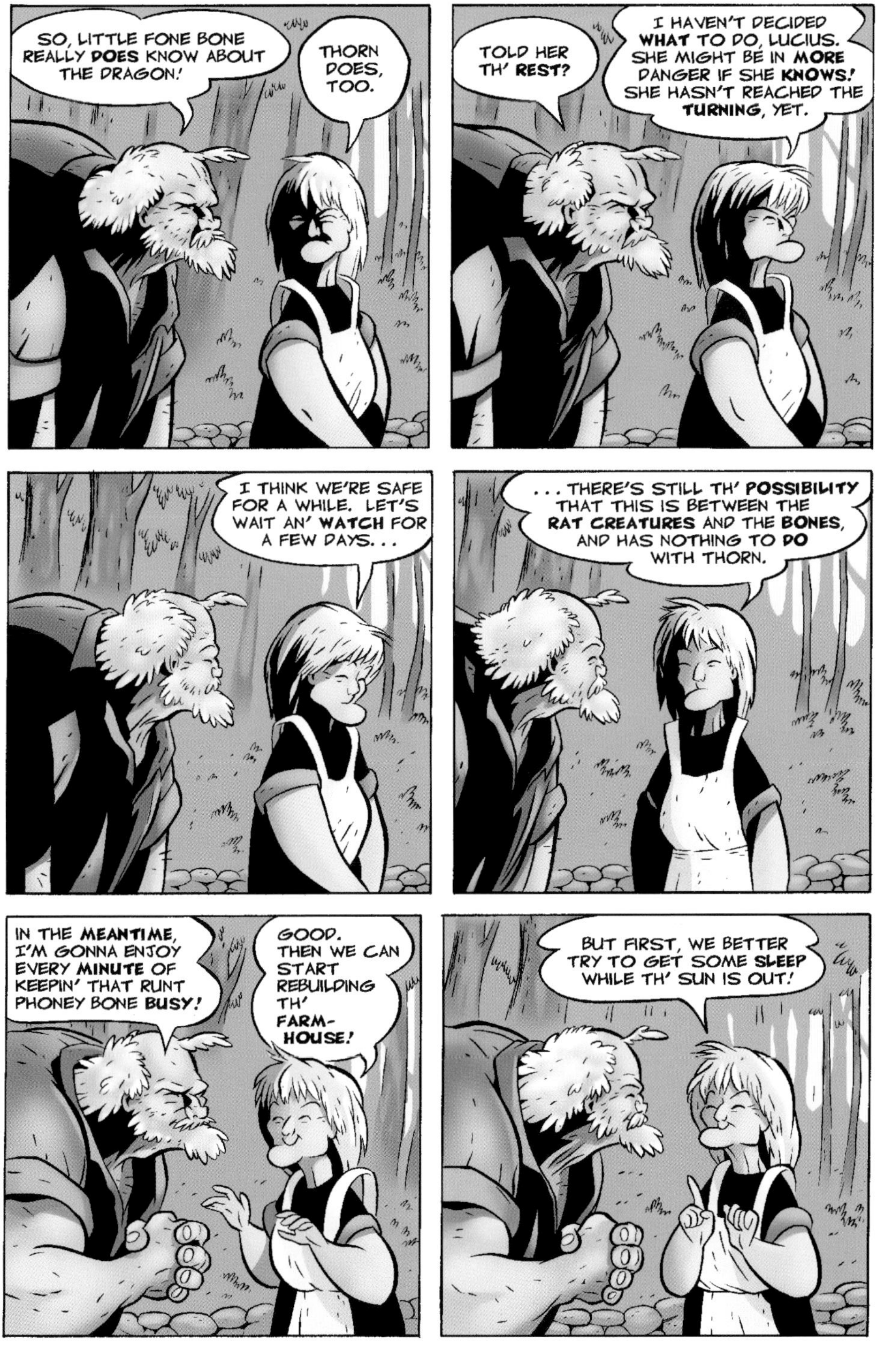
SO, LITTLE FONE BONE REALLY DOES KNOW ABOUT THE DRAGON!
THORN DOES, TOO.
TOLD HER TH' REST?
I HAVEN'T DECIDED WHAT TO DO, LUCIUS. SHE MIGHT BE IN MORE DANGER IF SHE KNOWS! SHE HASN'T REACHED THE TURNING, YET.
I THINK WE'RE SAFE FOR A WHILE. LET'S WAIT AN' WATCH FOR A FEW DAYS...
...THERE'S STILL TH' POSSIBILITY THAT THIS IS BETWEEN THE RAT CREATURES AND THE BONES, AND HAS NOTHING TO DO WITH THORN.
IN THE MEANTIME, I'M GONNA ENJOY EVERY MINUTE OF KEEPIN' THAT RUNT PHONEY BONE BUSY!
GOOD. THEN WE CAN START REBUILDING TH' FARM-HOUSE!
BUT FIRST, WE BETTER TRY TO GET SOME SLEEP WHILE TH' SUN IS OUT!

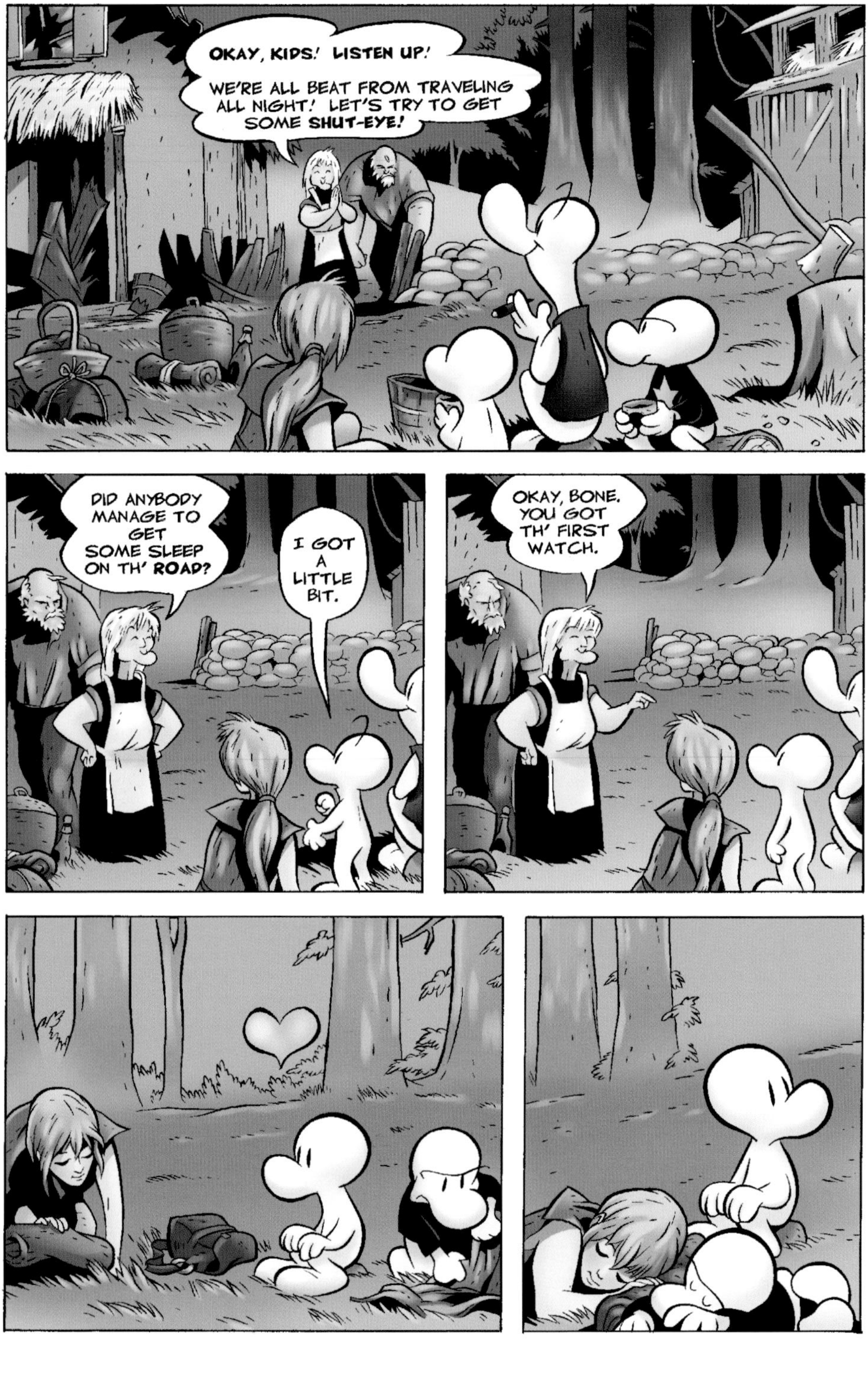
OKAY, KIDS! LISTEN UP!
WE'RE ALL BEAT FROM TRAVELING ALL NIGHT! LET'S TRY TO GET SOME SHUT-EYE!
DID ANYBODY MANAGE TO GET SOME SLEEP ON TH' ROAD?
I GOT A LITTLE BIT.
OKAY, BONE. YOU GOT TH' FIRST WATCH.

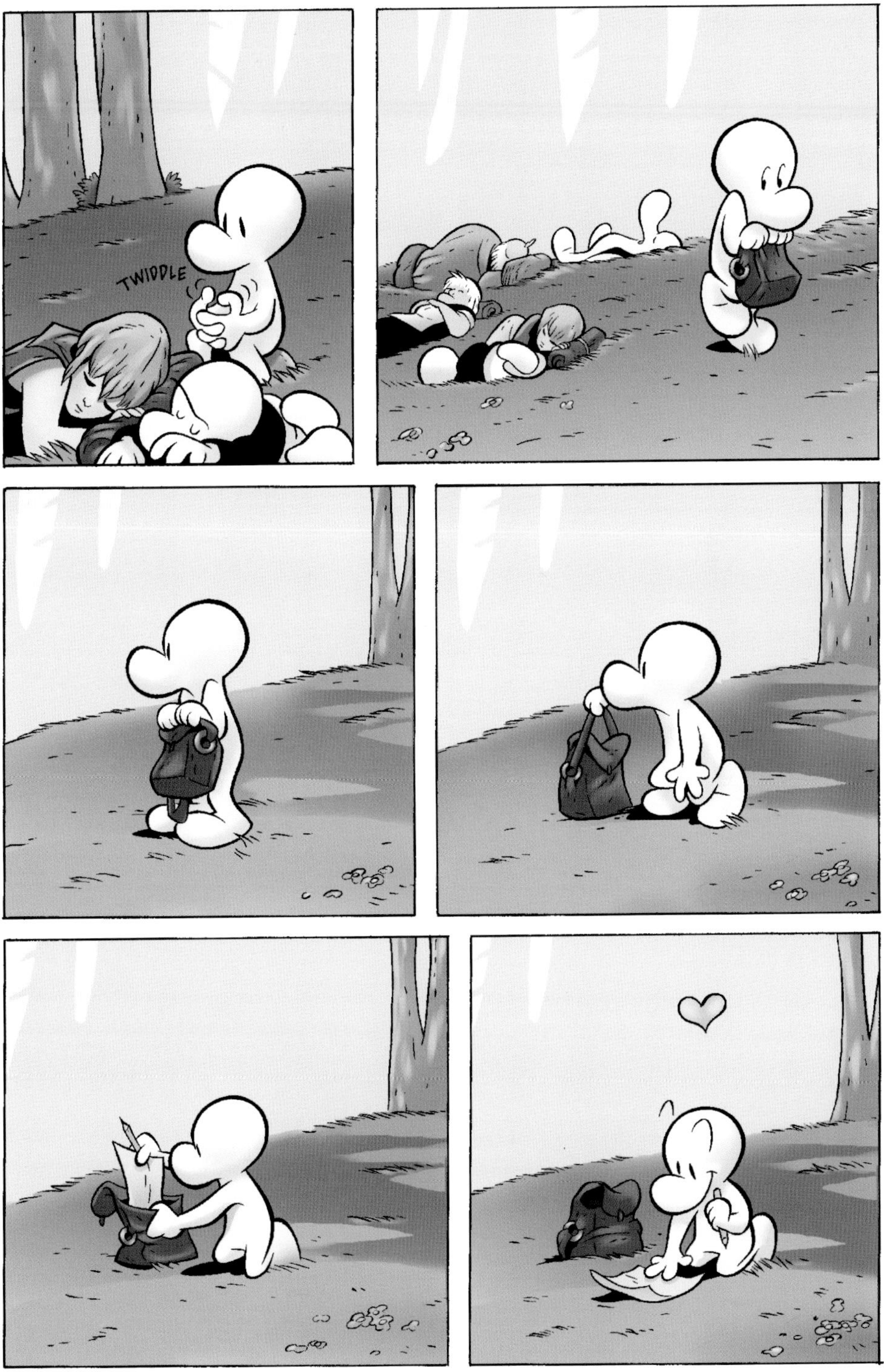
TWIDDLE

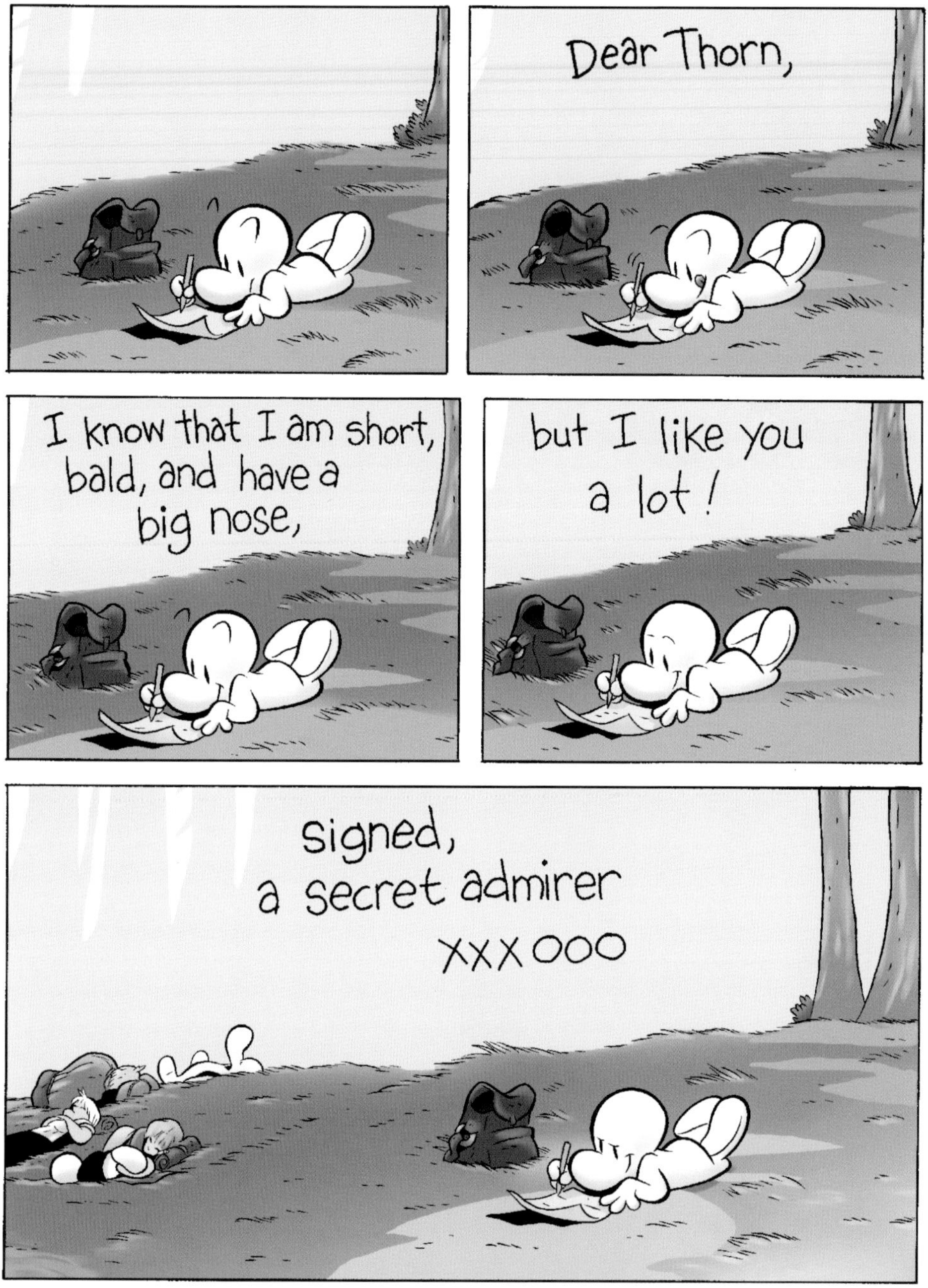
Dear Thorn,
I know that I am short, bald, and have a big nose,
but I like you a lot!
signed, a secret admirer XXX OOO

'Round and 'round
   OUR BUSY FEET GO

HURRY AND FURY
   AND APPLE-RED GLOW...

THE SIGHTS AND SOUNDS OF PLACES TO DO...

THE LAUGHING AND SHOUTING WILL NEVER BE THROUGH!

But...

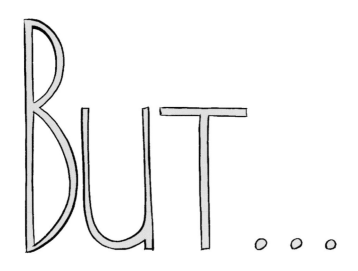

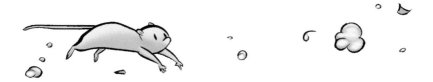

After all that running, the rest is best

A**ND THE BEST TO REST WITH
IS YOU.**

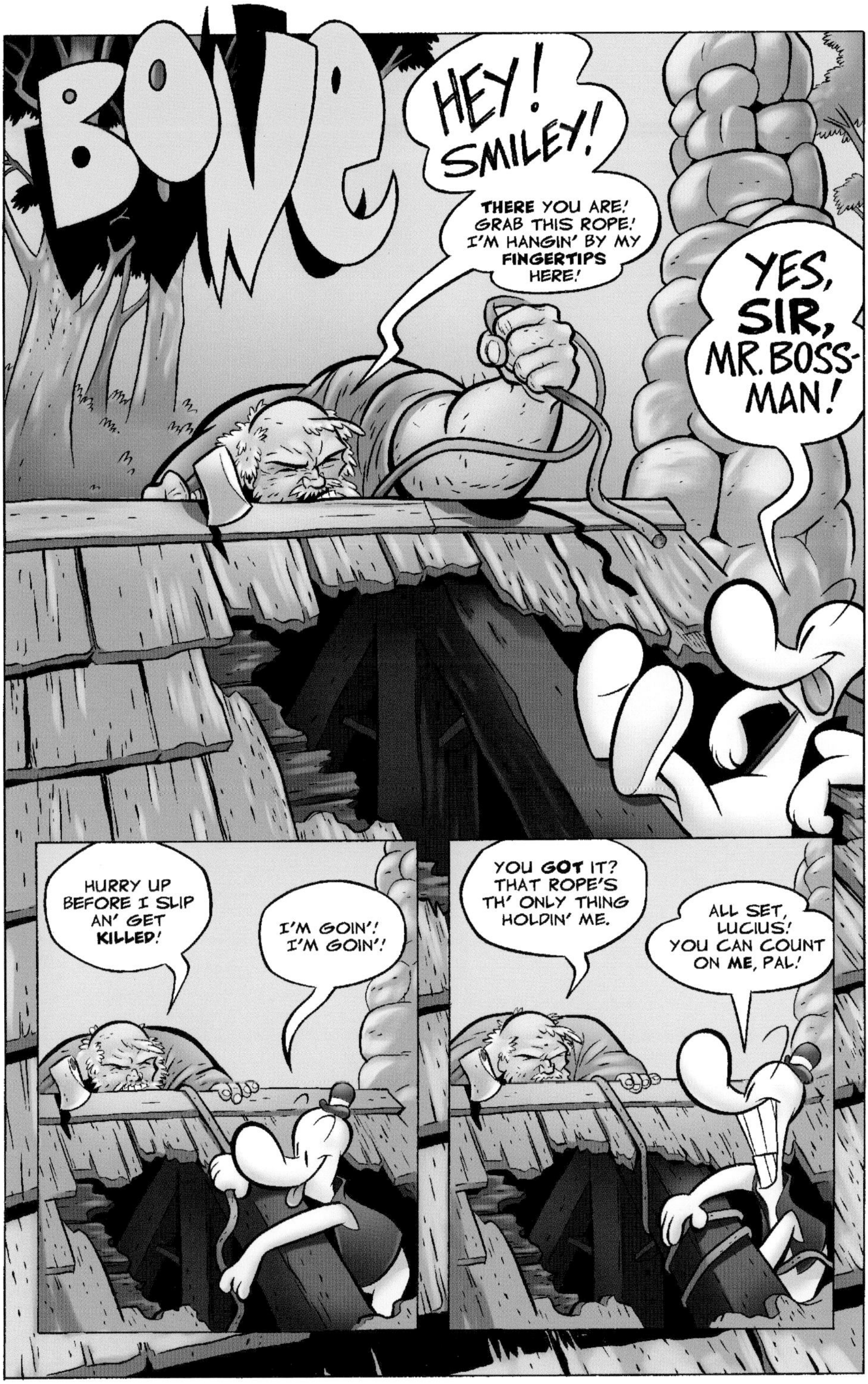
BONE
HEY! SMILEY!
THERE YOU ARE! GRAB THIS ROPE! I'M HANGIN' BY MY FINGERTIPS HERE!
YES, SIR, MR. BOSS-MAN!
HURRY UP BEFORE I SLIP AN' GET KILLED!
I'M GOIN'! I'M GOIN'!
YOU GOT IT? THAT ROPE'S TH' ONLY THING HOLDIN' ME.
ALL SET, LUCIUS! YOU CAN COUNT ON ME, PAL!

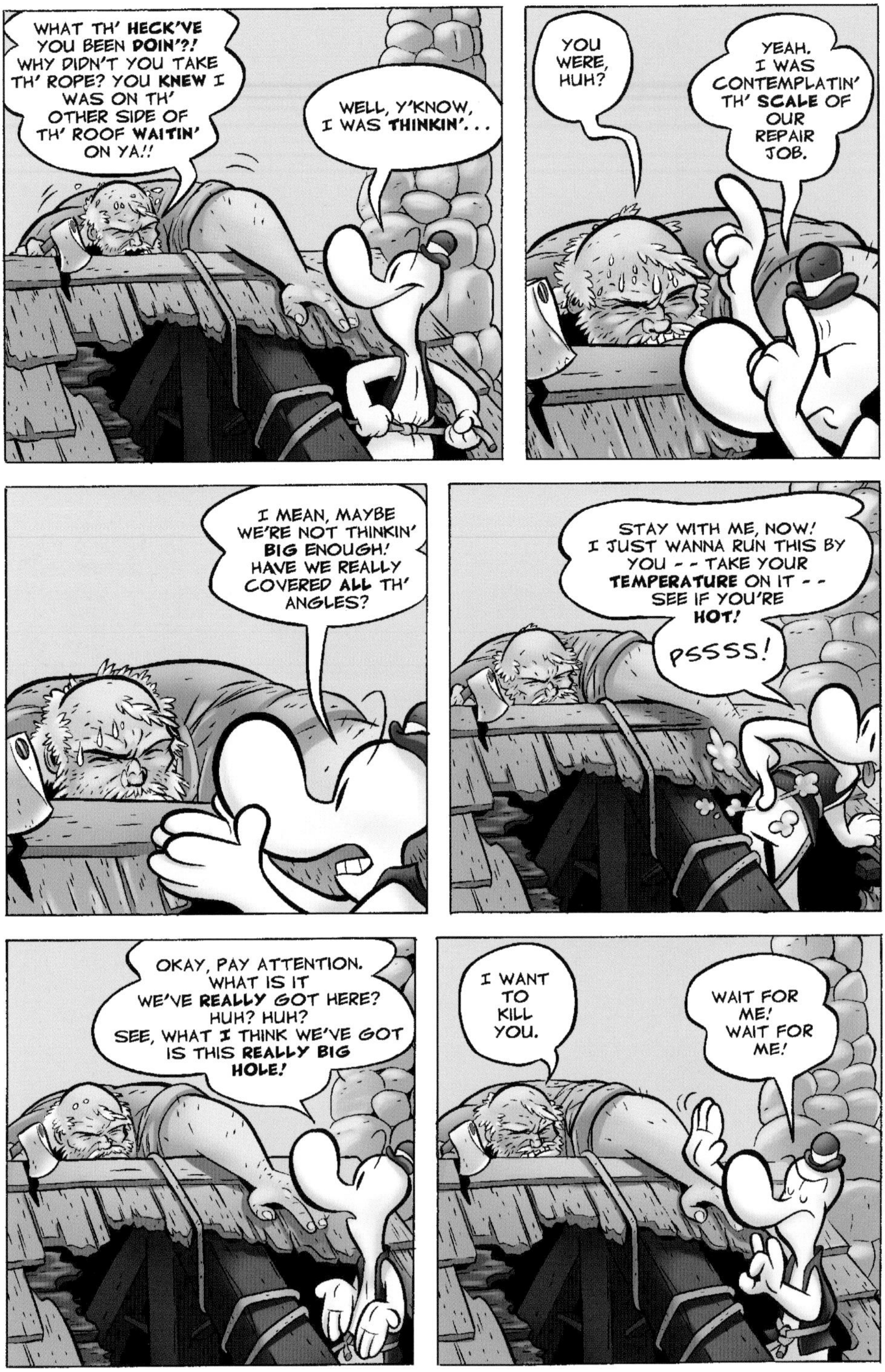
WHAT TH' HECK'VE YOU BEEN DOIN'?! WHY DIDN'T YOU TAKE TH' ROPE? YOU KNEW I WAS ON TH' OTHER SIDE OF TH' ROOF WAITIN' ON YA!!
WELL, Y'KNOW, I WAS THINKIN'...
YOU WERE, HUH?
YEAH. I WAS CONTEMPLATIN' TH' SCALE OF OUR REPAIR JOB.
I MEAN, MAYBE WE'RE NOT THINKIN' BIG ENOUGH! HAVE WE REALLY COVERED ALL TH' ANGLES?
STAY WITH ME, NOW! I JUST WANNA RUN THIS BY YOU - - TAKE YOUR TEMPERATURE ON IT - - SEE IF YOU'RE HOT!
PSSSS!
OKAY, PAY ATTENTION. WHAT IS IT WE'VE REALLY GOT HERE? HUH? HUH? SEE, WHAT I THINK WE'VE GOT IS THIS REALLY BIG HOLE!
I WANT TO KILL YOU.
WAIT FOR ME! WAIT FOR ME!

HOLD MY HAT FOR A MINUTE, WILL YA?

WE SHOULD TAKE **ADVANTAGE** OF THIS SOUTHEASTERN EXPOSURE. NOW, I DON'T KNOW ABOUT **YOU**, BUT I'M PICTURING A **GLASSED-IN ATRIUM**...

...AN' **HERE'S** WHERE WE PUT TH' **JACUZZI!**

BACK IN BONEVILLE YOU WERE TH' **VILLAGE IDIOT**, WEREN'T YOU?

ACTUALLY, I WORKED FOR MY COUSIN **PHONEY**. HE WAS TH' **RICHEST BONE IN BONEVILLE**, BEFORE THEY RAN US OUTTA TOWN. I DIDN'T WORK FOR HIM ALL TH' TIME, THOUGH. JUST KINDA DID **ODD JOBS** FOR HIM WHENEVER HE NEEDED SOMETHIN' DONE.

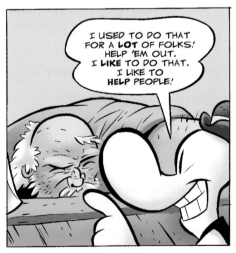

I USED TO DO THAT FOR A **LOT** OF FOLKS! HELP 'EM OUT. I **LIKE** TO DO THAT. I LIKE TO **HELP** PEOPLE!

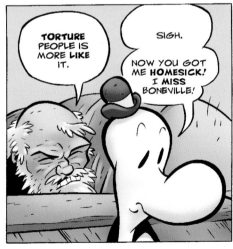

TORTURE PEOPLE IS MORE **LIKE** IT.

SIGH.

NOW YOU GOT ME **HOMESICK!** I MISS BONEVILLE!

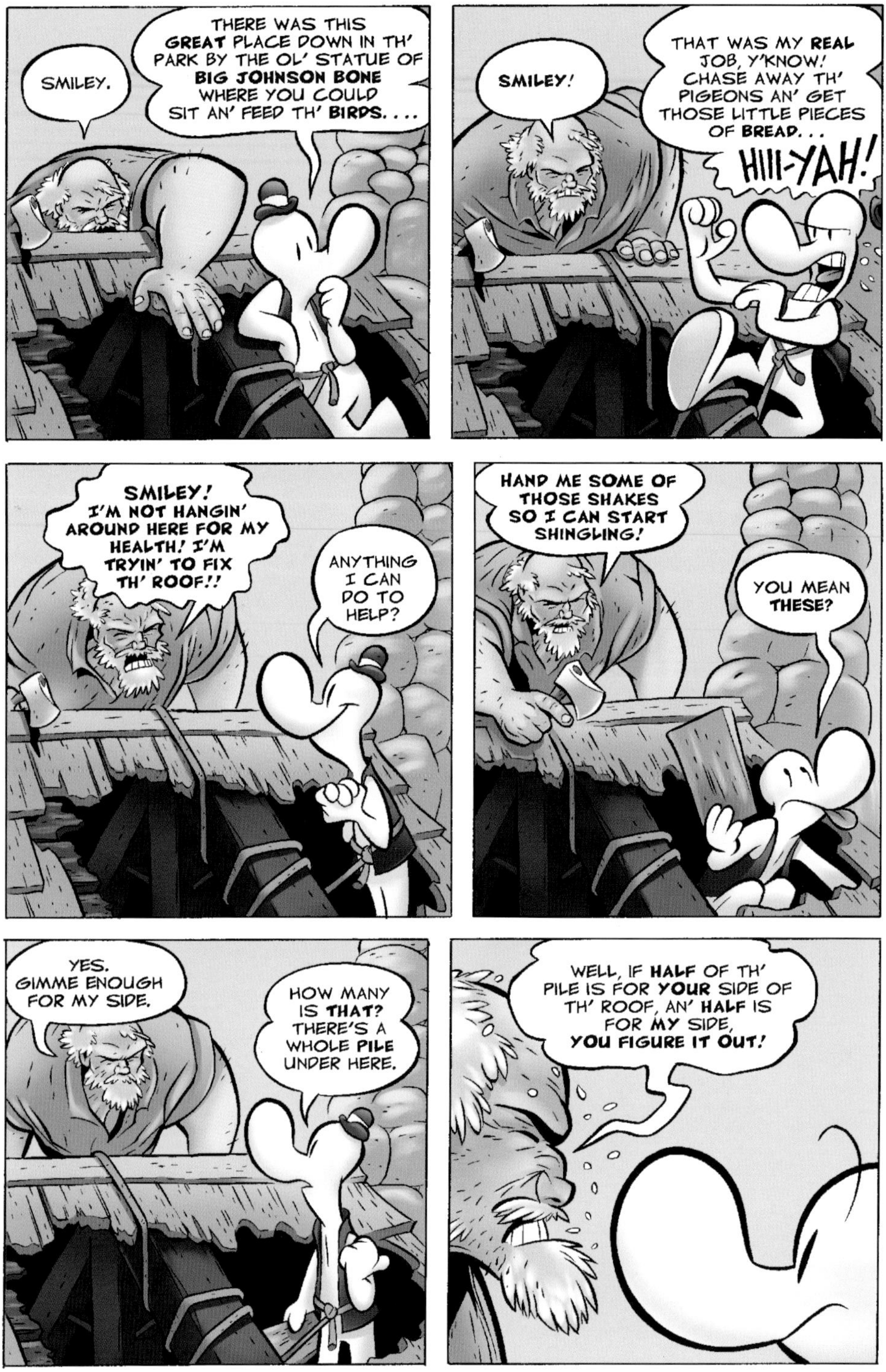
SMILEY.
THERE WAS THIS GREAT PLACE DOWN IN TH' PARK BY THE OL' STATUE OF BIG JOHNSON BONE WHERE YOU COULD SIT AN' FEED TH' BIRDS. . . .
SMILEY!
THAT WAS MY REAL JOB, Y'KNOW! CHASE AWAY TH' PIGEONS AN' GET THOSE LITTLE PIECES OF BREAD. . .
HIII-YAH!
SMILEY! I'M NOT HANGIN' AROUND HERE FOR MY HEALTH! I'M TRYIN' TO FIX TH' ROOF!!
ANYTHING I CAN DO TO HELP?
HAND ME SOME OF THOSE SHAKES SO I CAN START SHINGLING!
YOU MEAN THESE?
YES. GIMME ENOUGH FOR MY SIDE.
HOW MANY IS THAT? THERE'S A WHOLE PILE UNDER HERE.
WELL, IF HALF OF TH' PILE IS FOR YOUR SIDE OF TH' ROOF, AN' HALF IS FOR MY SIDE, YOU FIGURE IT OUT!

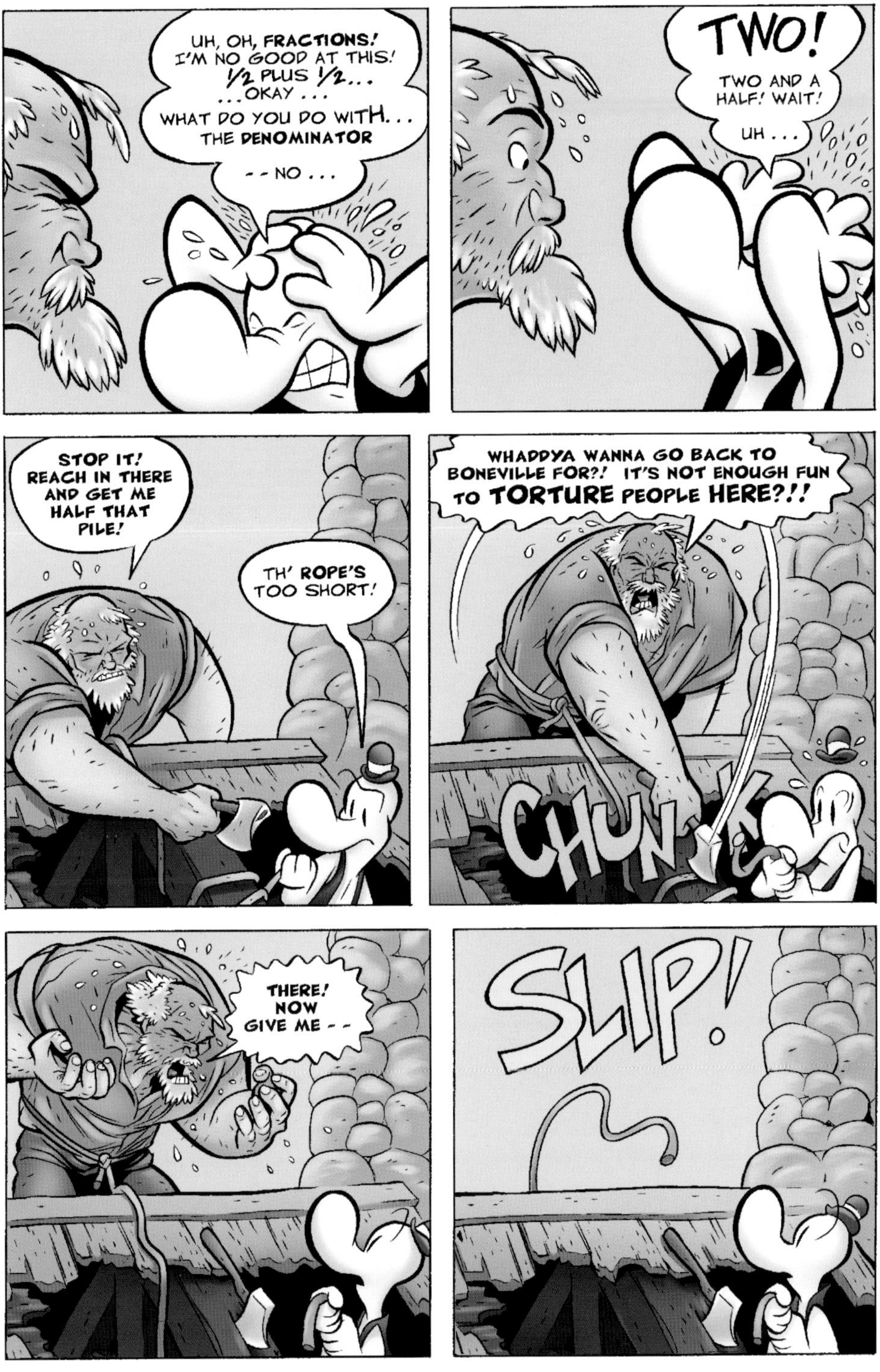
UH, OH, FRACTIONS! I'M NO GOOD AT THIS! 1/2 PLUS 1/2... ...OKAY... WHAT DO YOU DO WITH... THE DENOMINATOR
- - NO...
TWO!
TWO AND A HALF! WAIT!
UH...
STOP IT! REACH IN THERE AND GET ME HALF THAT PILE!
TH' ROPE'S TOO SHORT!
WHADDYA WANNA GO BACK TO BONEVILLE FOR?! IT'S NOT ENOUGH FUN TO TORTURE PEOPLE HERE?!!
CHUNK
THERE! NOW GIVE ME - -
SLIP!

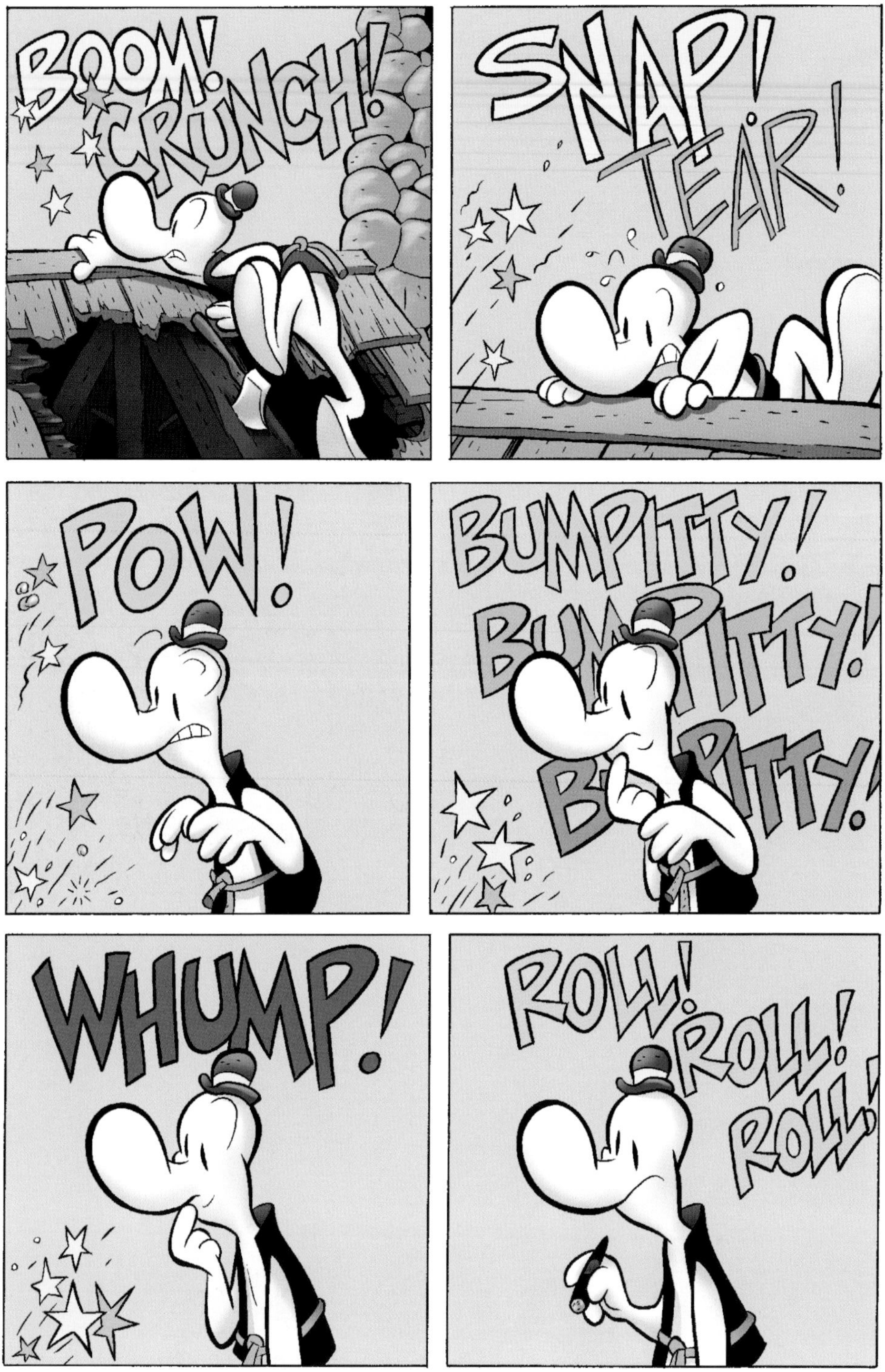
BOOM!
CRUNCH!
SNAP!
TEAR!
POW!
BUMPITTY!
BUMPITTY!
BUMPITTY!
WHUMP!
ROLL!
ROLL!
ROLL!

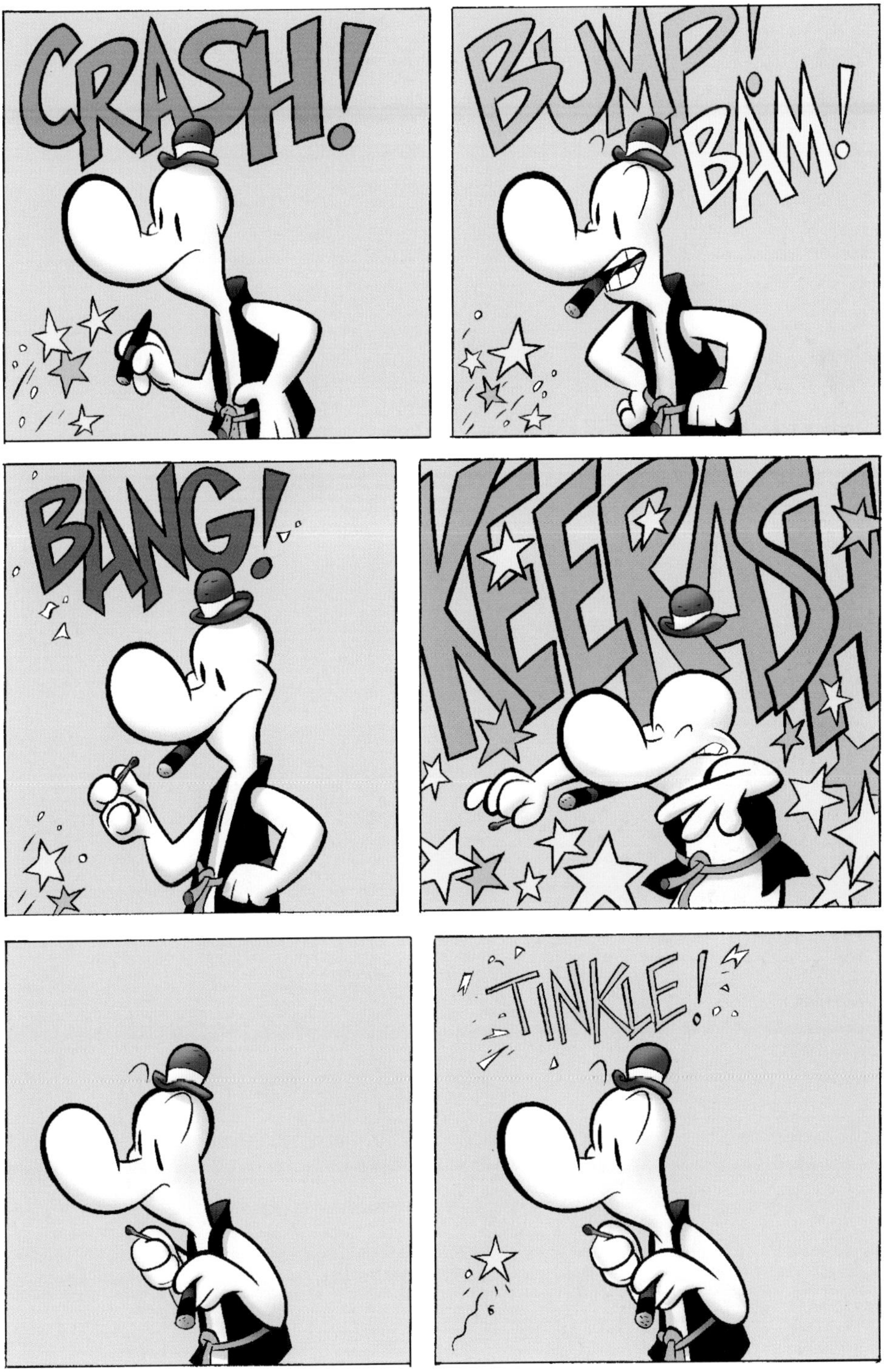
CRASH!
BUMP!
BAM!
BANG!
KEERASH
TINKLE!

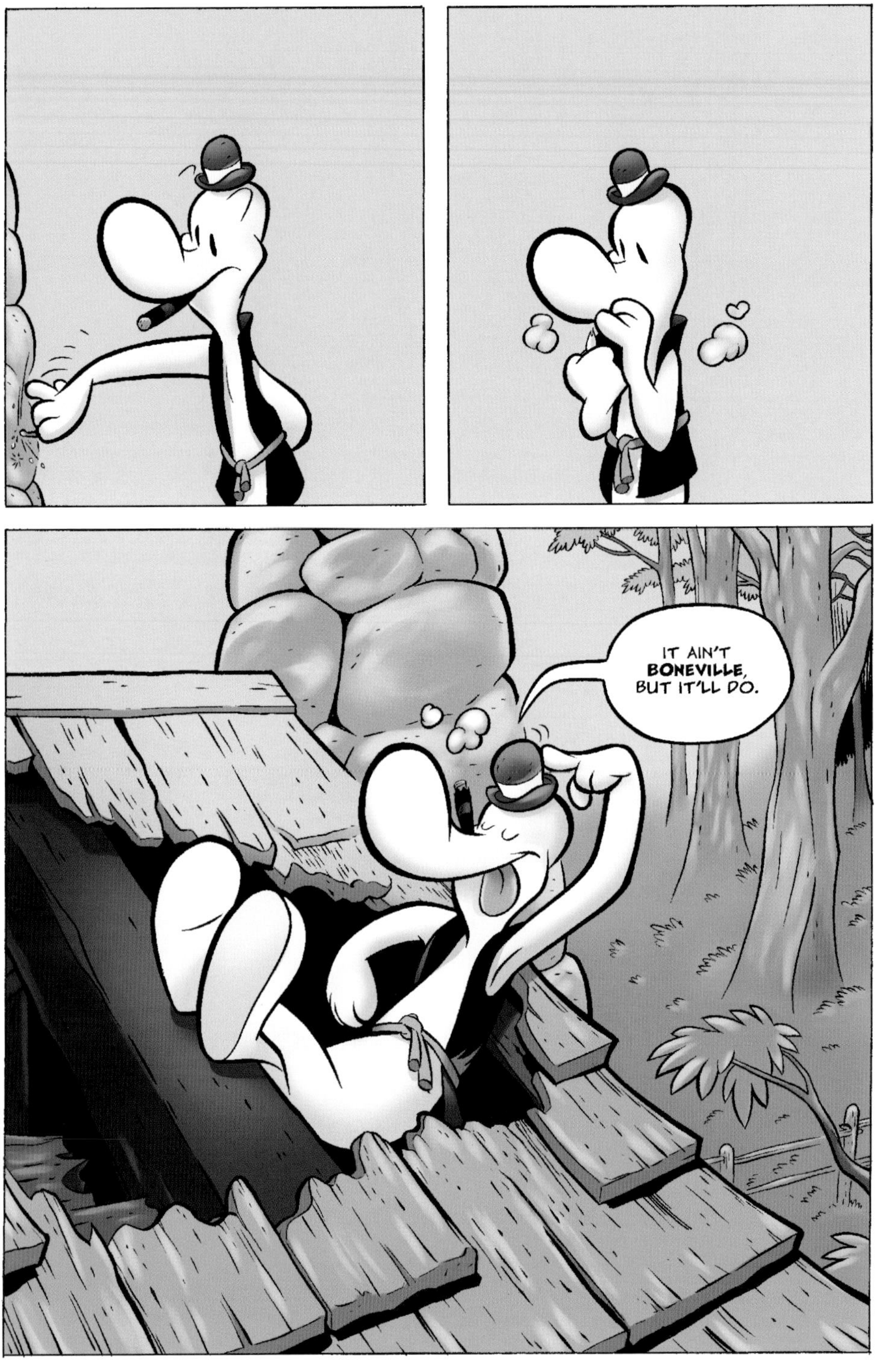
IT AIN'T BONEVILLE, BUT IT'LL DO.

...TO BE CONTINUED.

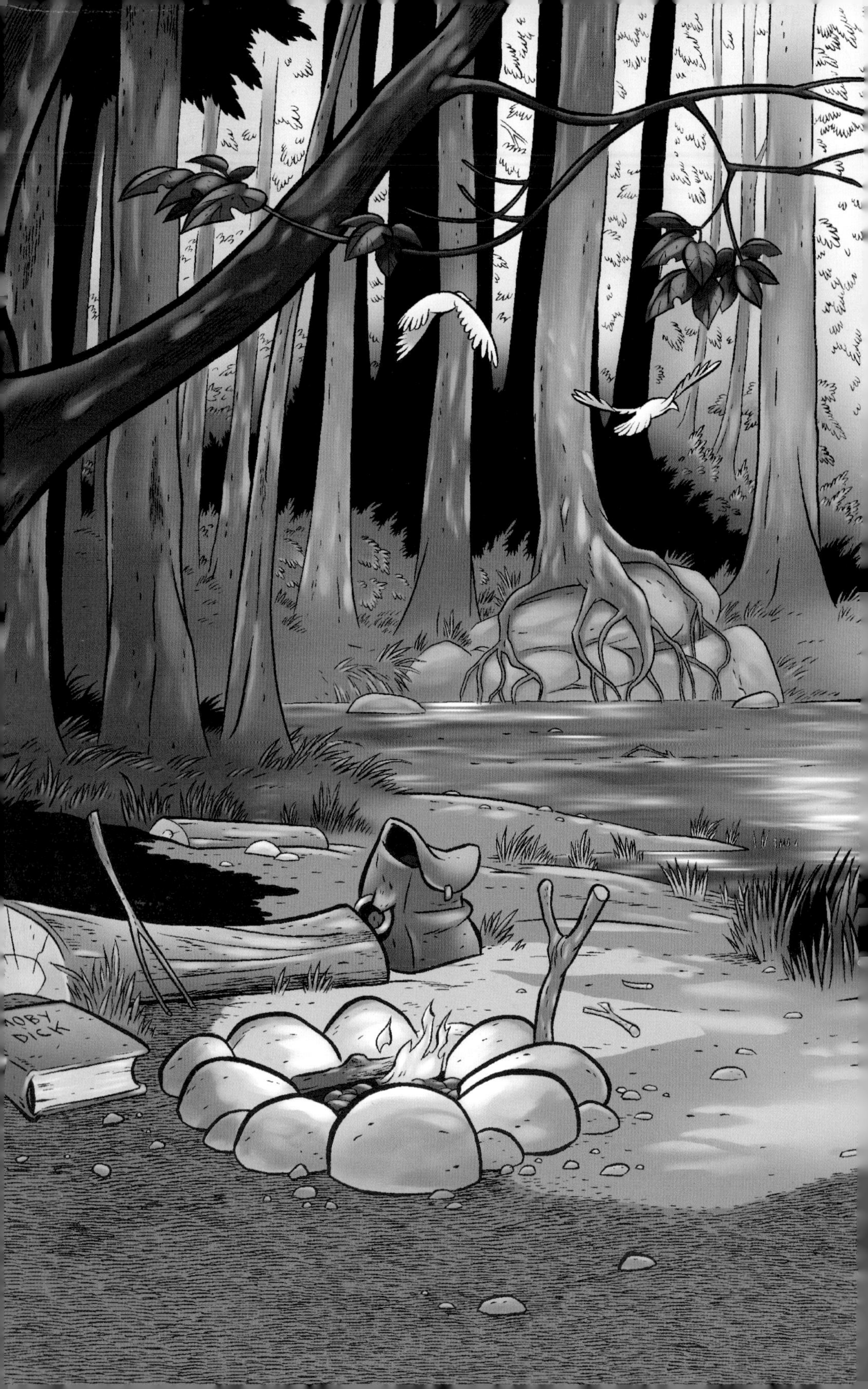
MOBY
DICK

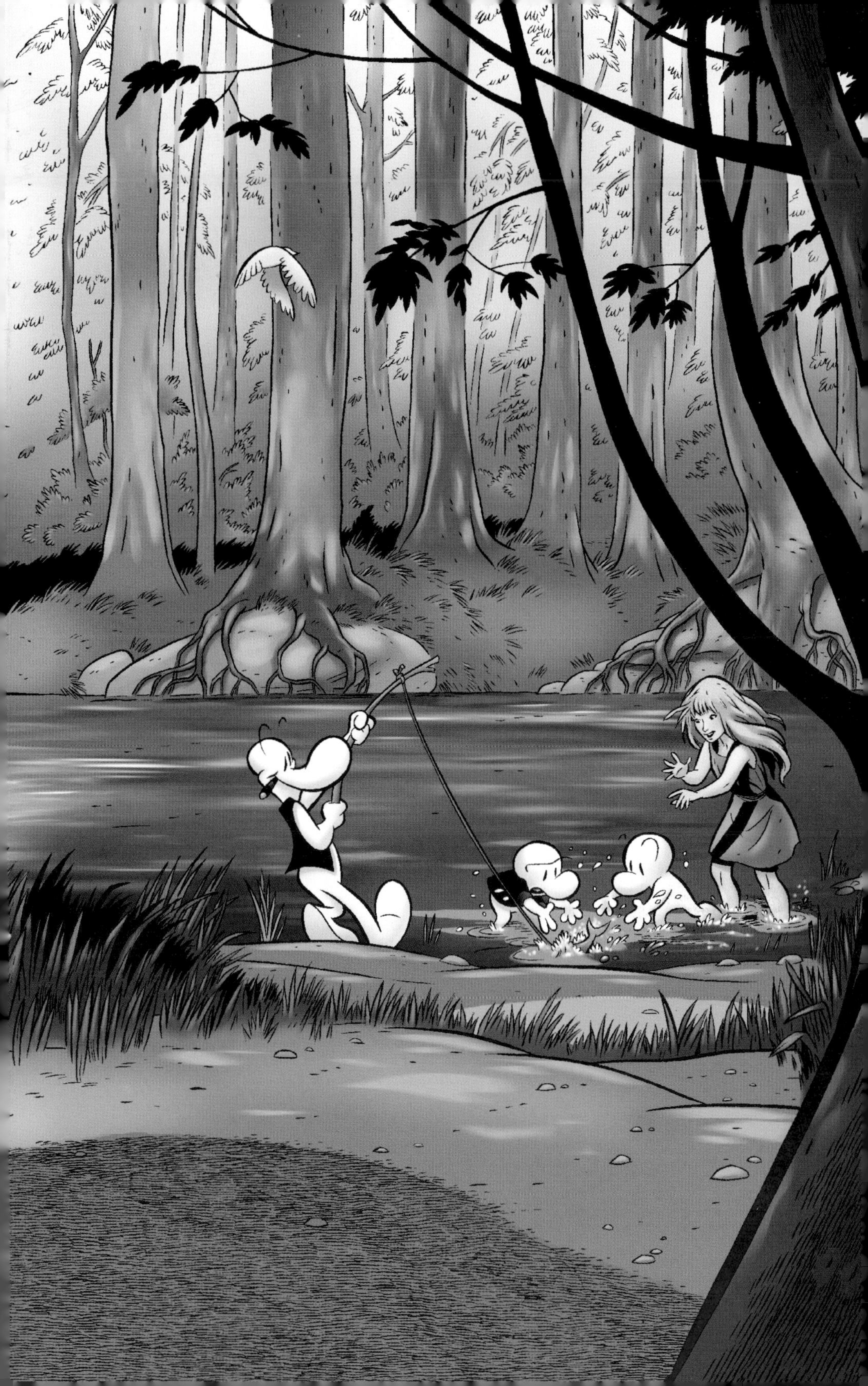

ABOUT JEFF SMITH

JEFF SMITH was born and raised in the American Midwest. He learned about cartooning from comic strips, comic books, and watching animated shorts on TV. After four years of drawing comic strips for Ohio State University's student newspaper and cofounding Character Builders animation studio in 1986, Smith launched the comic book *BONE* in 1991. Between *BONE* and other comics projects, Smith spends much of his time on the international guest circuit promoting comics and the art of graphic novels.

MORE ABOUT *BONE*

An instant classic when it first appeared in the U.S. as an underground comic book in 1991, *BONE* has since garnered 38 international awards and sold a million copies in 15 languages. Now, Scholastic's GRAPHIX imprint is publishing full-color graphic novel editions of the nine-book *BONE* series. Look for the continuing adventures of the Bone cousins in *Eyes of the Storm*.